MW00513150

To MaryAnn,
Best Wishes!
By – M. Joh...

SHADOWS AND DECEPTIONS

SHADOWS AND DECEPTIONS

By Bryan McLachlan

Four Seasons Publishers
Titusville, FL

SHADOWS AND DECEPTIONS

For information contact: Four Seasons Publishers
P.O.Box 51, Titusville, FL 32781

PRINTING HISTORY
First Printing 1999

ISBN 1-891929-15-1

PRINTED IN THE UNITED STATES OF AMERICA
1 2 3 4 5 6 7 8 9 10

ACKNOWLEDGMENTS

No amount of thank you's would be sufficient for my wife, Lisa. Her support and words of encouragement to keep me going during the times I wanted to give up were enormous. Many thanks to my children, Kayla and Connor for doing their best, as best as little children can, for giving me some quiet time to write this story.

I would also like to thank a dear friend of mine, Guy Clevenger, for his insight and for being my sounding board. A man couldn't ask for a better friend. And thanks to Danielle Martin for her conversations.

I also want to thank my publisher, James Roache, for taking a chance on a new author. Last but not least, there is WRM. Thank you.

PROLOGUE

It was eight o'clock in the evening in Beirut on the 1st of August 1983, and the day hadn't gone well for Lieutenant (Captain Designate) Marcus Kaderri, U.S. Army Special Forces.

Kaderri was sitting on a cropping of rocks a few miles away in the foothills of the Shuf Mountains. He watched through binoculars some Israeli small arms tracer rounds venture into the U.S. Marine perimeter next to Beirut International Airport. "I'm tired of the fucking Israelis taking pot shots at our guys!" Kaderri said in disgust.

"It's kinda hard to believe we're allies," said Staff Sergeant Robert Wolff. "You think they're just stray rounds?"

"No. It's been going on since we landed. The Israelis don't want us here. They figure if enough of our guys get killed, we'll pull out. And if they help a little, it just might make us move faster."

"Those motherfuckers want special treatment from us. They forget we're here on a nonpartisan mission. If I find the one pulling the trigger, I'll personally shoot the son-of-a-bitch."

Kaderri and Wolff were part of a Special Forces detachment that was training the Lebanese Army so they could take control of

Bryan McLachlan

their country and maintain peace once the UN sponsored Multinational Force, the Israeli Defense Force, the PLO, and all the other warring factions leave."

"What's on the agenda tomorrow, sir?" Wolff asked.

Kaderri lowered the field glasses and turned to face Wolff, whose outline was the only distinguishable feature in the fading light. "A little change in plans," Kaderri said. "Sergeant, tomorrow we train the Lebanese in sniping."

A week later, Kaderri and Wolff bounced along in their jeep as they drove along the rough road on their way to Beirut for a briefing. As they passed through the Israeli-controlled sector of Beirut, a fight erupted among three men on the crowded sidewalk. Two were dressed in civilian clothes. Kaderri thought he recognized the man wearing a Lebanese Army uniform. "Isn't that Sergeant Hassad?"

"Yes sir," Wolff said, "it is. It looks like he needs some help." Kaderri braced himself as Wolff slammed on the brakes and came to a screeching halt a few feet from the fight.

Feeling for the sidearm he hoped he wouldn't have to use, Kaderri leapt from the jeep. "Break it up!" he yelled as he grabbed the taller of the two men assaulting Hassad. A blow to Kaderri's mid-section from the shorter man caused him to release his grasp. Wolff then spun the shorter man around and dropped him with a punch to the jaw.

"I said break it up!" Kaderri said, grabbing the man again but this time in a choke-hold, and squeezing until the man's hands went up in surrender. Wolff helped Hassad to his feet and handed him his hat back.

" Sergeant Hassad, are you okay?" Kaderri asked. "What's going on here?" Kaderri's camouflaged shirt was rolled up past his elbow, and his forearm muscles rippled when he flexed his fists.

"I'll tell you what's going on here," said the man Kaderri was holding. The man spat disgustingly as Kaderri released him. "That man," he said pointing to Hassad, "is a PLO sympathizer and I'm arresting him for espionage."

"Slow down, pal," Kaderri commanded, holding up his hand. "Who the hell are you?"

"I am Major Ariel Steiner, and that unconscious man is Sergeant Horowitz, Israeli Defense Force. "And you", Steiner said pointing a finger at Kaderri "are intervening where you do not belong."

"Bullshit. This man is a sergeant in the Lebanese Armed Forces, which I happen to be training, and an American citizen."

Still pointing an accusatory finger at Kaderri, not bothering to look at Kaderri's name tag, Steiner shot back, "Listen, young lieutenant, you think you —"

"You take that finger out of my face right now or I'll shove it so far up your ass it'll come out your mouth." Kaderri turned to Sergeant Hassad. "What happened here, Sergeant?" Kaderri blinked the sweat out of this eye.

Still shaking from the fight, Hassad responded in a Brooklyn accent, "Sir, I was walking down the street when this man stopped me." He pointed to Steiner. "He said I'm under arrest for spying on the Israelis for the PLO."

"If you let me take him now," Steiner interjected, "I'll forget this ever happened, Lieutenant. If not, my men will help me forcibly remove him. And, you may get hurt in the process."

Now Kaderri was pointing his finger. "What evidence do you have that supports your accusations?"

"Not that it's any of your business, but we saw him walking distances to our positions yesterday. He was measuring us for an artillery strike." Steiner's voice was calm and steady.

"Well, Major, you're wrong," Kaderri said. "Sergeant Hassad was on the firing ranges with the rest of his unit all day yesterday. So why don't you help your sergeant up and leave. Now."

Wolff watched an Israeli foot patrol, complete with an M-113 armored personnel carrier, approach their position. "Sir," Wolff said, "we have some company."

Kaderri turned to see the twenty men form the IDF deploy around him. All were outfitted in full combat gear and armed with American made M16 rifles. "Shit," Kaderri muttered. The APC stopped in the road twenty meters away, its .50 caliber machine gun manned by the track commander and trained on Kaderri and Wolff.

The patrol leader approached and saluted Steiner. A smile spread across Steiner's face. "It seems, Lieutenant, that you are the one who is wrong. Now," Steiner said turning to Wolff, "release the prisoner to my men."

"Major, we have a problem here," Kaderri stated. "This man is not the spy you claim him to be. I won't allow you to take him."

Pulling a pistol from the small of his back Steiner said, "You are in no position to make any demands, release him, now!"

Kaderri surveyed the situation; every Israeli weapon was trained on him. He noticed the normal flow of people on the streets had thinned dramatically. He glanced at Wolff. Something was going down, and he and Wolff momentarily forgot the Israelis. Both men reached for their pistols.

"That is not a wise move," Steiner said, apparently oblivious to the developing situation. "My men outnumber you."

A band of PLO fighters had set up positions on the roofs of the building overlooking them. The roar of an RPG-7 being launched split everyone's ears. The trail of smoke raced toward the APC and slammed into its side, immediately followed by another. When the warhead detonated, the commander of the track was launched into midair, his body shredded by hundreds of steel fragments. Within seconds, greasy black smoke poured from the hatches of the armored vehicle. The three crewmen inside screamed briefly before they died. The hail of small arms fire that followed the launching of the RPG's was momentarily drowned out form the exploding APC.

As Kaderri and Wolff dove for cover behind the jeep, a bullet passed through the flesh of Kaderri's left arm above the elbow, feeling like a hot iron was placed there. The Israeli soldiers scramble for cover as they sought the direction of the fire, ready to return it violently. Three more Israeli soldiers lay dead, killed by hail from small arms fire. Two more lay screaming and writhing on the hot pavement. Kaderri was lying behind the jeep trying to stop the flow of blood from the bullet wound when he saw Steiner point his pistol at Hassad's head. "No!" Kaderri screamed. The pistol report echoed through the now silent street as the PLO withdrew.

Kaderri cocked his .45 and aimed at Steiner. The anger in his steel blue eyes erupted and his heart beat faster. "You motherfucker!

Shadows and Deceptions

You're not a soldier, you're a cold blooded murderer!"

"Like I said, Lieutenant, you are in no position to make any demands."

A few Israelis regained their positions around Kaderri and Wolff. Others went to help the wounded and search for the PLO. One soldier came up behind Kaderri and placed his rifle at the base of his skull. Another did the same to Wolff. Waving to the two men closest to him, Steiner instructed them to take Hassad's body. To Kaderri he said, "Get back in your vehicle and go your merry way. If not, you'll end up like him."

Kaderri's cheek twitched and his eyes bore a hole through Steiner. "One day Steiner. One day I will find you and blow your miserable ass away."

Steiner held his stare, but by the change in his eyes he was clearly taken aback by the cold finality in Kaderri's voice.

When Kaderri and Wolff arrived at headquarter an hour later, Kaderri jumped from the jeep before it stopped. Stepping through the flaps of the tent, he glanced around for Colonel Paul McKnight, the S-2 intelligence officer. Kaderri walked past easels covered with maps marked with red and blue pins, but could not find McKnight. The tent was vacant with the exception of a few mandatory people at their posts.

Seeing a sergeant sitting behind a row of radios, Kaderri sought him as a reference point. "Sergeant, where is Colonel McKnight?"

Without turning around to see who had asked him the question, the sergeant responded with a shrug. "Don't know, it wasn't my turn to baby-sit."

Losing his patience, Kaderri's voice boomed, "Get on your feet, Sergeant!" Wincing at the command, the sergeant saw the lone silver bar pinned in the center of the flash on Kaderri's beret. Since Kaderri was a Captain Designate, he was entitled to wear captain's bars, but chose to retain his first lieutenant's bars until he got his next assignment and command.

The sergeant immediately stood at attention and gave a textbook salute. "Sorry, sir. I thought you were someone else."

"Guess what? You were wrong!" Kaderri eyed the sergeant and did not return the salute.

"Yes, sir."

"Sergeant, next time, you better look before you speak. I could put your ass in a sling if I want to."

The sergeant swallowed hard. "Yes, sir."

"What brings you down here, Marc?"

Recognizing the voice of Colonel Paul McKnight, Kaderri spun around. A small, physically fit man wearing wire-framed glasses and dressed in camouflaged fatigues approached Kaderri as he was leaning into the sergeant.

"Good afternoon, sir," Kaderri said and saluted and then shook the outstretched hand of this former commander. "I need a few answers."

McKnight, in his thirties and young for a full colonel, looked at his standard army issue watch and ran his hand over his closely cropped dark hair. "Sergeant, let me know when my appointment arrives." McKnight led Kaderri to a vacant part of the tent where nobody could hear them.

"What can I do for you?" McKnight asked as he took a seat on a green metal folding chair. He gestured to Kaderri to take the metal chair opposite him. "What happened to your arm?" He pointed to the bloody battlefield dressing.

"I'll be brief. My sergeant and I witnessed an Israeli major execute a sergeant in the Lebanese Army, who was also an American citizen."

"You what? When did this happen?" McKnight leaned forward, resting his elbows on his knees. "An American you said?"

"Yeah, he's got dual citizenship. He was born and raised in Brooklyn, and moved out here when he was seventeen. The whole thing happened about an hour ago. We were on our way in for a briefing when we saw one of the Lebanese sergeants I was training caught in a fist fight. We went over to help him. While I was trying to explain to the major, who said my guy was a spy, that he was wrong, we were ambushed. During the ambush, the major pulled out his pistol and shot the sergeant in the head, twice."

"Marc, that is a matter for the LAF to handle, not us, and especially not Intelligence. What is it you want from me?"

"I want to know who he is, sir. He wasn't wearing a military uniform. I think he's a spook."

"What's his name, and what does he look like?"

"He said his name was Ariel Steiner. He's about five eleven, one seventy. He has light brown hair, long face, and brown eyes. He smiled when he pulled the trigger."

McKnight nodded. "He's Mossad, that's Israeli Intelligence, and is name isn't Ariel Steiner. It's Moshe Koretsky. He's a case officer, or what the Israeli's call a Katsa. Stay away from him. He's powerful and ruthless." McKnight didn't elaborate on how he knew who Koretsky was. "What else?"

"I told him if I ever saw him again, I'd blow his ass away. If I wasn't surrounded and outnumbered, I would have. Nobody does that to an American and gets away with it!"

"Watch yourself, he's the type to take out the threat before the threat takes him out. He's very good."

Kaderri sighed; still feeling more should be done. "Thanks for your help, sir." Kaderri stood as they shook hands and turned to leave. He glanced at the black man in a lightweight two-piece suit and mirrored sunglasses waiting by the radios and talking with the sergeant Kaderri had chewed out.

"You better get that arm looked at," the man said.

Kaderri didn't respond and walked past.

McKnight sauntered over to the sergeant and his appointment. "What did you say to the lieutenant to get him riled?"

The sergeant had an exceptional relationship with the colonel and knew he wouldn't get in trouble, but he swallowed hard anyway. "Sir, he asked where you were and without turning around to see who it was I said it wasn't my turn to baby-sit."

McKnight's eyes narrowed into slits. "That wasn't too bright, Ken, especially for a sergeant first class. What did he say to you?"

"Well, sir, he said he'd put my ass in a sling." His voice was shaky. Twenty years in the army could be thrown away if the lieutenant wanted to press the issue.

"That's it?" McKnight saw the hurt in the sergeant's eyes. "Don't worry, he forgot the incident occurred. Count your blessings. I've seen him take on colonels and win." He looked at his watch, nodded to the man in the suit and said, "Okay, let's get this over with."

Bryan McLachlan

CHAPTER ONE

Tuesday, May 19, 2:30 a.m.

Racing down Northern Boulevard, the white unmarked police cruiser had its grill lights flashing. The veteran officers were responding to a 911 call that a drug deal was in progress on the corner of Northern and Livingston. The lighted store fronts were a blur to the officers inside the car. It was a scene the officers were all too familiar with.

The police ventured into the Arbor Hill section of Albany with extreme caution. The inhabitants in the run-down area were known for hating authority, and sometimes shot at the police. When the police were called into the area, usually an unmarked car was first to respond to the plea for help, and the police rarely used the siren to attract unwanted attention. This call was no different. Officer Ronald Davies, the driver, spotted the dealers' brightly colored jogging suits as they were obviously trying to become enveloped by the shadow of an awning. Davies steered the car directly toward them. Next to him, Officer Peter Zacuran took the safety off his riot gun and poked it out the window.

The Caprice jumped the curb and screeched to a halt in

front of the unsuspecting dealers. The men were forced to press their backs against the brown brick wall of the Corner Deli to avoid getting hit. The glaring headlights blinded them long enough for the officers to spring from the car with their weapons trained on the chest of the two men.

"Don't move!" Zacuran ordered, standing behind the open car door, his finger nervously stroking the trigger.

"No problem man, I ain't gonna move," the bald one said putting his hands in the air. His face revealed his true fear.

"What's goin' on? We wasn't doin' nothin'," the other one, wearing a black and pink Nike warm-up suit said, his right hand slowly reaching for the small of his back.

"Take your hand away from your back, slowly." Davies ordered. Sweat covered his trigger finger as he clasped the pistol. He stepped away from the car and started towards the dealer.

"Hey man, whatever you say." The dealer in the Nike suit looked to his left, down the shadow filled street, and nodded.

"What the—" Zacuran turned to confront the danger, but never finished the sentence. The bullet impacted below his shield, slamming his body against the car.

"New target!" Robert Wolff, the spotter, said in an urgent, but hushed voice as he studied the new threat through his state-of-the-art AN/PVS-7A night vision goggles. "Right twenty meters. Next to the Dumpster. He's armed. It's an ambush. Shit! He just fired!"

No more 'sit and wait'. The adrenaline began a steady flow throughout Marcus Kaderri's veins. When the cops arrived unexpectedly, Kaderri thought he and Wolff might be out on the hit. All that changed when gunfire erupted.

"On target," Kaderri responded as they lay under the dilapidated billboard situated on top of the four-story apartment building diagonally opposite the Corner Deli. He peered through this night vision scope mounted on the silenced M14 rifle and watched the shoot-out below. Kaderri's field of vision through the scope was bathed in a lime green color, and he easily placed the cross hairs in the center of the target's forehead. With practiced expertise, he regulated his breathing and squeezed the trigger.

"Good shot," Wolff said matter-of-factly as the victim fell. The ambusher that shot the officer was dead, the back of his head blown away.

"Another target." Kaderri called out.

Wolff shifted his line of sight back to the drama unfolding at the Corner Deli. "Shit, good guy down. Take out the other two, right one first."

"Roger, got 'em." Kaderri saw the cop lying on the ground. He squeezed the trigger a second time. The 7.62mm round pierced the bridge of the terrified drug dealer's nose, exploding the head in a pink mist, staining the brick wall behind him. The body of the bald drug dealer slumped forward and draped over the hood of the car, twitching as a heavy stream of blood flowed down the hood from the gaping hole in his head.

The remaining cop on the scene and the dealer in the Nike warm-up suit traded shots as the firefight erupted. The dealer pulled the pistol that was hidden in the small of his back and pumped two rounds into the cop's chest. The dealer caught a round in this throat that tore out his jugular vein, causing blood to fountain with each beat of the heart. Both men crumpled to the pavement into unmoving heaps.

"Time to vacate," Wolff said, quickly stowing his gear.

"Right," Kaderri agreed and packed his gear. "Two kills."

"Two kills." Wolff confirmed the number.

They had to move fast before an army of police swarmed the area. It was the first time that Kaderri could remember that a cop was actually shot in Albany, New York. They had time to get away though, because they weren't the ones being sought. It would take some time before the cops realized that another shooter was involved.

Tuesday, May 19, 12:00 noon

"What's this city coming to when cops are shot?" Sara stated

3

as she opened the door to the seventeenth floor office. Stepping on the plush carpet, she brought lunch into Marc Kaderri's private office.

"Hey, Miss America!" Kaderri was happy to see her. "What are you talking about?" He took his nose out of the Wall Street Journal and gave the five foot seven inch stunning beauty a once over and smiled. Passionate, almond-shaped brown eyes topped with black eyebrows and split by a long, thin nose highlighted her oval face. Her full lips sat upon a chin that balanced her prominent, but delicate cheekbones. The long wavy hair parted over the right eye and framed her face as it fell over her shoulders.

She was wearing a royal blue and gold checkered form fitting knit dress that started as a turtle neck, and ended just above the knees. Down the front, a zipper ran the entire length, and her feet were covered in three-inch blue leather pumps. She shut out Marc's private secretary by closing the door behind her. "Lunch time? Already?" Kaderri glanced at his Rolex.

"Maybe if you stopped trying to sell insurance to everyone you'd know what's going on. On the noon news they have the story about the cops that were shot early this morning. And, it was runner-up, as you damn well know." Kaderri knew that the Miss America Pageant was a sore spot. Not because of coming in second, but because of political correctness.

"Not in my book," he quickly countered. "Is the report still on?" He asked from his brown leather wing back chair.

"Yes. I'll turn it on for you." Sara reached for the remote on the corner of his mahogany desk and turned on the twenty-six inch television located in the corn of his richly decorated office. "Maybe I'll turn something else on." Sara flashed her smile as she pulled the zipper open to reveal her voluptuous tan and toned body. A body that she had every reason to be proud of from constantly working out at the fitness club she owned. Her generous chest was supported by a black silk and lace bra, while her long shapely legs were bathed in sheer black stockings suspended by a matching black silk garter belt that accentuated her narrow waist curving into shapely hips. She

4

wasn't wearing any panties.

"Jesus! You look absolutely gorgeous." Kaderri's mouth hung open. "You know, I believe you are engaging in sexual harassment."

"How do you figure that?" Sara asked. "I don't work for you."

"True, but I can't touch!" Kaderri played along with the tease from his wife.

"You'll get your chance tonight." She zipped up her dress and strutted toward the door. It was their eighth wedding anniversary.

"You're not eating with me?"

"No, honey, I'm saving that for tonight!" Sara winked her long lashes coyly veiling her eyes. "Besides, I have to meet with a company rep who has some new exercise equipment."

"I guess I won't see you at the gym then. Good luck with your meeting and thanks for lunch," Kaderri said as she blew him a kiss and closed the door behind her.

Marc turned his attention to the newscast with a reporter interviewing a police officer. "Do you know what happened her last night, Detective? How are the police officers?"

"Both officers are in stable condition. Thank God they were wearing their vests. That probably saved their lives."

"What happened?" Michele Thorsen asked as she tossed her flowing blonde hair with a flick of her hand.

"What we know is that we have three dead black males, all in they're early to mid twenties. The officers responded to a call that a drug deal was in progress. We don't know what transpired after they arrived. We are conducting an investigation. Thank you." Detective Gary Trainor, Albany Police Department walked away from the reporter. The edited tape was over and the news anchor said they would update viewers when they received more information.

The special line on the phone rang, and only one person knew the number. Marc shut the TV off and answered it immediately. "Yes?" He listened for less than a minute. When the line was disconnected from the other end, he pushed a speed dial button.

"Crawford Enterprises," the pleasant female voice answered.

"Extension two-four-zero-three, please." Kaderri said, waiting for the connection.

"Optics," Chief Designer Robert Wolff, Ph.D. answered. "I'm glad you answered," Kaderri said. We have another appointment — Thursday. It's a vacant building on the corner of Third and Lark. I'll meet you inside at 9:15 p.m."

"Got it," Wolff said.

Marc put the receiver down, took a bite of his ham and cheese sandwich, and walked to the window overlooking the city. His mind was transfixed on the brief conversation.

Tuesday, May 19, 6:50 p.m.

The three story contemporary house in Loudonville, a well-to-do suburb of Albany, overlooked the small private lake. The soft, white floodlights and Temple lights illuminated the manicured landscape and were reflected in the calm water of the lake. Marc Kaderri drove his charcoal gray Porsche up to the cobblestone driveway and came to rest in front of the four-car garage. Sara's red Corvette occupied the third stall from the left. A Volvo was parked in the last stall. A Jeep Cherokee, used mostly in the winter and weekend getaways to their cabin in the Adirondack Mountains, was parked in the first stall. Marc smiled to himself in anticipation as he walked past the vehicles and stepped through the door that opened into the kitchen. A long inhales of his nose revealed a gourmet meal ready to be devoured. Making a quick stop in his home office to unload his briefcase and check his answering machine, he emerged into the elegantly decorated formal dining room.

Beautiful paintings of land and seascapes hung on the three oak-paneled walls; the remaining wall was made up of a large window that stretched from floor to ceiling.

As he stepped through the French doors onto the plush, beige carpet, the sight before him was exquisite. Sara was seated at the head of the eight seat, cherry dining table. The table was set with Wedgwood china, Oneida silver, and Waterford crystal wineglasses placed upon a rose colored tablecloth. Three covered serving platters were situated in the center of the table. The lit candelabra at the opposite end of the table gave the dining room a soft, warm glow. Next to Sara's chair was an uncorked bottle of Puligny-Montrachet, chilling in a silver bucket of ice.

With his hands behind his back, Marc walked over to Sara and gave her a deep passionate kiss. From behind his back her handed her a dozen long stem roses and a small wrapped box. "I could get used to this," Marc said. "Happy Anniversary."

"I bet you could. Now sit down." Sara brought the roses to her nose and breathed deeply, savoring the delicate scent. Placing the roses on the sideboard behind her, she unwrapped the gift. Once the paper was removed, she lifted the top of the box and pulled out a six-carat diamond tennis bracelet. "My God, this is beautiful. Thank you, honey," Sara said, before returning the deep kiss. Sitting back in her chair with a sheepish smile, she said, "You're present isn't here yet."

"Okay," Marc said shrugging, pretending he didn't care. He was happy for having eight wonderful years with Sara. "What are we having?" he said as he reached for his glass of wine.

"What?" Sara said, clearly shocked. "Aren't you the least bit curious what I got you?"

"All right, you win," he teased, "what did I get?"

"You're going to get a fat lip! Forget it. You'll have to wait." Sara reached for the large covered platter and removed the cover, releasing a delightful aroma. "Pheasant."

An hour and half later, dinner and dessert were finished. "Delicious, honey," Marc said. "That was excellent."

"Thank you." Sara stood up and pushed her chair under the table. Marc did likewise as she grabbed his hand and led him upstairs into the bedroom suite. He walked behind her as they ascended the stairs. His eyes studied the perfect shape of her tight buttocks, and the slender curve of the waist as it melted into the hip. Every time she stepped, he watched in awe as one cheek and hip would sway seductively. Walking through the doorway, Sara suggested, "Why don't you open the champagne?" Marc released her hand and walked toward the nightstand where a bottle of Veuve Clicquot Ponsardin was chilling on ice.

Marc popped the cork and poured the champagne. Turning to give one glass to Sara, he nearly dropped them upon seeing her. She was standing by the corner of the queen size bed with her dress gathered around her ankles. Her curvaceous body clad only in silk lingerie.

Marc's eyes slowly devoured her. With great delight, as always, he stared in wonder at the most beautiful woman on the face of the earth. Her normally trimmed pubic hair was shaved even smaller so only a small black strip remained. She stepped over her dress and strode toward him. "Let's celebrate."

She took her glass from his outstretched hand and sat on the edge of the four-post colonial bed. Her seductive brown eyes stared into Marc's steel blue eyes as he sat next to her.

"Happy eighth anniversary," Marc said as their glasses touched in a toast.

"Happy eighth." After the sip of champagne, Sara's red full lips zeroed in on Marc's mouth. The kiss began as light and feathery. Marc's tongue soon parted Sara's lips and explored the deepness of her mouth. His thrashing tongue was momentarily pushed back into his mouth by her tongue as she took over the exploration.

Marc's hands cupped her firm breasts and stroked her erect nipples staining against the lace fabric. A low, throaty moan surfaced from her as her breasts were freed by Marc's fingers unclasping the catch in the front of her bra, and lightly pinching her nipples.

Sara wasted no time in undressing Marc, stripping him to the waist, as their wet kiss continued. Gentle hands pushed him back with his head resting on the throw pillow as Sara's sensuous lips kissed his square chest and washboard stomach. Each kiss flamed the fire brewing in him. Soon, her lips came to rest at this waist. She suddenly stopped. "We have a problem."

Shocked by her statement, Marc propped himself up on his elbows. "What's the problem?"

With a mischievous smile and a gleam in her eye, she answered. "Your pants are still on." Marc practically tore off his trousers and boxer shorts so Sara could continue. She pushed him back on the bed and kneeled between his legs. Her fingers delicately but firmly wrapped around his erection as he felt the warmth of her mouth take him in. His testicles were being massaged with her other hand. He felt her take in his entire length until her nose buried in his pubic hair. Soon her mouth and hands began working in rhythm. Periodically she would bring her mouth to the tip and swirl her tongue around it, eliciting a deep moan as his hands clenched the bedspread. Marc felt the burning sensation building in his loins until he couldn't control it any longer. He could tell Sara sensed it also, she picked up the pace to a furious speed. Marc let go as a brilliant display of fireworks exploded in front of his eyes. When he caught his breath, he brought his hand down to hold hers. "My God, honey, that felt great."

Marc looked into Sara's sultry eyes, "Yes it was," she said, "but now it's my turn." She laid back on the bed and spread her legs, beckoning him to pleasure her.

Marc was eager to return the pleasure. Like Sara did, he kneeled between her legs and spread her a little wider revealing her inner pinkness. His tongue lightly stroked her and probed the opening, purposely avoiding her clitoris. He watched her hips rotate and his head was pulled in further by Sara's hand. "Oh, yes, yes! Just like that. Don't stop!" Her inner thighs pressing against his ears muffled her moans of pleasure. His tongue made wide circles around her labia and slowly circulated into tighter ones. The sweet smell of her tickled his nose, and he delicately drank her flowing wetness. He maintained the pace and began working on Sara's clitoris. He peered over her pubic strip and garter belt to watch her tight stomach muscles convulse in an orgasm that spread quickly throughout her body.

When she came back down, Marc was ready again. "How

did that feel?" he asked.

"That was absolutely beautiful," she said. "Now I want you in my pussy." Once again, Marc was pushed back on the bed. It was always enjoyable when Sara took control. He watched with eager anticipation as Sara straddled his waist and lowered herself onto him. He relished in her warmth. She moved her hips in a rotating motion as well as up and down. He met her thrust and quickly a sheen of sweat covered their bodies.

Marc's hands found their way to her breasts and skillfully kneaded them the way Sara liked. Her skin felt like silk as his hands roamed over her firm, smooth body. They gently picked up the pace and Sara leaned closer to Marc, pressing her sensitive breasts against his chest, her hair cascaded over his face. Marc reached down and grabbed her buttocks to help the pace reach a new speed. Her manicured fingernails sank into his shoulders as they climaxed together.

After a night of passionate lovemaking, Marc forced himself awake at 4:30 a.m., an hour before his usual time. The graphic scene of reliving his friend's death was fused into his memory forever. He, Wolff, Rufus "Ghost" Brown, and Steven Caron were walking down the street after a night of drinking. They were celebrating Steven's divorce from who he called "the wicked hag." They walked past a group of five young men sitting on the steps of an apartment in a group of row houses. Suddenly, a green pickup truck with two men in the bed sped past and opened fire on them with a burst of automatic weapons. The young men pulled their weapons and immediately returned fire.

Kaderri and his friends instinctively dove for cover. The event took six seconds. When it was over, Marc was clutching his friend Steven's hand while he lay bleeding on the damp sidewalk. Tears welled in Marc's eyes as he watched helplessly. Steven's life was pouring from a gaping hole in his chest to pool in the nooks and crannies of the gray concrete. They had been the innocent victims of a shoot out between drug dealers.

Sitting in bed fully awake, Marc looked at his naked wife to make sure he hadn't disturbed her. His emotions were boiling. His mind's eye was focused on the two men he and Wolff had eliminated at the Corner Deli, and the one hit he carried out alone last week after the first phone call. The two men he had killed were in a remote area where it would be some time before the bodies were found.

He remembered the sick scene of the policemen lying motionless on the ground; both wounded from the unsuspected gunfire. He knew he had made the right choice. Dealing drugs was wrong, and by what was taking place on the streets, it looked as though the law enforcement authorities needed all the help they could get. The people of the city needed to be free from this oppression.

Throwing the satin sheets aside, he slid off the bed, and strolled to the walk-in closet/dressing room. Closing the door behind him as he turned on the light, he parted some suits hanging on the rod. A black garment bag stood out. Pulling the zipper down, he saw a green, Class A United States Army uniform.

Above the right breast pocket was a black nametag with white lettering stenciled in. Above the nametag was a long, light blue rectangle with a gold musket and wreath placed in the middle. It was a Combat Infantryman's Badge. Just above the left breast pocket, were five rows of multi-colored ribbons, called a "salad", denoting the campaigns, medals, and awards the bearer participated in and won. Perched on top of the salad were silver wings surrounding a parachute and another set of wings surrounding a frontal view of a helicopter.

Just below the cut on each lapel stood a highly polished pair of brass crossed muskets, the symbol of the Infantry. Above the cut on the lapel, at the same distance the muskets were below the cut, was a highly polished pair of brass letters: U.S.

On the shoulder loops placed closer to the shoulder were a pair of connected silver bars, also known as "railroad tracks," identifying the rank of captain. In the center of the loop was a green tab with a unit crest. That crest was an erect knife covering the junction of two crossed arrows that formed an "X" behind the blade. At the base of the knife the words De Oppresso Libre, To Liberate From Oppression — the Special Forces motto — were written in a semi-circle that began and ended at each side of the knife's hand guard.

The patch on the left shoulder was a blue arrowhead with an upright gold sword with three lightning bolts across the blade. Perched on top of the patch were three separate tabs: Airborne, Ranger, and Special Forces. There was the same patch, minus the Ranger tab, on the right sleeve, indicating the unit he served in combat with.

A separate bag hung on the hanger that held the uniform. The contents being a green beret still intact with the unit flash and captain's bars attached in the middle of it. When worn on the head, the flash sits above the left eye.

Reflecting on what the uniform meant, something he was extremely proud of, Kaderri zipped the garment bag up. He sat on the bench in the huge closet and stared at himself in the mirror. The reflective glass revealed only the physical appearance of the looker. Kaderri looked closer. He stared into the eyes. The eyes were the gateway to the soul. The mirror didn't offer anything that couldn't be seen. It never revealed what was in the soul. Satisfied he was doing the right thing, De Oppresso Libre; he climbed back into bed.

Sara lay on her stomach with the sheets draping her buttocks. Her delicate breathing whistled softly through her nose, filling the room with a caressing melody that Marc found comforting and soothing. He slipped his hand under the sheet and ran his fingers the length of her leg coming to rest on her labia. Wiggling his fingers, she became aroused and awoke from her sleep.

Turning only her head to look at Marc through her long dark hair that covered her face, she asked, "You want it again?" She was clearly enjoying his probing fingers.

"I've decided not to run this morning, this type of exercise is more fun." She rolled over and spread her legs as Marc rolled on top. She reached between his legs and guided him into her wetness. Instead of the previously uninhibited sex, this time they savored each other as they made love.

Thursday, May 21, 9:14 p.m.

The corner of Third and Lark was an abandoned apartment building that was popular with the homeless and drug dealers. Marc arrived at 9:00 p.m. to make sure the building was clear and to determine which vantage point would be best suited for his needs. At 9:12 p.m. he stepped into a shadow in the hallway near the ground floor entrance and pulled his silenced 9mm Beretta from its shoulder holster. Another pair of echoing footsteps broke the stillness.

Lights from the city seeped through the boarded windows, casting an eerie glow that mixed with the dust and dirt of the rubble strewn in the hallway. The light compromised the outline of a man navigating through the debris. Draped over his left shoulder, a black nylon gym bag hung so it rested on the hip. The man's right hand swung loosely at his side, ready to grab the pistol stuffed in his trousers' waistband.

Marc targeted the pistol on the intruders head as he approached the secluded spot. He calmed his nerves to keep the pistol from wavering, and his heart rate tripled. It has been a while since he had been this close to a potential life or death situation. Though he killed before, it was something he never got used to or liked doing.

Cautiously, the intruder stepped around a pile of debris, his hand wrapped around the handle of the pistol, ready to use it if necessary. "Sierra One?" the voice asked.

"Roger, Sierra Two." Marc's voice drifted from the shadow he was occupying. He answered the call sign he used in the army. Recognizing Wolff, Marc exposed himself in the ghostly light. "Glad you made it. The building's clear and I got a spot on the third floor. Let's get set up." Both men holstered their pistols and ascended the creaky stairs.

Marc retrieved his duffel bag from under a pile of wood scraps as they approached the window that overlooked the corner of Third and Lark. Moving a few pieces of broken furniture and wood, both men prepared themselves for what Marc hoped wouldn't be a long wait. Unzipping the duffel bag, Marc retrieved his M14 rifle and one fully loaded, twenty round magazine slamming the magazine into the well of the rifle, he seated a round in the chamber, and attached the silencer.

Robert Wolff, Ph.D. was also digging through his gym bag. Grabbing the night vision scope he had "borrowed" from his lab where he designed telescopic sights, he handed it to Marc to mount on the rifle. The rifle and scope were previously sighted and zeroed, assuring them first shot hits. For himself, Wolff pulled the night vision binoculars from the bag, which were "borrowed," and a can of black grease paint to camouflage the exposed skin on their faces. Exactly four minutes from the time they moved to the window, they were waiting for their prey.

The alley that bordered Ramone's restaurant was usually quiet and abandoned. Occasionally, the side door from the restaurant would spring open when a member of the kitchen staff heaved a sack of trash into the dumpster. But tonight, the alley was the sight of a large drug deal. Kaderri glanced at the luminous dials of his watch. They read 10:31 p.m. A blue Mercedes turned right off third into the alley just short of the intersection of Lark. Right on time, he thought. The driver turned off the headlights and slid out from under the steering wheel. The passenger side door opened slowly. A monster of a man, standing at least six feet four, and muscles from head to toe, emerged from the seat in one swift fluid motion.

"Jesus Christ. That's the black Incredible Hulk," Wolff stated, observing the man through his glasses.

"You're not kidding. Looks like they're doing a recon." A smile spread across Kaderri's face after quickly studying the man. "All that gold he's wearing makes for a nice target." He followed him in the scope to a point where he met two men waiting in the alley.

All four came back to the Mercedes and stopped in front of the car. The rear driver's side door opened, and out stepped a man wearing a tailored suit, holding a leather briefcase. His blonde hair acted like a beacon in the night. That man was their primary target.

"Big Cheese is getting out," Kaderri said. It was the first thought that came to mind in describing the man.

"Look at those idiots," Wolff said. "They're all bunched together. A grenade launcher would be nice." A van drove down the alley and stopped in front of the Mercedes. Like the Mercedes driver, the van driver killed the engine and headlights and got out to meet the other five. "Show time."

Kaderri thumbed the safety on the rifle. Big Cheese and Musclehead had their backs to the snipers. The two men standing across from them had an unzipped duffel bag on the hood of the car. Bags of white powder were clearly visible through the night vision equipment.

"This should be easy," Wolff said. "Take out Big Cheese first and then Musclehead. Once they're out of the way, the others should be no problem."

"Roger." Kaderri placed the crosshairs on the back of Big Cheese's head. Taking a few breaths to relax his body, Kaderri took one last long inhale and let it out slowly. Halfway through the exhale, his body came to maximum rest. Timing the rhythm of his heartbeat, Kaderri's gloved finger squeezed the trigger between beats. A barely audible sound indicated that the bullet was rocketing toward its target. Before the bullet slammed home, Kaderri had Musclehead in his sights and fired again.

Wolff sat ever so still watching the scene through his glasses. The first bullet hit. "Good first shot."

Big Cheese was shaking hands with the man in front of him when the bullet hit. In horrifying slow motion, Big Cheese's head exploded. The eyes popped out, followed by the nose and chunks of bone and brain tissue. In a spray of blood, teeth, and flesh, the bullet exited the mouth and penetrated the other man's throat that was shaking hands with Big Cheese. On its descent, the bullet blew out the man's windpipe and

15

exited through the lung.

The back of Musclehead's neck was covered with gold. It afforded Kaderri a simple shot. All he did was aim at the center of the gold. When the bullet impacted with the gold, it deflected. Instead of severing the spine at the base of the skull, the bullet veered and tore through the jugular vein. Musclehead's huge hands clawed at his neck to stop the pulsating blood. He died a slower death than if Kaderri's bullet had stayed straight. The first two men were slow to react to the death of the three men. The van driver was quicker and bolted for what he apparently thought would be the protection of the van.

Taking advantage of the dealers' slow reaction time, Kaderri fired two more times with deadly accuracy. "Where's the driver?" Kaderri asked. His voice was cold and monotone.

"I have him in the van. Driver's side." Wolff answered with the glasses to his eyes.

"Got 'em." Kaderri spotted the driver sitting behind the steering wheel, trying to start the engine. For the last time that evening, Kaderri squeezed the trigger. The bullet blew through the windshield and tore through the forehead of the driver. Brains splattered over the interior would greet whoever opened the back of the van.

"You're getting better. Five shots and six kills. You can miss a target and still have a one shot — one kill ratio." Wolff paused. "What is it, Marc? You're cheek is twitching. When that happens, I get nervous."

"Look at the third table from the left in the restaurant." Kaderri's order was cold as ice.

Bringing the binoculars up once again, Wolff sought the third table inside the restaurant. Adjusting himself to get a clear picture, two figures came into view; one was partially hidden.

Kaderri waited momentarily and asked, "Is that him?"

Wolff's jaw dropped. "Holy shit. What's he doing here?" Wolff asked aloud. "We don't have time to kill him, it'll have to wait. Police will be all over this place."

Kaderri was still peering through his scope and putting steady pressure on the trigger.

"Marc, we'll get him later, we have to go!"

CHAPTER TWO

Friday, May 22, 10:20 a.m.

The police station had reporters swarming like bees on honey for information on the drug killings. A spokesman made a statement that they believed the killings were related to gangs from New York City trying to move into the area. Any help the public could give them would greatly be appreciated.

Detective Gary Trainor sat behind his metal desk in the glass enclosed office away from the noise and studied the photographs of the carnage left outside Ramone's from the previous night's shooting.

His partner of two months, Detective Keith Bernard, sat at his desk opposite Trainor. Bernard folded his arms across his broad chest as he leaned back in the chair, clearly amazed by the mess on Trainor's desk, and the office for that matter. "You know, your side of this office is pretty neat." He spied the coffee maker with three-day old coffee and half-empty Styrofoam cups scattered about. "If the health department saw this place, they would close it down. I bet your house is like this, too. Now I know why you don't have a girlfriend. When you bring

Trainor

his desk. It w...

something bet...

handed him the

"I think they'r...

"Cut the crap."

Bernard studied

commented. "I think

motherfuckers. These g...

day off when the shootin...

Bernard studied the pho...

photo, he paid close attention

then dumped the police repo... ...p of

the photos. Barnard quickly sc...

"Well, what do you think?" T... ...s he leaned back in his chair, interlocking his finge... ...ind his head.

Bernard dropped the papers in front of him and answered with a questioning look on his face. "Nobody took the weapons, the drugs, or the money. They were left there?"

"Yeah. Strange isn't it? I think we're dealing with someone who either has a lot of money or doesn't care about the weapons and drugs or—"

"Or what?" Bernard cut in, his eyes narrowed into tiny slits eager for Trainor's explanation.

"A professional hit man."

Bernard held his questioning look. "A professional hit man? Shit, you've been going out to the bars too much—or you've been reading too many of them books. What would a hit man be doing here in Albany? And, what was so important about these people?"

Trainor leaned forward and rested his elbows on a stack of paper where the desktop should have been showing. "First. No one heard any shots—"

"That's not that unusual." Bernard said quickly, interrupting for the second time. It was a habit that irritated some people, especially Trainor.

_____ mmed his fist on the
_____ t's unusual when six people
_____ n off. Second, no shell casings
_____ nce whatsoever was found indicating
_____ as in the area. Also, there was no return
_____ s never pulled their guns. The person or per-
_____ pulled this off are good. Real good. Plus," he shoved
_____ hotos back in front of Bernard, "who would leave two
hundred seventy thousand dollars in cash and cocaine, and three
MAC-tens"?

"We have Ids on everybody. Three are locals, who we've arrested before on minor drug charges. The other three are from Peekskill. The one with the suit had a driver's license that said his name was Allen Stroehmann. He owned Stroehmann Storage, which is a small storage facility on the Hudson River. We figured the other two were with him. We're waiting for the Peekskill police to fax us any information on him."

Both men sat quietly for a moment. Bernard finally broke the silence. "Isn't there a new storage facility being built down at the port with the same name? I wonder if it's the same company?"

"It's a place to start looking, but I'm more interested in finding the people who pulled the trigger. I still can't figure out why no one heard any shots."

"Six less druggies on the street is great, no matter who killed them and how." Bernard smiled and snapped his fingers. "I got it. Silencers."

"Silencers?" Trainor was bewildered.

"Yeah. The weapons were silenced. That's why nobody heard any shots."

Trainor reread the report and studied the photos once more. None of the victims pulled their weapons. When the bodies were found, their weapons were still in their holster. "Shit. That makes sense." He leaned back in his chair again, let out a big sigh, and thought to himself; amateurs don't kill six people before the victims have a chance to shoot back. These people are good.

This was going to be a tough case to crack, and it was only Gary Trainor's third case as a homicide detective.

A half-hour later, a quick rap on his office door by a uniformed police officer woke him from his reverie. Looking up, he motioned the officer to enter. "There's a reporter here to see you," the officer said, pointing to a shapely blonde with long, flowing hair that cascaded over her shoulders standing ten feet away on the other side of the counter. She had a round, pleasant face, a long nose, and thin lips. Only her blue, wide-set eyes showed hostility. Her blue tailored skirt hugged her hips and ended three inches above the knee, revealing a beautiful set of legs. The matching blazer with padded shoulders and chinched waist, combined with a red camisole, accentuated her flattering waist and bust. She was attractive, he thought.

"What should I tell her?" the officer asked.

Trainor furrowed his brow as he cast a quick glance in her direction. It was too early in the morning for her. "Tell her I'll be ready in a minute." The officer left to relay the message as Trainor shuffled the reports and the newly arrived fax from the Peekskill Police Department on his desk, mostly to conceal the file on the drug killings. He knew that that was what the reporter was after. Satisfied that wandering eyes couldn't see anything, Trainor stood to meet her.

Tugging on his pants, he stood in the doorway and motioned for her to enter his office. She walked past him without a word and took one of the seats. Closing the door as he shook his head in disbelief at her arrogance, Trainor regained his seat behind his desk. "We meet again, Michele Thorsen, what brings you here today?" He didn't offer to shake her hand.

She flipped a few pages in the spiral notepad that was resting on her crossed legs. Her right hand cradled a gold Cross-pen, ready to write down any information that Trainor was willing to give her. "Detective Trainor, you know exactly what I want."

A smile spread across his face. He allowed his hazel eyes to travel in a slow and exaggerated sweep as he undressed Thorsen, coming to rest on her exposed thigh. Trainor rarely had the opportunity to respond to a statement like the one she just offered, and he wouldn't let it pass. He liked to piss off the reporter any way he could. Making some kind of sexual remark always worked. He just didn't know how close to home his remarks hit. "I was wondering when you would come to your senses. Shall we meet in your bed or mine?"

Thorsen's already hostile eyes turned deadly. "You male chauvinist pig! That's all you men ever think about."

"I see you still haven't found a sense of humor. Once a liberal, always a liberal." He noticed she was about to go ballistic and backed off when he saw the slight outline of a rectangular object in her right blazer pocket. "What is it that you came here for?"

"I've been assigned to cover the story on the drug killings. And I'm getting the complete runaround."

That would explain why she was in a bad mood. Except she wasn't getting the runaround, she was told everything else the rest of the press was told. The simple truth was that the police had no idea what happened. "Which one's?" Trainor asked, "We have had quite a few in the past week."

Thorsen launched right into the interrogation. "The killings outside of Ramone's restaurant last night. Are these killings related to the ones in which the two police officers were shot?"

"No idea," Trainor answered truthfully.

"What were the victims' names? Did they have prior convictions?" Her pen was ready.

"I can't give the names. The next of kin haven't been notified yet." He watched as Thorsen shifted in her seat, obviously getting irritated.

"How many people were involved and what kind of gun or guns were used?" She was clearly trying to hold her temper.

"We don't know how many people were involved, or what kind of weapon or weapons were used." That was a half-truth, he thought.

Thorsen lost it. She threw her notepad on the desk and slammed her feet on the floor as she stood in front of the desk. "Trainor, you can be a real shit! This is a major story, and the public has a right to know what's going on. You--"

Trainor held up his hand, cutting her off in mid-sentence. "Calm down, Thorsen. I'll fill you in with what I can. But first, I want your word that what I say here stays here. I'll give you the okay when you can air your story with the information I give you. Agreed?"

She started to protest. "You can't do that!"

Trainor remained calm and shrugged. "Yes, I can. For reasons of my own, I'm talking to you." He pointed to the crowd of reporters outside his office. "Look behind you." She turned to look out the window. "I can bring any one of those reporters in here and tell them what I can tell you. The PR officer usually handles you people, but for reasons of my own, I'll keep you up to date on what I think the real story is— not the department's. In the meantime, you go on the air and report the same bullshit that every other reporter does. Agree or get out," he said firmly. The truth of the matter was that he had no idea what the real story was, the investigation was just beginning.

She didn't have time to think long; Trainor was offering a one-time chance for exclusive information. "Agreed."

"Good. Sit your ass down and shut up. " She did and Trainor tossed her the notepad. "Here it is in a nutshell. We have no suspects or solid leads in either case. I will tell you what we do have. A lot of dead bad guys and two wounded cops. Every victim is local and tied into drugs, with the exception of three victims from Thursday's killings. Those three were from Peekskill, a city in Westchester County north of New York. Two were small-time drug dealers, and then there's the guy in the suit." He purposefully left out Stroehmann's name— the next of kin had been notified so he could have given out his name. He knew Thorsen was a good reporter, and if she got hold of Stroehmann's name, who knows what kind of damage she could do.

Thorsen's pen was busy scribbling, not missing a single syllable.

"Now, I don't believe these killings to be somebody moving into somebody else's turf like we've said. That's just a theory of mine." He received a frown for that comment.

"Why?" Thorsen didn't want to be lied to.

"At both sites, all the drugs, drug paraphernalia, weapons, and money were left. No one picked them up. The police took possession of all the material before you people could get pictures of it."

"So?"

"That means that whoever killed these people isn't interested in the drugs, weapons, or the money. We're dealing with people who are very professional and we don't know why these druggies were killed." He reached for the photographs of the crime scenes and placed them in front of Thorsen. She grimaced when she saw the photographs of the practically headless corpses.

"My God, what did this?"

"As far as we can tell, one bullet to each victim." Trainor scooped up the photographs and placed them back in the folder. "That's it. That's all I know." He decided he had said enough and abruptly ended the conversation. He reached across the desk and grabbed the notepad out of her hands.

"Give me that back, I need those notes," Thorsen demanded, her eyes wide with shock at Trainor's actions.

"I don't want any record of me mentioning this." Trainor tore the pages into tiny pieces and tossed them into the circular file next to his desk. He stood with his hand outstretched. "Give me your tape recorder."

"I don't have a tape recorder," she said defiantly. She had underestimated Trainor's intelligence and scrutiny.

Trainor let her see his dark side. "Don't fuck with me. If you do, I'll make your life miserable and see to it that you get your press pass lifted. Give me the recorder in your blazer pocket." Knowing he had her, she reluctantly reached into her pocket and handed it over. He took out the micro-cassette and handed the recorder back to her.

"Why me?" she asked as she put the recorder back in her pocket.

"What do you mean?"

"Why did you choose me over the other reporters? She rose from the chair and threw her handbag over her shoulder.

"Because you have a great body, and I wanted to stare at it while we talked." That was only partly true, and not the only reason. Trainor had switched tactics again to keep her off balance.

"S.O.B.," she said and stormed out the door.

CHAPTER THREE

Monday, May 25, 1:15 p.m.

Morris Street was the perfect setting for the current occupant of the house. The spacious and tastefully decorated three-bedroom house was located in a quiet residential middle class neighborhood in Albany. It blended in with the rest of the neighborhood that consisted of houses of like design.

Mossad owned the house on Morris; it was their safe house that Moshe Koretsky operated from in Albany. Officially, Mossad always told the United States government that they wouldn't operate against or in the United States. They lied. The operation Koretsky was conducting was exactly that. Though he wasn't operating directly against the United States Government, he was operating against the citizens and the law. Albany, New York was an inconspicuous and advantageous place for Mossad to work. The city and the Port of Albany weren't scrutinized by the Customs Service like the international ports of New York and Miami. For that reason, Koretsky picked Albany for his current operation.

"Well, sir, my contact was eliminated," Koretsky spoke into

the receiver of the secure telephone as he sat on the sofa that faced out the bay windows. The call was placed to Tel Aviv, Israel. He listened impatiently as his boss asked the questions of who killed his contact, Allen Stroehmann. "I don't have any idea who pulled it off," he said flatly, " but I'm confident that there has been no leak and the operation is not in jeopardy. Obviously, our timetable has been thrown out of whack, but I'm working on a solution this very moment. I'm still going to meet the carrier on the docks." His boss was satisfied and disconnected the call.

Koretsky's mind was racing. He had to find another replacement, and fast. Under normal circumstances, Koretsky would have aborted the operation under the pretense that the operation was compromised. But, he had been in the field of espionage for twenty-odd years and his gut instincts told him that the operation wasn't in jeopardy, and that his contact was eliminated for an entirely separate reason. He grabbed his L. L. Bean windbreaker from the tree stand on his way down the stairs. Pausing just before he opened the door, he checked to make sure his jacket covered the Makarov pistol stowed in his trousers' waistband at the small of his back. Satisfied it was hidden, he closed the door behind him and hopped into the brown Ford Taurus.

Driving the city streets at the posted speed limits, Koretsky reached his destination at two o'clock. He circled 60 State Street three times from various locations to make sure he and the building weren't under surveillance from any counterintelligence teams from the CIA or FBI. He drove past the twenty-story building and beared right at the top of the hill; where State merged with Washington Avenue and Eagle Street. That was where City Hall was located. He continued up Washington, past the mammoth structure of the New York State Education Department building, and parked in front of a small antique shop. From there, he continued his security precautions by walking up Washington a few blocks, stopping to pretend to glance in the store windows, only to use the reflection to see if anyone was following him.

Crossing the street and continuing his walk, he paused to hail a taxi that took him across town where he continued his counter-surveillance on foot. After a while, he switched cabs again. This taxi took him back to the juncture of Washington, Eagle, and State via a circuitous route where Koretsky exited the cab in front of the Court of Appeals.

Through his sunglasses, he surveyed the park across the street to see if he was being watched as he exited the car. His eyes came to rest on a man sitting under a tree reading a newspaper, but dismissed him as what he appeared to be. In his line of work, he was always on the lookout for something out of the ordinary. Blending in with the rest of city folk, he took the sidewalk south on Eagle past City Hall and a statue of Philip Schuyler. He turned left on the descent down State Street, passing various clothing shops and the crowded Capital District Transportation Authority bus stop.

Coming to the intersection of Pearl, he crossed against traffic and paused at the entrance of 60 State Street, making sure he was at the right building. He checked once again to see if he was being followed. He wasn't. It was three o'clock when he bounded up the steps through the glass doors, nodded to the security guard and located the brass directory fastened to the marble wall next to three pairs of elevators. He glanced at the names on his search for Miller, Katz & Kaufmann, Attorneys at Law. It was the most powerful and successful law firm money could buy in the Capital District. Reading through the names on the brass directory, he found the firm's name located on the eighteenth floor. He didn't notice the name located under the law firm's, Kaderri Financial Services.

The carpeted and panel lined elevator opened in the suite on the eighteenth floor. Upon stepping out of the elevator, he was greeted by all types of green foliage surrounding the elevator's frame. He almost bumped into a tall, handsome, light-skinned, black man smartly dressed in a Poplin suit waiting to get on the elevator. "Excuse me," Koretsky said stepping out of the other man's way, whose arms were full of overflowing manila folders.

"I'm sorry, I should have been looking."

Dismissing the incident, Koretsky took three determined strides and came to the receptionist's desk. The gold plated nameplate on the mahogany desk read, "Ms. Waters."

Ms. Waters, a pretty young lady with short, red hair, and deep beautiful green eyes looked up from her computer monitor at Koretsky, then back at the appointment book. Nobody was scheduled for any appointments. "May I help you?" she asked.

"I'd like to see Joshua Miller."

"I'm sorry, sir, but you don't have an appointment scheduled." She flipped a few pages on Miller's appointment book. "His next available time is next Thursday, I'd be happy to schedule an appointment for you then."

"This is very important," Koretsky said. He didn't like to be told no.

"I'm sorry, but Mr. Miller is very busy. . .

Koretsky's eyes narrowed to slits. "You tell him that Ariel Steiner is here to see him."

The receptionist looked him full in the face. "I cannot interrupt him when he is in consultation. I'm sure you understand."

Koretsky was losing his patience. "If you want your job to be here tomorrow, Miz Waters, you tell him Ariel Steiner is here."

The coldness in his voice apparently changed her mind. She sighed and picked up the phone and dialed Miller's extension. "Mr. Miller, there is a gentleman here to see you. I told him you were in consultation... His name is Ariel Steiner. . . right away." She turned with a skeptical look to Koretsky. "He will see you now."

"See you tomorrow, Louise," Marc Kaderri said to his secretary as he departed his office.

"You're leaving early on a Monday?" She said, glancing at her watch surprised at the time. Kaderri rarely left before six, but then again, he never was predictable.

"I'm going to work out."

Louise sometimes wished she were his wife, or better yet, his mistress. But, she knew he would never entertain the thought of cheating on his wife. Louise's heart always melted when she looked into his steel blue eyes. He had short, light brown hair that parted down the middle and touched the tip of his ears. His square jaw and flat cheekbones gave his face a handsome quality that many women found attractive. His oval face was weathered from his time in the Army. Giving him character and ruggedness.

Louise even told Kaderri that she fantasized what it would be like to make love to him. Having his powerful arms cradling her naked body as he carried her to the bed. She thought of running her fingers through his short hair as their bodies entwined. She knew he'd be magnificent. But, she realized it would never be, and there was nothing wrong with fantasizing.

"Work up a good sweat." A smile spread across her face.

Kaderri slipped the Porsche next to his wife's Corvette in their reserved spots in the parking lot of A Better Body. It was a huge club, complete with six racquetball courts, six indoor tennis courts, and an indoor track. It had an Olympic size swimming pool, without diving boards, two saunas, and six hot tubs of various sizes. The two aerobics rooms were for beginner and advanced classes. The huge weight rooms were complete with free weights, Nautilus exercise machines, stationary bicycles, stair climbers, and every other exercise machine imaginable. There were even heavy bags for the want-to-be boxers. He strode through the glass doors, waved to the receptionist and leaped up the stairs into Sara's private office.

He quickly changed into a pair of shorts and T-shirt that stretched across his broad chest and shoulders. He descended the stairs and entered the weight room. A deep inhale through his nose revealed the scent of sweat, and various types of deodorant working overtime. Glancing around the weight room, Kaderri looked for a weight bench that was open. The room was filled with all shapes and sizes of bodies. Male and female alike. Large and small. Lean and fat. Some women wore tight multi-colored spandex bodysuits that showed off their curvy shapes. Some wore sweatpants and sweatshirts to hide their bodies, working energetically so that one day they could wear the tight spandex bodysuits. The same with the men. Some were monstrous. Some wore skimpy tank tops and short, tight shorts to show off their hours of hard work. Like some of the women, some men wore sweats to hide their bodies. Probably hoping that one day, they too, would have the muscles and physique like the monsters. Amid grunts and groans of people trying for that one last repetition and words of encouragement from spotters, Kaderri found a bench on his first stop in his hour-long workouts. He lifted weights for strength and conditioning, not to bulk up like a body builder or manufacture beach muscles to impress the ladies. Kaderri worked his upper and lower body on alternate days, except for Sunday, which was his day of rest. He worked through various types of bench presses, upper and lower arm exercises, and upper and lower back exercises. Finishing his workout with one hundred eighty pounds on the shoulder press, he felt a smooth hand glide up his right sweaty biceps. The other hand quickly covered his eyes. The delicate fingers moved up his shoulder, climbed his neck, and circled his ear. Warm breath flowed into his ear attached to a delicate voice.

"Care to join me in working up a bigger sweat? I have a private office where you can work on lower back exercises."

"Depends," Kaderri answered as the delicate fingers moved to his chest and soft kisses were placed on his neck.

"On what?" the once sultry voice shot back. The kisses ceased and fingernails slowly began to sink into his flesh.

"If my wife isn't around, I'll gladly join you." He spun around to allow Sara a seat on his lap and gave her a kiss hello.

"You're early. What's up?" Sara asked.

"I've got some work to do tonight, so I wanted to get my workout done early. I just finished and I'm headed up to the shower."

"Ooh, can I lather you up?" Her devilish smile flashed across her face and she slowly wiggled on his lap.

"You bet!" He knew she was joking this time, though they'd had intimate encounters in their private shower.

"Hey," she stood abruptly, "do you like my new outfit?" Kaderri studied the red, white, and blue spandex thong bodysuit and matching shorts. "It's part of your anniversary present."

"It looks fantastic on you, but I don't get it." Kaderri furrowed his brow. He wondered what his wife was up to this time.

"Look closer." She pointed to her left breast. Amid the colored geometric shapes, there was a logo for the NFL team, the Giants. He loved the Giants.

"Hey, I like that!" His smile turned into a questioning look again. "What does that have to do with my anniversary present?"

The receptionist, who was waving to Sara and then pointed to a Federal Express courier next to her, caught Sara's attention. She turned to Kaderri. "You'll see." She smiled, gave him a kiss and left to sign for the package. He smiled to himself and watched in awe—as did many others in the gym—as Sara glided across the gym floor.

Kaderri wandered the complex to make sure things were in order, especially in the men's locker room. He strode past the whirlpool, stopping to chat with a few of the members he knew. Turning the corner, he was in the section that provided lockers for members who paid their membership fee on an annual basis. A huge man, standing six inches taller than Kaderri's six-foot frame, and twice as wide with a long blonde ponytail, had his head in the locker, sniffing deeply. Kaderri walked over to him, knowing what he was doing. Kaderri tapped the man on the shoulder, "Hey pal, what's up?"

The huge man turned to see who interrupted him. "Go away," he said, not making any attempt to hide the cocaine. His wide set brown eyes were already glazed over, and the white particles that didn't make it into his nostrils clung to his mustache. He turned his head back into the locker and snorted more cocaine.

Kaderri looked at the company provided monogrammed nametag glued to the locker. It read Greg Sander. "Sander, get rid of the nose candy and get the hell out of this club. Your membership is terminated." Kaderri didn't think about the eighteen hundred-dollar annual membership fee the club would be losing, and didn't care.

Sander stood to his full height, pumping his huge arms and pointed a finger at Kaderri's chest. "Get the fuck out of here before you get hurt." Spittle clung to the strands of his blonde mustache that hung over his upper lip.

With fire in his eyes, Kaderri responded. "I'm not going to tell you again. Get rid of the coke and get the hell out of this gym." Kaderri didn't back down from Sander's threat. He balled his fist and took a step forward to reinforce his position.

Sander responded by swinging his huge arm at Kaderri's head and missed. Anticipating the move, Kaderri ducked and countered with a blow to Sander's stomach. The punch had little effect. Sander's stomach was like iron. Before Sander could react, Kaderri immediately landed a solid punch at the exposed kidney. Then another, and another. He scored direct hits as Sander winced and tilted in pain. "Had enough?" Kaderri asked. The flame in Kaderri's eyes grew brighter and more menacing as he looked directly into Sander's.

Sander answered with an inaccurate jab to Kaderri's head that missed again. He was no match for Kaderri's experience in hand to hand combat and black belt status in the Korean martial art, Tae Kwon Do. Deciding to finish the one-sided fight, Sander's outstretched arm left his ribs exposed, and Kaderri took advantage of the shot. Kaderri quickly pivoted on the ball of his left foot so his left heel and right hip were pointing at Sander. He tucked his right leg by bringing his knee up to his chest. With extreme power, Kaderri released a sidekick under Sander's outstretched arm. The bottom of this foot landed with a sickening crunch as he easily broke two ribs. He quickly followed with a roundhouse kick with his left foot to the solar plexus, knocking the air out of the behemoth. Sander crumpled to the carpeted floor gasping for air and gently holding his sore ribs.

Kaderri looked down at Sander dispassionately, who was looking up at him with tears in his eyes. "It looks like you need some help," Kaderri said. He grabbed Sander by his ponytail with this left hand and grasped a fistful of shorts with the other and lifted him so he was on his hands and knees. A cry of pain emitted deep from within as the hair was pulled from its roots and the elastic leg band on his under shorts cut into Sanders testicles, adding to the extreme pain from the broken ribs. Applying a little force to the wounded man, Kaderri pushed him forward until his head slammed into the wall of blue lockers.

Kaderri leaned over Sander, seeing if he was stupid enough to get up and try to fight back when a pair of strong hands grabbed both of his arms. Kaderri's first instinct was to turn and punch the owner of the hands, thinking they might belong to a friend of Sander's. He quickly surmised that if they were, he would have been blindsided already.

"Okay, buddy, that's enough. He's not gonna get up."

Kaderri eyed the black man standing in front of him. He noticed the man in the gym before and assumed he was a member, but was he a friend of Sander's? "Who are you? Are you a friend of his?" Kaderri asked warily, stepping back and preparing to fight him if necessary.

"No." the man held up his hands. "I'm Detective Keith Bernard, Albany Police. Who are you?"

Kaderri relaxed and let his guard slip, but just a little. The man in front of him didn't display any badge, but he did speak with confidence and authority. "I'm Marc Kaderri. My wife owns this place. Do you have a badge, Detective?"

"You need help, Marc?" asked one of Kaderri's weightlifting partners as he emerged from the hot tub wrapped in a towel. He looked ready for a fight.

"No thanks, Jim, I got it under control. But get Sara, will you?" His friend stood there for a second longer before he left, making sure Marc really didn't need his assistance.

34

Bernard fished his badge and ID out of his back pocket and handed it to Marc to examine. As Kaderri studied the badge, Bernard helped Sander to the bench that was between the rows of lockers.

Kaderri handed the badge back to Bernard. "Okay, detective, arrest the son-of-a-bitch."

"Arrest him for what?" Bernard asked. "All that I saw was you beating the crap out of him."

"How about possession of a controlled substance?" Kaderri was annoyed, but then thought Bernard probably hadn't seen the entire episode. He took a deep breath that filled his lungs and relayed the incident up until the point where Bernard intervened.

Bernard reached into Sander's open locker and pulled out a vile of cocaine. "Well Mr. Kaderri, it appears you maybe right."

Another man emerged from the spa dripping wet, clinging to his towel wrapped loosely around his waist to prevent it from falling off. He looked at Sander sitting on the bench, his face contorted in pain and holding his broken ribs. "What's going on here?" he demanded.

"I got it under control, Gary." Bernard answered. "Go get an ambulance for this guy, and have two uniformed officers accompany him. I'll meet them at the hospital and book him for possession once he's fixed up." He threw Sander a handkerchief to stem the flow of blood from his forehead.

Apparently seeing that he wasn't needed, Trainor left to call the ambulance and uniformed officers.

Sara arrived with Jim, who still appeared to be ready to fight. She walked up to Kaderri and Bernard, looked at Sander who was now holding a handkerchief to his cut forehead, and cradling his ribs. She quickly became concerned and placed her hand on Kaderri's arm. "Are you okay, Marc?" she asked. "What's going on?"

"Yeah, honey, I'm fine." Kaderri introduced Sara to Bernard, and quickly explained to her what happened.

The arrival of the paramedics interrupted the conversation. Once Sander was gone, Bernard said, "I'm going to need the two of you down at the station."

"Right, Detective," Kaderri answered for both of them.

Monday, May 25, 3:10 p.m.

Despite the help of Gary Trainor, Michele Thorsen knew what the police were doing. She decided to find out on her own if the two incidents were related, and try to uncover who the killer was. If she was successful in breaking the case, or covering it successfully, she was hoping that her journalism career would expand into the international arena.

Reviewing her notes, she completed a summary. One full week had gone by since the shoot-out involving the police on the corner of Northern and Livingston, and four days since the six bodies were found in the alley outside Ramone's. Nine people dying violent deaths in six months was unheard of in Albany. Nine in one week took an act of Congress. Many news stations and reporters were airing stories of all kinds across the radio waves and television screens. None were accurate. All focused on what the police were feeding the hungry reporters—New York City gangs and drug pushers trying to expand their territory. The information they were getting was tightly controlled and not accurate either.

Dressed in a matching green leather mini skirt and blazer that covered a white cotton tank top, Michele combed the streets of Albany to get some answers and the feelings of the cities' inhabitants.

It was four o'clock in the afternoon and some of the office workers were leaving early. Armed with her microphone and cameraman, Tony Patten, she positioned herself on Washington Avenue, just outside the Alfred E. Smith State office building. She spied a well-dressed man in a blue two-piece suit and polished black shoes. He looked like the intelligent type. "Excuse me," she said politely, "What's your opinion on the recent drug murders?" She thrust the microphone in the man's face.

"Uh, well, uh, I think they're unfortunate." He looked into the camera.

"In what way?" She asked another question hoping to elicit a more substantive answer. She stuck the microphone back in his face.

"Uh, those people shouldn't have been killed. Hey, am I gonna be on TV?"

Thorsen pulled the microphone back and thanked the man for his time. She turned to Patten, "That was a waste. He is definitely one of those 'dumber than you look' types."

Next, she came up to a heavyset mother with three small children in tow. Hoping this one would give a more literate answer, she posed the same question. "What's your opinion on the recent drug murders?"

The lady seemed to be ecstatic that the reporter asked her and gave a matter-of-fact answer. "Those no good swines deserved it! I hope more of them get it that way."

"Do you really mean that?" Thorsen asked, amazed at the lady's conviction. "Those people are now dead, some may have had families."

"You bet I mean it, honey." The lady raised her voice a few decibels. "And what about the families of the people they kill? Slime like that spread their filth all over this place. Pushing those drugs and gettin' little children involved. They should all die!"

"Are you getting all of this?" Michele whispered to Tony out of the corner of her mouth. He nodded. A small crowd started gathering to see what the lady was so enraged about. This was the perfect highlight for the news segment, Thorsen thought.

"I agree with her!" an anonymous voice shouted from the crowd. The group of ten or so people shouted in agreement. Thorsen asked a few other individuals the same question when the crowd dissipated. By 5:30 p.m., both her and Patten moved into Arbor Hill, the northern section of the city that was abundant in low-income housing and rampant with drugs. On the streets there, the answers were quite different. She came to two black men who were sitting on overturned garbage cans. "Guys, what are your opinions on the recent drug murders?"

The man wearing a black baseball cap and a jogging suit answered first. When he spoke, he butchered the English language. "Man, I tell you, they should find those dudes who popped them and shot them, too. Those dudes were just trying to make a living."

"Like yeah," the other one said. He was dressing a similar manner but his vocabulary was much better. "They were exercising their rights of freedom. Freedom to do what-ever they want."

The first one interjected with a laugh. "They was using the free enterprise system in America."

"Hey man, that's right!" They gave each other a high five. "Free enterprise."

Monday, May 25, 5:45 p.m.

Bernard finished the report on the arrest of Sander back at the precinct. Trainer's side of the office was still a mess. "Gary, what do you think of that guy, Kaderri?"

"Well—" Trainor started to answer.

"I think he could have killed Sander in a heartbeat," Bernard said quickly. "Do you agree? I wonder where he got that scar on his left arm? It was pretty ugly." He suddenly got a sense of déjà vu.

"I don't know. I didn't see the fight—" Trainor said, trying to answer the questions but was cut off again.

"I saw it in his eyes. " Bernard's' thoughts carried him away back to the fight at A Better Body. When he arrived at the scene, he heard the smaller man ask the bigger man if he had enough. He watched with fascination as the fight continued for another three seconds. In that short time he studied the obvious victor, Kaderri, thinking that he had seen him before. After intervening to prevent any further damage to Greg Sander after his head was rammed into the locker, Bernard was thankful that Kaderri didn't offer any resistance. Despite all of his own training and experience, he was no match for the speed and skill that Marc Kaderri displayed. Jesus Christ, Bernard remembered, rubbing the palms of his hands. Kaderri

38

was a force to be reckoned with. It took a certain type of man to be calm and extremely self-confident one minute and extremely violent, but not reckless, the next. Marcus Kaderri knew how to control his power and emotions like few men did. They were the trademark of a highly disciplined man who was accustomed to using them and wasn't afraid to use them. Despite his size, Kaderri had more power and strength than his physical appearance led on.

A moment late, Bernard heard Trainor's voice. "Keith? Hello? Are you in there?" Trainor waved his hand in front of Bernard's face and got no reaction.

"I'll be back, I gotta make a private phone call." Bernard sprinted from his chair and raced down the hallway through the front doors to the pay phone outside the station.

"Keith!" Trainor called after him. "Where are you going? What's going on?"

Monday, May 25, 7:30 p.m.

Two attorneys, Kaderri like to call them ambulance chasers, sat opposite Kaderri in his conference room. White and yellow sheets of legal paper covered the walnut top of the circular table. Somewhere in the mess was the proposal for a buy-sell agreement Kaderri offered that the attorneys needed. The incident at the club earlier that day was locked deep in the chambers of this mind along with the drug dealers he and Wolff had eliminated. Now it was time for business.

"Don't you two see the need for the agreement?" Kaderri asked. He had been going over this for the past hour and a half. This was his second meeting with the attorneys.

"Not really," Henry Jakab answered.

"Let me get this straight. Are you married?" Kaderri pointed to Jakab. He nodded. Kaderri turned to the other partner, Alfred Moore. "Are you married?"

"You know the answer to that." Moore held up his left hand to show the wedding ring on his stubby finger.

Kaderri went over the basics of a buy-sell agreement for the third time. Lawyers thought they knew everything. If all lawyers were like those two, he thought, well, no wonder the country was in the shape it was in. Kaderri continued in the most rudimentary way, "Al, if Henry dies, do you want his wife to become a partner in the firm?"

"Absolutely not," Moore answered.

"Henry, if Al dies, do you want to become a partner with his wife in the firm?"

"No," Jakab answered.

"Well, without a buy-sell agreement, if one of you dies, your spouse owns your half of the business. That's the law, and you two should know that, being divorce attorneys. Married couples own things jointly. I'm surprised you don't already have it set up. You could write it yourself."

"Then why are we here talking to you, an insurance agent?" Jakab asked.

Kaderri was losing his patience. He hated the high and mighty attitude lawyers carried. "Because you need to fund the agreement," he said sternly. "Where is the money going to come from to buy out the dead partner's spouse? Only an idiot would got to a bank and ask for a loan."

"Why is that?" Moore asked. He seemed to be the brighter of the two.

"First, you have to see if you can get the loan. Second, you have to pay back the loan and the interest. Doing it that way is bad business. It costs more money."

"Then what do you suggest?" Moore seemed to be following Kaderri's logic.

"Buy a life insurance policy on each other. It's cheaper on the dollar, and extremely flexible. Using an insurance contract is the proper way to fund a buy-sell."

"I see your point," Jakab answered.

Kaderri hashed over the numbers with the lawyers and came out with the proper policy. It was eight o'clock in the evening when he shut his office door.

Monday, May 25, 7:55 p.m.

Moshe Koretsky was dressed smartly and casually for a

stroll on the docks at the Port of Albany. The calves of his tan Levi's Dockers and Timberland boat shoes were splashed with specks of mud from walking through the unavoidable puddles. He arrived to meet his contact, Pedro, a deck hand from the Liberian registered freighter Whispering Sea, moored at its pilings. Koretsky watched the freighter's crane unload its cargo of steel spools from its deep bowels for shipment to various sites across the country. He was always amazed at how something so big and heavy could float on water. But, Koretsky wasn't interested in the steel, only one small two-foot by two-foot wooden box that was contained deep within its bowels.

Koretsky watched from the shadows as Pedro carried his fit, muscular body with pride and a "don't fuck with me attitude". He was reading something in his hand, but what, Koretsky couldn't determine from that distance. After a moment, Pedro's path took him out of Koretsky's view.

The crimson orb in the sky descended behind the city of Albany, making for a wonderful picture of the city skyline. The structure of Albany's tallest building, New York State's Office of General Services, pointed skyward like an arrow aimed at the heavens.

Long shadows stretched across the docks as the ship's floodlights stemmed their creeping advance. Koretsky stood in the shadow of the new storage facility, Stroehmann Storage, and glanced at this watch. It read eight o'clock. Muffled footsteps from rubber-soled shoes heading toward him heightened his senses while the adrenaline flowed freely through his veins. He pulled the Makarov from his waistband, attached the silencer, and held it with the tip of the barrel level with his ear and pointing skyward. He loved this part of the job, the excitement, the danger, the chance of death.

A figure appeared with the footsteps. A muscular man that stood just shy of six feet with a wooden box carried on his shoulder approached Koretsky's position. "Don't move," Koretsky said, placing the pistol in the center of the man's forehead. The man stopped, tense, but not frightened. "Too bad it's not raining."

41

Koretsky waited for the proper response. If the man responded incorrectly, Koretsky would fire twice and walk away. If the man said a specific sentence, Koretsky would be alerted that the man was compromised and the exchange wouldn't take place. If he responded correctly, things would go as planned. He hated playing these stupid games with code words, but he knew they were necessary for operational security.

"Rain is the fruit of all life," the man responded correctly in a Latin accent.

"Let's get this over with, Pedro." That was all Koretsky knew to call the man standing in front of him. He lowered his weapon from Pedro's forehead.

"You have something for me?" Pedro asked calmly, his right hand was behind his back.

"Yes." Koretsky reached slowly into his windbreaker and pulled a folded manila envelope from the breast pocket of his shirt. "Open the box first," Koretsky ordered.

Pedro squatted and placed the box at his feet. He pried the top off with a Swiss Army knife that he pulled from his trouser pocket. He stood and took two steps back so Koretsky could examine the contents.

Koretsky eyed Pedro suspiciously, the same way he did everybody, no matter how long he knew them. It was one thing he always did in the game of spying. With his left foot, he lifted the top slightly to peek inside. But he didn't actually look. He was looking at Pedro's eyes, which were locked on the box.

In the coming darkness, and the last traces of the sun boring into Pedro's eyes, Koretsky raised the pistol to Pedro's forehead once again; knowing it would be hard for him to see it.

"What the fuck you doin'?" Pedro asking in a calm voice. But the look in his eyes betrayed the terror that gripped him like being wrapped in a wet blanket.

Koretsky looked directly into Pedro's eyes and a thin smile spread across his face. "Goodbye." Koretsky cold-heartedly fired twice in rapid succession, placing two bullets between Pedro's eyes and blowing out the back of his skull. Pedro was dead before his body hit the ground.

Koretsky had had no choice but to eliminate Pedro. Even though the exchange went as planned, he had to go on the assumption that Pedro was compromised like his previous contact, Stroehmann. He couldn't take the chance of getting compromised himself.

Koretsky placed the pistol back in his waistband and the empty envelope back in his pocket. He gave Pedro's body a quick search to see if there was anything there that could incriminate him. He found the piece of paper with the name and address of the prostitute, and stuffed that into his pocket. Scooping up the wooden box, he headed for his car, leaving Pedro's body where it lay.

CHAPTER FOUR

Monday, May 25, 9:25 p.m.

"Thanks for the company, Tony," Michele Thorsen said through slurred speech as she sat on the wooden stool at the bar in The Steer House. The upscale restaurant was famous for its meat entrees, serving only the choicest cuts of beef and steak. If you wanted a Porterhouse grilled to perfection, or filet mignon with a delicate Bernaise sauce, The Steer House, located on James Street, was the place. It was one of the few places she frequented. She and Tony had put in a long day walking the streets, and the day's success wouldn't be aired on that evening's news. It had been a long time since she was drunk, and after a day like the one she just had, she thought she deserved to get a little tipsy. Her self-imposed two-drink limit went out the window.

"Are you sure you're going to be okay?" Tony Patten asked as he threw a ten-dollar bill on the bar to cover the last round of drinks and tip.

"Yeah, I'll be fine. See you tomorrow." She held up her white Russian in a toast to Tony.

"Be careful, don't hook up with any strangers. Are you sure you don't need a ride home? You've been hitting the sauce pretty good." Obvious concern was in his voice.

"Go home to your wife and kids, Tony." Michele winked to the older man and father of two. She found it both annoying and flattering when he showed his paternal instincts. "Good work today, it should be aired tomorrow night." Tony patted her on the shoulder and turned to walk out of the bar.

Sitting in a booth in a dimly lit corner of the bar, Robert Wolff, sat nursing a cold bottle of Samuel Adams lager. He sat in the same booth that he, Kaderri, Rufus "Ghost" Brown, and Steven Caron had been sitting in the night Steven was killed in the drive-by shooting.

That night was also the first time that Wolff and Kaderri had met Ghost. Steven and Ghost had been friends since Army basic training, and had kept in touch after graduation when Steven joined Special Forces and Ghost moved into the Quartermaster Corps. Although the three men had served together they never served together on the same team. When they left the Army at different times, it was ironic that they all settled in the same area.

Being the shy type, Wolff sat in his corner and observed the crowd. It was Thursday night and he hoped that some attractive woman would approach him. He didn't like the Friday and Saturday night crowds; they were too rowdy for his taste.

He observed a woman slowly getting drunk at the bar on white Russians. He admired her shapely legs in the green mini skirt that hiked up high on her thighs. He knew he had seen her before, but couldn't put his finger on it.

Swallowing the last of his beer in one gulp, Wolff worked up the courage to approach her. Spying the recently vacated stool, Wolff stood to work his way through the tables. He stopped briefly to dislodge the stone stuck in the bottom of his shoe. When he looked up, the stool was occupied. He couldn't make out the face from his angle, but the back of the man's head was very familiar. When the man turned to catch the bartender's attention, Wolff caught his profile. The sight of Moshe Koretsky sent a shivering chill throughout his body. His hand instinctively went for the 9mm Smith and Wesson tucked into the small of his back. He had started carrying it after he had spotted Koretsky at Ramone's.

Thinking that people might be watching him, he diverted his hand into the back pocket of his trousers to check that his wallet was still there. Slowly, he sat back down into his obscure booth and observed the two at the bar.

Michele Thorsen glanced with unsteady eyes at the man who gracefully sat in the stool next to her. He wasn't that good looking, but he had a ruggedness that drew her attention. Too bad, she thought, he had a growing stomach. She finished off her white Russian.

"How are you tonight? What can I get you?" asked the mulatto bartender. He smiled a bright smile against his darker skin as he stood behind the bar and looked over six highly polished brass beer taps.

"I'll take a scotch and water and give her another white Russian." The man threw a fifty-dollar bill on the bar.

"Thank you. . ." Michele slurred, not knowing the man's name.

"My name is Ariel Steiner. You're welcome." He held out his hand for Michele to shake.

"Michele Thorsen." She shook his strong, callused hand, "How'd you know I was drinking white Russians?"

"That's what it looked like. And if I was wrong, you or the bartender would have corrected me." He flashed a disarming smile. "This may seem like a pick-up line, but I have to ask. You are too pretty to be sitting here alone. Are you with someone?" Steiner looked around to see if anyone was walking over to kick him off the stool.

"No, I'm not. I was having a drink with my cameraman, but he went home to his family." She took a sip from her fourth drink.

"Cameraman?" He cocked an eyebrow. "What do you do for a living?"

Michele stared at him in disbelief. He didn't know who she was? Well, maybe he doesn't watch much TV. "I'm a reporter," she said.

"Ah, that explains the cameraman. I must say, you are a very beautiful reporter."

Michele took another sip. Here is another guy that is only after one thing. Why can't he ask about my job? "Ariel, what do you do for a living?" She tried to take the focus off her physical appearance.

"I'm in the import/export business."

"What do you import?" Michele became curious. Her reporter instinct took over; it was a habit that got her into trouble on more than one occasion. Many times, she turned good male prospects away by being too nosy. But, she still asked the questions.

"Wines," he answered quickly. "Are you working on any interesting stories?"

Michele's attitude changed. Maybe there was hope for men after all. This guy was interested in her work. "I'm working on the story of all the drug killings here in the past week."

"Drug killings?" Steiner sounded shocked. "I'm sorry, but I'm not from around here."

"Yes, there have been. . . a lot." She couldn't remember how many. This guy's an out-of-towner, which would explain why he didn't recognize her.

"Michele, tell me more about these murders." He ordered another white Russian for her a club soda for himself.

Robert Wolff studied the two at the bar with intensity. A figure blocked his view, and he looked up to see who the idiot was.

"Here's another beer, Doc." Rufus "Ghost" Brown said and placed the bottle in front of him. Wolff didn't notice. "What the hell are you looking at?"

"Thanks. That girl in the green. . ."

"Ah, looking for action tonight?" He slid into the booth across from Wolff. Ghost just got off duty from his part-time job. "She is definitely a looker." He turned to look at her. "Do you know who she is?"

"No," Wolff answered.

"She's a reporter. Michele Thorsen." Ghost was usually on duty when she came in and always served her.

Wolff snapped his fingers. "That's where I saw her, on TV. She's dong the story on the drug killings." His eyes never left the bar. He was staring at Koretsky.

"Something else is up," Ghost asked. "What is it?"

"That guy sitting next to her, what does he want?"

"Probably the same thing you want." Ghost smiled.

"Answer the fucking question!" Wolff kept his voice low, but hard. A few people glanced over at the use of his language. A high-class clientele visited the bar and most disliked the use of foul language.

Ghost held up his hand to quiet his friend. "Whoa, slow down, buddy. I asked what he wanted to drink, not if he wanted to take her home to fuck." His delicate features turned harsh. "Jesus Christ, Doc. Steven told me I could trust you and Marc with my life, but he also said to never cross you. Now I think I know what he meant."

"Sorry Ghost. I didn't mean it." He noticed Ghost's face relax.

Rufus "Ghost" Brown was a mulatto. The product of a white mother and a light-skinned black father. His features were more Caucasian than Negro and people found it hard to believe he was of mixed race. "Why is that guy so important?" Ghost glanced over to Koretsky and then back at Wolff.

"You don't want to know," Wolff answered pouring his beer into the glass and taking a sip. He then added, "If the situation warrants, I'll fill you in."

Ghost didn't press for more information. "Listen," Ghost lowered his voice and leaned across the table. "I have info on another deal. The target's name is Slapper."

"I'm listening." Wolff watched as Thorsen and Koretsky

stood and strode toward the door. Koretsky was holding her arm to keep her steady. "Let's go." Wolff rose to follow.

Monday, May 25, 11:40 p.m.

Michele Thorsen's two-story townhouse in Bethlehem, a well-to-do suburb south of Albany, was stylized without being expensive. Being only fifteen minutes from the bar, it seemed the logical place to go.

Michele lay spread eagle on the queen size bed with her arms wrapped around Steiner's neck. Both were stark naked as Steiner lay on his side next to Michele. He was kissing her delicate neck as his right hand rubbed her blonde pubic mound. He adjusted his position to let his mouth sink to her firm creamy breast so he could take an erect rosy nipple into his mouth.

"Ouch!" Michele said as his teeth sank too deep. His hand wasn't any gentler. "Take it easy, Ariel."

"Your body is so beautiful," he commented. He then roughly pushed two fingers into her dryness.

Michele was extremely drunk, but amazingly his roughness started to awake her desires. She remembered that she didn't like rough sex, but this time it was different. Maybe it was because it had been too long since she'd had a lover. He began moving his fingers harder, and his mouth alternated between nipples, causing her to become very wet and a tingling sensation that started in her abdomen spread to her breast and throughout her body.

It had been six months since she'd last had sex, and she missed it dearly. She never had anybody satisfy her desires, mostly because she had to control the session. If it didn't go the way she wanted, she'd stop participating, leaving her lover to do all the work.

She vividly remembered the last lover she was with. A very good-looking, twenty-eight year old contractor she met at The Steer House. He was well built, and well endowed, and let her have her way with him. While she was straddling him upon her bed, he lifted her up with his strong arms and laid her on her back. To that, she had immediately protested. "No! I have

49

to stay on top! Get off of me!"

"What the hell are you talking about?" Her lover stopped thrusting.

"I have to get on top," she demanded.

"Listen," he said, "you were on top for a long time, now it's my turn." He started thrusting again in a smooth, fast pace.

Michele tried again to get on top and regain her position of control, but he was too strong. She resigned herself to lay there and let him do the work. Angered that she couldn't get her way, she lay her hands at her sides, and didn't move.

When her lover finished, he quickly got dressed. As he was leaving her bedroom, he closed with a parting shot. "You really are a bitch." It was another disappointing encounter. She always had the assumption that he didn't care about her desires, he was only concerned about getting it on with a beautiful woman.

She moved her hand down between Steiner's legs to grab him, hoping his size would make up for his lack of tenderness. But, the rougher his hands and mouth became, the more excited she became.

This wasn't supposed to happen this way, she thought. She was supposed to be in control. Her mind told her to get out of this, and quick, but her body was enjoying it.

"Roll over," Steiner ordered. He twisted her so she was now on her stomach with her head hanging over the bed; her long blonde hair fell over her face like a waterfall.

She felt her legs being spread open. A hand stroked her inner thighs, causing her to lift her buttocks in the air. For a brief moment, she felt vulnerable and embarrassed, but then he entered her. He didn't fill her like the last lover, but he felt good. Her embarrassment and vulnerability dissipated when he began thrusting. Unlike an experienced, careful lover who started slow and smooth, Steiner was hard, fast, and uneven.

She managed to bring herself up on her hands and knees, and began to meet his thrusts. His strong hands grabbed her waist and pulled her onto him. A loud smack resounded throughout the bedroom as the slick skin of their bodies collided. An unfamiliar sound rang in her ears, replacing the smack of their bodies. As it grew louder, it sounded like a high pitched wail. She was startled to learn that the noise was coming from her. My God! She thought. Her surprise turned to shock when she called out, "Harder! Goddamnit!" It was if someone else had taken over her body. She grasped the sheet tighter and dug her toes deeper into the queen-sized bed for support. This was incredible, she thought.

By Steiner's noises and actions, it was evident he was enjoying himself immensely. His strong hands grasped her just above her hips to give him the extra power he needed when she told him to go harder.

Even though she was getting sore from Steiner's hard, wild thrusting, Michele couldn't get enough. It felt so good. Her desires were finally being fulfilled.

Suddenly, the room began to spin. Oh, no, she thought. Bed spins. She tried to focus on the floor, but Steiner's clothes were thrown all over it. She thought she noticed the tip of a pistol barrel poking out from underneath his shirt. Because of the alcohol, and her rocking body, she wasn't sure. Her stomach began to rumble. She tried to push the acid down that was clawing up her throat, but like the sex, it was beyond her control. "Stop!" she cried out.

"Huh?" Steiner said, surprise in his voice. "No." he grabbed her waist harder so she couldn't get free. His wild movements became more frenzied and the sound of his body smacking into hers became louder.

Enjoying the rough sex as she had never enjoyed sex before, and not wanting the unsurpassed pleasure to stop, she had to. As much as she tried, she couldn't control the gurgling and rumbling in her stomach. It was time to move and move now.

"Ariel, stop!" She kicked at his legs and wiggled herself free of his grip. She slid off the bed and landed with a thud. It was a good thing she had new padding installed under the carpet. She tried to stand but fell again. Using the night table for support, she stood on wobbly legs and made an erratic beeline to the master bathroom. Once inside, she slammed the door and bent over the toilet. Her stomach heaved and threw the contents into the blue water.

Ten minutes passed since she bolted into the bathroom and she was still throwing up. There was a rap on the bathroom door. "Are you ok?"

"I'll survive," she answered. That was soon followed with a moan and another heave of the stomach.

"It's fair to say the evening won't continue. I'll call you soon."

Michele emerged from the bathroom when she heard the faint click of the front door open then shut. Steiner was gone. She tried to focus her eyes on anything that was stationary. She couldn't. God, did her head hurt. If it hurt this bad now, she could only imagine what her head would feel like in the morning. She found the bed and collapsed. The bed wasn't spinning this time and she was fast asleep.

Monday, May 25, 9:00 p.m.

Kaderri pulled the Porsche into his driveway, and his stomach was telling him it was still hungry. The Big Mac, large fries, and Coke didn't go far. He hated eating this late at night, but his stomach wanted more food.

He slid the car into the garage and noticed that Sara's Corvette was missing. He walked into the kitchen, opened the refrigerator, and grabbed a cold Samuel Adams from the top shelf. Continuing on his way, he turned right off the kitchen into his home office, and deposited his leather briefcase on the sofa and checked his answering machine. There weren't any messages.

He grabbed the bottle opener and popped the top off the bottle, sailing it toward the wastebasket. The beer flowed freely from the bottle and splashed against his dry throat. Being a good and dutiful beer drinker, he grabbed a pint glass from the cupboard and poured the rest in. It's a sin to drink a great beer from the bottle, he thought.

Walking back into the kitchen, he grabbed two more Samuel

Adams and a bag of banana chips that Sara had bought. He wished she would buy ordinary snacks like potato chips. After untying the knot in his tie, he bounded up the stairs taking two at a time. He went into the master bedroom and the spa. Quickly undressing, he tossed his Brooks Brothers suit over the back of one of the two wingback chairs, threw his tailored shirt, socks, and underwear next and settled into the ninety-eight degree water.

Kaderri leaned his head back and let his mind drift like a stick floating down a stream. The drifting brought him back to his premature discharge from the Army and the beginning of the success he was now.

Not sure of what he wanted to do with his life, he had thought long and hard about his future. The skills he learned and practiced in the army weren't extremely marketable. He could have joined a police force somewhere, or taken a civil service job upon his discharge, but he wanted no part of that. An infantryman's skills just weren't in demand. But, he never had any regrets about serving his country. He only wished he could have continued his career on a full-time basis. He unconsciously rubbed his knee where the six-inch scar revealed where the shattered cap had been replaced.

But, he was happy. He had settle in the Capital District of New York, mostly because Sara opened A Better Body a year before he was discharged.

Kaderri had happened to be present when an insurance agent was giving Sara a quote on her liability and content's coverage on A Better Body. The entire sale took fifteen minutes, and that intrigued him.

"May I ask you a question?" Kaderri had asked the agent.
"Sure."

"How much money did you make on this sale?" Kaderri was usually quiet, but when he spoke, he was always blunt and to the point. He actually surprised himself by asking the question. That type of question was totally out of character for him. He was always the person who respected privacy and was quick to tell someone to mind their own business.

The insurance agent thought for a brief second before he answered. "Not much on this one, but somewhere in the neighborhood of a thousand dollars."

"What? That kind of money for what. . ." he glanced at his watch, "fifteen minutes?" Kaderri was really intrigued now. So, he asked the next question, this one being much bolder. "How much do you make in a year?"

The agent seemed like he was about to tell him to mind his own business, but realized Kaderri wasn't going to ask for a rebate on the price. The man was genuinely intrigued. "Well, I'm proud of my income. It was one hundred forty-eight thousand dollars last year."

"How can you make that much selling insurance?" Kaderri asked.

"It's not easy, I can say that. You work hard, put up with a bunch of bullshit." The agent went on to explain that insurance agents did more than sell insurance. They set up retirement programs such as 401k's, deferred compensation, the financial aspects of estate planning, mutual funds, and the list went on.

"I can honestly say that I never knew any of that," Kaderri admitted.

"Most people don't."

"How can I get involved in this?" Kaderri asked, leaning his elbows on the table.

"I own my own agency. Are you serious about getting involved?"

"Absolutely. I just got out of the army as a captain and I'm looking for a job."

"What did you do?" the agent asked.

"Eleven Bravo."

"I served in Vietnam, infantry too." The agent checked his Gucci watch and gave Marc a business card. "Listen, I have another appointment to go to. Call me tonight at my home, and we'll get together about getting you licensed. The job is yours if you want it." The agent seemed to have a soft spot for infantrymen.

54

"Sounds great. I'll call you later." They stood and shook hands.

Sara was giving him a strange look. Once the agent left, she asked, "You want to be an insurance agent?"

"I've got nothing to lose. Besides, look at the money he makes."

Marc Kaderri began his career the next day. It took him three months to go through the licensing process to become a fully licensed agent. Through hard work and sixteen hour days, six and one-half days a week, he made seventy thousand dollars his first year. But, he knew he could be better. Using the determination that earned him his Green Beret, he pushed himself and over the years, he furthered his education to become a Certified Life Underwriter, a Chartered Financial Consultant, and a Certified Financial Planner.

During his second year, he broke into the lucrative business market, setting up retirement plans, and got extremely lucky when he stumbled onto an estate planning case. One of his clients referred Kaderri to his elderly uncle, who owned four automobile dealerships and a construction company in the area. Kaderri sat down with the man and pointed out how much in tax the man's family would owe the government after his demise. To the man's dismay, and Kaderri's delight, the man was grossly underinsured. If he died, three quarters of his estate would go to both State and Federal governments. So, Kaderri wrote him a big insurance policy to cover the taxes enabling the family to inherit the entire estate, virtually tax free. The man was so happy with Kaderri, that he connected him to all his wealthy friends.

In his second year, his income doubled and he opened his own agency. His current income hovers around three hundred thousand; and combined with Sara's one hundred six, his military pay, their investments and rental income on the two family houses they own, they could easily afford the cars, the three quarter of a million dollar house, and the cabin in the Adirondack Mountains.

Marc Kaderri was living a great life. All except for the fact that his friend, Steven Caron, who saved his life, was murdered in cold blood by drug dealers.

Twenty minutes and another beer later, Sara flew in like a whirlwind to say she was home. She gave him a kiss hello and disappeared into the bedroom as fast as she arrived.

"Where were you?" Kaderri asked form the swirling water of the spa. She was being mischievous again.

"I had a problem at the club. No big deal," Sara answered from the bedroom. "How'd everything go with your appointment.

Kaderri let out a big sigh. "I hate ambulance chasers, but I made five thousand dollars on the buy-sell I set up for them."

"Well, after the day we had today, maybe this will help you feel better." Sara walked up to the spa wearing her satin bathrobe and carrying a Macys's shopping bag.

He was familiar with the bag. Macy's and Victoria's Secret were Sara's favorite stores. He assumed that she spent a large sum of money again, but he asked anyway. "What's that?" He pointed to the bag with his beer glass.

"Part of your anniversary present." She was wearing a huge smile that extended to her eyes. She threw him a towel to dry his hands and she sat back in the other chair that didn't have his clothes on.

Kaderri was like a child at Christmas when it came to opening gifts. He opened them like a child too. Sara handed him a box that would normally hold a necktie; wrapped in New York Giants gift-wrap. He tore off the paper on one pull and threw it into the wastepaper basket. His eager hands pulled the top of the box off and expected to find a Giants necktie. He was wrong.

He unfolded the tissue paper carefully and found sixteen tickets to the eight home games played in East Rutherford, New Jersey. His mouth hung open. "Holy shit!" Kaderri yelled. He got his long sought season tickets.

Marc?" Sara called as she reached into the bag again.

He looked up just in time to catch the autographed football heading straight for this nose. "My God, Sara, is this for real?"

Kaderri was overwhelmed.

"Yeah, dummy, it's real."

"How did you manage to get these? I thought season tickets were sold out for what? Ten, twenty years?" He picked up the football and read the autographs written across it.

"If you really want to know," Sara said smiling. She stood and shed her robe. I modeled this for a poster."

Kaderri stared in awe at Sara's beautiful body. She was wearing a very skimpy thong bikini that had the same geometric pattern as the bodysuit she had been wearing at the gym. Her large, firm breasts overflowed the tiny triangles that tried to contain them. Somehow, the name Giants was printed into the small space on the left breast. The bottom of the bikini was the smallest piece of material he'd ever seen. It fit snugly over her crotch and one thin strip wrapped under her and went up the crack between her buttocks. It looked more like a G-string than a bikini.

"You modeled that for a poster? When?" Kaderri loved for Sara to wear seductive clothing, but only for his eyes. He wasn't happy with what she did.

"I did this a few months ago when you were out of town on one of your seminars." She kept smiling. "A member at the club knows I was runner-up in the Miss America bullshit and put me in contact with the company who's in charge of the pictures. Besides, I posed with two of the players who covered most of me."

"What part wasn't covered?"

She leaned forward and put her hands on her knees. "They got a great shot of my tits." She juggled them and they almost popped out. Suddenly, she apparently noticed Kaderri wasn't amused. "Marc, stop being so conservative. They offered me ten thousand dollars to model this and the bodysuit I had on at the gym today. Every team in the league is having the same thing done. They're promoting a new line of swimwear and exercise clothing. I turned down the money for season tickets. They're yours for as long as you like."

Kaderri's demeanor softened. He should have known better than to question Sara. She was a brilliant and capable woman. Besides being runner-up in the Miss America Pageant where she was Miss New York State, she wasn't just a stunning face with a knockout body. She earned her MBA and utilized her business skills by purchasing the gym and making a profit every year since she bought it four years ago at age twenty-five.

"Okay, okay. So I'm a little overprotective. I'm sorry. Do we get a copy of the poster before it gets distributed?"

"You don't need the poster, you have me," Sara said, untying the top of her suit to release her breasts and sliding the bottoms off in a seductive dance. Gently she slipped into the water and straddled Kaderri's waist.

"Good point." He barely got the words out when Sara laid a passionate kiss on his mouth.

"Now, isn't that better than a poster?" Sara asked.

"Hmmm. That was nice, but I need more convincing. I never kissed a poster before." He reached behind his head and pressed the button to turn on the bubbles in the spa. With a rush of air entering the pipes, the bubbles exploded on the surface of the water.

Kaderri cupped one of Sara's breasts and brought the nipple into his mouth. Slowly and methodically he worked his tongue in small circles around her nipples and sucked it to erection. Sara's hands pulled his head closer as he continued a steady rhythm.

Sara moaned at his touch and reached down into the bubbly water to grab him. She slowly stroked him to full erection, and as usual, he was huge and ready to fulfill her desires. She grasped him and inserted the swollen tip into her, stopping to squeeze him with her strong muscles. Slowly she let go and lowered herself a little more, only to stop and squeeze again. Then she raised herself until he almost popped out. She repeated this process until he was all the way inside her, easily stretching and filling her.

The last time that she rode him down and squeezed him with her muscles, he blurted out in a passionate moan for her to stop. Even though he loved her moist tightness, her teasing was getting the best of him. He grabbed her tiny waist to prevent her from continuing her tease and to keep him from going over the edge.

He felt Sara's hand sliding up his muscular thigh and into his crotch where she began to fondle his testicles, and began to lightly scratch him with her long fingernails. A shiver rippled throughout his body when she grasped him harder and began to rock back and forth.

Sara had him in as far as he could go and began stimulating her clit by rubbing against him. Her breath came in short breaths and she began to shake as a warm ripple spread throughout her body. She arched her back, thrusting her breast into Marc's face, and moved faster as one spasm after another rocked her body. Her hands grappled Marc's neck and drew warm blood as she climaxed and her scream of delight echoed above the sound of the turbulent water.

Spinning around so now she faced away from Marc, Sara continued to straddle him and rocked her hips. Kaderri was slowly losing his staying power and fought to control his stamina. He reached around her with one hand and squeezed her soft, satin breast. His other hand reached down between her spread legs and massaged her erect clit. He placed light kisses on her slick back. He watched with delight as a series of shivers and goose bumps spread like wildfire across her bronzed skin. The motion of her body slamming against Marc's caused a continuous wave action in the spa that spilled the steaming water over the edge. "How does that feel?" he said in short gasps. He was almost to the majestic point.

"Don't stop!" She was reaching another orgasm.

Their moans hit the apex simultaneously. Like the force of a crashing wave slamming onto a beach, Sara and Marc climaxed together. Marc caught his breath as she collapsed against his chest. He wrapped his arms around her chest and squeezed her tight.

"Marc, what happened at the gym today?" Her voice was soft; almost afraid to ask as if there was a part about her husband that she didn't know.

"What do you mean? I thought we went over that at the gym and then at the police station."

After shutting off the bubbles in the spa, she turned to face him. "I guess I mean, well, what did you do in the Army?" She pulled at a strand of hair.

"What kind of question is that? You know what I did." He studied her nervous face through the rising steam of the water.

"Not really. The time in Germany we spent actually together was relatively short. I didn't see much of you; you were always on field exercises. Then I moved back here to get the gym opened."

"Sara, I was in Special Forces. I did a lot of teaching, and things along those lines. Some things I can't talk about."

"Did you teach people to do what you did to Greg Sanders?"

Marc took a deep breath. He didn't want to get into this now. Actually, most of what he did he couldn't tell her. He cradled her face and looked into her beautiful brown eyes. "Yes, Sara, I taught people martial arts. But let's not get into this now." The protective curtain came crashing down that isolated Kaderri and his thoughts and feelings. Once the curtain fell, it would be a while before it was raised. He leaned forward, gave her a soft kiss, and left the spa.

Sara felt scared as she watched Marc walk away. Her eyes focused on the ugly scar that wrapped around his knee. The usually kind and gentle man that she had married had changed. Or had he? Was this a side to her husband that existed, but that he never revealed? She thought she knew her husband inside and out, but now realized that there was something foreign. She always thought they were best friends first, lovers second, and could talk to each other about anything. Anything, she realized, except for his experiences in the Army. She had heard and experienced the camaraderie that the service instilled in people, but she was never exposed to the in-depth details of her husband's duties. Even together with Robert

60

Wolff, the details of their Army life were never revealed.

Marc Kaderri was usually quiet and rarely got involved in anything that didn't affect him. When the two of them went to outings and parties, Marc would rarely start a conversation with anyone he didn't know, and when he engaged in some idle chitchat, he never opened himself up. Actually, she thought, he was quite boring unless you knew him. Sara was the one who was friendly and outgoing, capable of striking up a conversation with a potted plant. With his quiet reserve, Sara was amazed at how successful he was in the insurance business.

But when she looked into his eyes after the fight at A Better Body, they were cold, but full of fire. It was that look that scared her. It was a look that she never saw before and hoped she would never see again.

Fortunately for her, she would at the most crucial time in her life.

CHAPTER FIVE

Tuesday, May 26, 7:00 a.m.

Detective Gary Trainor knelt next to Pedro's cold, lifeless body. The police photographer finished snapping pictures, and the outline of Pedro's body was already traced in white. The back of Pedro's head had been blown out, and a dark red pool dotted with shards of skull and pieces of brain fanned out on the concrete. The two holes in the center of his forehead were rimmed with dried blood and gunpowder.

"You look like shit," Trainor said to Michele Thorsen, who appeared on the scene. He glanced away from Pedro's body to look at her. Her hair was combed, but there wasn't any hairspray to keep the wavy blonde hair in place after she curled the ends under. She wasn't wearing any makeup except for the rose colored lipstick smeared across her thin lips. Trainor happily pointed out that she'd missed a corner.

Thorsen snorted. "Shut up asshole. And good morning to you, too." She rubbed her temple. "Now that the formalities are over, what happened here?" Michele tried to bring out her professionalism.

"The only thing we know right now is he was murdered last night." Trainor put his finger to his lip and said, "Officially, we don't know who he is yet, but his ID says his name is Pedro. He was a crewman on the Whispering Sea." Trainor pointed to the freighter still tied to its moorings. "We're waiting for someone to identify him."

"Is this murder related to the other ones?" Michelee whispered, avoiding looking at Pedro's corpse.

"Don't know yet," Trainor answered truthfully. "Too much to drink?"

Michele nodded. "My head is pounding like a bass drum from too many white Russians."

"I thought you liberals didn't know how to have a good time." Trainor wanted to piss her off. He was going to yell something to rattle her already scrambled brain, but decided not to. He wasn't cruel. He's had many mornings like the one she was experiencing. "Look," he continued, "you're in no condition to work this morning, go back to bed. I'll call later and fill you in."

Michele stared at Trainor with a skeptical look, working her mouth in preparation for a response. "You're right. See you."

Tuesday, May 26, 12:35 p.m.

Trainor sat behind his usually messy desk and stared at Betty Freeman sitting across from him. He was lucky to find her during the day, for she rarely worked in her profession during the daylight hours. In fact, it was like finding a needle in a haystack. It was by chance that Trainor saw her in the vicinity of one of the upper-class downtown hotels. Up to this point, she was unknown to the detectives. Her eye makeup was a light shade of purple and green, and her fake eyelashes had a thin coating of mascara. An unfiltered Camel cigarette clung between her expertly painted red lips. Her long, red hair was combed but somewhat skewed. Even without makeup, it was obvious that Betty Freeman was a very pretty woman. And her beautiful eyes were a deep green.

Her attire was decent. She wore a white lace teddy under a blue blazer, and a red cotton mini skirt that she said accented her hair. "Do I get my one phone call?" She asked out of the blue.

"Who's the special person you have to call?" Trainor asked.

"I got business to take care of," Betty shot back. "Besides, do you have probable cause for bringing me in here?"

"Slow down." Detective Keith Bernard walked into the office and sat on the desk. He opened up the file he was carrying and studied the list before him, He looked up and into Betty Freeman's eyes. "What do you know about probable cause?"

"Something I heard about."

"So, Miss Freeman, tell me who you were with last night." Bernard asked politely. "How many were from the freighter, Whispering Sea?"

"I don't know what you're talking about," Betty had a smug look on her face. She seemed to be trying to play the game to the best of her ability, which wasn't much.

"Cut the bullshit!" Trainor snapped. "We talked to the crew of the Whispering Sea. How do you think we got your name? We brought you in here to cooperate, not to arrest you for prostitution. But, if you don't cooperate, I'm sure I can find enough evidence to put you behind bars." He took a breath to let his threat sink in. His eyes narrowed into slits and he leaned into Betty's face so their noses were almost touching. "Which is it going to be?"

"What's this all about?" Betty asked.

"The murder of one of the crewman."

Her hands began to tremble. "Murder?"

"Yeah," Trainor said. "The guy who was killed was supposed to visit you. We want to know if he did, and what time."

"Now, answer my question." Bernard stated.

"I wasn't involved in any murder. " Betty said, visibly shaken. She took a deep breath before she continued. "I was with three guys. Two were from the Whispering Sea."

"Describe them," Bernard said bluntly.

Figuring that she had nothing to lose, Betty went into as

much detail of the action she had last night. She stated that she always looked at the faces of the men she was going to perform with, but never asked their names. She also tried to judge their demeanor and character, hoping to get out of a situation that could be life threatening before she even got into it. Betty Freeman wanted to live a long life, and had a reputation of being damn good at what she did. She didn't want it to end abruptly and violently. She had more important things to do in her life.

"Thank you for the vivid detail, and your future plans, Miss Freeman," Bernard said. "But, can you remember anything about the men, besides their performance? Age, build, anything along those lines?" Trainor was scribbling the information on a legal pad as Betty recounted the events.

"Detective, call me Blossom," she said with a grin.

"Why is that?" Bernard asked.

"Because when I spread my legs, my pussy blossoms like a flower when the sun's rays warms them."

"We'll call you Miss Freeman," Trainor said. "Can you remember anything at all? Did they say or do anything out of the ordinary?"

"Detective, everything these people do is out of the ordinary." She sat for a while in silence replaying the night in her mind. Things were starting to materialize. "The last guy I was with was rough. He wasn't from the boat."

"What time was that?" Trainor asked.

Betty thought for a moment. "About one-thirty in the morning."

"You said he was rough. Did he hit you?"

"No. Not that way." Her eyes searched the ceiling for an answer. "He wasn't housebroken. He pushed and poked as if no one ever taught him how to fuck. He was rough."

"Can you remember anything else?" Bernard leaned closer.

"He had a small dick and was lousy. Wasn't worth shit," she said disgustingly. "But he got his money's worth."

Bernard snorted. "I meant about his features, what did he look like?"

"Oh." She hid a sheepish grin. "White guy, and he wasn't circumcised. And he was in his forties." Betty searched her memory for more details. "His stomach was starting to show the signs of old age, and he had short, light brown hair."

"What about his facial features?" Trainor took a quick glance at his own stomach then asked his next question as he looked up from his writing pad. "Can you think of anything else?"

"Hmm." She snapped her fingers in satisfaction. "Brown eyes and long face. He dressed well." She rummaged through her handbag looking for another Camel, but withdrew a crushed pack of Marlboro's. Bernard tossed her a lighter before she could find one in her bottomless pit. "Wait!" she yelled, sitting up straight in her chair. Trainor and Bernard both jumped at her outburst. "When he was getting undressed and then dressed, I could swear the guy had a gun. But, I couldn't actually see it. I thought he might be a cop because he wasn't anybody I've fucked before who carried a gun. I have a few regulars who carry guns, but this guy wasn't one of them."

"How did he act?" Bernard asked.

"Like the gun was part of him. I mean he looked like he was used to carrying it. If it was a gun, I think he carried it in his back." She pointed to the small of her back. "He reached back there and put something on the ground next to the bed before we got it on, and it wasn't a wallet. Most of the guys I'm with who carry guns brag about having them. Not this guy."

"What's else?" Trainor pushed.

"His eyes," she whispered. The thought of them made her shiver.

"What about them," Bernard asked and leaned forward.

"They were scary, blank. They showed no emotion, like they were dead." Her body shuddered involuntarily.

"Anything else?" asked Trainor.

"Nothing." Betty Freeman felt she had done her duty and wanted to get back to work.

"One more moment, Miss Freeman, then you can go," Bernard said and left the room. He came back a few minutes later with a large book and placed it in front of Betty.

"What's this?" she asked.

"Those are mug shots of criminals", Bernard answered. "Do you think you may be able to pick out the man you just described?"

"Sure, I'll try." Betty opened the book and scanned the pages of photographs. There weren't that many criminals in the book so it didn't take long for her to finish. "He's not in there."

"Are you sure?" Trainor asked. "You went through that book pretty quick."

"I would know those eyes if I saw them, detective. He wasn't in there."

Bernard stood. "One more thing," he said. "Can you sit with our artist and describe him to her?"

Betty agreed and left with Trainor to go see the artist. Within fifteen minutes, Betty Freeman came back with the police artist and a sketch of the last man she was with. She sat down as both Trainor and Bernard looked at the drawing.

"Thanks, Miss Freeman, you can go now. We may contact you again," Trainor warned.

"Come and see me for fun next time." She stood, threw her bag over her shoulder, and walked out the door.

"Well, Keith, what do you think?"

Bernard thought about that for a moment. "There is a lot more there than she's letting on."

"How so?" Trainor asked

"Her vocabulary was erratic. She spoke at times like she was educated, and other times she acted like a prostitute."

"Did you notice that her fingernails were manicured?"

"No I didn't," Trainor admitted. "Were they?"

Keith Bernard thought a moment before he said anything else. "Come to think of it, her skin tone was in excellent condition, and her teeth were clean, white, and even."

It became clear to the detectives that Betty Freeman wasn't a street-walking prostitute. "We're going to have to call her back," Trainor said.

The phone was picked up on the second ring. "Yes?" The husky male voice said.

"I found him." The traffic in the background caused the caller to cup his free hand over the phone.

"Can you grab him?" The voice was impassive.

"Not yet," the caller reveled.

"Keep me informed. Anything else?"

"No, sir."

The line went dead.

Tuesday, May 26, 3:00 p.m.

A knock on the door startled her. Michele didn't have that many friends, and the ones she did have lived out of town and would call before making the trip. So, who would be calling? She walked to the door timidly and pushed the curtain away form the window that ran parallel to the doorframe. Her skepticism vacated her when she saw Gary Trainor standing as nonchalant as ever.

She tied the belt on her white terrycloth robe tighter before she opened the door. "Hi, Detective."

"Hi, Michele," Trainor said happily. "May I come in?"

Michele moved away to let him pass and closed the door behind him. "Come on, let's go in the living room." She led him down the small hallway into the sunken living room." It was decorated with a white leather sofa and loveseat that had a glass cocktail table placed in front of them. Two brass sculptures flanked both sides of the fireplace that was across from the sofa. A large picture window allowed the sunlight in and brightened the room with a warm glow.

"Nice place you have here," Trainor said truthfully.

"Thanks."

"How does a reporter afford a home like this? You don't make that much do you?"

Michele resented him asking her personal questions. Asking personal questions was her job. "If you must know, my parents have a lot of money."

"Ah, that explains a lot."

"Explains what?" She said sharply.

"Nothing. You look much better compared to the last time I saw you. Feeling better?"

She nodded. "A pot of coffee, lunch, and six hours of sleep helped tremendously." She studied her watch again; the hands read three o'clock. She had called in sick, which was something she rarely did. "So why are you here?"

Trainor sat on the sofa; Michele sat on the loveseat to his right with her back to the window. "Like I said at the murder scene this morning, I came by to fill you in."

"Yeah, right." Michele left for the kitchen to get a pad of paper and a pen, the thought of hitting the big time with the story raced through her mind. "Can I get you anything?" She called to Trainor politely as she could. For her, being polite took a lot of effort.

"Got a Coke?" He shouted back.

"Diet."

"Fine."

She emerged from the kitchen with a tray and placed it on the cocktail table, each one grabbing their soda and settling down in the soft leather. "What have you got?" She had her pen and paper ready.

"You have your tape recorder on?"

"No," Michele answered truthfully. She didn't want a repeat of the last fiasco.

"I can't give you the name of the deceased yet, we haven't been able to locate the next of kin," Trainor said.

"Is he a local?"

Trainor thought for a moment. "No."

"Can you tell me where he's from?"

"From talking to the crew members of the Whispering Sea he *was* from New York City."

"And?" Michele prodded him for more information.

"And what?" he asked back.

"Goddamnit, Trainor. Can you be a little more forthcoming with the information?" She was getting angry, especially because she wasn't getting her way.

"I'm answering your questions," Trainor replied. "You have to understand that I'm a police officer in the middle of an investigation, not your personal encyclopedia."

Michele snorted. It was time to change tactics, the straight questions weren't working. She had to get him to open up. She rose abruptly and walked into the kitchen, trying to cool down and think of a way to get to him. She grabbed two more sodas from the refrigerator and a bag of potato chips from the cupboard. As the saying goes, a way to a man's heart is through his stomach—maybe it worked for information, too.

Arriving back into the living room, she found Trainor studying the photographs of her family on the stone mantle above the fireplace. Why was he doing that? What was he up to? "Got some chips," Michele called to his back.

Trainor turned to face her. "No thanks, I had a big lunch. Lots of cholesterol and fat." He patted his stomach. "Is this your family?"

"Yes. Why?" She remained standing.

He turned to face her. "Just curious. Why are you getting so defensive?"

Michele had no reason to, but avoided the question and sat back down on the loveseat. "Can we continue?"

Trainor sat back on the couch and thanked her for the soda. "What else do you want to know?"

Okay, she thought, now we're getting somewhere. "Is the victim's death related to the other murders — drug murders," she corrected herself, "that have occurred in the city?"

"No, as far as we can tell."

"How can you be sure?" she prodded.

"Looks like a different MO."

Michele waited for Trainor to explain the police department's reasoning, but when he didn't, she asked him through clenched teeth, "What's different?"

"Well, most significantly, this guy was shot up close. He had powder burns on his forehead. Most likely he knew who and was looking at the person who pulled the trigger."

Dammit! There's more to it than that. Patience, Michele

told herself, or she wouldn't get anywhere. "Are you saying that the victims in the previous murders didn't know who the killers were?"

An astute observation. Trainor silently applauded her on figuring out that bit of information. The next one would be harder. "Yes, that's what we believe."

"But how?"

"You're a reporter that had been at one of the crime scenes. And, I showed you the pictures of the other. Put them together and figure out what you don't have."

Michele's mind replayed the scene where the cops were being rushed to the hospital in the ambulance, and the bodies of the drug dealers lay dead. The one sprawled on the hood of the car, the other next to it on the ground. The third was next to the dumpster. "Two of the victims were shot in the head on the night of the nineteenth. Isn't that a connection?" Michele though she had something there.

"No."

"Why not?" Michele shot back. She also hoped to get a substantive answer out of him.

A thin smile spread across Trainor's face, obviously he was having fun, but was also teaching Michele how to analyze and dissect the scenes from her mind. "Because the victims on the night of the nineteenth were shot once each, the victim at the port was shot twice." He ended his explanation there. "Now, what else did you see and not see?"

Michele was getting irritated, hating these stupid games. He was becoming an asshole again. "I don't know."

"Jeez, I thought reporters were better than that. Let me help you out." Trainor finished off his soda before he continued. "The victim who was killed at the port had traces of cocaine on him, but there were no drugs."

Thorsen caught on. "Right! And at the other scenes, all the drugs and money were left."

"You should learn to think a little more, it may help you out."

"So, that's why you don't think there is a connection?"

"You're getting smarter," Trainor chided. He rose and asked directions to the bathroom.

Michele watched as he walked down the hall, her mind thinking of another way to get the information out of him that she knew he was holding back. She wanted to be the one to break this story so bad she could taste it. She heard the toilet flush and made her decision, a hasty one, and one she hadn't thought out. Visions of being the next high profile reporter clouded her judgement.

As soon as Gary Trainor sat back down on the couch, Michele sat next to him and put her plan in motion. "Can we finish?" she said, being overly friendly.

"There isn't much left to say," Trainor answered.

"I think there is." Michele untied her belt and shed her robe, revealing her naked body. Her delicate right hand slid up Trainor's leg to his crotch, as her other hand grasped his hand and placed it on her soft breast, encouraging him to squeeze it and take advantage. She placed her mouth on his and laid a passionate kiss, her tongue probing deep within.

After a long moment, Trainor detached his mouth and pushed her hand away from his growing erection. "Knock it off, Thorsen!" he yelled. "I'm surprised at you, stooping to sex to get information."

Michele looked up at him in bewilderment, unable to believe her ears. She thought men would do anything to get a piece of ass, and she knew that hers was a real nice piece. Thinking he was joking, she tried again.

"Nice try." Trainor stood abruptly and headed for the door, leaving her on the couch in a state of shock. Before he left, he said, "Thorsen, I'm a professional, something you're not. You had everything. Everything! You had me in your hip pocket, only you. I gave you all the information I could. For obvious reasons, some of it I couldn't. But now, you went and fucked it all up." He closed the door gently when he left.

Shit. That didn't go well, horrible actually. Michele didn't bother to go after him, knowing it would be fruitless. She remained on the couch thinking, what now?

Thursday, May 28, 6:45 a.m.

Frustrated, angry, and bewildered were just some of the thought that were going through Michele Thorsen's mind as she lay in her bed and stared up at the ceiling. She still couldn't believe that Gary Trainor had turned her down. She was hoping that she could have her way with him, or that he would be rough like Ariel Steiner. Steiner awoke sexual desires and delights that she had never thought possible.

The chance Trainor had had to bed her was literally at his fingertips, but he had turned her down. His charges that she was unprofessional in her attempt to exchange information for sex hurt somewhat, but she refused to believe it. No man would turn down sex with the likes of her unless they didn't like women. That had to be it, she thought. Oh my God. Gary Trainor must be gay and doesn't want anyone to know, she thought. He used his speech on professionalism to hide it.

Michele shook at the frightening thought from her mind, rolled out of bed, and headed for the shower. Turning on the hot water, she let the exhilarating streams wash away her depressing thoughts of Trainor and switched them to the more erotic and pleasurable thoughts of Ariel Steiner.

To add to the pleasure, she began squeezing her breasts and pulling hard at her nipples. She became aroused and put her fingers between her legs to stimulate herself even more. To increase her pleasure, she turned the water stream to her clitoris. Michele's last few sexual encounters were huge disappointments and this was the one way she could get sexual gratification. This has to change soon. There was just no substitute for a hard cock, she thought.

In a matter of minutes, a warm wonderful sensation spread from the groin and radiated throughout her body. She sat down in the tub so she wouldn't lose her balance as waves of pleasure began shaking her body. Deeper and deeper she pushed her fingers in to intensify her pleasure and moans of delight were released from deep within. Concentrating on the orgasm, she slowing let herself come down, wanting to hold on to the gratifying moment for as long as possible.

Now that her pleasure making was finished, she grabbed the soap and continued with her shower. While lathering up, she reflected on her encounter with Steiner, and cursed herself for not getting his phone number. But, she vaguely remembered between her bouts of vomiting, that he said he would call her. She wondered if he meant it, and hoped that he did.

Thursday, May 28, 4:30 p.m.

"The evidence at the crime scene seems to indicate that the murder of the individual at the port is not related to the other murders." Michele Thorsen was giving her report from outside the police station. "The police have yet to comment any further on the recent rash of murders that have devastated Albany for the past few weeks. They are still asking the public for any help that they can give and all information will be kept confidential. This is Michele Thorsen for Channel Eleven News."

Tony Patten kept the camera focused on Michele for another three seconds then he cut the picture. "Nice work, Michele."

"Thanks, Tony." Michele walked up to Tony and handed him her microphone. Silently, they both walked over to the van where Tony opened the side door and stowed the camera. Michele made her way around the other side and got in the passenger side.

After the camera was secure, Tony jumped into the van, slid the door closed behind him, and made his way forward to the driver's seat. "So how did you make out the other night?" He fished the keys out of his pocket and started the van.

"I think I left shortly after you. I woke with one hell of a headache."

"How many more drinks did you have?" Tony pulled out into the traffic and made his way back to the station.

"I don't remember. Some guy was buying them for me."

"Some guy?" Tony smiled. "Did you—"

Michele put her hand across his mouth to shut him up. "The discussion is closed. The night didn't turn out the way I wanted it to, and don't ask which way was that."

Keeping one hand on the wheel Tony raised the other in surrender. "On the story we're doing, did your cop friend give you any more information that the police aren't releasing?"

"More?"

"Yeah, more." He smiled again. "You are the only one who has stated that the evidence found at the crime scene indicates that the two incidents are unrelated."

"Officially, no. But, he is keeping me informed on what is really going on. Besides, he didn't tell me that. It was deduced from the evidence that was at the scene. I can't help it if none of the other reporters aren't as observant as I am."

"Michele, do you really expect me to believe that?"

"Yes, I do." She tried to hide her smile.

"What do the police really believe, or more correctly, what does your source believe?"

"Nothing really. They are at a loss as to who and why these murders are being committed."

"Then why don't you go on the air with this? The police covering up information is a story unto itself."

"I know, but I gave my word."

"Oh, come on, Michele."

Michele started getting annoyed. She didn't like all the questions and was going to put a stop to it. "No more, Tony. I gave my word and that's it." She would keep her word only until the time it suited her to break it.

The remainder of the short ride back to the station was filled with idle chitchat. None of it had to do with work or their personal lives. Tony let Michele off at the front of the three-story concrete building and then went to park the van. Michele walked into the lobby and made her way to the stairs instead of the elevator, ignoring the people in the lobby. She bounded up the stairs to the second floor where her desk was located with the other reporters. The floor was open except for the two conference rooms at each end and a small office that was converted to hold the coffee maker and a couple vending machines. A rectangular table with six chairs was pushed off to one side. The dozen desks in the main part of the floor were set up in pairs pushed together facing each other. Thorsen's desk was opposite Barbara Toomey, the court reporter, with whom she got along with on occasion.

Michele arrived at her desk to find a single red long stem rose in a glass vase and a bottle of 1985 Roederer Cristal Champagne with a red ribbon wrapped around its neck. She was impressed by what she saw; the champagne went for well over a hundred dollars. Immediately, though, she became very suspicious. She had no idea who would leave her these gifts, and for what reason. She searched for a note, but none was found. She looked around the open floor to see if someone was eyeing her to see her reaction. But, there didn't seem to be anyone interested in her gifts.

Barbara Toomey came up behind Michele and sat down at her desk. "Hi Michele," Barbara said.

"Hi Barb," Michele said back. "Do you know who left these?" She pointed to the rose and champagne.

"Some guy came in here about an hour ago and was asking for you. I told him you were out in the field and would be back later."

"Did you get his name?" Her curiosity was now peaked.

"No," Barbara admitted, "but he asked if he could leave those. Did he leave you a note?"

"No, nothing." Michele held up the bottle. "But he has very good taste in champagne."

"I believe I also have very good taste in women," a male voice said.

Michele looked up in surprise to see Ariel Steiner standing at the side of the desk, a small smile spread on his lips.

"Hi, Michele," Steiner said. He looked over to Barbara and extended his hand, introducing himself before Michele had a chance to. "Hi, I'm Ariel Steiner."

Barbara shook the outstretched hand. "Barbara Toomey."

"Hi, Ariel," Michele said. "What brings you down here?"

Before he could answer, Barbara winked at Michele and excused herself. "It was nice to meet you, Ariel."

"Likewise." Steiner shifted his focus back to Michele. "I remember when I left the other night I said I would call."

Michele's face turned pink in embarrassment. He made that statement when she was praying to the porcelain god and he was on his way out the door. "I'm so embarrassed by that night. I'm not usually like that."

"Like what?"

Michele knew what he was alluding to and quickly said, "The alcohol. I rarely get drunk."

"Oh, I see." His smile came back. "Another reason why I came by was to ask you if you would like to go to dinner."

"Tonight? Now."

"Yes, now."

"Ariel, I don't know." The first thought that came to mind was that he wanted to sleep with her again. Typical male, Michele thought. There was no doubt that she wanted to finish what they started, but she was going to be in control. "I have to shower and change---"

"No, no, no. Nothing fancy, just a quick bite. I have some work I have to do tonight, so it can't be that long."

"Oh." Once again this man surprised her. He wasn't out to just get back in her pants. He just told her that he didn't have time for it. "Deal. Where to?"

"You pick the place, and I'll follow in my car."

Thursday, May 28, 5:10 p.m.

Trainor's desk was still a mess despite a promise he had made to himself to clean it up and keep it neat. Files, photographs, pads of legal paper that were both used and unused, and an unbalanced stack of paper covered the desk. There was a tiny space left open where he had room to place half a legal pad on the desk to take notes. The other half was hanging off and bent down under the weight of Trainor pressing it against the desk. At the moment, he was thinking about the opportunity he had had with Michele and he cursed himself for being professional. Her body was exquisite, and it would have been fun to screw her. But he resigned himself to thinking that he had made the right decision. Under different circumstances, he would have jumped at the advance. Her skin was soft and tender, and her breasts were large and firm, just the way her liked. She did have a remarkable body, and it was one her would love to explore, but not under these circumstances. He let his feelings and the passionate kiss go on a little longer than he should have. She was a good kisser!

"How's it going, Gary?" It was a deep male voice.

Trainor dropped his pencil and pushed his chair back. "Hey, Lieutenant." He looked up at the plump man who wore his suspenders to hold up his pants, not for fashion.

"Are you making any progress?" Lieutenant Robert Chiles asked, placing a meaty hand on Trainor's shoulder.

"Slow. Real slow."

"Any ideas of what's going on?"

"No. There are no clues as to who pulled these hits off. And I don't think they're related."

"What do you mean no clues?" Chiles' voice deepened.

"That's it, no clues. Nobody saw anything. Nobody heard anything, and nobody on the streets is bragging that they know who pulled these off. There is absolutely nothing incriminating at the crime scenes. There are no shell casings, no bloody footprints. Even the dog came up blank."

"Yeah, I found that strange when I read the reports. Anyway, Gary, go home." Chiles patted him on his shoulder and said, "I have confidence in you; I know you'll find them."

"Thanks," Trainor said.

"And one more thing."

"What's that?"

Chiles lowered his voice and his eyes flashed. "Keep the sketch under wraps."

Before he could say anything, Trainor watched his boss turn and leave. Shaking his head, he thought about what his boss had just told him. Rarely did Chiles come out into the detectives' area and give some encouragement. If he did come out of his office, it was usually to chew some poor detective out. Automatically Trainor's defenses had gone up. Was it a subtle hint to get results fast? Or was it what it appeared to be a vote of confidence. But, why keep the artist's drawing under wraps? he thought. Trainor reached for the unwrapped package of Tums and popped a couple into his mouth.

Andre's Bistro was located on Madison Avenue just up from the Empire State Plaza. A small place with California yuppie food dominating the menu. Michele Thorsen was digging heartily into her huge Caesar Salad. To play it safe she had a half bottle of Chardonnay and a promise to limit herself to one. Steiner, at the moment, picked at his chicken teriyaki, obviously eating it with little delight. His second Chivas and water seemed to make the meal worth his while.

Michele was filled with mixed emotions about being with the man she knew as Ariel Steiner. She felt excited, apprehensive and lustful, yet cautious. The man across from her was not very handsome, yet he wasn't unattractive. There was something about him that kept her attention.

Throughout dinner, the conversation flowed smoothly about everything under the sun. Michele felt that she could trust this man. She didn't know why, and she never felt this trust in a person so quickly after meeting them. After some small talk Michele asked what she thought was a rightful question. "So, Ariel, where do you stay; when you are in town?" After all, he knew where she lived.

"At the Hilton." Though that wasn't true, he kept a room at all times at the Hilton since he began his operation in Albany. If Michele or anybody else went to the Hilton looking for Ariel Steiner, they would find that he was registered there under Wine Importers Limited. "I'm in town for a few weeks then off to Miami."

"Oh, really," Michele said a little more disappointedly than she had intended. She hoped he didn't pick up on it and felt sure that he hadn't. Then she added, "I like South Florida, but I prefer the Keys."

Steiner cocked an eyebrow and smiled. "Of course, plans change like the weather and I may not go."

"That they do," she smiled and said in agreement.

"So, Michele, what have you learned about the drug killings?"

She swallowed her mouthful of food and wiped her delicate lips with the linen napkin before she answered. "Nothing concrete except that it appears that the victims were murdered by the same killer."

"Killer? You know it's only one person?"

"The police don't know that for sure, but they know that it's not gang warfare or the like."

"How so?" Steiner asked.

"My source informed me."

Steiner raised an eyebrow. "And who is your source?"

A smile spread across Michele's lips. "A good reporter never reveals her sources. But, I can tell you that the body found at the docks isn't related to the other murders."

Steiner now listened intently, but made the effort to not let his face reveal any emotions. "How do they know that?"

"Whoever killed that man was definitely interested in the drugs. They were taken from the victim. With the other murders, all the drugs and money were left."

"I guess you really take your job seriously to observe that much detail."

Michele winked and said, "I'm just good. And that's not the only thing I'm good at."

Steiner smiled and looked at his watch. "Oh! I have to go, Michele." He stood and dropped a hundred-dollar bill on the table to cover the bill. "Thank you for having dinner with me. I really enjoyed it." He turned to walk away.

"Ariel, wait!" Michele called after him. She rose from her chair and walked toward him.

"Yes, what is it?"

"That wonderful bottle of champagne you left me."

"Enjoy it, it's very good."

Without thinking, Michele blurted out, "Come over to my

place tomorrow at eight, we'll open it then."

"Eight o'clock then." He leaned over to kiss her on the cheek, but she turned her head to meet his lips and gave him a soft passionate kiss.

"Until then."

Friday, May 29, 9:15 p.m.

The candles lit the living room in a soft glow. The uncorked bottle of Roerderer Cristal champagne was turned upside down in its ice bucket on the coffee table. Michele and Steiner sat next to each other on the sofa sipping the last of the delicious nectar from crystal champagne glasses.

"That was a wonderful dinner, Michele," Steiner said.

"Thank you. Did you get enough?"

"Yes, thanks. I'm stuffed."

Michele kicked off her pumps, leaned back into the soft sofa, and put her feet up on the coffee table, wiggling her toes. She made sure the slit of her skirt revealed her naked thighs. "I love to do that at the end of a day."

"Do you now?" Steiner did the same thing. "I like to do that, too."

"Ariel, would you like some coffee? I can put on a pot." She was hoping he would say no.

"No, thanks I haven't' t finished the champagne yet."

All day, Michele had been waiting for this moment. She drained what was left of her champagne, put the glass down next to the ice bucket, and stood up. She pulled her blouse over head and exposed her bare breasts. Then, just as quickly, she whisked off her skirt and panties standing naked in front of Steiner. "Ariel, I've been waiting for this moment since the first time we met." She took a step closer to him so he had to look up to meet her eyes. "We have to finish what we started."

Steiner still hadn't moved, obviously in awe of the beauty looming in front of him. She stood with his face even with her small tuft of blonde pubic hair. Before he could do anything with it, she stepped over to him and sat on his lap. She took one of her nipples and danced it in front of his face. She reached down to his crotch, unzipped his pants, and took out his erection.

Steiner took the offered nipple into his mouth and began sucking and biting, hard like he had done the last time. With his free hand, he still held the champagne in the other; he reached around her firm buttocks and plunged a finger into her wetness.

Michele moaned in pleasure and started pumping his cock. "Harder," she commanded, "suck my tits harder!" She found that rough sex was what she craved and wanted him to give it to her. She began moving her hips on his finger for more stimulation and decided she needed something bigger.

She pulled away from his face and moved off of him and on to the sofa. There she kneeled on the cushion and placed her hands over the back of the sofa, thrusting her ass toward Steiner. She looked back over her shoulder through her blonde hair at Steiner and said, "This is where we were last time. Ariel, stick your dick in me and fuck me hard!"

Steiner quickly stripped and stood behind her. He paused momentarily to admire the view before he shoved his cock deep into Michele's wetness. He grasped her thin waist for support and pulled her against him. The sound of their skin smacking against each other echoed throughout the living room. Soon, Michele's moans drowned out any other sound. Taking control, Ariel thought that if she wanted to be fucked hard, he was happy to comply with her wishes. Besides, that was the only thing he knew how to do.

CHAPTER SIX

Saturday, June 6, 10:40 a.m.

The Corning Preserve was a small stretch of real estate that ran along the western back of the Hudson River in Albany. Broadway marked the Preserve's western boundary with an overpass of Interstate 787 that also followed the river. A blacktop path snaked its way through the Preserve, following the river northward for another five miles and exiting the city limits.

The path was filled with joggers and cyclists on their Saturday morning exercise excursion. Numerous sunbathers stretched out on blankets getting a head start on bronzing their bodies dotted the big grassy areas. The buds on the shade trees exploded into full bloom and offered protection for those who didn't like the sun or wanted to escape the heat. Groups of people tossing a Frisbee or baseball were about, as were lovers strolling hand in hand.

Blending in with the population enjoying the Preserve, Marc Kaderri and Robert Wolff walked along the same path. Kaderri and Wolff were hard at work; their eyes focused through Ray Ban sunglasses on the spot that the next drug deal was supposed to take place. The shadow from the ramp of the overpass afforded a place that was obstructed from view from almost every angle. An excellent spot.

"This is going to be a tough shot," Kaderri stated. "Got any idea?" He put a handful of cashews in his mouth.

Wolff looked around. "I can't see any place that will keep us hidden from view and afford an easy shot. The escape route will be even harder."

"Let's keep walking, we'll find something."

Luis "Slapper" Varcasia sat quietly in the torn and faded recliner watching a rerun of his favorite cartoon, He-man. It was a cartoon he thought he could relate to. In Luis' small mind, he thought he had the same powers as the cartoon character.

He sat in the middle of the bare walled living room in the one-bedroom apartment with a marijuana cigarette the size of a cigar hanging precariously from his bottom lip. Streaks of sunlight poked through the tattered shade that was held up with thumb tacks and tape. Slapper thought he was somewhat of a bad ass in the local drug trade, but not bad enough. He wanted the reputation of being the badest motherfucker in town, and soon he hoped he would have that designation. He got his nickname when he was fourteen for slapping his mother around when she confronted him about all the school days he missed. That was six years ago.

Sitting across from him stuffing a piece of last night's pepperoni pizza into his mouth was Slapper's right hand man, Hector Romero.

"Slapper, man," Romero said, standing to his full six foot height, "when are we gonna pop them dudes?" They had a score to settle with a rival group of dope pushers that ripped them off before Slapper could sell his precious merchandise to some other addict.

The end of the joint glowed brighter as Slapper inhaled, then handed it to Hector. When Slapper answered, his voice was heavily accented in his Puerto Rican drawl. "Sunday morning, man. Tomorrow."

Slapper reached for a piece of the stale pizza on the coffee table without taking his eyes off the television. "Listen Hector, man, you gotta be cool 'bout this. You fuck this up and we are dead. Got it?" He butchered the language, speaking phonetically.

"Yeah man. Let's go over this once again, I want to be with my woman." Hector sat back on the torn couch and popped a beer. He handed the joint back.

"I changed something."

"You what?" Hector blurted, evidently stunned by the revelation. It was supposed to be simple. Hector was going to wait in the car while Slapper was dealing with Francisco. Slapper was going to shoot Francisco while Hector covered Francisco's driver.

Slapper shut the television off and leaned forward. He looked into Hector's eyes. "I'm meeting Francisco at the Preserve. We're supposed to be selling him a kilo of coke. He said he'd pay us for the last one he stole. Guess he wants to make up. Of course, we ain't gonna do that, man, he already fucked us on one and ain't gonna fuck us again. You gonna be hiding in the trunk —"

"It ain't gonna be locked, man." Hector sat at the end of the couch.

"No shit, asshole." Slapper rolled his eyes at Hector's stupidity. He sometimes wondered why he put up with him. "If it's locked, you won't be able to pop him."

"Yeah, right," Hector settled back on the couch. "Wait. Why me?" Realizing what Slapper said.

"'Cause I say so. I'm the only one who is getting out of the car. It's gonna be me and him and one driver each. Keena's driving. When I rub my head and move away from Francisco, you pop him."

"What about Francisco's driver?" Hector wasn't that stupid.

"Man, he'll be driving away so fast to save his ass we won't worry 'bout it."

A cautious smile spread across Hector's face. "You gonna trust him? He fucked us once. Maybe he got somebody in the trunk too." Hector was thinking.

"Don't worry, man, everything be cool." Slapper turned the television back on. "Nobody fucks Slapper twice. Besides, Keena will be parked right next to Francisco's car. He'll shoot the driver if he has to."

Hector stood in the dirty, run-down, Arbor Hill housing project apartment. He was clearly having second thoughts about this hit. "You gonna be carrying a piece?"

"Yeah." Slapper was watching another cartoon.

"I'll see you later. I'm gonna meet my woman." They tapped fists and Hector turned away.

"Later," Slapper said as he turned back to the television to live in another fantasy. "Hey," he called to Hector; " I gotta meet with some dude The Man hooked me up with after the hit."

Saturday, June 6, 1:15 p.m.

Once again Gary Trainor was behind his desk. His feet were propped up and he was leaning back in his chair. A manila folder shielded his face from the activity outside his office. This was the last Saturday he was going to work in a month, and he was happy about that.

Keith Bernard was sitting in the same fashion opposite him. He was studying a photograph of Pedro's corpse. More photographs covered his desktop.

"What do you make of all this?" Trainor asked dropping the folder. He was beginning to get worried.

"Has this ever happened in Albany before?" Bernard asked, picking up another photograph.

"Not that I can recall. How did you handle this sort of shit when you were a detective in New York?"

Bernard laid the photograph gently on a stack of others in the center of his desk. "The same way we're doing it here. Asking lots questions, following up on leads. Nothing different."

Trainor studied his partner. He had only been working with him for a few months and he hadn't been able to get to know him in that short of time. Trainor knew Bernard wasn't telling him the entire story. There was a side to Detective Keith Bernard that Trainor wanted to know about.

A knock on the door changed his thoughts. He waved in a uniformed officer holding an ordinary manila folder. It was the ballistics report on Pedro.

"What does it say?" Bernard asked before Trainor read the first line.

Trainor looked over the top of the report at Bernard. "Let me open the damn thing!" He scanned the report quickly and blinked.

"Well?"

Trainor read it again, but slower this time. A crease split his forehead. "Shit," he flung the report across his desk to Bernard.

Bernard quickly read the report and said, "That puts a damper on that theory." His eyes searched for a particular paragraph that caught his attention.

Trainor stood and paced the office. "Doesn't that bother you?"

"What?"

"That we're not getting any closer to solving the drug killings," Trainor said impatiently.

"Calm down, Gary. Don't let this get to you," Bernard said patiently. "Things don't always go as we like." It was a comment he knew too well.

"Yeah," Trainor sat back down after grabbing two cups of old coffee. He handed one to Bernard.

"Thanks. Now, what do you make of the ballistics report on Pedro?" Bernard handed the file back.

The frustration began to build again. Trainor searched the desk for the ballistics report on the killings outside of Ramones.

Bernard waited patiently.

"I have no idea. All that I know is that the bullets don't

match. And that probably means the two incidents aren't related."

"Good point." Bernard tossed another file to Trainor. "The ballistics from the shooting where our people were shot and the ones where Stroehmann and his cohorts were assassinated match. I think it's safe to say that those are related."

Bernard's terminology didn't escape Trainor.

"Assassinated? When I mentioned a professional hit man you laughed your ass off. Why the switch?"

Bernard looked slightly uncomfortable. "I think we have another problem on our hands." He gave Trainor a deadpan look.

"Like what?" Trainor leaned forward, resting his elbows on the desk.

Bernard made sure the door to the office was closed and that nobody could overhear them. He straightened his blue and white striped tie before he spoke. "The ballistics report on Pedro said the bullet was a nine millimeter."

"Big deal. Nine millimeters are common. We carry them." He took a gulp from his lukewarm coffee.

Bernard held up his hand. "The bullet was slightly larger than a nine millimeter short and slightly smaller than a nine millimeter parabellum." He said, sounding like a lecture.

Trainor wondered where he was going with this. He read the same information in the file. "What's your point?"

"Have you ever seen that type of ammo before?" Bernard asked. "Do you know what weapon uses that kind of ammo?"

This was no time to be macho. Trainor answered truthfully, "No."

"A Makarov uses that ammo." Bernard's voice was calm and flat.

"A what?"

"A Makarov. It's manufactured in Russia."

Trainor placed his face in his hands. The investigation took a new twist. What was somebody doing with a Makarov in Albany? The implication was enormous. Was it possible that an international gun running operation was operating in Albany? "Oh, shit. I need a big drink." Trainor wasn't ready for something like this. First, the inordinate amount of killings. Now, foreign weapons. All he had to do was solve them, and figure out if they were connected.

Bernard stood. "I think I'm going to make another trip down to the docks."

"Good idea."

Bernard walked out the door of the police station and headed toward the pay phone on the way to his car.

Trainor waited until his partner shut the door then unwrapped another roll of Tums antacid tablets. It was his second roll.

Saturday, June 6, 2:20 p.m.

Moshe Koretsky handed the sealed Federal Express package to the driver who stood patiently at Koretsky's kitchen table. The driver wasn't just a Federal Express employee; he also worked for Mossad as a *sayan*, or "helper." The sealed package was the box of heroin Koretsky had received from Pedro.

The driver knew better than to ask what the contents of the package were and Koretsky wasn't about to offer. The package was going to a corporation that was set up as a front. It had all the legal papers, store front, and mailing address. It just didn't conduct any business. It was one of many of Mossad's intricate deceptions working throughout the world.

The package was on its way to the dummy corporation, Galaxy Incorporated, located in the Bronx. From there, it would change packaging and be shipped to a legitimate food company in Manhattan. And from there, the package could be shipped with real food to anywhere in the world, including exported kosher food to Israel.

Once in its desired locations, the package would be sent to the right people. Throughout the entire journey, nobody would ask what was in the package. Only a select few knew what was really going on.

This particular package was to be used in Manhattan. It

would end up in the hands of another Mossad Katsa, or case officer, who would sell it on the street for a five hundred percent profit. The money would then be funneled through a series of bank accounts and be accessible to Mossad headquarters in Tel Aviv, Israel. Mossad would use the money to fund its operations throughout the world.

By using the drug money, it was untraceable and Mossad never had to justify the price of its covert operations to the Israeli government. The government simply didn't know about the money, or some of the operations that the money was used to fund.

Koretsky waited until the courier was on his way before he called Tel Aviv. He pressed the button on the side of the phone to make sure the connection was secure. The phone rang once before it was picked up.

"I'm looking for Henry," he said the code phrase for the day. He carried a small leather bound book, called a Seven Star, filled with telephone numbers in code that only he could decipher. If someone found it, they would mistake it for a series of notes or phrases from a college textbook. The book was used for both sending and receiving information. The voice on the other end was unfamiliar to him.

"Henry who?" The question meant Koretsky had to verify himself.

"Henry's flowers were delivered yesterday to his mother."

"Wait," the voice on the other end ordered.

Three minutes elapsed when another voice came on the line. This one he recognized.

"Hello, Moshe." It was Mossad's director. He had become personally involved with the Katsas who worked in the United States.

Koretsky didn't waste any time in getting to the point. "Hello, sir. The package is on its way. We should make over two hundred thousand dollars."

"The money is going into the Galaxy account, correct?"

"Yes, the money is going into that account. I'll contact you at the next scheduled time." The call was disconnected.

Satisfied that things were going as well as could be expected, Koretsky walked over to the bar and poured a double
shot of Chivas Regal. It was unfortunate that his contact,
Allen Stroehmann was eliminated, but his supplier and attorney, Joshua Miller, promised him that he'd soon have a new
one.

Koretsky still had a lot of work to do. Stroehmann's storage facilities were perfect for his operation. Ships carrying the
drugs that Koretsky ordered would pull into port and store
the narcotics in the self-storage containers. Once stored,
Koretsky would pick up the drugs and arrange for them to be
shipped to their destinations. The operation in New York had
worked well, but the New York City Police had gotten close
to discovering him a few times. He began looking for an inconspicuous location and found Albany to be the perfect location. He didn't have to worry about an army of police like
New York.

Koretsky wasn't interested in dealing; he left that to the
locals. He also wasn't interested in becoming a kingpin either.
All that he wanted to do was make enough money to fund
operations that would promote the existence of Israel and the
demise of any anti-Semites — no matter where in the world.

Saturday, June 6, 8:45 p.m.

"What was Koretsky doing?" Kaderri steepled his hands
under his chin. His eyes narrowed into slits and he leaned forward in his seat at the dining room table in Wolff's house.

"He left with Michele Thorsen. That TV reporter who's
reporting on our work." Wolff walked into the kitchen to get
another round of beers. It was their second and last.

Kaderri, Brown, and Wolff were in Wolff's spacious two-
story colonial outside of Troy, a city north and east of Albany on the opposite side of the Hudson River. They had spent
three hours planning the following day's mission.

"Ghost and I followed him to Thorsen's house." Wolff
popped the tops on the Samuel Adams and regained his seat.

"And?" Kaderri looked at him intently.

"He didn't stay there for long, maybe a half hour."

Brown entered the conversation. "We tried to follow him to see where he lived, but we lost him."

"He's good, Marc." Wolff rubbed his tired eyes. "I don't think he knew we were tracking him."

"Who is this guy?" Brown said in exasperation. "You guys seemed obsessed with him. What has he done?"

Kaderri told him the story of when the Israelis were taking pot shots at the Marines who were stationed at Beirut International Airport. He described the scene in Lebanon when Sergeant Hassad was murdered, and the subsequent conversation with Colonel McKnight. He went into further detail describing the time when he and Wolff spotted Koretsky sitting at the table in Ramones.

Brown's face contorted in anger. He had a friend who was among the 243 servicemen who were killed in the bombing of the American compound in Beirut. It could have been prevented if the Israelis had shared their intelligence.

"Let me know what I can do to help get this motherfucker."

"We'll let you know, Ghost." Kaderri didn't want Ghost involved too deep. This was his and Wolff's fight. But, if Ghost could use some of his contacts in the shadowy world of Albany, well, he wouldn't hesitate to use him. He turned to Wolff. "Do you have any idea of what he's doing in Albany?"

"I'm clueless, Marc."

Ghost let out a long, loud belch to break the tension. "I'll tell you one thing, the drug dealers and pushers are beginning to run scared. The job we're doing is working."

"How do you know?" Kaderri asked.

"I've been serving white Russians to Michele Thorsen for a long time. She was telling me at the bar about her latest story."

"When did this happen?" Wolff asked.

"Before you made goo goo eyes at her, buddy." Ghost smiled.

"What did she say?" Kaderri's curiosity was peaked.

"Basically, she said that people are happy the dealers are

getting their due. The cops are, too, but not the way we are going about it. She also ran into a couple of guys who said the dealers were starting to run scared. They're starting to be more careful in their selection of places to deal. Some are starting to deal indoors instead of on street corners."

"Okay. Let's get to sleep, we've got to be in position by zero five hundred." The three said good night and turned in. Kaderri lay in bed thinking about Sara. It bothered him that he lied to her about that night. He told her that he would be playing poker all night. It was something that he, Wolff, Brown, and Steven Caron did on a monthly basis. Sara referred to it as the monthly male bonding meeting. It was agreed by all that they would cancel the poker game since Steven's death. It wasn't the same without him. But, the cover was perfect for what they were doing.

Kaderri began thinking again. He fought down a wave of nausea as the vivid memory of Steven's death played over and over in his mind. He was happy his work was having the de- sired affect, but it was time to concentrate on Moshe Koretsky. Kaderri remembered what his father had always told him that "When you believe strongly in something and you know it's right, morally and ethically, go for it with all your energy. But make sure it doesn't hurt anyone else." For now, he pushed the thoughts out of his mind to concentrate on his mission in the morning. Kaderri rose from the bed and checked his equip- ment for the third time. He'd perform the fourth check again tomorrow.

Situated on the long, folding table, the equipment was laid in an orderly fashion. Kaderri picked up the trusted M14 and ran his hand over the smooth stock. The weapon felt like an extension of his body. He loaded a magazine and chambered a round to make sure it was operating smoothly. It was. Raising the weapon to his shoulder, he peered through the scope and pretended to sight the weapon on a drug dealer. The level of hate boiled inside him, even at the imaginary sight of a drug dealer. He stroked the trigger and pretended to fire. A smile spread across his face as he watched the dealer drop dead.

Another kill for the good guys. He ejected the magazine and the chambered round and loaded it back into the magazine.

He placed the rifle down next to his ghillie suit, a camouflaged suit that was made of an old flight suite and irregular sized strips of brown, tan, and green burlap to break up the shape of a human and blend in with the natural surroundings. They were the real camouflage suits that the professionals used, not the ones that the hunters purchase from catalogs or sporting goods stores. Next to the ghillie suit was a slender, long, flat black box that held his terror weapon. If there was time, or the situation warranted, he would use the weapon to make his message clear.

The rest of the table was covered with camouflaged battle dress uniforms, face paint, combat boots, and voice activated headsets to communicate with each other without compromising their positions. They always had to be careful of ham radio operators picking up their signals. Satisfied that everything was in order, Kaderri laid back down on his bed and his thoughts of hatred drifted from drug dealers, to finding and killing Moshe Koretsky. The knowledge that he would have his day settled him into a restful sleep.

Sunday, June 7, 5:30 a.m.

Another beautiful Sunday was on tap for the Capital District. The bright yellow sun rose triumphantly over the eastern bank of the Hudson River. Its rays stretched out across the brilliant blue sky and reflected off the greenish-brown water of the river. The calls and grunts of a crew team gliding down the center of the river echoed across the silent waters. The oars splashed lightly when they entered the water as the rowers propelled themselves faster with each stroke.

The sun rose behind the prone position of Marc Kaderri and Robert Wolff. Perfect for a sniper about to engage in his deadly art. Anyone who looked in their direction would be blinded by the celestial object. But, at the same time, that person would be illuminated by it.

Kaderri and Wolff lay among the few trees and scrub brush

on the western shore of the river. It was a position they weren't happy with. An ideal distance for a sniper to hit his target was at least six hundred yards. Kaderri and Wolff were at one hundred fifty. That distance would normally make them more susceptible to being spotted. If they had to, they would lie and wait for hours until the opportune time to move. To break up their human form and blend in with the natural surrounding, they each wore a ghillie suit. Kaderri knew it was virtually impossible to see a man when he was wearing one of them.

They had been in position for the past hour. Kaderri had his familiar M14 rifle resting on the grass in front of him and the long, flat black box lying next to him. Wolff had his 20-power spotting scope and a silenced 9mm Smith and Wesson pistol. Not one had said a word since they arrived.

The wait continued.

Kaderri heard muffled footsteps coming from his left. He turned his head slightly to see a jogger heading his way. Shit, he thought. That was one thing they didn't need. The man bean to slow to a walk. Shit again. Kaderri's heart began pounding and the adrenaline flowed through his veins. His right hand reached for the six-inch scuba knife he had strapped to the outside of his boot. He wouldn't kill the innocent bystander, but he would give him one hell of a headache if necessary by hitting him with the flat steel bottom of the knife.

Incredibly, the jogger stopped six feet away. He began searching in each direction. Kaderri held his breath. There was no way anyone could know what they were doing or where they were. He gripped the knife tighter, ready to strike hard and fast. He wasn't going to put all of his confidence in the ghillie suit like he'd done before. The last time he did that, he was commanding an A-Team in Afghanistan with Steven Caron and Jesse Hughes and it almost cost him his life. During a firefight with a Soviet patrol, he had his kneecap shattered.

The jogger took one last quick look and suddenly dropped his shorts and relieved himself on the small tree next to Kaderri. Time seemed to stand still as Kaderri silently urged

the man to finish and be on his way. Once the man was finished and continued his jog, Kaderri let out a sigh of relief.
Now, the only thing he had to worry about was if the jogger
came back.

Sunday, June 7, 6:45 a.m.

Nothing happened in the twenty minutes that the car sat
in the parking lot of the Corning Preserve. Just the sound of
the big eighteen wheelers that rumbled across the bridge overhead echoed in the parking lot below added to the chatter
from the few seagulls flying over the river. Hector was getting
anxious. Francisco was ten minutes late. The trunk smelled
terribly, and the only air he was getting was from the tiny
opening he was looking through.

Slapper sat in the passenger seat of the worn green
Chrysler New Yorker unaware of the time that passed. "You
know what to do?" Slapper asked his driver, Keena.

Keena nodded.

"Keep that piece out of sight." Slapper nodded to the sawed
off shotgun Keena had on his lap. He looked out the window
and spotted Francisco's white BMW gliding into the parking
lot. Slowly and confidently, he emerged from the car and rapped
twice on the side of the trunk to alert Hector that Francisco
was spotted.

As agreed, Francisco arrived only with his driver and pulled
alongside the passenger side of the Chrysler so both cars
were facing the same direction. Francisco rose from the small,
white sports car and stretched his large frame. He wasn't smiling.

"Hey, 'Cisco! Good to see you, man." Slapper tried to lighten
the mood.

"Cut the shit. Put your piece on the ground and kick it
away." His eyes roamed the parking lot, searching for any signs
of an ambush. As a gesture, Francisco pulled his pistol from
his waistband and placed it on the ground and kicked it away.

For a brief moment, Slapper thought about blowing Francisco away himself. But then if he did, word on the street would be that Slapper couldn't be trusted. It was a warped thought, but the blame would be on Hector for shooting Francisco. He would stick to his original plan and let Hector take the heat. Slapper followed suit. Besides, Francisco was too close; he'd be able to counter his move if he tried. Francisco was also in better shape and faster than Slapper. "There," Slapper said thickly. "You happy? Now let's get this over with. You owe me a lot of money, man."

Kaderri was happy everything was going as Rufus "Ghost" Brown said it would. He watched with predatory eyes as the BMW pulled up to the parked Chrysler and the two men met. Kaderri spoke to Brown in his headset. "Showtime, Sentry."

Brown was patrolling the road system in the area for any signs of police or stray vehicles. They were using code names in the event that someone picked up their transmissions.

"All clear," Brown's voice flowed through the tiny earpiece stuck in Kaderri's ear. It was the words he was hoping for. Minimal traffic and no police officers.

Wolff heard it, too. In a barely audible whisper, Wolff spoke to Kaderri. "Let's reach out and touch someone." He brought the binoculars to his eyes.

Kaderri surveyed the scene before him. Things couldn't have been better. The two men standing were thirty feet away from the cars were arguing about something. Good. They would be distracted while he eliminated the two drivers. It's easier to bear down on someone on foot than driving away in a car. "Driver's first."

"Roger." Wolff focused the binoculars.

The driver of the BMW sitting behind the wheel filled Kaderri's 10-power Unertl scope. The first thing Kaderri noticed was the man's eyes. They were shiny and brown, rimmed in red. The man was either tired or on some sort of drug. It didn't matter, thought Kaderri. The familiar rush of adrenaline coursed through his veins. All thought of the men he was about to kill was erased. They were no longer men; they were targets, not paper ones, but ones that dealt in death and misery. A smile spread across his serious face. This would be the last time these bastards would spread their menace.

He placed the crosshairs just below and behind the man's left ear, guaranteeing a deadly and messy hit. Kaderri went for head shots most of the time. Barring any unforeseen events, such as sudden gusts of wind or jerky movements from the target, headshots usually guaranteed a kill, but more importantly, it sent a clear message. He wanted to instill terror in the drug dealers.

The butt plate of the rifle fit snugly in his shoulder and his cheek rested against the stock. *Okay, motherfucker,* he thought, *time to meet your creator.* His gloved finger put pressure on the trigger. The rifle jerked lightly in his hands as the bullet raced toward its target, the gas operated weapon fed another round into the chamber. The brass deflector attached to the rifle's ejector port guided the spent shell casing straight down, instead of ejecting it straight out where it could be lost. It made it easy to pick up the spent brass casings when finished shooting.

The 7.62mm match grade bullet passed through the open windows of the Chrysler and tore through the BMW driver's head, blowing out the entire right side of the skull and exiting through the windshield. Brains, tissue, bone fragments, and blood splattered across the interior of the sports car. The man fell across the passenger seat.

"Good shot." Wolff spoke like he was on a firing range.

Kaderri next placed the crosshairs on the back of the other driver's head that was straining to see what happened to the other driver. "Second shot." Kaderri squeezed the trigger again. Like the first shot, this was true to is mark. The bullet hit in the base of the head. The man would no longer have a face that could be recognized.

"Good shot."

Kaderri watched as the two dealers continued their discussion thirty feet away from their parked cars, totally unaware that their drivers were dead. Their conversation was getting animated and then abruptly the larger man turned towards his BMW and stopped dead in his tracks. He turned back to Slapper and said something.

The conversation the two men began ended abruptly. Kaderri placed the crosshairs on the larger man's head and squeezed the trigger. In slow motion he watched the man's head explode in a pink mist that resembled a ripe watermelon being hit by a baseball bat. Blood geysered from the exposed artery as the heart continued to pump blood to the nonexistent brain. Slapper stood there motionless, plainly trying to figure out what happened. In morbid curiosity he watched the body twitch as if it were being shocked by electricity.

Slapper instinctively went for his gun ten feet away. It was a costly mistake.

"Good shot." Wolff was getting tired of saying the same words. In a moment he would be saying something different.

Methodically, Kaderri put the crosshairs on Slapper's heart. A body shot was easier on an erratic moving target. He squeezed the trigger. The bullet rocketed toward the target, but missed its intended point. "Shit." Kaderri snorted through clenched teeth.

Slapper turned to pick up the pistol just as the bullet hit. Instead of piercing his heart, the bullet practically tore off his right shoulder.

"You hit the right shoulder. He's still up." There was no sign of any urgency in Wolff's voice.

"I got him." Kaderri squeezed the trigger again. Click. From experience with weapons, he knew immediately that a round was jammed. He tried to clear it, but it wouldn't budge. Damn!

"He's getting away." Wolff hissed as he dropped the binoculars and drew his pistol. It also had a brass deflector. He emptied the fifteen rounds from his silenced pistol as fast as he could squeeze the trigger. It was almost impossible to hit a moving target at one hundred fifty yards with a pistol. But, Wolff was qualified as an expert. Two rounds hit Slapper in the leg, while the other bullets nicked at his feet or punctured holes in the cars behind him. "Got him in the leg," he announced. Slapper flopped on the pavement like a fish out of water.

Kaderri tried in vain to dislodge the jammed cartridge, but it wouldn't cooperate. Things weren't going as planned. Time for option two. He threw the rifle down in disgust and snapped open the sleek, black box next to him. He pulled out what looked like a camouflaged fiberglass rifle stock with a mounted 3-power scope and a square ring the size of the fist on the tip called a tow claw. Next he pulled out the limb, a piece that looked like a miniature compound bow. With practiced, quick efficiency, Kaderri fastened the limb to the stock, placed his foot in the toe claw, and pulled the string back until it locked in place. Sliding the razor sharp, double bladed broad-headed bolt into place, he thumbed the safety on the crossbow and sighted it on Slapper.

Wolff was replacing the spent magazine with a fresh one when he noticed that Kaderri had the crossbow assembled and ready to fire. "You need a spotter?"

Without thinking, Kaderri rose to his knees and watched as Slapper crawled on his shattered leg and dragged his shoulder to the car. "No," Kaderri answered. Some of the burlap strips of his ghillie suit partly obscured his vision, but not enough to hamper his shot. Slapper was almost to the car and reaching for the trunk when Kaderri fired. The one hundred fifty-pound draw of the string propelled the eighteen-inch bolt at two hundred eighty feet per second.

Just over one and one-half seconds later, the razor sharp tip sliced through Slapper's back. The momentum of the bolt slammed him against the car and imbedded into the rear quarter panel, leaving him stuck to the car in a grotesque prayer. Dark red blood flowed from the holes in his body, around his knees and spread across the blacktop.

The entire ambush took three minutes. Kaderri talked rapidly into the throat mike as the sniper team packed their equipment, paying careful attention to pick up every spent shell casing. "We're pulling out."

"Roger. All clear." Brown's calm voice was reassuring. He

would be waiting on the roadside of Interstate 787. There was another parking lot further up the highway, but it would have taken Kaderri and Wolff too long to get there. Time was critical.

Kaderri and Wolff made their way north along the river for a half-mile where they met Brown with a blue pickup truck that he had rented in nearby Vermont. As a precaution, he had put on New York license plates. He had a corner of the tarpaulin pulled back and empty boxes placed on the side of the road. To the occasional motorist passing by, it looked like he was re-packing his cargo.

Kaderri and Wolff lay hidden from view on the grass hill on the side of the highway mixing their equipment with the boxes Brown had scattered. Each box had one side open that allowed the two men to insert their equipment in; concealing it from the few motorists who passed by. When all the equipment was packed, Brown gave one last look in either direction for any traffic. At six thirty on a Sunday morning, there was hardly any traffic at all. Brown signaled to them. First Wolff, then Kaderri rose from the grass and hopped into the bed of the truck.

Brown closed the gate and secured the tarp. He jumped into the cab and eased onto the highway.

Hector Romero had more problems than he could handle. His mind was racing for answers. In total fear he watched silently from the small slit in the trunk of the car at Francisco's and presumably Slapper's death. He couldn't figure out how Francisco's head could explode without a sound. For a brief moment he thought he and Slapper were set up, like they set up Francisco. Especially when he saw Slapper crumple to the ground screaming and holding his shoulder. With his pistol ready, he was about to leap out of the trunk blazing away to help when a hail of bullets slammed into the trunk, including the one that shattered his collarbone.

He continued to watch as Slapper went down in another scream, this time holding his leg. Hector thought it would be better for his health and well being if he remained hidden. Slapper was by himself on this one. He silently urged Slapper on as he crawled to the car. What he saw next made him tremble. A small bush one hundred fifty yards away lying quietly along the shoreline grew to the size of a large bush, with one lonely, protruding branch pointed in his direction.

Slapper was almost to the car when Hector heard a smack, immediately followed by a thud that rocked the car. The force of the bolt slamming Slapper's body against the car locked the trunk. The sight of the bolt, dripping with Slapper's blood, protruding into the trunk caused Hector to urinate and defecate in his pants. It took all his might to keep from screaming. Hector was trapped inside with an extremely painful and bleeding collarbone. His only hope of escaping was if Keena let him out. When Keena failed to do just that, he assumed that Keena was dead. Hector would have to wait until someone came along to let him out. Eventually, he passed out from the terror, excruciating pain, and loss of blood.

CHAPTER SEVEN

Sunday, June 7, 7:30 a.m.

Gary Trainor scowled at the ringing phone. There was enough of the bright morning sunlight seeping through the shade that he didn't have to turn on the bedside lamp. He stared at the bright red numbers glowing back at him from the digital clock on the nightstand and didn't like what he saw.

Wiping his unshaven face, he let out a groan and answered the phone in a groggy voice. "Hello?" It was too early in the morning for him

"Detective?" The voice on the other end identified herself as an officer from the police department.

"Yes?" What did she want on a Sunday morning? It better be important.

"Detective, we have a report of a multiple homicide—" He cut her off, sitting upright in bed. "Where?"

"At the Corning preserve parking lot. Officers are on the scene."

Trainor thought for a moment. There were other detectives on the force. "Why are you calling me?"

"Orders from the captain. He said they need you ASAP. I already contacted Detective Bernard."

Trainor let out a big sigh. "I'm on my way." He hung up the phone. Rubbing the sleep out of his tired eyes, he stumbled out of bed and headed for the shower. Definitely not a great way to start a day.

Sunday, June 7, 7:55 a.m.

A half dozen police cars and three ambulances filled the parking lot of the Corning Preserve. The officers on scene already taped off the area with the familiar yellow tape. A police photographer was busy taking snapshots of the bodies before they were removed to the coroner's office. A quick thinking officer kept the few reporters at bay. Many of them monitored the police radios and had arrived almost as quickly as the police had.

Detective Gary Trainor inspected the headless body first. He was careful not to step in the huge pool of blood and goo that ran from where the head should have been. Various gold chains of all sizes some with medallions and charms attached, glistened in the rising sun as they swam in the dark red pool. Trainor fought down the vomit working its way up to escape out his mouth.

"Any idea who it is?" Trainor asked the uniformed officer who was the first one on the scene. The reporters apparently realized that he was the man in charge and shouted at him to let them in. He acknowledged their presence with a snort. The officer's face was pale, almost gray. Like the other officers in Albany, he wasn't prepared for anything like this. He flipped through a pocket size spiral notebook. "We think his name is Francisco Solarz. We got it off the driver's license in his pocket. Of course, we can't identify him by his face." The officer was clearly just as shocked and dismayed as anyone.

"Take it easy, Henry." Trainor sympathized with the man, but he couldn't let the officers lose control.

Detective Keith Bernard walked over to Trainor. As usual, Bernard's face showed no emotion. "You have to take a look at the other three." He took Trainor by the arm and led him to the parked cars. He made another statement, this time in a barely audible whisper. "Same as the other drug murders. The drugs are still here along with the money and weapons."

Trainor briefly stared at Bernard. Now he knew why he was called to the scene. He shook his head before he took in the body still impaled on the car. He shuddered at the sight. A pool of dark red blood had formed at the man's knees. His arm dangled at the shoulder by a few strands of muscle, and his broken leg lay twisted in an awkward position. Trainor fought down another wave of nausea. At least this one still had his head. *What do the others look like?* He thought.

Bernard seemed to read his mind. "Look in both cars." This type of carnage didn't seem to bother him.

Trainor stuck his head in the Chrysler and noticed the driver was laying face down. By the mess in the car, he knew the victim didn't have a face. The cabin of the car was stained red with blood and pieces of brain. An eyeball lay on the floor staring back in yet another pool of blood. There was a hole in the windshield where the bullet had exited. "Jesus Christ!" He stepped back from the car and held his stomach.

With hesitant steps, Trainor stepped over to the BMW. Bracing himself for the carnage, Trainor looked in on the driver. The sight was jut as grotesque. Trainor's stomach couldn't take it. He dropped to his hands and knees and let his stomach heave.

A half hour later, the bodies were identified and removed to the coroner's office, except for Varcasia's, he was still impaled on the car and a tarp was thrown over the body. Another officer was using a pair of bolt cutters to cut the bolt and release the body. A pair of tow trucks arrived to take the cars back to be thoroughly searched. Detectives Gary Trainor and Keith Bernard stood next to a squad car, each sipping from a container of orange juice and munching on powdered donuts that another officer had been more than willing to leave the scene to purchase.

"What do you think happened here?" Trainor asked.

"I don't know, but it was definitely a one sided fight. I counted six holes in the car, not including the ones that killed the victims. The two guns we found lying on the ground were never fired. Nor were the guns the victims in the car were carrying. These people probably never knew what hit them."

"Except for the guy who's stuck to the car," Trainor added. "It's got to be the same people that pulled off the hit on Stroehmann." He took another sip of his juice before continuing. He shook his head. "They left the guns, the cash, and drugs." Both remained silent lost in their own thoughts when one of the two truck operators ran over.

"Hey, there's blood dripping from inside the trunk of the Chrysler."

Trainor had just taken a bite of his donut. He spoke around his mouthful. "Blood from inside the car?"

"Yeah!"

Bernard grabbed a crow bar from the tool chest in the back of the tow truck. He walked around to the back of the car and smashed the lock on the trunk. The key would have been easier, but they wanted it for fingerprints. He was just about to lift the trunk when Trainor stopped him.

Trainor looked at the trunk and drew his pistol. They had no idea who may be in there, in all actuality; this might be the killer they were looking for. He moved off to the side of the car to cover Bernard and pointed his pistol at the trunk. If the man inside tried to shoot, he would be the recipient of a point blank 9mm slug.

The tow truck operator moved away without having to be told.

In one brisk, fluid motion, Bernard broke the lock, raised the trunk, drew his pistol, and stuck it in. Trainor did the same. The sight before them was extraordinary. A Puerto Rican man lay shaking in a fetal position trying to point his gun at whoever opened the trunk. His eyes were wide with fear and his dark skin was ashen white from the loss of blood that still flowed from the jagged tear where his exposed collarbone broke through the skin. Part of the trunk was rusted out letting the

Shadows and Deceptions

blood drip onto the pavement below.

The man dropped the gun when he saw the uniformed police officer standing behind Bernard. He wasn't going to die like the rest.

Trainor stared in disbelief at the pathetic man in the trunk muttering something incomprehensible. Trainor thought he said something about a tree shooting Slapper. That would have to be deciphered later. Right now this man needed medical attention, or they weren't going to get any answers. "Get the paramedics!"

Discovering the gruesome sight when the officers arrived, they mistakenly forgot to search the trunk. They had apparently thought that all the blood on the ground belonged to the victim stuck on the car.

In solemn silence, Trainor and Bernard watched the ambulance exit the parking lot and race toward the nearest hospital. Trainor hoped the man would make it, they needed any information stored in his brain. They needed a break in the case.

Sunday, June 7, 3:45 p.m.

Within Albany Medical Center's antiseptic recovery room, Hector Romero lay sound asleep recovering from six hours of surgery. When he arrived in the emergency room, he was in shock from loss of blood and almost dead. The doctors who operated on him said he was a lucky man.

Detective Gary Trainor wanted his prized possession protected from any attempt on Hector Romero's life. He had to be debriefed concerning the mass murders at the Corning Preserve. This man could be the killer they were looking for. But, Trainor kept his options open and thought this man might not be. If he wasn't, the killer or killers may come back to silence him before he could talk to the police. For that reason, Trainor placed a uniformed officer to stand watch with instructions to use whatever means were necessary just short of shoot first, ask questions later—to keep people away.

Trainor sat in the lounge with his hands between his knees,

107

twiddling his thumbs to keep from barging in on the doctor checking on Romero's recovery. The eight cups of coffee didn't do much to steady his nerves either.

Finally, the doctor emerged from the room. Trainor stood, "Well, Doc, can I question him?"

The doctor gave him a puzzled look. "Are you a relative?"

"No. I'm a detective." He flashed his badge and ID. "I need to question him on his involvement in a few murders."

The doctor thought for a moment then said. "Go ahead, Detective, but don't expect too much from him. He's still out of it for the most part."

"Thanks." Trainor nodded and stepped through the door.

Hector Romero lay still in the hospital bed. IV bottles hung from their racks as clear liquid flowed into the veins on both arms. Trainor smiled. Bastard probably hoped they were filled with drugs instead of saline, or whatever antibiotic he was receiving. A heart monitor wheeled behind the bed kept track of Romero's strengthening heart. Good, he thought, he was going to live.

"Who are you?" A soft hoarse voice escaped from Romero's dry cracked lips.

Trainor pulled out his badge. "Detective Gary Trainor, Albany Police." He slid the only chair in the room over to the side of the bed and whipped out his small spiral notebook. His right hand clicked the pen. "I need a lot of answers from you."

An hour later, Trainor left the hospital more confused than before, and no closer to solving any of the murders.

CHAPTER EIGHT

Wednesday, June 10, 11:45 a.m.

The dust that rose and hung in the hot humid air blotted out the beautiful crystalline blue sky. The huge dumptrucks and earth movers were busy moving tons of earth from the every widening hole that was soon to be another strip mall on the already over crowded stretch of highway. The early June sun beat down on the heads and backs of men stripped to their waist, turning their already bronzed skin a shade darker.

Greg Sander hauled cinder blocks six at a time from the stacks that were fifteen feet away from the trench where they were going to lay. His sweaty body was cut and scratched from the laboring work that he didn't have to do. The laborers on the job site couldn't figure out why the mason, Sander, would do their job along with his own. It was against union regulations, but no one was going to put in a grievance on this violation.

Sander dropped into the trench after dumping the last of the six blocks. He paused briefly to tighten the rubber band that held his ponytail, and rub the white medical tape that was wrapped tightly around his broken ribs. It hurt like hell every time he moved, but it reminded him of what had happened and what he had to do. He grabbed his trowel and began laying the blocks.

Greg Sander was a very good mason, even considered the best by some. But since his arrest on cocaine possession, he has become a different man. He used to be a hot headed, quick tempered, insolent idiot. But not anymore. Since the arrest and his initial hearing, for which the judge let him free on his own recognizance because he was a first time offender, he hardly spoke to anyone. When he did, it was in one-syllable answers to any questions. He never started a conversation with anybody, and would only carry on one in limited words with his long-time friend, John Hendricks.

Sander also insisted that he didn't need the help of the laborers. His reasoning being that he could do the job himself and needed the time to think about his future and what the arrest had done to him. He told his foreman that the arrest had changed him, and that he had a new goal in life.

Surprised by the new ethic that Sander displayed, the foremen agreed to let Sander try it his way. Maybe the arrest did wake him up, and maybe it made him a better man.

"Hey, Greg!" John Hendricks called out over the growing roar of a passing dumptruck. "Catch."

Sander looked up in time to catch the overloaded turkey sub and a can of soda. "Where did you get this?"

Hendricks sat down on one of the blocks and made a hasty table with a piece of plywood and another block. He jerked his thumb over his shoulder to a shiny silver truck with one side of it open. A crowd of hungry construction workers was lined up waiting to place their order. "Over there at the roach coach."

Sander pulled a block over for himself and bit hungrily into the sandwich and muttered a thanks. The nourishment quickly quieted his grumbling stomach. For what seemed like an eternity, both men sat there in silence chomping at their lunch.

"What's going on in that thick head of yours?"

Sander shook out his thoughts. "What do you mean?"

"Shit, Greg. Ever since you got arrested you've been on Mars. What gives?"

Sander shrugged. "Do you know of any other exercise clubs in the area that are as good as A Better Body? I need a place to work out."

He shook his head. "No, man. There ain't any as good, but there are a lot of other ones."

Sander snorted.

"Hey, man, why don't you try to get your membership back?"

Sander's eyes turned cold and his voice hard. "When I go back to that place, someone is going to get hurt real bad."

"Greg, man, if you go back there again, that guy Kaderri will probably do the same thing to you again. Isn't getting the shit knocked out of you once enough?" He drew his sweaty hand across his mouth instead of using a napkin. "Well, time to get back to work."

Sander was lost in his thoughts again and didn't notice that his friend had left. Ten minutes later, a harsh reminder from his foreman that he was lucky to be there, working after his stupid arrest brought him back to the present.

Wednesday, June 10, 12:30 p.m.

Michele Thorsen should have been in her office preparing her next segment for the nightly news or been out combing the streets for information with her cameraman. But, she wasn't. She was working in her backyard, taking advantage of the hot sun. She sat comfortably in the chase lounge wearing a skimpy pink bikini with a sweaty pitcher of iced tea and a half-eaten chicken salad sandwich perched on the folding table next to her. Soft rock music flowed gently from the portable radio that was hidden under the table, to keep it from melting in the sun.

Scattered around her were notebooks and newspapers filled with information on the drug murders. The murders themselves were beginning to attract national attention, and that was competition she didn't need. She picked one newspaper up

111

off the freshly cut grass, and intently read the story. This one happened to be the New York Times. By the third paragraph, her fears and apprehension subsided. The writer of the story was very vague and had no concrete evidence about the murders or who committed them. He, too, believed the police story that the murders were related to dealers expanding their territory from New York City. Trading the Times for a local paper, The Daily Gazette, the story printed on the first page said the same thing.

Michele still had the inside edge on the rest of the reporters. Well, she thought she still did. That edge was Detective Gary Trainor. She made a mental note to stop by the station to get a few answers she needed and to find out why he picked her to confide in above all the other reporters. She hated it when she couldn't get an answer. She was at a loss to his reasoning. She knocked herself out on more than one occasion trying to answer the question herself. What compounded the situation was that he hadn't asked for anything in return. Was he holding out for a later time? He just kept telling her not to reveal anything until he gave her the okay.

This time, she would have to tread water. She was utterly shocked when her sexual advances had been turned down. It was another blow to her ego when she realized she couldn't control the information that she wanted. Maybe she didn't try hard enough. More seductive clothing may help, too. No, he was mad that she had tried that, more correctly, he was royally pissed. Better not try that again.

Somewhere in the caverns of her brain, she respected Gary Trainor more than she would readily admit. It took a lot of willpower to turn down someone with her looks and open advances. Maybe she was becoming attracted to Trainor.

The radio announcer rambled off the time in between songs and it reminded her to put more suntan lotion on. Grabbing the bottle of Hawaiian Tropic, she squirted a liberal amount on her arms and rubbed it in. She quickly applied the lotion to her chest and stomach and began spreading it on her legs when she spotted her extremely fat neighbor staring at her from his second floor kitchen window.

She snorted in contempt and disgust. It was obvious that he was undressing her with his eyes, and probably was hoping she would sunbathe naked. A devilish smile spread across her face. The guy was probably excited, she thought. Why not egg the fat bastard on a little more?

Pretending not to see him, she reached behind her back, unhooked the clasp of her top, and pulled the strings tied behind her neck. Draping the top over the back of the chair, she stood and stretched with her interlocked fingers pointing towards the sky, causing her to thrust out her naked breasts. Still standing as she finished her exaggerated stretch, she grabbed the suntan lotion once more and applied it to her breasts, rubbing it on slowly and seductively.

It was no secret that Michele hated her neighbor. She always said that when the temperature rose above sixty, he started to sweat. Every time he saw her, he would always stare and never failed to make advances. When she first moved into her house, she thought he was just playing games. After all, she knew that her body was well proportioned and a pleasure to look at. But she soon realized he wasn't playing games and was indeed serious. Relations between the two were quickly severed, and she built a six foot high solid wood fence around her back yard to keep him and his prying eyes out. But, that didn't daunt his efforts. He peered out his upper floor windows to continue his staring.

Deciding that he had seen enough, she put her top back on, looked in his direction, and gave him the finger.

Clearing her mind, she got back to work. Wiping some stubborn grass clippings that had stuck to her lotioned body that dropped from her notebook when she picked it up, she leafed through a few pages to her notes on the first conversation with Gary Trainor. As she read the barely legible handwriting, her mind was racing to remember anything he said that she had forgotten to write down. She cursed, thinking it would have been much easier if he'd let her take notes or keep the recording.

Finally finished reading her notes on the interview, she determined that there wasn't anything she missed. Charging forward, she flipped a few blank pages until the noted began again and stopped to consult the scribble containing the street interviews. Deciding they had nothing to do with what she was looking for she closed the notebook and risked a peek at her neighbor. He wasn't there anymore.

Taking a short break, Michele ran a sweaty hand through her blonde hair that rested on her shoulders. She refilled the glass with more iced tea. Realizing the phone ringing was hers, she ran to the kitchen to answer it. By the time she reached it, the ringing stopped. *Damn*, she thought, she had to be the only person in the world without an answering machine. If it was important, she reasoned, the caller would try again.

Now that she was inside, she decided to take a shower and pay a visit to Gary Trainor.

Wednesday, June 10, 3:25 p.m.

"Oh, shit, Thorsen, what do you want now?" Detective Gary Trainor threw down another folder on top of a huge teetering pile that was ready to topple off his desk. Like usual, he wasn't in the mood to deal with any reporters, especially Michele Thorsen since the stunt she had pulled earlier. "Go talk to the Public Relations officer, I'm busy." He turned away from her and reached for the two-hour-old coffee.

"Hi Detectives," she said as she stood in the door.

"He's in another good mood. Though you should have seen him earlier," Keith Bernard commented from behind his desk. "He was playing Mister Hyde again. You know. Bloodshot eyes, fangs protruding from his mouth." Bernard pulled his upper lip back to reveal his set of perfect teeth. "And the drooling would put a rabid dog to shame." He received a dirty look from Trainor. "I'm out of here."

Michele stifled a laugh at Bernard's animated story, and took a seat, "I'm not going to be long, Detective, you don't have to leave." A look of embarrassment was on her face.

"I'm going to be the referee," Bernard said. "The mood that Gary's in, Michele, I'm afraid to be left alone with him. And, the congenial mood that you appear to be in, he'll eat you for lunch."

Trainor's face was twisted in anger, and it took a lot of energy to calm him down. He could feel his face redden, "You didn't answer me, what do you want?"

She held up her hand to quiet Trainor before he launched into her. She reached into her purse, pulled out a small white envelope, and handed it over to him.

"What's this?" Trainor said, fighting to keep his anger in check. She still didn't verbally answer his question, but he surmised the answer was contained in the envelope.

"It looks like an envelope," Bernard said.

"Shut up," Trainor snapped.

"Read it." Thorsen turned and walked out the door.

"Well?" Bernard stood from behind his desk and walked toward Trainor. "Are you going to read it, or shall I?"

"Mind your own fucking business." Trainor sat in his chair and dropped the envelope in the middle of his desk. He stared at for a few minutes deciding if he should open it or throw it in the garbage. Finally, he stuck his finger in the corner of the sealed envelope and split the top open. Inside was a delicately designed invitation to dinner at The Steer House on Saturday, June 13 at 7 p.m.

"What does it say?" Bernard's said cheerfully, trying to lighten Trainor's dark mood. He caught the invitation that Trainor tossed. "Whoa! Your presence is requested to join me for dinner at The Steer House on Saturday, June 13th at 7 p.m." Bernard read further and said, "She's even going to pay for it!"

"I don't think I'm going."

"What? Why?" Bernard said, clearly dumfounded at his remark. "You're nuts for not going with her. She's beautiful, and who knows, you may get lucky!" he raised and lowered his eyebrows a few times for effect.

"She already tried that," Trainor admitted.

"Tried what?"

Trainor refilled his lukewarm coffee and popped another Tums in his mouth. "She tried to seduce me." He didn't go any further.

"When did this happen?" Bernard asked, obviously wanting to hear the details.

"After we found Pedro's body at the port. I went back to her place to fill her in, like I promised, and she guessed correctly that I wasn't telling her everything. She knew I couldn't tell her everything, but she pressed anyway." Trainor shrugged his shoulders.

"And?"

Trainor sat behind his desk. "She took her robe off and...you can figure out the rest."

"Did you give in?" concern in his voice. "We're in the middle of a murder epidemic and we don't want things to get out of control."

"Fuck no! What do you think I am?" Trainor shouted, then his voice softened and he smiled. "But it would have been fun."

Bernard couldn't help but laugh, and then turned serious. "I was hoping you would say that."

"Now that they were on the subject of the murders," Trainor pursued it further. "Did the lieutenant tell you that Narcotics is getting involved in our investigations?" There was genuine scorn in his voice. Trainor thought there was no reason for Narcotics to get heavily involved in a Homicide investigation.

"What? Why the hell would he do that?"

"He thought because drugs were involved, it may help us find the killers faster."

"There wasn't any trafficking involved, all the drugs were left at the scene," Bernard said, staying silent for a moment. "But then, the murder of Pedro was different."

"True," Trainor admitted as he thought back on the murder investigation. They found traces of cocaine and plastic from a bag on the knife that Pedro was carrying, but the drugs were missing. "I guess he has a point there."

"Who's being assigned to this?" Bernard asked.

"Chris Dinwiddie." Trainor said through clenched teeth. Dinwiddie was the most inept Narcotics officer on the force.

"I haven't been on the force that long, but I've heard horror stories about his investigation practices."

"I'm sure that what you've heard is all true, and probably flattering compared to what he's really like. I used to be in Narcotics and worked with him. He's useless." Trainor popped another Tums in his mouth and continued "With the connections that I still have in Narcotics and on the streets, we don't need them to get involved, especially *Dickwiddie.*"

"You were in Narcotics?"

"Yeah, just over a year." Trainor didn't go any further.

"Why did you get out?" Bernard asked.

"I'll tell you why." A high pitched nasally voice shot though them.

Trainor felt a shiver course through his body when he heard that man's horrible voice and watched Bernard's face twist in pain. A mousy man stood defiantly in the doorway staring down at Bernard and Trainor. The man has his hands on his small hips, and his head was too big for his tall, skinny body. His neck was long and skinny also, resembling the neck of a Thanksgiving turkey ready for the chopping block. The gold wire framed glasses sat unevenly on his crooked nose, that has obviously been broken at one point and ill repaired. His greasy black hair was parted over his left eye and reached the bottom of his collar. He looked like a typical geek, right down to the ill fitting clothes and acne-scarred face.

"He was removed from Narcotics for using excessive force and his inability to work with others."

"Who are you?" Bernard asked sourly.

"That is Chris Dick-Dinwiddie." The hatred in Trainor's voice hung in the air with each word.

Bernard stood and offered his hand to Dinwiddie, "I'm Keith Bernard, nice to meet you, Chris."

"Detective," Dinwiddie answered and nodded, grasping the offered hand.

"We were just talking about you," Bernard said, trying to

lighten the mood. He pulled a chair from behind a desk.

"I can just imagine." He took a seat in the offered chair.

"What do you want, Dinwiddie?" Trainor spat. Dinwiddie opened the files he was carrying and laid the papers out in a neat row on the deck. "I'm here to confer with you on our joint operation."

"Confer on a joint operation? Where the fuck did you learn to talk?" Bernard asked as he laughed aloud.

"I said 'our' joint operation, and I don't find your humor funny."

"You still don't have a sense of humor," Trainor commented. "Every time you try to put on your mad face, Dinwiddie, you look constipated."

"Now that that's cleared up, where do you want to start?" Bernard certainly tried to diffuse the situation by getting back to the case that they were supposed to be working on. He directed the question to Dinwiddie.

Dinwiddie pulled a folder from the middle of the row. "Let's start with our interview with Betty 'Blossom' Freeman."

"What about her?" Bernard asked.

"I want to know what she said about Pedro's murder."

"Nothing," Trainor lied. He wanted to keep Dinwiddie in the dark for as long as possible.

Dinwiddie threw down the file in disgust. "Goddamnit, Trainor! Quit fucking with me!"

Trainor felt his face become hot. He stood and got right into Dinwiddie's face. He wasn't about to let another case go down the sewer because of Dinwiddie. It didn't matter that they were nowhere near solving it.

Bernard reached out and forced Trainor back in his chair before the punches started. "Sit your ass down!" He looked over at Dinwiddie who was still standing behind the desk and spoke to him with authority, "Sit your ass down, too."

Bernard waited a few minutes to let things simmer before he continued. "How did you know about Betty Freeman?"

Dinwiddie ran his hand through his greasy hair before he answered. "She's a confidential informant."

Trainor shot out of his seat. "What?"

"Sit!" Bernard commanded, pointing to the seat.

"She reports to me once a week," Dinwiddie said, proudly pointing to himself. "And I've been gathering evidence on the drug trade that her drunken customers from the ships brag to her about."

"Well, well, Dinwiddie, you surprise me," Trainor said, "I didn't think you were capable of anything along those lines of police work."

Before Dinwiddie could respond, Bernard cut him off. "Well, Chris, your good news may be the break we are looking for."

Moshe Koretsky sat quietly as the sun shone through the huge floor to ceiling plate-glass windows in the conference room that was elegantly decorated with a rich, deep, teal carpet, and a solid oak oval table. Its highly polished finish was reflecting the sun and gleaming like a mirror. Hung on the walls were various collages of past members of the Bar Association, and a copy of the first multi-million dollar contract the law firm of Miller, Katz & Kaufmann had drafted twenty years ago.

The three partners, Joshua Miller, Nadine Katz, and Albert Kaufmann were all in there mid forties. They had started one of the most successful law firm in the Capital District upon graduating from law school.

Besides graduating from the same school and being Jewish, Moshe Koretsky also knew of something else that the three attorneys had in common—he used this to his advantage. Although they never knew them, all three attorneys had relatives who had been lost in the concentration camps during World War II. Miller had also lost his brother and father fighting the PLO and Egyptians. Because of that common thread, the lawyers were perfect candidates to become *Sayanim's*-Jewish helpers outside of Israel.

Joshua Miller, the senior partner, sat commandingly at the head of the table. His immaculate tailored, gray silk suit and red paisley tie were striking against the maroon leather chair.

His salt and pepper hair was just short of collar length and parted on the left.

"When is the next freighter leaving for Israel?" Koretsky asked from his seat next to Nadine Katz. It was one of the rare occasions that Koretsky visited the firm. He wanted to remain anonymous, but sometimes he had to expose himself.

After consulting with her manifest, she said, "Tomorrow."

"I assume my shipment will be on board," he said sharply. Koretsky didn't like surprises, and the fact that another ship was leaving tomorrow was a big surprise.

"Yes, it will, Mr. Steiner," Albert Kaufmann said. "We are competent, you know."

"If you're so competent, why didn't you tell me a ship was leaving tomorrow? I have customers that need—"

"That's enough," Miller said, cutting off Koretsky. "We apologize. It won't happen again."

Koretsky flashed Miller an icy stare for cutting him off, but, spoke with a calm voice, "Of course you're competent."

If Miller saw the look, he did a good job of ignoring it. "Well, I think we covered everything. The same procedures will be used for the loading and unloading of Ariel's package, so everything is safe and secure."

Both Kaufmann and Katz rose and left the conference room, leaving Miller and Koretsky behind. Koretsky was thankful for that. It saved him from throwing them out so he could have a serious conversation with Miller.

Once outside the conference room, Nadine Katz challenged Kaufmann, "Al, why do you give him such a hard time?"

Kaufmann's face was red with anger, and he took a deep breath before answering. "I don't trust that guy. He's up to something."

"Like what?" she pressed. "He's shipping his material off to Israel, our people's homeland. What's wrong with that?"

"Has he ever told you what type material he's shipping?" Nadine thought before answering. She sought the answer in her memory. "I think it is computer chips, or something to do with electronics."

"I don't believe him. He's up to no good."

"But Al, he said he's doing it for Israel. And besides, he assured us that nobody is getting hurt by it, or that it is illegal. Doesn't that mean anything?"

Al was silent for the moment. "You're right, I guess, but I still don't trust him." He looked back into the conference room as Miller and Koretsky continued their private conversation.

Nadine didn't want to continue this discussion in the open air where the secretaries and staff could overhear. One of the paralegals walked past and reminded her of some work she had to catch up on. "Rufus?"

"Yes?" Rufus "Ghost" Brown turned to face her.

"I forgot to finish the depositions on Walker, can you bring the file over to my office? I am also going to need your help on chasing some info."

"I'll bring it right over."

The door was closed and privacy assured in the conference room. Both Koretsky and Miller waited until Katz and Kaufmann moved far enough away from the door before they continued their private conversation.

As Koretsky walked softly around the table, he could feel Joshua Miller's eyes on him. There was no doubt in his mind that he intrigued Miller. Koretsky had wealth, power, knowledge to events and circumstances that Miller would kill for. Koretsky knew when a ship was going to be late leaving or arriving from port. With that pertinent information passed along, Miller could negotiate shipping contracts in his clients' favor due to lack of competence on the carrier's part. How many people would want to do business with a company that was late getting the merchandise to the warehouses, which in turn would make it late getting it to the people who needed the product, which would mean less profit?

But there was more to Moshe Koretsky than having a well-placed source feeding him information on departure and arrival times for merchant ships. He led Miller to believe that he was an import/export merchant dealing mostly in wine, but also dipped into electronics. And, he didn't do anything to dispel Miller's belief that he was a member of one of the world's largest terrorist organizations, the JDL, or Jewish Defense League.

Moshe Koretsky watched as Nadine Katz moved away with her paralegal before turning to Miller. "What the fuck is going on? Why haven't you gotten me a new contact?"

Clearly shocked by Koretsky's sudden outburst, Miller stammered his feeble response, "What?"

Koretsky moved to the opposite end of the table, his face hot with anger. "Why haven't you gotten me a new contact?" He slammed his fist on the table for emphasis.

Miller recovered quickly and attempted to show Koretsky he couldn't be intimidated. He rose and walked over to the portable bar, poured himself a glass of bourbon, and reclaimed his seat at the head of the table.

The battle of wills had begun. Koretsky immediately saw what Miller was doing and decided to play the game too. *Fine* he thought. He sat down at the opposite end of the table and stared directly into Miller's eyes. After two minutes of staring, without as much as a blink, Koretsky saw Miller's composure start to crack. First he blinked, and after three minutes of total silence, Miller averted his eyes from Koretsky. "I'm still waiting for an answer to my question," Koretsky said. He still hadn't blinked, his facial expression set in stone.

Miller suddenly knew he couldn't compete with the man across from him. Pulling a cigarette from the gold holder in his inner jacket pocket, he took one for himself and offered one to Koretsky, who declined. Flicking the monogrammed Zippo lighter, he lit the cigarette and inhaled deeply, savoring the nicotine before answering. "Your last contact was Luis Varcasia."

The name rang a bell, but Koretsky couldn't place it "The name's familiar."

"He was the guy who was stuck on the car with the arrow," he looked Koretsky right in the eye.

"What's going on here, Josh? That's twice this has happened." Koretsky was getting pissed. Every contact he was supposed to meet that Miller had set up was getting murdered.

Miller ran his hand through his hair. "I don't know, Ariel, but if anymore of my people get killed, I'll lose my network. First, there was Rudolph, who was killed in the gun battle with the cops. Then, Stroehmann, and now Varcasia. I also don't know if what the police are saying about rival drug dealers fighting for turf is true or not."

"Why not?"

Miller let out a big sigh. "Of all the drug related murders in the city in the past few weeks, most of the people killed were mine."

Koretsky immediately caught on to what Miller was saying but didn't let on. So, the motherfucker suspected him on knocking off his people. He decided to play dumb and let Miller take his own course. "How many people have you lost?"

Miller thought for a few seconds before answering. "I lost three of my lieutenants, not counting the little shits who do most of the work."

"That's a lot of people," Koretsky admitted. "Do you have the resources to replace them?"

"Replacing that scum is no problem, it'll just take time to get the right people in place. I'm just worried about losing people faster than I can replace them, which will cut into profits."

"Good point." Koretsky's mind was working overtime. The problem that Miller had was serious enough to be concerned. The time it would take to replace those people would cut into the money that Mossad needed to fund operations, and Koretsky wouldn't let that happen. "Who else can you set me up with?" Koretsky wanted to get back on the main reason why he was there.

Miller gave him a skeptical look as he ground out his cigarette. "I'm going to have to check, Ariel. My people are running a bit scared at the moment at meeting new people."

That's twice Miller eluded to his suspicions regarding Koretsky. "I see your point." Koretsky stood and walked toward the door.

"Where are you going" Miller said in genuine surprise.

Koretsky stopped with his hand on the doorknob and turned to face Miller. " "Your retainer is cancelled, Josh. If you ever accuse me of killing your people again, I'll make your life so miserable, you'd wish you were dead."

"Wait—" Miller's plea ended with the closing of the door as Koretsky walked away.

On his way out, Moshe Koretsky locked eyes with the pretty redhead, Ms. Waters, as he walked past the receptionist's desk. "Good day," he said.

"Good day," she parroted.

Koretsky stared a little longer than he intended, and for a brief moment, he saw the subtle change in her eyes that looked like she recognized him. He, too, felt like he had met her before, but he wasn't sure.

"Good work, Rufus," Nadine Katz said from behind her desk.

"Thanks. Is there anything else?" He noticed she was staring out into the lobby through her Venetian blinds. He turned to see who she was staring at. "Who is that guy?"

Ghost's question startled her. "Huh? Oh, his name is Ariel Steiner."

Ghost stared through the blinds and locked eyes with the man who walked with a purpose. For a brief moment, Ghost had the uncanny feeling that he just looked at the devil himself, and that scared the hell out him.

CHAPTER NINE

The top of Kaderri's desk couldn't be seen. Paper, partially completed forms, client files and all other types of paraphernalia were piled into one big heap. It was Marc Kaderri's monthly cleaning of his files. Once a month, he would sift through all the files of the prospects he saw to generate new business, finish up old business, or throw out the file completely because there was no hope in making any money.

For the most part, Kaderri's personal filing system was horrible. He stored the information mostly on memory, and more than once he forgot to call clients back. He knew he had to join the technological age in computer storage, but he rationalized that it would take too much time to find a system, implement it, and store all the information in a computer's memory. He was concerned with making money.

He read one particular file in which he had forgotten to call back the owner of a small business who wanted to set up

125

a retirement program. There was a Post-it attached to the file that said to call back in the beginning of June, which was almost two weeks ago. He cursed himself for being late. Somehow, he hoped there was still a chance for writing the business. As he cursed himself, his phone rang. But he had trouble reaching it. By the sound of the ring, he knew it was Louise on his intercom.

"Marc," Louise said as she walked through the open door in her stocking feet. "I see it's that time of the month again."

"Hi," he said. "I don't know who's time of the month is worse, yours' or mine."

"Very funny."

"Why did you buzz me?"

"Ghost is in the lobby."

Kaderri thought for a moment and looked at his watch, it was well past lunch and Ghost rarely stopped by unannounced. "Okay, send him in."

"Marc," she said as she moved in front of his desk, "when are you going to get a filing system that works?"

Kaderri furrowed his brow. "How do you keep track of everything out there?"

Simple, I'm organized." She smiled smugly, "Marc, I could handle a filing system for you and your clients, but that would cut into the work I do now. To really run your office more efficiently, you need to hire someone else."

"Okay, smart ass," he said with a smile, "effective Monday you're promoted. You find the system that can do what I want and need. Plus, you hire someone to take your position."

"And what about compensation?" she asked with a straight face.

"What about it?" Kaderri teased.

Louise leaned her hourglass figure forward and placed her hands on her hips. "If you—"

"Okay, okay. An extra fifty a week, and maybe a bonus when the system is ready."

"Is the bonus physical?" A devilish smile spread across her face and she wiggled her hips for accent.

Kaderri smiled and shook his head. "Show Ghost in."

Louise turned and swayed her hips seductively. "Oh, Marc," she said before she exited. "If it helps in your decision about the bonus, I'm a true redhead."

Before he could comment, she was out the door and replaced by Ghost walking in and closing the door behind him.

"Hi, Marc." There was a sense of urgency in his voice. Kaderri gestured to the small round table in the corner of his office that overlooked the city. "Take a seat." After both men took their seats, Kaderri said, "What's up?"

"That guy, Koretsky—"

Kaderri leaned closer, his emotions starting to boil. Unconsciously, his hands balled into fists, a knot formed in his stomach, and the twitch started in his cheek. "What about him?"

"He was in my office today, and he's going by the name Ariel Steiner."

The news hit Kaderri like a sledgehammer. After all the years, after spotting him at Ramones, Kaderri finally had Moshe Koretsky. Kaderri couldn't believe his luck. Moshe Koretsky was in the same building. He felt both elated and alarmed at the same time. Knowing that Koretsky had business in the building, would make him easier to track, but the warning that Paul McKnight gave him in Beirut about being careful also came to mind. Kaderri frowned slightly, "What was he doing there and when did he leave?"

"I don't know why he's there, but he was talking to the three partners, then just to Josh Miller alone."

"Did you get anything on tape?"

"No, they were in the conference room."

Shortly after Steven Caron was gunned down in the street, Ghost had overheard a one-sided conversation Joshua Miller had had with what was obviously a drug supplier. It was at that time that Ghost had approached Kaderri and Wolff with his newly found knowledge and suggested that he go to the cops with the information. He'd said he hoped that somehow there was a remote chance that the police would find the killers of Steven Caron.

Kaderri and Wolff then suggested that they handle matters on their own, with Ghost having a very limited role. Marc Kaderri was the last person expected to take the law into his own hands. On the battlefield, though, it was a different story. He didn't fight fair. But, in the civilian world, it was a different world. But in the end, Kaderri had persuaded him that the police couldn't handle everything on their own, and the liberal judges who pushed their lenient philosophy into the criminal justice system. By pooling their talents, they could relieve some of the pressure that was placed on the police force, and put one hell of a dent in the local drug trade. The three men now had a source where they could get information on local deals and trades, and eliminate them. The only remaining question was how to get the information without jeopardizing themselves or their intentions. They had decided that the best way was to place a microphone in Joshua Miller's office and a tape recorder in Ghost's desk. He happened to be right next to Miller's office. It was a risk, but one they were willing to take. Joshua Miller seemed to be the only partner involved in the drug dealings, so his office was the only one bugged.

"Damn!" Kaderri said.

"Sorry," Ghost said, feeling like he failed.

"There's nothing to be sorry about, Ghost." Kaderri rose and peered out the window. "Do you have any idea what transpired?" He spoke to the glass.

"No, but Koretsky was pissed, and Miller looked as though he was surprised by what was said."

Kaderri thought for a moment, wondering why Koretsky was seeking the advice of an attorney, and especially the firm of Miller, Katz & Kaufmann? Hundreds of thoughts raced through his brain. What did Koretsky want? What was he doing there? Was he connected to Miller in any way? Ghost calling his name interrupted his thought process.

"Marc? I gotta get back upstairs."

"Okay, Ghost, I'll be in touch. Thanks."

As Brown turned to leave, Kaderri said, "Wait a minute." He found a piece of paper and scribbled a quick note on it and handed it to Brown. "Can you get this?"

Brown studied the note with shock and amazement. "Are you serious?"

"If I wasn't, I wouldn't have asked you, would I?"

"I guess not." He looked at the note again. "Yeah, I can get it for you, but it's going to be expensive."

"Thanks."

"Where were you today?" Hank Warren asked.

"Working, where else would I be?" Michelee Thorsen said to her boss.

"I called your house, and you didn't answer," Warren said with added vigor.

Thorsen knew he was after something, and wasn't in the mood to play his version of Simon Says. "Hank," her blue eyes challenged him, "what is it that you want?"

"Come with me."

She was led past the news room and the production room. She waved to the people she could stomach and ignored the ones she couldn't stand, which was most. At the end of the hallway was Hank Warren's office that adjoined a private conference room. Before she reached the end of the hallway, she questioned Warren on what was going on. To her annoyance, he ignored her question.

He paused briefly with his hand on the doorknob and turned as if to be sure Michele Thorsen was still behind him. Warren opened the door and stepped into the conference room. Sitting at the pine conference table was a acne scarred twenty-year-old male with oily brown hair and heavy black-framed glasses that held half-inch thick lenses. When he stood, she noticed that he was hunched over, and he could easily have reached six feet if he would stand up straight.

Michele Thorsen," Warren offered, "meet Richard Armstrong."

Michele didn't like to be surprised, and found it hard to

hide her displeasure at the situation. Warren apparently picked up on it before she had a chance to spit out some vulgar statement.

"Michele," Warren turned to face Michele and said softly, "that geek in front of you has some extremely interesting information that you will find invaluable."

Michele Thorsen stepped away from her boss and extended her hand and smiled to the geek. She sat down opposite him and opened a fresh notebook.

Moshe Koretsky was on the secure line to Tel Aviv. He checked in with the director at his check-in time to update him on his current assignment. He had to convey the news that he really didn't want to.

"I had to cut relations with Miller," Koretsky said.

"Repair them," the director ordered, obviously not caring why they were cut in the first place.

"But, sir, he hasn't come through for me in the past few weeks. He needs a cooling-off period. Beside, he's accused me of knocking off his contacts."

"Have you?" the gruff voice asked.

"Only one. But, that was necessary for operational security, and only after I got the merchandise. Miller's other suppliers were killed before I met them. Obviously, killing them before the transaction was complete wouldn't be in the mission's best interest."

"Things are moving faster than anticipated. We need more money, so you are going to have to reestablish a relationship with Miller. There isn't enough time for you to look for a new supplier." The director's voice was final.

Koretsky knew better than to argue. The only thing he could do was say, "Yes, sir."

The line was disconnected from the other end first. Koretsky sat there dangling the receiver thinking about how he was going to get Miller to supply him with the drugs. Finally replacing the receiver back in the cradle, he ran a hand over his stubble and decided to take a shower. The warm water usually cleared his head and allowed him to think straight.

It didn't take long for a plan to formulate.

The move from the hot June sun and into the cold air-conditioned building made Michele's nipples stiff and push through her bra and light cotton blouse. The geek in front of her was staring at them, which pissed Michele off. She only wanted people to stare at her body when it was her choosing and for her advantage—not for the pleasure of someone else, especially when he looked like the man across from her.

"So, Richard, what do you have?" Her question broke his stare.

"Let me say first that it's really great to be here with you!"

"I'm glad you feel that way. Now, what do you have?"

"Right. Right. I'm a ham radio operator, and I get to talk and listen to people on the radio."

Michele immediately decided that his was a complete waste of her time and was going to strangle her boss for it. "That's very interesting, but what's the point?"

"I get to listen to people on the radio, and not just the type of radio you have in your car."

She frowned and shook her head, still not understanding his point.

"I'll make it simple for you," he said.

"Thank you," she said

"I listen and talk to people on short wave radio, and listen to radio waves. I can listen to people talking in Montreal, captains talking to other captains on the high seas. Depending on the atmospherics, I can sometimes listen to people who think they are talking on pretty secure channels."

"So you can eavesdrop, that's what you're telling me?"

"I never looked at it that way." He thought for a moment then added, "No, it's not. What I'm doing is legal. If I tape it, then it's illegal."

"What does this have to do with me?"

Richard Armstrong reached under the table and placed a cassette recorder on top of it and pressed the play button.

What she heard made her heart skip a beat.

Wednesday, June 10, 5:10 p.m.

Betty "Blossom" Freeman was sitting at the counter in a coffee shop sipping her heavily sugared luke warm tea. A half eaten corn muffin was on the plate in front of her. She was wearing a short, brown skirt with a white blazer over a stretch lace camisole. Her attire would also be proper in a business office. Right now, she didn't even resemble a hooker. Her idle conversation with the counter waitress stopped when a man sat on the stool next to her.

"You're good looking. Do you turn tricks?" he asked through a drunken stupor.

Betty looked him over quickly before answering. His hair was askew and in knots and his teeth were yellow. A blast of his putrid breath signaled that he hadn't brushed his teeth in a month. His wardrobe was worse than anything that she had seen. He was also the ugliest and most decrepit bum she had ever seen. There was no way she was going to turn any tricks for this guy. She flipped her long red hair off her shoulder and said, "Get lost."

"Want to?" He pulled out a wad of money from his pocket trying to impress her, but it was mostly singles. He didn't seem to be willing to take no for an answer.

"I said get lost."

The man became furious. He grabbed Betty's arm and put his face in hers. "I have money. All women fuck for money, and you're gonna---"

Suddenly the man's arm was wrenched off of Betty's and twisted violently behind his back. Another hand grabbed his hair and jerked his head back until he was looking up into the white eyes of a big black face.

"Want to take a ride?"

"Man, that fucking' hurts, let me go. Who are you?"

"Police." Keith Bernard lifted the man off his stool and helped him through the door. He threw him across the sidewalk and slammed him into the side of the unmarked police car parked on the street.

When Bernard returned, Betty sniffed. "I can take care of myself," She said defiantly.

"Isn't there something you forgot to tell me?"

"No."

"Hi, Betty," another more familiar voice said.

She turned to see Chris Dinwiddie sitting on the opposite stool. "Oh, shit."

I've told you everything I know," Betty said from her slouched position in her metal folding chair.

Keith Bernard stood and walked from his side of the table and slowly circled the interview room twice without saying a single word. He knows Betty's eyes were following his every move.

"Are you going to say anything?"

Bernard kept circling like a hawk.

"Detective?" she called out nervously. She looked over at Dinwiddie for support.

Bernard pulled his gun from the holster and worked the slide. He kept circling.

"What are you doing?" she said, her voice filled with fear. "Detective!" Her eyes pleaded to Dinwiddie.

"What the fuck are you doing?" Dinwiddie asked, trying to sound tough, but his voice revealed his nervousness.

Bernard reached his chair and stood there for a moment, staring down at the prostitute. Her eyes were wide with fear. Good, he thought. He had her. Now, to make sure she would cooperate to her fullest extent, he raised the pistol and placed it on the center of her sweat soaked forehead.

The door opened with a click and Trainor walked in. He stopped dead in his tracks when he saw his partner pointing the pistol at Betty's head. Chris Dinwiddie was sitting at the end of the table, and his face was filled with terror.

Bernard saw Trainor and the (*oh, shit!*) look on his face out of the corner of his eye when he walked in, but didn't ease his stance. "Sit down, Gary."

Not knowing what Bernard was up to, he sat down in the remaining seat and watched Bernard act out his role.

"You got to do something, Gary!" Dinwiddie said from his chair. "He's crazy."

Trainor looked over at Dinwiddie and shook his head in disgust.

"Are you going to cooperate, Betty?" Bernard asked. He put pressure on the trigger.

She looked like she was too scared to speak. Her body began to tremble.

"I'll take that as a no." He looked into Betty's eyes and pulled the trigger.

The loud click was drowned out by Dinwiddie's scream.

The overpowering smell of urine suddenly filled the room. Betty passed out. Her head falling forward onto her chin.

"Whoa. Is that you who pissed your pants, Dinwiddie?" Bernard asked, a wry smile formed on his lips.

"You mother fucker—"

"Sit down!" Bernard gestured to the seat with his gun. "It's not loaded you asshole."

"I'm going to report—"

"Leave now." Bernard commanded.

"I will not" Dinwiddie shot back. Bernard's voice was unusually calm, but the look on his face could freeze water. There was no doubt that Bernard was in total control.

Trainor watched in fascination as Bernard took control of the situation. Actually, he was always in control, it was Dinwiddie who had lost all control. He had to admit to himself, that he had lost it for a moment also. He stared at Dinwiddie's back as he left the room.

Bernard holstered his weapon, leaned forward across the table, and lifted Betty's head by her chin. She was still unconscious. He slapped her face a few times to wake her up, and on the fifth slap her eyes opened.

It took a minute for Betty's eyes to focus on Keith Bernard, and when they did, she screamed and jumped out of her chair.

"Shut up and sit back down." Bernard said.

Betty looked between her legs and noticed her skirt was much darker. She also noticed the absence of Dinwiddie and looked up to search the room. She began to shake even more.

"Now, are you going to cooperate?"

"Yes," she said in a whisper.

Bernard sat across the table, his face impassive to her obvious discomfort. "Why didn't you tell us you were a confidential informant for Dinwiddie?"

Silence.

Bernard unsnapped his holster.

Betty's eyes popped open. The trembling shook her body. In a wild and rapid voice she spat out. "He told me not to say anything to anybody, including other policemen."

"Why?" Trainor asked from his sea at the end of the table.

She slowly turned her eyes to face Trainor. Her head never moved. "B-because you wouldn't believe me."

Bernard thought about that one for a moment. He realized she was probably right. The last thing most people wanted was trouble form the police, or any more trouble. He knew that many would say anything to get out of any trouble they were in. So, if Betty Freeman said she was a CI, Bernard and Trainor wouldn't have believed a word of it.

Casting the thought aside, Bernard wanted to continue with the interview. He didn't have any more information on Pedro's murder, but after talking with Chris Dinwiddie, he now knew that Betty Freeman knew much more about the drug running operation at the Port of Albany.

Bernard was positive that his scare tactics worked, but he wanted to see if she would cooperate to her fullest extent. He asked a few questions that he already knew the answer to.

"Betty," his voice was calm, face impassive. "Who is your pimp?"

Not ready for this line of questioning, she hesitated before answering. "I don't have a pimp."

Good answer. "So, you keep all the money you make? Nobody gets a cut?"

More hesitation. "That's right. Why are you asking about

135

my business?"

Trainor tapped the pencil on the paper when he answered, "We ask the questions, you don't."

Bernard asked another question. "Who are most of your customers?"

"Officers from the ships that are in port," she said.

"Do you work the streets?" Bernard asked.

"Sometimes," she said hesitantly.

"When?" Bernard immediately picked up on it, but chose not to pursue it. It could wait.

She fidgeted in her seat, the urine was getting cold and uncomfortable. "When a ship ain't in port."

"Do you do drugs?"

"Sometimes."

"Expand on that answer."

She took a deep breath to calm her nerves. "I use coke or smoke a joint when the night is over and I have no customers. I never use them when I'm working. It's too dangerous."

"Do you use them on a regular basis?" Bernard asked.

"No. Only after the hard days."

"Who supplies the drugs?" Trainor demanded.

Betty hesitated. Her face showed that she didn't want to reveal the name.

"Answer the question!" Trainor shouted.

Betty lowered her head and whispered, "Two people." She hesitated again. "One is Chris Dinwiddie."

Trainor's face registered shock, but he quickly recovered before she looked up. Bernard wasn't surprised at the answer. It made sense. By supplying his CI the right amount of drugs— just short of enough to become addicted—Dinwiddie could keep a tight grip on her. "Who's the other one?" Bernard asked.

"I don't know."

"I'm tired of fucking around!" Bernard yelled. He thought he was on to something. The second name that Betty was going to reveal was a surprise. She answered all the questions correctly, now it was a new territory that the officers were chartering.

Bernard pulled his pistol from the holster and cocked it.

"Okay, Okay! I'll tell you what I can, just put that thing away!" Betty screamed. Nobody had ever threatened her with a gun.

"We're listening," Trainor said. His pencil was ready to write down the name.

Betty watched in anticipation as Bernard slid the pistol back in its holster. Breathing deeply, she answered, "He's a Jewish lawyer."

The police detectives ears were still waiting for the name of the lawyer when they both realized that she had finished talking.

"That's it? A Jewish lawyer?" Trainor blurted.

"He also tells me when a particular ship is going to be in port, and that I will be busy."

Bernard asked the next logical question. "Have you ever met this guy?"

Betty fidgeted in the cold urine again. She searched her memory for the right answer. "I met him once about three years ago, right after I started turning tricks."

Bernard wanted to go slow with this. Like all good police officers, his gut told him they were on to something. He decided the information she was about to release was too important. He called in a female officer to take Betty Freeman to the showers to get cleaned up.

Trainor stared hard at Bernard after Betty left. "Is that how you interrogated people in New York?"

Bernard stared back.

"Are you going to answer my question?"

"I question people in a manner I see fit." Bernard answered calmly. "If you didn't like it, Gary, you could have left with Dinwiddie. Besides, we're making progress."

"You know Dinwiddie is going to tell the lieutenant what you did here." He put another Tums in his mouth.

"So be it."

After sitting in silence for some time, Trainor rose and headed for the door. "I have to take a leak."

When Betty Freeman returned to the conference room she was alone with Bernard and immediately began to shake.

Bernard offered her a clean seat and sat down opposite her. "Are we ready to begin again?"

She didn't answer.

"Listen, I want to show you a picture. Let me know if he was the last man you were with the other night." He took a three by five picture out of his back pocket and handed it to her.

She immediately nodded. "Yes, that's him. Who is he?"

"Somebody you don't want to meet again." He put the picture back in his pocket just at Trainor opened the door.

"Are we ready to begin again?" Trainor asked.

"No, Gary, I think we're done." He turned to Betty and said flatly, "you may go." He rose from the chair and opened the door for her.

After she left, Trainor asked, "Has the lieutenant been in here to see you?"

"No, why?" Bernard leaned against the wall and folded his arms across his chest.

"It's been more than a half hour since Dinwiddie left threatening to get the lieutenant. I figure he'd be in here to question you about your unorthodox and unacceptable interrogation procedures."

Bernard kept his face impassive. "Strange how things work. Isn't it?"

CHAPTER TEN

Friday, June 12, 6:00 a.m.

The sun was beautiful at this time in the morning. Birds of all species sang out in beautiful melodies. Marc Kaderri had a bead on his target, two hundred yards straight ahead and up a small incline. An easy shot for a professional. Robert Wolff was behind and off to his left observing what he knew to be a simple shot. Concentrating upon the target, Kaderri dug his feet into the ground to stabilize his body, took a breath and let it half way out.

Then the sound of the crack.

Wolff watched with naked eyes as a broad smile spread across his face. "Nice shot, Marc," Wolff said then exploded with laughter.

"Shit." Kaderri watched the little white ball go straight for one hundred fifty yards, then bank right and sail another forty. The golf ball landed over a row of tall pine trees that lined the immaculately groomed fairways. Kaderri couldn't figure out why he played this stupid game with a passion. Though he didn't play the game well, he most certainly looked the part. He wore tan pants with a black and white checkered pullover shirt.

It was easier in theory and on TV than in reality to hit a ball straight and into a hole in the ground. With the way he was playing lately, he felt he personally kept the ball manufacturers in business. Disgusted with his tee shot, he slammed the club back into the bag and trotted off to find his ball.

Three shots later, Kaderri caught up with Wolff on the green. Kaderri noticed Wolff's ball was pin high, eight inches from the cup, while his was on the first cut, sixteen feet from the cup. "Show off," Kaderri said with a smile.

"If I had sunk it," Wolff said, "then you could call me a show off." He played with a two handicap.

"Then I wouldn't be playing with you." Kaderri laughed. "Oh, by the way," he pointed to Wolff's bright yellow trousers. "I like your pants." He laughed harder.

"Thank you, sir," Wolff said taking a bow and pulling at his shirt. "And the powder blue shirt matches well."

By the time they hit the sixth green, the light and jovial conversation turned to one of seriousness. Kaderri told Wolff, "Ghost stopped by my office and informed me that Moshe Koretsky was paying a visit to Joshua Miller."

"What? What kind of visit?" Wolff's brown eyes narrowed.

"I don't know," Kaderri admitted. "We didn't get any of it on tape. The conversation took place in the conference room."

"Shit. We'll have to put a listening device in that room," Wolff said.

Kaderri placed his tee in the ground and noticed there were two golfers finishing up on the green behind them. The conversation that he was having with Wolff was more important than the game right now, and the last thing he wanted was an ornery pair of golfers pushing him. He picked up his tee and motioned for the pair to play through.

The pair of golfers were good enough that their tee shots put them far enough down the fairway where they couldn't hear Kaderri's and Wolff's conversation.

"Did Ghost say anything else?" Wolff asked.

"No," Kaderri answered. "But I asked him if he could get me an M forty A one." The M40A1 was the U.S. Marine Corps sniper rifle. It was actually a modified Remington 700 bolt action .308 rifle that could fire a round at 2,550 feet per second with deadly accuracy.

Marc Kaderri had been trained by the Marine Corps at the U.S. Marine Corps Scout/Sniper School in Quantico, Virginia. That was before he went to Beirut and took his A-Team into Afghanistan. Because of his training and the experience of using the M40A1 in real combat, he chose to use that weapon instead of the M24, the army's version of the Remington 700.

Wolff almost dropped his club when Kaderri told him that. "What?" he said in disbelief.

"If I knew you would react like that, I would've told you just as you were going to hit the ball."

"Can he get it for you?"

Kaderri nodded. "Do you have any new toys to mount on it?" he asked. The toys he referred to were the next generation of telescopic scopes that the military services were going to use for their weapons. Dr. Robert Wolff was one of the designers of the new scopes.

"Yeah, I got some new stuff that just tested out perfectly. You'll like it."

It was at that moment that Marc Kaderri made the decision that he would stop at nothing to see Moshe Koretsky's eyes in the scope before he pulled the trigger.

"Good," Kaderri answered. He hit the ball and it sailed three hundred yards—one hundred straight and two hundred to the right.

Friday, June 12, 4:00 p.m.

"Thanks for switching, Tim, I appreciate it."

"No problem, Gary."

Gary Trainor now had the weekend off, starting with Friday night, which also happened to be in one hour. He told a fellow detective, Tim Worth, that he had an extremely busy weekend planned and dinner at The Steer House Saturday with a real winner.

Trainor balanced the grocery bag and twelve pack of beer between his arms and chin. With his free hand, he fumbled with the key to the front door, cursing himself for not having the key ready when he got out of the car. After three tries, he finally inserted the correct key into the keyhole and opened the door.

Making his way through to the kitchen, he dropped the groceries on the table and popped a beer. The cold liquid felt soothing against his throat. Deciding he wasn't hungry, he put the groceries away and popped another beer. After the events of the past few weeks, he thought a twelve-pack might be sufficient to make him forget things for a while. He had originally planned on taking advantage of the time to rest, but, on his way home from the store, he swung by the police station and picked up two boxes of files. There was absolutely no way he could rest until he found the murderer or murderers that were decimating the city's inhabitants.

So, instead of having a weekend to rest, he was now prepared for a weekend of down right hard work that would push his brain to the limit. He spread his files across the table and popped his third beer.

Friday, June 12, 7:30 p.m.

Ramones Restaurant was crowded with early diners. Moshe Koretsky sat in a dark corner with his back to the wall so he could observe the entire dining room. He had a clear view of the front door as well as the door to the kitchen.

As he nursed a scotch and water, he didn't have to wait long before his dinner guest arrived. Approaching the table with a look of skepticism and relief was Joshua Miller. He offered his hand to Koretsky, which went unshaken, before he sat down. The waiter who showed him to the table took his drink order and disappeared. "It's nice to see you, Ariel," Miller said as he placed the linen napkin across his lap.

Koretsky didn't respond.

"So what is this all about?" Miller said bluntly.

"I'm offering you a second chance," Koretsky said evenly. What Mossad's director had said to Koretsky was none of Miller's business, and he wasn't about to find out.

"A second chance? How kind of you, Mr. Steiner," Miller said. A sarcastic smile spread across his lips.

"Don't fuck with me, Miller," Koretsky said in a hushed voice.

"I haven't decided if I want to do business with you again," Miller responded, obviously trying to get the upper hand and recover some of his pride that was badly tarnished in his previous conversation with Koretsky.

Koretsky was in no mood to play games, and he decided to put Miller over a fire from the outset. He pushed a brown nine by twelve envelope across the white linen tablecloth.

"What's this, an early payment?" Miller opened the envelope and pulled out two photographs. His face went white and he immediately clenched his teeth. The fire that he had in his eyes when he came into the restaurant was now extinguished. The first photograph was a picture of a pretty redhead with her head buried deep in Joshua Miller's crotch, and the second was him lying on top of the same girl with her legs wrapped around his waist. In both pictures, the lighting was dark enough to obscure the woman's face.

"How—" Miller began to ask, the embarrassment evident on his face.

"Like I said, don't fuck with me. You have no idea who you're dealing with. You're way out of your league. You accused me of killing your people without any evidence, and then you come in here on your fucking pedestal. I have the reamainder of the roll of film. What would you say to your wife?"

Miller's head shot up from looking at the photograph. "My God."

"Thank you for the drink, Josh," Koretsky stood, "Have the name ready for me tomorrow. Good night."

Friday, June 12, 8:10 p.m.

The colossal gray cumulonimbus clouds grew more threatening with every passing moment. They seemed ready to tear their seams and dump massive amounts of water on the late commuters who were unfortunate enough to get caught in the massive thunderstorm.

For once, the forecasters were right. The storm started right on time with a sudden unleashed fury.

The Troll turned up his collar to keep the drenching rain off his neck. The Troll, a black, short man who had long arms, a short torso and a fat, meaty face with a large flat nose was built like a brick outhouse. He waited by the public telephone like he was instructed to do for fifteen minutes at the same time everyday. Extremely annoyed that he had to wait in the storm for a phone call that he knew would never come, he contemplated leaving for shelter.

Suddenly, the phone rang. It took him a moment to realize that the sound was actually the phone ringing. In the four months that he had waited for the phone to ring, it had rung only once. That had been on the second day in his new employment. And that was apparently to test his trustworthiness. He was actually a little nervous, trying to figure out why he was being called on now. Was he in trouble? He couldn't think of anything he had done wrong. He picked up the phone on the fourth ring. "Troll," he said as casually as he could.

"You are to meet a man tomorrow at Linda's News and Coffee Shop. You are to sit on the third stool from the right and be drinking a soda." Joshua Miller ordered.

"What's his name? And why am I meeting him?" The Troll was suddenly worried that he was being set up.

"You don't need to know his name, he will identify himself. You are to give him three packages, but charge him for two."

"What? Are you sure?" That's alot of money we'd be losin'"

"Don't ever question my authority again!"

He swallowed hard at his stupidity. "Yes, sir."

"Meet him at six o'clock. And Troll, be careful."

144

The line was disconnected and The Troll stood in the rain for a moment holding the phone. His employer was never known to tell any of his people to be careful. One thing was for sure, if his boss told him to be careful, he would heed his advice.

Friday, June 12, 8:40 p.m.

The thunderstorm lasted for twenty minutes and was followed by two more over the next three hours. A few times the lights blinked, threatening to go out in one of Albany's finer restaurants. Instead of sitting where they were, Marc Kaderri wished he was back with Sara on their living room couch repeating their spectacular love making that they'd had earlier in the day.

After an exquisite dinner, they proceeded to a show at the Palace Theater that turned out to be extremely boring. The private balcony they were sitting in was dark enough that Marc could have fallen asleep, and no one would have ever known. A few times, Sara whacked him with her elbow to wake him up. Finally, to combat the boredom, and because he was extremely horny, Marc let his hands wander.

Sara was wearing a tight black sequined dress that came down to mid thigh with spaghetti straps. The neckline scooped low both in front and in back. It was obvious she wasn't wearing a bra, there was no room to hide it. Diamond and gold rope earrings hung from her lobes matching the sparkle in her eyes. A strand of black pearls intermixed with diamonds wrapped around her long neck. She was a sight that made heads turn, both male and female. But because of her beauty and the way she carried herself, she looked extravagant instead of risque'. She was the pinnacle of grace, elegance, beauty, and sex.

Marc looked as admirable as his wife. He was wearing a dove gray and chalk stripe custom made suit that accented his powerful athletic physique. He wore a white, French cuff shirt clasped by large solid gold cuff links. His matching tie and pocket square brought his appearance to near perfection. He would not have been out of place as the cover photo for GQ. That's what Sara had told him. Not one for jewelry, which he thought drew unnecessary attention, he only wore his gold Rolex on his left wrist along with his wedding band. He left the jewelry and the attention for Sara. Actually, the huge gold eagle cuff links had been Sara's idea. Being very patriotic, she had bought them for him as a gift which he enjoyed, but he would have been happy with an average size pair of cuff links.

In the darkness of the balcony, Marc traced his hand up Sara's naked thigh, she wasn't wearing any stockings. He caressed up to her crotch where he happily discovered that she wasn't wearing any panties either.

Sara quickly responded to his touch. She pulled her dress up to her waist, rotated her hips forward and spread her legs. Marc knew the prospect of making love on the balcony while the show was performing on stage and having hundreds of people in the audience so close excited her even more. By no means an exhibitionist, the danger of getting caught in the act of copulation was thrilling.

Marc could feel her instant heat. Instead of putting his fingers in her, he traced his fingers around her, and enjoyed her soft, delicate skin.

He knew his fingers would drive her crazy. His strong but gentle fingers worked their way from her knee up her leg, brushed across her opening and back down the other leg. After the third time, she stopped his hand and pressed it to her, begging that he would put his fingers in. "Put your fingers in me!" she hissed.

He didn't.

Marc's erection pushed the front of his trousers. He knew he would soon need relief. He looked over at Sara in the light that emanated from the stage. She was absolutely beautiful, and more importantly for the moment, going absolutely crazy. He was enjoying the tease. Like her, he wanted to have her right then and there, but he continued to let his fingers do the walking.

He brought his hand back to her crotch and toyed with

her velvet pubic strip. The hair was short and soft and the strip wasn't more than two inches long and a half inch wide. As he rubbed her hair, he silently wondered how she kept it so soft. Sara's had quickly grabbed his hand and tried to force it into her. He resisted, and to make her suffer more, he pulled his hand free. She caught on and let go, so he replaced his hand. He moved his hand lower pressing her exposed clitoris, his fingers hovering over her opening.

Marc watched Sara lick the sweat that formed on her upper lip. He knew he was driving her insane. His hand stopped on her, feeling her excitement grow even more. His fingers moved lower, slower to her opening. She pressed her hips forward, trying to cause one or more fingers to go in. His fingers began a gentle massage to her labia, and finally back to her clitoris. "Please!" she begged. She gripped the soft upholstered cushion of her seat to keep from screaming out in ecstasy from his touch. "God," she moaned, "it feels good! Goddamn, put the fingers in!"

Finally, he moved his fingers lower. Still moving them in a massaging circular motion, one then two fingers went in. Sara let out a loud moan. She grabbed her husband's wrist with both hands so he couldn't pull them out and furiously pushed his fingers in and out.

After a shuddering orgasm, Sara shrugged off the straps of her dress so that it was completely around her waist. Jiggling her now exposed, large, firm breasts she whispered in Marc's ear, "Let's finish this." She moved her hand to Marc's groin and squeezed his erection. "You need to be satisfied."

A little apprehensive of getting a blow job in public, Marc glanced around to make sure they weren't being watched. It was dark enough in the balcony that it was almost impossible to tell if anyone was occupying them, let along having any type of sex. He desperately needed to be relieved, but he felt awkward hanging out like he was.

Marc unzipped his pants and pulled himself out. Sara left her seat and knelt between his legs. Her warm breath tickled the tip before her soft lips expertly and lovingly took him in her mouth.

Her wet tongue worked its way around his erection in a slow and deliberate fashion, adding pressure at certain spots, and lightly touching other areas. Soon she took him in her mouth and her nose went as far as it could, and the warm wet feeling of her mouth covering his entire erection was exquisite.

Marc searched the audience for anything that would expose them. Satisfied that nobody was watching, Marc relaxed and settled back in his chair, enjoying the art that Sara was performing. He reached down and fondled Sara's breasts.

Suddenly the actors on stage stopped performing and the curtain began to fall. Act two was over.

"Stop!" Marc said and disconnected Sara's Mouth.

"What's wrong?" she asked.

"The act is over!"

Marc hurriedly stuffed himself back in his pants and Sara quickly stood and pulled the shoulder straps up and the rest of her dress down to her thigh. Since she was standing, she pretended to stretch to cover her quick dressing. When the light came on to full power, all was normal in the balcony.

Well, not really.

Marc was left hanging, and so was Sara. The play had one more act, but Marc and Sara weren't interested. As soon as the second intermission began, Marc grabbed Sara's hand and practically ran for the car. Marc figured that if anybody was watching, they would think they were running to the car to escape the torrential downpour and the ferocity of the thunderstorm.

Marc Kaderri thought about taking his wife in the Corvette right in the parking lot. Because of the torrential rain, most people caught in it would make a dash to the nearest shelter, thus keeping prying eyes away. But, the Corvette was too small to do it right.

Instead of driving the distance home, Kaderri drove to the cloest and second most private place he knew of, A Better Body.

148

Once Sara got the door to the club open, she pulled her dress off and pulled Marc behind the reception counter.

Marc practically tore his trousers off, sat in the receptionist chair and eagerly awaited for Sara to finish what she started in the balcony. He didn't have to wait long. Standing totally naked, Sara rubbed her hands over her body, lifting and squeezing her breasts to heighten the sexuality of the situation. She seductively licked her lips and knelt down. Once again, Marc felt her warm mouth take him in. "Oh, God." he moaned. In a matter of minutes, Marc grunted and lost control.

Sara continued and made him hard again. This night was not going to be one of gourmet lovemaking, but one of wild abandon. Sara disengaged her warm mouth and immediately straddled his exposed hard cock. She sat facing him interlocking her fingers behind his muscular neck. Leaning back, she rotated her hips forward so she could get all of him deep inside her. Sara sighed as he continued to grow even bigger.

Marc grabbed her around her slender waist so she wouldn't fall and to give her support for her thrusting. The rotation of Sara's hips caused her to arch her back and stuff her large, firm breasts into Marc's face. His mouth found one of her erect, inviting nipples and hungrily took it in his mouth.

Ten minutes later, Sara let out a loud scream and shuddered in Marc's arms. Her body convulsing as Marc was still inside her added to her pleasurable orgasm. Marc was tired of sitting, and he couldn't get any thrusting power. He stood, holding onto Sara and kept himself inside her. She wrapped her long legs around his waist, and he walked up the stairs to her office.

Once inside the office, Marc placed Sara on the couch. He laid her on her back and she raised her legs, locking her ankles behind his neck. This allowed him the freedom of moving any way he wanted. She was warm and tight and felt great. Her hot skin seemed to melt around him. He alternated between long, hard, fast strokes that rocked the couch and long, soft, slow ones that made her writhe under him. All Sara could do was enjoy the pleasure and give it back to him.

Tiring of the same position, Sara got on her hands and knees. Marc stood behind her and took in her perfectly shaped buttocks. After stimulating her a little more with his hands, he reentered her with all his lust. As he moved himself in and out of her, he leaned over her back and squeezed her breasts and erect nipples. In return for her great delight, she reached underneath and gave him a firm squeeze. Soon they found a comfortable and satisfying rhythm. Finally, Marc couldn't hold back any longer and let himself go with an explosion.

Sara turned around, wrapped her arms around Marc's neck and gave him a deep passionate kiss. "Oh, Marc, that was wonderful!"

Marc reached down and squeezed her firm buttocks. "You are absolutely amazing," he said. "I'm going down into the sauna. Care to join me?" Even though nobody else was in the building, Marc threw on a pair of shorts he kept in the closet. He always felt strange walking around naked where strangers could be.

"No thanks." Sara said. "I'm going to do some work on the computer while I recuperate. But, don't be too long, I'm enjoying the night." She squeezed his shrinking erection for emphasis. "Get it ready."

Friday, June 12, 11:40pm

Sara Kaderri was working on her computer that was behind her desk with her back to the door. Surrounding her were the decorations of the office. There was a photograph of her, then Sara Flannery, dressed in a green evening gown accepting the crown of Miss New York State. There was another picture, this one much larger, above the computer that showed her being awarded runner up in the Miss American Pageant.

Decorating the rest of the walls were numerous photographs of her modeling bathing suits, and a huge poster with her in a skimpy bathing suit surrounded by a bunch of football players. Amidst the photographs were two diplomas from the University at Albany, one for a degree in Business Administration, and the other for an MBA.

Sara heard breathing behind her and assumed it was Marc. It wasn't uncommon not to hear Marc when he walked. "That was quick, you were only gone for ten minutes," she said to the computer monitor. "Which, of course, is okay." She placed her hand in her crotch and started stimulating herself. "I'm really horny, come over here and fuck me again."

"That's the idea."

Sara spun around at the strange voice. Terror immediately gripped her. She couldn't do anything but sit there and tremble. She was frozen with fear as if a giant glove wrapped itself around her. Standing in front of her desk was a man, totally nude, standing at six foot six. He had a huge cocaine induced erection and a full roll of duct tape in his hand. His blonde hair was in a ponytail, and his eyes were glazed over and bloodshot. White tape was wrapped around his mid-section to keep his broken ribs from moving. Instantly, Sara recognized Greg Sander, the man who Marc had beaten up in the locker room for using cocaine.

"After I fuck you good and hard, you're going to die."

Sara tried to say something, but Sander reached over the desk and clasped one hand over her mouth. He grabbed the back of her head with his other hand and lifted her off the chair. He dragged her around the desk and made her stand, obviously wanting to admire her exquisite body.

Her mind began to overcome her initial fear and she tried to think of a way to get out of the room or to hold him off until Marc came back. The first thing that came to her mind was to kick him in the groin and scratch his eyes. With as much strength and bravery as she could muster, she swung her leg with all her might. Her kick caught Sander in the upper thigh, not doing any harm.

He shoved her to the floor before she could scratch his eyes. "Nice try, bitch," he laughed. "I'm going to enjoy hurting you."

Utter confusion swirled in Sara's head. She saw she couldn't crawl through the door so she curled into a fetal position for protection. *Marc has got to come back!* She thought frantically. Where is he? Then the thought struck her that Sander may have already killed Marc. That sickening thought caused her to tremble even more. She had to get out. *My God*, she thought, she was going to be raped. Despite the lessons her husband had taught her in self-defense, Sara was enveloped by a paralyzing fear that she never thought possible. At that moment, she lost control of her bladder.

With a sweep of his hand, Greg Sander cleared the top of the desk, scooped Sara off the floor like a rag doll, and dropped her on the desk. He picked up a picture of Marc off the floor and placed it next to her head so she could look at it "Take a good look," he said "It's the last time you'll see him."

Sara tried kicking again, but only got air. The thought of not seeing Marc was too much for her. Sander twisted her until she laid flat on her back with her arms and legs hanging over the desk. Like vise grips, Sander locked his hand around Sara's delicate writs and held them outstretched above her head. He pinned her legs together between his and used his free hand to pull hard at one of her nipples and used his mouth to bite the other.

Sara screamed in pain and frantically tried to kick, scratch,writhe, anything to get away from him.

Tiring with her nipples, he moved his hand down to her tiny pubic strip. The scream that erupted from Sara was quickly quieted by a forceful slap.

After ten beers, a frozen pizza and two burritos, Gary Trainor felt like he was going to explode. He also felt like he was trying to climb a mountain of mud in a hurricane. He wasn't making much progress on the murders.

He had to move from the kitchen to the living room floor where he would have more space to spread out the files. He brought the beer out with him, saving him from having to get up, walk to the kitchen, get a beer and go back to the living room. He also had a roll of Tums that was now half eaten.

After reviewing all the files, he was left with more questions than answers. Since May 19th, he had two cops shot in a drug raid that left the two perpetrators dead, one shot by Officer Ronald Davies, the other had his head blown away by a single bullet fired by someone else. Another drug dealer, who shot Officer Peter Zacuran, was killed by a single gunshot to the head. The Medical Examiners report and ballistics confirmed they were killed by the same type of bullet, a .308 or 7.62mm in military terms.

Then on May 21st, six more drug dealers turned up dead in the alley behind Ramone's restaurant. All victims were killed by 7.62mm bullets. Actually, one bullet killed two men. And the incredible thing was that nobody had heard any shots. It was apparent that this included the victims because nobody had their weapons drawn. Obviously silencers had been used, and whoever used them were professional.

Trainor picked up the file for the horrible morning of June 7th. Four more dead bodies. A literal blood bath where each victim was killed from the same weapon, except the last victim. Trainor was amazed that the last victim had been hit by presumably three different weapons. The weapon that killed him was, unbelievably, a bolt fired from a crossbow.

The last victim, found alive in the trunk was no help. The only thing he kept saying was, "The tree was shootin' Slapper." That victim and suspect, Hector Romero, was the only witness to anything. Trainor kept him away from all reporters. The press didn't seem to have any idea that a witness even existed. There was the real possibility that the person, persons or whatever would try to eliminate Hector Romero if they found out he had been at the scene. And Gary Trainor wanted to keep him alive.

Another murder, this one seemed totally unrelated, was gnawing at his stomach. The murder of Pedro at the docks appeared to be a simple drug deal rip-off. But, Trainor's gut feeling said that it was somehow related to all other murders. Why? That he couldn't answer. There was nothing in common with the other murders. But, somehow he knew it fit.

One thing that Trainor was sure of was that Pedro's murderer had visited the prostitute, Betty "Blossom" Freeman. The communications officer of the Whispering Sea told him during the interview that he personally gave Pedro the name and address of the prostitute on a piece of paper. That paper wasn't found on Pedro. And Betty Freeman was able to help a little. She gave vivid details of her customers' sexual performance, and helped the artist with the sketch, but he couldn't circulate it.

Something about that gun, Keith Bernard called it, a Makarov, a Russian made gun. There had been no other reports of that type of weapon used in any shooting since Pedro's body was found. And the killings of the drug dealers were by someone or somebody who knew how to handle a weapon and not get caught.

Trainor knew that wasn't due to luck, but due to professionalism. Once again, the thought of a professional assassin moved to the front of his brain. But why would an assassin want to hit these people? What did they have in common besides drug trafficking? There was no other correlation that he could find.

Trainor made a note to make another trip to the hospital, and pay another visit to Hector Romero, and to question Betty Freeman again. He had a gut feeling that she was holding back a tremendous amount of information. A vision of the last interview with her appeared in front of his eyes. She was dressed in expensive, well-tailored clothing. And her make-up was very neat. She didn't look like a hooker who walked the streets. Obviously she was a call girl.

Trainor was on to something. Rejuvenated, he popped another beer and a Tums and fingered through more files.

Kaderri decided he'd better empty his bladder before he cooked himself in the sauna. Once in the bathroom, he decided he better empty his entire system. Fifteen minutes later he emerged and made his way through the dimly lit corridors to the sauna. The way to the sauna brought him past the main doors to the club. The thunderstorms subsided, giving way to a full moon that brightened the parking lot and illuminated the lobby. The sight of a pick-up truck parked next to the Corvette, sent a shiver down his spine and give him an uneasy feeling in his stomach. Something wasn't right. His senses were heightened and he sensed extreme danger. The last time he felt this way was when he was in combat. The first thing he thought of was Sara. A muffled scream echoing through the silent building justified his suspicions.

Marc raced to the stairs and took them three at a time. When he reached the top, he noticed the door to Sara's office was closed. His mind raced through two scenarios simultaneously. One was that someone was in there with a weapon to Sara's head. Or, someone was in there without a weapon doing God knew what. Kaderri didn't have a gun. He had to decide if a trap was being set for him.

Hundreds of thoughts raced through his brain, but the entire process took less than two seconds. He knew that whoever was in the office, was no match for him in hand to hand combat. He lowered his shoulder and crashed through the wooden door.

The sight before him was repulsive. Sara lay on her back on the top of her desk with her wrists and ankles taped together behind her head. A steady stream of blood flowed from one corner of the tape that covered her mouth and dripped down her neck to form a small pool on the desk. A wild look of terror shot from her normally beautiful almond shaped eyes. Greg Sander had his full erection poised at Sara's anus, obviously ready to enter her. Sara was wiggling her body to make it more difficult for him to penetrate her, but it was obvious that she would soon lose the struggle.

Before the shattered door hit the floor, Kaderri scanned the room, noted that Sander was the only one there, and tackled him away from Sara. He placed his shoulder on the taping around Sanders rib cage just under the armpit, and drove through Sander, knocking him into the wall and re-breaking Sander's ribs.

Kaderri used Sander's slow response time to his advantage.

Seeing Sander slumped against the wall, Kaderri delivered a kick to the groin and gave him a punch on the top of his head. Sander, now unconscious, fell forward, his face making contact with the floor with a crunch. Kaderri wanted to kill him, but Sara needed his immediate attention.

He pulled a pair of scissors out of the top drawer and quickly cut the duct tape that bound her hand and legs. Because of the blood flowing from beneath the tape, he would have to be more careful with the strip across her mouth. He had no idea of what type of damage was done to her mouth.

As soon as her hands and feet were free, Sara jumped off the table and into Marc's arms. Like water flowing out of a garden hose, tears flowed from Sara's eyes. Her body trembled from the hell she had just gone through, and the joy that Marc wasn't dead and had found her. She pulled the tape off her mouth. "Oh, thank God!" Sara said in a shaky whisper.

He squeezed her tighter. He too was scared and noticed his hands were trembling. "I'm here, honey, I got you." he said. "Everything's going to be okay."

Sara cried even more and clung to him tighter.

Marc gently picked her up and placed her on the couch. He knelt next to her and gently brushed the hair away that clung to her tear soaked face and examined the cut on her mouth. Both her upper and bottom lips were split near the corner of her mouth. He gently touched her swollen lips and learned that three of her teeth were loose. A nasty bruise was already forming.

Marc, I'm sorry," Sara said. She placed her face in her hands to hide her embarrassment.

"For what?" He pulled her hands away from her face and held them.

"For letting him do this to me," she said. "I tried to get away, but couldn't. I'm so, so sorry."

"Oh, honey, it's not your fault. It's nothing to be sorry about." He gave her another tender hug and held her for a long moment. He was beyond mad at Sander, there was no doubt that man would not live. He also felt scared for Sara. He couldn't ever possibly relate to what she had gone through. At the same time he also felt scared for himself for almost losing his wife.

Kaderri let go to look for the phone to call the police and an ambulance, but Sara held on to one of his hands for reassurance. He spotted the phone on the opposite side of the desk and crawled over to it. He placed the receiver next to his ear to see if there was a dial tone and quickly dialed 911.

It took two rings before the call was answered.

As soon as he heard the phone being picked up on the other end, he started talking. "I need an ambulance at A Betty Body. My wife was just raped."

"Slow down sir," the female voice on the other end said. "Can you repeat what you just said and give me your name?"

Shit! "My name is Kaderri. My wife was raped and we are at A Better Body—"

"The health club?" the voice said suddenly.

"Yes, the health club. She needs an ambulance."

Sara let out a loud scream that was inhuman.

Sander was starting toward Sara. The blood flowing from his nostrils and a cut across the bridge of his nose streaked his chin and chest. In his drug induced state, he didn't feel the pain of either his ribs or his nose, and didn't see Kaderri behind the desk until he stood up. Sander locked eyes with Kaderri and stopped in his tracks.

Kaderri dropped the phone. "You're dead motherfucker," Kaderri stated flatly. He moved his body between Sander and the couch that Sara was on to make good on his threat.

Instead of meeting the challenge, Sander ran out the door.

Letting Sander go for the moment, Kaderri quickly picked up the phone. "Did you get that?" Kaderri asked.

"What's going on?" the voice asked.

"Just send an ambulance to A Betty Body!"

"Okay, sir, one is on the way. Keep yourself calm, it's important for your wife to see you calm. What's your wife's name?"

Kaderri knew the voice on the line was being professional

and doing her job, but Kaderri was as calm as the dead sea. He was anxious to get Sander before he got too far away. He also knew it was important that they get as much information as possible. He spoke into the phone as if he were on a battlefield talking on a radio. He used short, concise sentences that got to the point and off the air before enemy tracking devices could spot where the radio transmissions came from. "Her name is Sara," he answered. "She's in her office at the top of the stairs."

"Mister Kaderri, can you meet the ambulance from where you are?"

"I won't be here. I'm going after the son-of-a-bitch." He hung up the phone, took an oversized towel from the same closet that held his shorts and placed it over Sara. Though she was still crying and shaking from the ordeal, she was more in control of herself. "An ambulance is on its way honey. I'll meet you at the hospital." He gave her a hug and a kiss on her forehead, and bolted out the door.

"Marc!"

The adrenaline was flowing and his emotions were cold. His thoughts were on one purpose. He jumped down the stairs, fished the car keys out of his trouser pocket that were still on the floor, hopped into his shoes and ran out the door into the moonlit parking lot. Standing in only his shorts, his eyes and ears began searching for Sander's big Ford pickup truck. He could hear the ambulance and police sirens growing louder.

Suddenly, he spotted the truck turning north out of the parking lot, heading toward Interstate 787.

Before he jumped in the Corvette and started the powerful engine, Kaderri grabbed a handful of rocks off the ground. The tires squealed and left a six foot strip of rubber on the blacktop as Kaderri worked his way through the six gears to catch up to Sander.

Keeping one eye on the extremely light traffic and one on Sander's truck, Kaderri took the ramp to 787 North. It didn't take long before the speedometer passed one-hundred ten miles an hour. It didn't take long to catch up with Sander. Kaderri had to be careful. Though his car was one of the fastest on the road, Sander's huge diesel pickup was powerful, too, and big.

Kaderri had to figure out how to get Sander off the road without getting crushed in the process. The only tactic Kaderri could utilize was to use the Corvette as bait and hope Sander's reflexes and driving ability were slow. He was also counting on the cocaine to really impair Sander's judgment.

Kaderri slid up on the left next to Sander, hoping Sander would know who was chasing him. It worked. Sander immediately jerked the wheel to the left to squash the Corvette. Kaderri, anticipating the move, slammed on the brakes and clutch and watched the truck dart ahead. Placing the car back in gear, Kaderri pressed the gas pedal to the floor and glided his way through the gears. The engine growled as the machine responded like a finely tuned machine.

He pulled the Corvette to the right and became parallel with Sander's passenger side door. He grabbed a few rocks and tossed them at the truck. The only purpose they had was to make Sander jerk the truck so it would flip, or run down the embankment and into the Hudson River.

Anticipating that Sander would try and run him off the road, he slammed on the brakes so Sander would miss him.

But that didn't happen. Instead of trying to run the Corvette over, Sander turned the opposite way. He crossed the three northbound lanes, broke through the guardrail that separated the north and southbound lanes, broad sided a southbound passenger car, and turned to follow the southbound highway back into Albany.

Cursing aloud, Kaderri slammed on the brakes, furiously downshifted and turned the car around in the middle of the highway to follow Sander's truck through the hole in the guardrail.

The few police cars that were now in pursuit followed Kaderri. By the time the police cars went through the hole, Kaderri and Sander were three miles away.

Once again, it didn't take Kaderri long to catch up with

Sander's truck. Noticing that the highway and the ramps were quickly filling with police cars, Kaderri was determined to get his hands on Sander before the police did. He currently had the mentality of a juvenile or a caveman. Kaderri was going to protect his woman at all costs. Nobody was going to hurt Sara Kaderri without getting seriously hurt themselves. And Marc Kaderri knew many ways to seriously hurt somebody.

Checking to make sure his seatbelt was tight, Kaderri closed the gap on Sander's truck and pulled alongside. Because of the height difference between the massive pickup and low slung sports car, the two adversaries couldn't look into each other's eyes. But Kaderri could sense Sander's eyes upon him, and he knew Sander felt his.

Kaderri's time was running out, the police were closing. His quick comment to the 911 operator that he was going after the son-of-a-bitch who raped his wife had apparently released a flood of police cars that began a massive search.

He had only one chance to get the truck off the road and then kill Greg Sander, assuming that he would survive his stunt. Kaderri pushed more gas through the fuel injectors and raced far out in front of Sander.

Kaderri jammed on the brakes and spun the car around one-hundred-eighty degrees. With a squeal of the high performance tires, he gunned the engine and pointed the sleek nose of the Corvette toward the front of the oncoming truck. Sander kept his truck straight and true. If Kaderri didn't move out of the way, the truck would win the violent head-on collision that was about to happen.

The distance between the vehicles was one hundred yards. Kaderri estimated that he had no more than two seconds. He turned the wheel quickly to the left and then back further to the right. The car responded immediately. The bright headlights to the truck were right before his eyes. Kaderri tightly held the wheel with his right hand, laid-across the passenger seat and covered his head with his left arm, and slammed on the brakes.

160

A bone jarring collision shook the Corvette. Because of lying low across the seat, the inflating airbags didn't keep Kaderri from slamming his head into the dashboard and opening a two-inch gash above his ear. A millisecond after the collision, the truck's diesel engine roared in Kaderri's ears as the truck passed overhead. The tempered glass across the interior as the rear tire of the cabin erupted on the truck tore through it.

Kaderri heard the metal screeching on the pavement and saw a brilliant display of orange and white-blue sparks fountained as the metal from the overturned truck scraped, flipped and bounced across the pavement.

The speed and violent turning of the Corvette caused the truck's left front wheel to ride up the nose of the Corvette, acting like a ramp, instead of a head-on collision. When the wheel hit, the car was at an angle that afforded the car to survive the crash. The huge tire rode up the nose and over the car's left wheel well and put the truck at an unbalanced angle. As the Corvette continued on its path, the truck's rear tire slammed into the rear of the car's cabin, forcing the truck to flip.

Kaderri climbed out of the twisted roof and sprinted toward the overturned truck. Greg Sander was slowly opening the door of the truck when Kaderri arrived. Because he hadn't been wearing his seatbelt when he flipped over the Corvette, Sander was a bloody mess. He had evidently bounced around the cabin of the truck until it came to a stop. If it wasn't for the roll bar and cocaine, Sander wouldn't have survived the crash.

"Your're mine, motherfucker!" Kaderri yelled, reaching up and pulling the door open. Sander promptly fell to the pavement. Before Sander could get up on all fours, Kaderri kicked him in his broken ribs. A sickening crunch signaled more ribs were broken as Sander rolled in front of the overturned trucks headlights.

A passing motorist screeched to a halt to offer help. "Get out of here!" Kaderri yelled. The motorist sped off.

Sander rose from the pavement and squinted at Kaderri through the rivers of blood that flowed from the cuts across his forehead and nose. He steadied himself and seemed to prepare to fight. The halogen lights provided an eerie back light as if the two men were in a ring.

Kaderri knew this was the last time he would see Greg Sander.

Sizing up the situation, Kaderri went for the obvious shot, Sanders naked groin. Because of the cocaine, the man still had a hard on. With his lightning speed, Kaderri placed a kick into the groin. The hard rubber sole of the wing tip caught Sander's testicles and ripped them wide open. An animalistic scream so horrifying erupted from deep within Sander that it caused Kaderri to hesitate before he placed his second kick.

When Sander bent over to clutch his torn groin, Kaderri place his second kick across Sander's forehead, opening the cut even further and catapulting Sander onto the hot under-carriage of the truck. Another scream erupted from Sander when his flesh made contact with the hot metal. It hissed and smoked as the searing skin burned.

Sander pulled himself off the truck and collapsed to the pavement.

By now, almost half a dozen police cruisers coverged on the scene and surrounded the two men. "Hold it, Mister Kaderri!" one officer yelled in Kaderri's ear and grabbed his tightly muscled arm. It was obvious that the cop didn't want to get in between the two combatants. Firmly, the officer led Kaderri away from Sander to a cruiser.

Kaderri's chest was heaving slightly from the ordeal and turned to look into the cops eyes. He didn't attempt to resist. Two cops rushed over to where Sander lay.

"You are Kaderri, right" The officer asked after he got no response.

He nodded. Confused about how the cop knew his name, he asked. "How do you know my name?" Kaderri read the officer's nametag. It read Franks.

"We don't get too many 911 callers," Franks said with a

faint smile, "that say they are going after an attacker, especially after they give their name." Then he added, "Beside, I'm a member of your club."

Then Kaderri asked the all important question that was first and foremost on his mind. "Do you know how my wife is?"

Marc Kaderri felt like a heel for leaving his wife's side, but she had seemed in control of her emotions. If she wasn't in control or was still in danger, there was no way he would have left her. No matter how he rationalized it, he shouldn't have left her. He could have tracked down Greg Sander and killed him later.

"She's at Albany Medical Center being examined."

Kaderri nodded an acknowledgment, but a foreboding feeling about Sander suddenly heightened his senses. He still had his eyes on Sander who was being attended by one of the police officers who was also an Emergency Medical Technician.

"As soon as this is settled, Marc, I'll take you there. I like Sara. I hope everything—"

"Shit!" Kaderri yelled.

Suddenly a loud growl broke the night silence and the EMT applying a compress to Sander's head was suddenly thrown backwards. Greg Sander stood to his full height and lifted the assisting officer off the ground by the throat with one hand, punched him once in the face, and then tossed him aside like a rag doll.

Two more officers rushed to subdue Sander, but were pummelled. Sander tossed one officer over the flipped truck before he had a chance to do anything. The second officer drew his billy club and swung at Sander. But Sander caught the officer's hand, crushing it in his own, and then knocked the officer over his head with the club. Once again, the cocaine made Sander oblivious to pain and gave him superhuman strength.

Greg Sander stood perfectly still despite his bleeding torso, and then began scanning the group of people before him. The

163

compress had fallen off his forehead and blood continued to pour out. Only the bloodshot whites of his eyes were visible behind the red mask of blood. Those eyes found Kaderri and both men charged at each other.

Kaderri jumped up and to the left as Sander charged past. Kaderri kicked him in the temple with his right foot. Sander took three more steps and fell to the ground, his momentum causing him to slide across the pavement and stop at Officer Franks feet. Franks quickly tried to cuff Sander, but Sander grabbed Franks' ankles and pulled his feet out from under him. Sander then punched Franks across his abdomen once he hit the ground.

Kaderri watched in astonishment as Sander once again rose to his feet. He knew that the easiest way to stop Sander was to exploit his wounds. The taping around his broken ribs was illuminated by the police cruiser spotlights, and made an easy target. His torn groin, forehead and broken nose were the other targets. Kaderri decided he'd have to hit Sander with a flying side-kick. If he didn't and stood still waiting to take on Sander in his drug induced state, Sander's strength and weight would win out.

Sander began a dead run aimed directly at Kaderri, a terrifying growl bellowing from his mouth. Unlike Sander's wild flailing and brut strength, Kaderri timed his every move. At Sander's speed, Kaderri needed to take three steps for maximum effectiveness. The force of his kick to his face should snap Sander's neck like a twig.

Just as Kaderri was ready to take his second step, a familiar but wholly unexpected cracking sound of 9mm bullets cooking off at close range sounded in his ears. He instinctively hit the pavement and Sander immediately stopped in his tracks and stood straight up from his running position. Six holes burst from his chest as new blood streaked his torso. Three more shots echoed and Sander arched his back and fell backwards.

Kaderri turned his eyes away from the corpse, looked over it and found Franks sitting on the ground, his back against the car, a smoking pistol held in his hand. Another officer was leaning over the hood, his smoking pistol held in outstretched hands.

By now, the highway in both directions was filled with speeding police cars, ambulances, and television reporters.

"Can I see her? How is she?" Marc Kaderri asked the emergency room doctor. The cut above his ear was stitched and bandaged, and hurt like hell.

The doctor reached out and grabbed Kaderri's forearm. "She's a remarkable woman, Mister Kaderri." Her hand was soft and gentle. "She's doing fine, and resting. She was concerned for you. When I told her you were out here waiting for her, she fell into a deep sleep."

"Can I see her?" He repeated the question, this time a little impatiently.

The doctor gestured with her clipboard toward a small conference room. "Come with me, Marc, I want to fill you in on what happened to your wife."

Kaderri followed the tall, thin dark-haired doctor to the small conference room and took a seat opposite the doctor. "Is she okay?" Kaderri's voice was low and menacing and he looked straight into the doctors green-eyes. It was his intention to let the doctor know he did not want to get the runaround. And if he frightened her, so be it.

She got the message.

"Okay," she began, "Sara was raped, but it wasn't bad."

Kaderri exploded. "What!" When he stood, the chair flew out from behind him, and he leaned over the table. His face inches away from the doctor's.

The doctor immediately realized her words came out wrong. She shook her head, clearly trying to ignore the flush that was flooding her cheeks. "Sorry, that didn't come out right."

Kaderri was still standing. His fingers rapped around the edge of the table were turning white from the vise-like grip he had. He was also ready to throw the table and the doctor out the door." Explain," he said through clenched teeth.

The doctor, visibly shaken by the man in front of her, took a deep breath, and began to explain. She gave Kaderri a complete report on Sara's body from the head down. "Sara was beat up, but no bones were broken. She lost one tooth that was replaced, and her mouth is going to hurt like hell. We put sutures inside her mouth, and it doesn't look like there will be any scarring.

"Her breasts and nipples were bitten and bruised, we gave her a Tetanus shot for the bites. Her wrists are bruised also, as a result from the attacker's grip and subsequent binding with the tape."

Kaderri sat down, but kept staring into the doctor's eyes.

When he didn't say anything, she continued. "For the good news, if you could call it that, when the rapist entered her, he pulled out before any bodily fluids mixed. He ejaculated on her stomach and pubic area. Though we did find some semen inside—"

"I assume you are running tests, and you will find that the semen is mine if you want a sample."

"Sara said the same thing."

"Anything else?, Kaderri didn't like this doctor. She had no bedside manner and talked with a casual flair. But Goddamit, he thought, this was his wife they were talking about.

"Other than a little battered, your wife will have a one-hundred percent recovery. I do suggest that you both may want to seek counseling to get over this horrible incident."

"Thank you. May I see my wife?" It was more of a statement than a question.

Marc Kaderri slowly pushed the door open the private hospital room. The woman who was the greatest joy in his life way lying peacefully asleep in the bed. An intravenous tube stabbed into the vein on the back of her delicate right hand. The sheet and blanket were drawn up tight to her chin, covering every portion of her except her head and exposed arm that had the intravenous needle sticking in her hand.

Hurriedly but silently he moved to the bed. He saw the

bruises that Sander had given her. Her eye was puffy and discolored, as was her jaw. The stitches in and on her lips were barely visible. He had to admit the doctor did a remarkable job on the sutures. He had to look real close to see if there would be a faint scar, if one at all.

He gently brushed her hair away from her cheek with one hand and wiped a tear away from his eye with the other. He stroked her cheek a few times and bent down to give her a kiss.

Sara stirred at her husband's touch and opened her eyes. She tried to smile but the cut and sutures made it difficult. The smile was in her eyes, and it was the biggest smile she ever made. "Hi," she said. She started to say something else, but Marc cut her off.

"Shhh. Don't talk, honey, go back to sleep." He clutched her hand, and her grip on his hand was firm.

"I'm glad you're okay," she said in a whisper.

"I'm glad you're still alive." He began to sob. "Now, go back to sleep."

Sara smiled and nodded. She immediately fell back to sleep, taking comfort knowing that her husband, her lover, her protector was once again by her side. She didn't let go of his hand.

Kaderri reached out and pulled over the lone chair and sat down. His mind immediately replayed what had transpired. His reactions from the time he had heard Sara scream up till now had been instant and detached. Now that the rush of adrenaline subsided he had time to think. The thought of losing his precious wife was too much. And for the first time since he could remember, Marc Kaderri cried like a child.

CHAPTER ELEVEN

Saturday, June 13, 5:50 a.m.

When Marc Kaderri emerged from the hospital room, a tear hung precariously from his eyelash, and his stomach was hollering for food. When he looked down the hallway to start toward the elevator, he saw a familiar black face staring back at him from one of the chairs across from the elevators. It was one he wasn't especially happy to see but he wasn't surprised either. He was still wearing the hospital greens that were given to him last night.

"Marc, is Sara okay?" The black man extended his hand.

It wasn't the greeting Marc had expected, and he realized that the question was genuine, not routine. "As well as could be expected, I guess. She's sleeping." Kaderri shook Detective Keith Bernard's hand.

"That's good to hear."

There was more to Bernard's presence than being concerned about the welfare of his wife. So, Kaderri said, "Obviously you're after something, what is it?"

"Blunt, aren't we?"

"I've had a lousy night, Detective," Kaderri answered with an icy stare. "I'm tired, hungry, and I don't want to play games." He pushed the down button.

The elevator's bell 'dinged' signalling the arrival of the car and the doors slid open. It was empty. Kaderri walked in and held the door for Bernard. "I'm going to the cafeteria, you want to join me?"

"I was just going to ask you if I could buy you breakfast," Bernard admitted as he jumped up from his seat and stepped inside the elevator.

The ride to the first floor was quiet, and once they reached the cafeteria they both ordered two egg sandwiches with bacon, and large coffees. Bernard paid the overpriced bill and found a table out of the way from the few doctors and customers that were there.

"Thank you," Kaderri said when he sat down.

"You're welcome. Now, will you tell me what happened last night?"

Kaderri finished chewing before he answered. "What do you have to do with this?" he asked. "Is this official?"

"Officer Franks knew about the first run-in you had with Greg Sander, we sometimes work out at the club together. And since I was the investigating officer on that case, he thought I would like to know about last night."

Kaderri looked hard and long into Bernard's eyes. "You still didn't answer my question."

Keith Bernard clearly studied the man in front of him, and thought a long, tense moment before he answered. "Yes, it's official. It has to be determined if you are going to be brought up on attempted murder charges."

"Your people killed Sander, not me, what's the point?" Kaderri immediately became suspicious.

Bernard put his egg sandwich down and opened up his hand. "One," he ticked off one finger, "you threatened to go after somebody, we have it on tape. You can't do that."

Kaderri felt the blood run from his face. "That motherfucker was raping my wife! And it was premeditated!"

169

"How do you know?" Bernard asked.

"I hope you're a better detective than that," Kaderri challenged. He took another bit of his sandwich. He had to fill his mouth with something before he said something he would regret.

Bernard took the challenge in stride. He deserved the comment. "You're right," Bernard said, "I am a better detective." "It's obvious it was premeditated. But I just have to do my job." Then he added, "Understand?" The time it took to answer gave Bernard more time to study the man across from him.

Kaderri stared at Bernard and nodded. Still not sure what to say, he finished off his breakfast.

"Now, number two," Bernard ticked off another finger, then thought a moment. "Aw, fuck it!" He leaned back in the cushioned chair, rubbed his hand over a tired face, and gulped at his coffee. "Marc, can you tell me what happened?"

Kaderri still hadn't blinked. He washed the remainder of the sandwich down with his coffee and nodded once he placed the cup back down on the formica table. "I'll give you the highlights."

Bernard nodded his understanding. "Fair enough."

Kaderri began. "My wife and I went to a boring show and left earl—"

"Why?" Bernard cut him off. He also took out his pad to write everything down.

Kaderri was annoyed at being cut off. The man said he wanted highlights not details. Kaderri tried to use a little psychology on the detective before him, and a little shock. "Because we were horny," Kaderri's attempt at shock turned into anger. As he continued, he felt the blood rush to his face. "And the club was the closest place where there was enough room to fuck properly!"

Bernard sat there open-mouthed. Surprise covered his face.

"Now, Detective," Kaderri said through clenched teeth, "do you want details or highlights?"

"Sorry, Marc. Highlights would be fine."

Kaderri took a deep breath, finished his coffee, and continued. "After we were finished, I went downstairs to the crapper and sauna. On my way to the sauna, I saw Sander's truck outside the door, and heard Sara scream. I ran upstairs, broke down the door. . ." he choked and rubbed his face. "And I found Sander. . ." He shuddered at the sight in his mind.

Bernard stopped writing.

Kaderri took a deep breath and continued. "I knocked him into the wall, broke his ribs again, and gave him a sledgehammer that knocked him out. I ran to my wife, untied her and called 911. Sander got up, came toward my wife, saw me, and ran out the door. I chased him and the rest is history."

Bernard only nodded.

Marc Kaderri sat there for a long moment and stared at Bernard. The whole conversation had been bizarre. *What the hell kind of cop was this guy?* he thought. Who in their right mind would want to pursue attempted murder charges on a man who got into a fight with another man. The police wound up fatally shooting Sander after he beat up five police officers. Kaderri began to have a strange feeling that Bernard wasn't who he said he was.

"Another cup of coffee, Marc?"

The question shook Kaderri from his thoughts. "Yeah, thanks."

"Cream and sugar?"

Kaderri nodded. "I have to make a phone call."

The early morning sun was bright and brilliant, and promised to be a beautiful day. But, the bright sun was completely blocked out by a thick shade and heavy curtains that covered the windows in the upstairs bedroom.

Robert Wolff, Ph.D. was in ecstasy. He awoke to the extremely delightful warm sensation of a mouth wrapped around his erect penis. His "guest," he couldn't remember her name but thought it was Jennifer, was a sexual dynamo. She just couldn't seem to get enough of anything. After she brought him out of a deep sleep, she disengaged her mouth and straddled him.

He just lay there and let her do all the work. It was their fifth time since they had come back to his bed. She wasn't the best looking woman, but she had a nice body and loved sex. It had been too long without the feel of a woman, and he didn't really care what she looked like, Well, he did have his standards, as long as she wasn't the size of a tuna fish or a double bagger, it was fine with him.

Jennifer methodically moved and began to screech every time she worked him deep. The screech annoyed him, but her expertise was worth the little inconvenience.

Suddenly, the phone rang. *Who the hell is that?* he thought. He looked at his guest bouncing up and down and noticed her eyes were shut tight, concentrating on what she was doing. She seemed totally oblivious to the phone. He glanced at the red numbers on the clock next to the bed. He cursed. It was 6:45 in the morning.

He decided to ignore the phone and enjoy the pleasure. He lifted his head and took one of her straining nipples into his mouth.

The phone was now on its fourth ring.

Wolff grabbed her buttocks and pulled her forward. She got the hint and began moving back and fourth instead of up and down.

Seven rings. Damn, he forgot to turn on the answering machine.

He cursed again. Obviously the caller thought it was important. If he answered it, he could get rid of the caller quick, and get back to the serious business of fornicating. "What?" he shouted into the phone. Jennifer didn't stop.

"It's about time you answered the phone."

"Christ, Marc, this better be important. I'm in the middle of a great lay—"

"I'm at the hospital."

He didn't really comprehend what Kaderri said. Sometimes Kaderri would drive by and see another car in his driveway.

He'd then call and harass him hoping to interrupt him in his carnal delights. All the previous times, it had been somebody from the lab going over the latest problems and Wolff had welcomed the interruption. Not this time.

"Then you better find a room because you are going to need one after I beat the shit out of you." With his free hand he squeezed the nipples dancing in front of his face.

"Sara was raped."

That got his attention. Marc would never joke about anything like that. "Whoa. What?" He sat straight up and stopped the girl from sliding. But, she didn't get off.

"I'm at Albany Medical Center. I need a ride home. I'll be in the cafeteria."

"I'm on my way." He hung up the phone, regretfully, and quickly disconnected the hot woman. He threw on sweats and ran out the door.

"You want anything else?" Bernard asked from his seat. He decided not to get another cup of the bitter coffee.

"No, thanks." Kaderri sat down and took a sip of the steaming coffee.

"Listen, Marc, I hope everything turns out okay. I have to go. If I need anything else, I'll call you at your office." Bernard extended his hand.

"Thank, you." Kaderri shook Bernard's hand, but eyed him suspiciously. What else could this man want?

Kaderri felt physically and emotionally drained. He had been on an emotional roller coaster before, like the one when Steven Caron died in his arms, but the roller coaster he just rode with Sara was a doozie. Sitting alone and staring into his coffee, he couldn't help but think about the loss he almost incurred. Life without Sara was unthinkable.

A nurse who he recognized from Sara's floor walked by and he got her attention.

Saturday, June 113, 7:20 a.m.

Detective Keith Bernard sat outside the hospital on one of

the concrete benches and wished he smoked. His mind was transfixed on Marcus Kaderri. That was one cool customer, he thought. Once again he had the strange feeling inside that he had met this man before. And during the interview, his eyes kept gravitating toward the nasty scar on Kaderri's left elbow. For a brief moment when he looked into Kaderri's eyes, he saw something behind them. It was the look of a calm, cold, and calculated. . .killer. Bernard saw that look in men before. Men who were hard, who saw death up close, came close to death and dealt it out. But it was from men who didn't like killing. The killing was necessary, not wanton. It was the look of a combat veteran. The look of a warrior. A special kind of warrior. The uneasy feeling that he had met this man before came back. The look in Kaderri's eyes, his mannerisms, and the nasty scar above the left elbow gave him a sense of déjà vu.

As he rose to leave, he ran into Michele Thorsen. She was alone, dressed in a tight pair of blue jeans and a black T-shirt. Her oversized bag was draped over her shoulder. "What brings you here, Michele? Isn't it a little early?"

"Hi, Detective," she said. "I understand that Marc Kaderri, the man involved in last night's shooting is in there."

Bernard shook his head. "You don't waste any time, do you? How do you know his name? And what do you want with him?" He moved slightly to block her from entering the hospital.

"I was at the scene," she said.

"Well?" Bernard asked. He wanted the answer to his second question.

"What?" she said a little indignantly. "Isn't it obvious?"

Bernard just stared.

"All right. It's a major story, and I want to interview him. It's not every day that I get to interview someone who attempted murder. Oh," she said, "can you comment on anything?"

There was no way he was going to volunteer any information even if the case was cut and dry. "Now, Michele," he wiggled his index finger, "you know we can't comment on a shooting that is under investigation, especially when a police officer is involved."

"Okay," she said resignedly, "but what about Kaderri?"

For Christ's sake, he thought, the guy's wife was just raped. Couldn't they once give somebody a break. Bernard knew he couldn't stop the press, and he knew how brutal they could be. He would try to help Marc Kaderri out as much as he could by warding Micheee Thorsen off. If he couldn't do that, at least he could try to channel her line of questioning.

"I have to warn you," he smiled. "Marc isn't what you are going to expect. He's not going to be the easiest person to interview, and his head hurts like hell from the accident."

"Detective, I've been around a while. I've interviewed all types of characters, I'm sure I can handle this one. But thanks for the advice." She turned to walk away.

"Michele?" Bernard called after her.

"What?"

"Have fun at dinner tonight with Gary."

Saturday, June 13, 7:30 a.m.

Michele Thorsen walked up to the reception desk in the main lobby at Albany Med. "Hi." She put on her charm for the handsome young man and asked, "Could you direct me to Sara Kaderri's room?"

"Hey," he smiled. "You're—"

Michele put her fingers on her lips and winked. "Keep it between us, okay?"

"Sure, but, the lady who got raped isn't seeing anybody, but her husband is in the cafeteria eating breakfast."

"Thanks," Michele said, knowing the man's eyes were following her.

The cafeteria was still empty, mainly due to it being Saturday. During the week, Medical and Pharmacology students packed the cafeteria to grab a quick meal and discuss a patient's problem or the work assignment they had just completed. So, in the absence of the extra bodies running around, it was easy for Michele to spot Marc Kaderri.

The partially carpeted floor masked her footsteps and she quietly walked up to him and was ready to ask if she could sit down.

"Thanks for coming." Kaderri said without looking up from his coffee cup. He obviously heard her footsteps or sensed her presence.

"Excuse me?" Michele was startled by what he said. Kaderri looked up from his coffee at the strange voice. "I'm sorry," he said with a tired smile. "I thought you were somebody else."

"May I sit down?" She looked at the strikingly handsome man before her. His piercing, steel blue-eyes looked right into hers, when he spoke, they didn't roam her body like most mens eyes did. His smile smoothed out his rugged features, causing her heart to skip a beat. His broad chest stretched the green surgical shirt and his chest hairs popped out at the collar. His powerful arms rippled with his taught muscles. The simple gold wedding band glistened around his finger as did his Rolex watch around his wrist.

He hesitated before answering. "Yes, Miss Thorsen, you may."

"Thank you," she simply said. She noticed how disheveled Kaderri looked and thought that with him being in his tired state, she could get all the information she wanted out of him. She turned on her charm again. She flipped her flowing blonde hair and slightly pushed her chest out for effect. It was a trick she learned, that worked, to distract males and get the information she wanted. As they focused their concentration on her extremely appealing curves she would extract the information she wanted out of them.

The only time her tactic didn't work had been with Detective Gary Trainor.

The phone was picked up on the second ring. "Yes," the husky male voice said.

"I need you to pull a file, if there is one."

"Jesus Christ, It's Saturday morning! Do you know what

time it is?"

"Yes, sir, but it's important," the caller said.

"It better be." The voice was joking. "What's the name?"

"Kaderri, Marcus A. I've just had an interesting conversation with him."

"I know him personally, what do you want with his file?"

"Curiosity. So he does have a file."

"You've met him before," the husky voice stated.

"I have?" The caller became very curious. "Where?"

"Beirut."

"I think we need to meet."

"Agreed, Get to the airport. I'll have a plane ready for you."

"Yes, sir."

"How is your wife?" Michele asked in her best concerned voice.

Marc Kaderri didn't answer and looked at her with suspicious eyes. It took a moment for him to realize that she was doing a story on him or his wife.

"Have you been here all night, Marc?" It was obvious that he had been. His beard wasn't shaved, his hair not combed. . . and he was wearing the surgical greens.

He simply nodded, then asked, "Are you people trained to ask stupid questions?" He didn't give her a chance to answer. "Why do you want to know about my wife?" There weren't too many people who knew what happened to Sara Kaderri.

For some reason, that she couldn't explain, the man across from her excited her, aroused her and frightened her. But, all he did was sit there." What was it about him that brought out these feelings? "I thing rape is such a horrible crime, and I'm always concerned about the victim."

Kaderri tried to hide the anger, and he almost succeeded, but the flash in his eyes gave the truth away. "What makes you think my wife was raped?"

"I was at that horrible accident last night and I overheard two officers talking." She learned the hard way when not to press a subject, and it was obvious that this was one of those times. She had to clear her mind, before she asked any more questions about the accident and subsequent shooting. "Would you like another cup of coffee? Or something to eat?" she asked. "I'm a bit hungry." She stood slowly, stretched and in the process jutted her breasts and tight buttocks out further for Kaderri to see.

"No thanks, I've had breakfast already. Besides, I'm waiting for someone to pick me up." He didn't take the bait.

"Oh." She would have to work quickly. Another rejection on her sex appeal was unexpected. She sat back down, breakfast and coffee would have to wait. She reached into her bag pulled out her spiral notepad, Cross-pen and miniature tape recorder. "Now, can you tell me what happened last night?" She turned on the tape recorder.

He reached across the table and shut off the tape recorder. "You were at the scene last night, along with other reporters. You know what happened."

Michele became annoyed at his action, but kept the annoyance masked from her face. She didn't like people taking control of the situation. She was a reporter, and that was her job. She kept her voice calm and understanding, playing the part of the sympathetic listener perfectly. "I understand your reluctance to talk about the horrible incident last night, but you were involved in a major story that the public would like to know about." She clicked the tape recorder back on.

Kaderri leaned slightly forward and stared deeper into Thorsen's eyes. It was as if he was looking through her eyes into her soul. His voice was calm, steady, and menacing. "What I was involved with last night is over and done with. It's nobody else's business. I saw you at the scene last night, Miss Thorsen. You know what happened. Why don't you leave it at that?" He clicked off the tape recorder.

Like any good reporter, Michele remained undaunted. "But, people would like to know the circumstances behind the incident."

"There is nothing else to say."

It was obvious that she had her work cut out for her. "Can

I get some background information on you so I make sure I have all the facts straight?"

"Why don't you tell me what you have?"

Michele frowned. This had never happened to her before. She had never been completely denied anything in a story before. She had always been able to elicit some sort of answer. This wasn't good for her career. Two major stories and she had nothing concrete. She had nothing to lose or hide. "Okay," she said. She recalled the incident from memory. "What I have is that you and Greg Sander were involved in a car accident, which was immediately followed by a fight. During the fight, the police arrived and found Greg Sander beaten up and unconscious. He woke, beat up a bunch of cops, and the only way they could stop him was by shooting him."

"You have the whole story. There is nothing else that I can add, except that he was high on cocaine."

"How do you know that without the results of an autopsy?"

"Like you said, I was involved in a fight with the man. I saw him up close and personal," he said. "Besides, the police told me they found a bunch of it in his truck."

She began writing, believing he was starting to open up. She leaned forward and rested her breasts on the table. "Why did the two of you get into a fight?"

He still didn't take the bait. "You'll have to ask the police. I have to go, my ride is here."

She spun around to see who he was talking about.

A man approached the table with a purpose. He looked tired and concerned. His oval face was unshaven and he wore a baseball hat to hide his uncombed and unwashed hair. His gray sweats made him look like a bum. "How are you, Marc?" He walked over to him and placed his hand on Marc's shoulder.

"I've been better."

"How is she?"

"Sleeping."

"Hi," Michele said, not wanting to be left out.

"I'm sorry," Marc said, "Bob, this is Michelee Thorsen. Michele, this is Robert Wolff."

179

Wolff grinned sheepishly. He too did not let his eyes roam. "Excuse my appearance." He extended his hand, "Nice to meet you."

"Nice to meet you, too." She shook his outstretched hand.

Wolff turned to Marc. "Can I go see her?"

"Yes."

Just like that, the interview was over. Michelee sighed and watched the two men walk away.

Saturday, June 13, 9:00 a.m.

Marc and Wolff sat in silence around the kitchen table in Kaderri's air-conditioned house. The ride back to the house had also been quiet. Marc was too tired to talk and Wolff didn't know what to say. Wolff knew that it wasn't the right time to ask what happened or if the right time would ever present itself. In time, Marc would fill him in on the details on what happened.

Wolff broke the strained silence. "Marc, do you need anything?"

Kaderri shook his head.

"When Sara gets released, I'm going up to the cabin for a while." Kaderri was talking about the three-bedroom log home on 145 acres in the Adirondack Mountains that had a beautiful view of Mt. Marcy, the highest point in New York State.

"When does she get out?" Wolff inquired again. He thought Marc told him earlier but he had forgotten what he had said.

"Monday."

Wolff saw the hurt in Kaderri's eyes and immediately changed the subject. "Marc" Wolff said, "let me help you up to bed. You don't look too good."

"Thank you for your two cents." His small smile was genuine.

Wolff helped Kaderri get to his feet and followed him up the stairs to the master bedroom. As soon as Kaderri saw the king-size bed, he fell face down upon it and went right to sleep. Wolff took Kaderri's shoes and socks off and threw a blanket over him.

CHAPTER TWELVE

Saturday, June 13, 10:45 a.m.

The last man that Betty "Blossom" Freeman slept with was the key to the murder at the self-storage buildings. In fact, Gary Trainor knew in his gut that, that was the man who killed Pedro. But that was just another one of the unsolved murders that plagued the city.

Trainor knew from the evidence that the murders were drug related. But, the other unsolved murders weren't so clear. More answers were needed and every day new questions popped up.

Trainor felt somewhat refreshed after eight hours of sleep, though he did have a slight hangover. He was up till all hours in the morning studying the information on the murders. He'd read page after page of information, deciphered it, and read it again. He was surprised that nothing new had turned up. Even the information that had been collected from the canvass after each murder revealed nothing. There was absolutely no information on the streets about the murders. Trainor hoped that somewhere, someone would brag that it was them who pulled off the hits. But there wasn't even a sniff of that floating in the air.

Trainor left his kitchen table for the shower.

Being the bearer of a gold shield that had 'City of Albany Detective' written on it, allowed him certain privileges. One of those-being able to see suspects in a murder investigation at his leisure. When he was done with his long, hot shower, he drove to Albany Medical Center to question Hector Romero again.

Up to this point, there were no attempts made to end Hector's life while he was recovering from his wounds. The guard that was originally placed outside the hospital room door immediately after the shooting was no longer needed and the hospital room looked as inconspicuous as any other. As Trainor approached the room, voices inside were in a hushed but heated discussion that spilled into the hallway.

"Hi, Hector," Trainor said to the man lying in the bed. He was wearing a pair of his own pajamas and had the sheets pulled up to his waist. His right arm was in a sling to keep the strain off the collar-bone and an empty glass was on the tray next to the bed. Despite his appearance of improved health, Hector Romero still had IV tubes in his veins. Both Hector and his mother looked up at the strange voice.

Trainor looked at Hector who quickly averted his eyes. But when he looked at Mrs. Romero, hers were full of hope.

She moved away from the side of the bed and stood right in front of Trainor. "Did you find the son-of-a-bitch that did this to my baby." It was more of a demand than a question.

"No. I'm here to question your son on his involvement in the murders," Trainor answered.

"My Hector did nothing wrong. Nothing!"

"Ma!" Hector shouted. "Why don't you go?"

She looked at him and nodded then closed the door when she left.

Trainor looked at the empty bed in the semi-private room. "Still alone in here?"

"What do you want Detective? I'm tired." Romero still

hadn't looked into Trainor's eyes.

Trainor pulled over a chair and took out his notepad and pen. He moved his pistol in his shoulder holster so it was more comfortable and then sat down. "You're smarter than that, aren't you?"

"I thought we went over this?"

"I need better answers. You weren't in that great of shape the last time we talked. You had a hole in your collar-bone, you pissed and shit your pants, and were bleeding to death. Remember?"

He finally looked up into Trainor's eyes. "How could I forget."

"Good, now let's get started."

Hector groaned.

"You and Slapper were going to pop Francisco for ripping you off in your last dealing with smack."

"Yeah."

"Then what happened?" Trainor asked.

"Man, I got to go through this shit again? I told you what happened. You must think I'm nuts."

"You said that a tree shot Slapper. Is that the story you want to stick with?"

"Yeah, man, that's what happened, except it was a big bush instead of a tree."

"Okay, a bush. Now, tell me again what you saw."

Hector Romero let out a loud sigh and began. "I was in the trunk getting ready to pop 'Cisco when his fucking head exploded, man. I mean it just exploded. No sound, nothing. Then I saw Slapper get hit, man. I was gonna go help him, but I didn't know what was going on. So, I stayed in the trunk. And when I didn't hear anything from Keena, I thought he would be able to help Slapper. But when he didn't go help, I said to myself they be on their own, I'm safer in the trunk."

Hector was getting agitated so Trainor let him catch his breath before he prodded for more information.

"What else?"

Romero took a deep breath. "Slapper got up and started

running to the car. Then, bullets hit him and came flying into the trunk where I got hit." He rubbed his taped collarbone. "And I still didn't hear nothing, man, except for Slapper screaming. Then I looked out the trunk and saw the little bush grow right before my eyes. No, man, wait. There were two bushes. Both got bigger, but I only saw one grow before my eyes."

"Was that the one with the branch?" Trainor asked.

In an embarrassed whisper, Romeo acknowledged, "Yeah, man, the one with the branch."

"How far away were the bushes?"

Hector thought for a moment. It was hard for him to think of measurements before a traumatic experience, now it was just about impossible. "I think, man, 'bout three-hundred feet."

Then what happened Hector?"

He stayed silent for a moment. When he began to speak, it was haltingly. "I couldn't see Slapper anymore 'cause he was close to the car and then I heard a thump, felt the car rock and then the fucking arrow came through the car!" He went silent as he replayed the scene in his mind and shuddered.

"Detective, man, can you tell me what happened to everybody? I mean how did they die?"

"Do you really want to know?"

Romero nodded. "Yeah," he whispered.

"Starting with Luis, he got hit in two places. In the leg and in the shoulder."

"Yeah, man, I seen those two."

"What's called a bolt, or arrow, from a crossbow cut through his heart and impaled him on the car. His body was the thump you heard and what caused the car to rock. Your colleague, Keena—"

"He was driving," Hector volunteered.

"Took a bullet in the back of the head that blew away his face. And so did Carlos, the guy behind the wheel of the BMW."

"No noise, man, I didn't hear no noise on that either."

"You didn't hear anything on that hit either?"

"No."

"What about when Francisco's head got blown away?"

"No, man, I already told you. I didn't hear nothing."

Trainor's wheels began moving, and he almost kicked himself for not seeing this earlier. "Hector, did you hear anything out of the ordinary?"

"Like what, man?"

"Footsteps, pistol hammers locking, any type of noise?"

Hector thought for a moment then spoke. "No, man, there was nothing else moving. I didn't even hear another car go over the bridge."

Trainor walked to the bed and picked up the white buzzer that signaled the nurse's station and pressed the button. A moment later a metallic voice came through the wall mounted speaker above the bed. "Yes?"

"Can you get the doctor in here?" Before he could add that it wasn't an emergency, two nurses and a doctor burst through the door.

"What's wrong?" the doctor asked as he made his way to the bed.

"There's nothing wrong, Doctor. I want to ask you if I could take him for a few hours. But before I could tell the nurse it wasn't an emergency, you were already in here. Sorry."

"That's it?"

"Yes."

"Who are you?" The doctor asked, visibly annoyed at the screw up.

Trainor took out his badge and showed it to the doctor. "Detective Gary Trainor, Albany Police Department."

"I assume that it's important."

"Very. I'm in the middle of a murder investigation, and he may be able to provide some answers."

"He can go, but only for a few hours. He has to stay in a wheelchair and a nurse stays with him."

"Thank you." Trainor picked up the phone and dialed as the doctor and nurses left.

Saturday, June 13, 11:40 a.m.

The police van slowed to a stop next to the police Chevy Blazer that held one of the police department's K-9 units. The parking lot in the Corning Preserve was crowded with automobiles and the Preserve itself was full of people. Trainor stepped from the air-conditioned van and immediately began to sweat in the hot, humid air. The officer who was driving wasn't needed and apparently had no interest in venturing out into the heat to see what Trainor was doing. He remained in the air-conditioned van.

The officer in the Blazer got out with the squat, mean looking, brown and black German Shepherd attached to a short leash and walked over to Trainor. When they stopped, the dog immediately sat by the officer's leg and began to scan the area. "What's up, Gary?" Officer Kurt Schneider asked in a slight German accent.

"Hi, Kurt." Trainor bent down and rubbed the dog's jowls with both hands and pulled at his ears. "And how are you, Dumptruck?" The dog wagged his tail and affectionately turned his head to Trainor's legs.

"Who's the guy in the back?" Schneider pointed to Hector Romero in the back of the van.

"He's the guy we found in the trunk after you left." The humidity was getting oppressive and dark circles quickly formed under Trainor's arm pits and a dark strip quickly spread along his spine.

"What do you want from us?" Kurt wiped his sweaty face with a hankerchief he took from his back pocket.

"Hector says he remembers seeing a couple of bushes grow before his eyes. There may be something that Dumptruck can pick up."

"Bushes grew? You have got to be kidding?"

"Nope." He turned to see Hector in the wheelchair being lowered on the rear door ramp. When it was down, the nurse wheeled him over to the two officers.

Dumptruck immediately began to growl. The hair behind

his neck stood straight and he rose off his haunches.

"Stay." Officer Schneider commanded the dog.

"Keep that fucking dog away from me, man." Hector said.

Trainor looked at the nurse and saw her frown. He turned back to Romero. "Watch your mouth!"

Hector didn't take his eyes off the dog. The sweat on his face wasn't just from the heat. It was obvious he was petrified of the animal.

"Okay, Hector, show us where the bushes grew."

"Down there by the water," Hector pointed in the direction. The nurse pushed the wheelchair, the two police officers and Dumptruck were right at his side.

"Hold it" Hector said. A few small trees and some scrub bush marked the spot that was about 20 feet away from the sloping shoreline.

"Is this it?" Trainor asked.

He looked at the trees and brush more closely and nodded that this was the right spot. "Yeah."

Kurt Schneider gave Dumptruck a command to begin a search but there were too many scents to pick from. It would have helped if Dumptruck had a matching scent to search for.

"Hey, Hector where did you see the bushes grow?"

"Right there, man," he pointed to a space between a bush and a small maple tree.

Schneider brought the dog over to the spot to have him sniff it more thoroughly but had no success. The grass was flattened in the spot that Romero pointed to, but that could have been from anyone or even the hard rain that fell the previous night.

"Anything?" Trainor asked.

"No, he doesn't have anything to go on, and besides too much time may have passed. Too many things could have happened here. That's twice we struck out here, Gary."

Trainor looked back to the spot where the murders had taken place and then back over his shoulder to look across the river and squinted. The sun was much higher in the sky than it would have been in the morning, but he realized that the shooters had the advantage. They had a clear shot at the victims, who were clearly illuminated by the sunlight and at the same time, had the sun to their backs making it almost impossible to look in that direction.

"Hey, Romero."

"What?" he answered as the nurse spun him around in the wheelchair to face Trainor.

"If the sun was over the horizon, facing this way, and you were in the trunk looking that way," he pointed to the spot under the bridge, and then over the water, "how come you were able to see so much?"

"What are you talking 'bout?"

"The sun. The sun was over there and you were looking right into it. How could you see so much?"

"I was in the trunk and the trunk lid blocked the sun."

Trainor got right in Romero's face. "You sure?"

"Yeah, man, I'm sure." He stared back at Trainor. Suddenly, his eyes widened. "You still think I had somethin' to do with all them people gettin' popped?"

"Let's just say you aren't out of the picture. Besides, you were dealing with a controlled substances and were planning to commit murder."

Hector Romero was silent.

Trainor told the nurse to put him on the ramp and then turned to Schneider. "Do you have anything pressing, Kurt?"

"No, do you need us?"

"Yeah, I want to check something out." He went to the van and told the driver to take Romero back to the hospital.

Both Trainor and Schneider helped the nurse lock the wheelchair in the back of the van and then watched it drive off.

"Where is your partner?" Schneider asked.

Trainor turned and looked at Schneider like he came from Mars. "That's a good question, I have no idea." The wheels were turning in his mind. "I haven't heard or seen him since, I can't remember," he said absently. He reached into his shirt pocket and unwrapped a roll of Tums and popped one into his mouth.

"Anyway, what is it that you need from me and Dumptruck?"

"I want to go over to the scene on Northern Boulevard where our guys were hit, and then the vacant building where Stroehmann and the gang were killed."

"By Ramone's?"

"Yeah. I want to see if Dumptruck can pick up anything."

"Let's go," Schneider said. He loaded Dumptruck and then both Trainor and he jumped in the Blazer.

Saturday, June 13, 12:50 p.m.

The officers and Dumptruck were at the intersection of Northern and Livingston. They were inside the air-conditioned Blazer eating Pastrami sandwiches on rye with mustard and washing it down with Coke that Trainor had bought at the Corner Deli. It was safer for them in daylight.

"Let me ask you something, Kurt," Trainor said. He was looking out the window at the building across the street.

"Go ahead."

"You handle Dumptruck very well. Better than any of the other officers we have. It's obvious that you didn't learn everything here."

"Thanks. No, I learned how to handle dogs in the German Army."

"No shit?" Trainor blurted. "What else did you do?"

"Besides a scout, where I worked with dogs, I was trained as an infantryman and a sniper."

Trainor wiped the smile off his face. "Sniper?" He could have kicked himself for not thinking of this earlier. What better way to catch a sniper than to ask one. The police department had their own sharpshooters, he could have asked one of them. Kurt was there now, it would do just as well to ask him.

"Yes," Kurt's face showed concern like he said something wrong. "Why?"

"If you wanted to kill somebody right here," he pointed to the spot where the officers and drug dealers had been shot, "where would you go?"

Kurt Schneider thought about it as he looked out the windshield and door windows. His view was obstructed so he got out of the vehicle. "Where were the victims when they were hit?"

Trainor got out also and pointed to the spot. "One was facing that way, he had his back to the wall and the other one by the dumpster facing the cruiser."

Schneider looked at both locations and asked, "Where were the victims hit?"

"The two that the sniper took out were head shots. Both were on the bridge of the nose."

A smile spread across Schneider's face. "The guy is a good shot."

"Why are you smiling?" Trainor was curious at Schneider's smile.

"Professional admiration."

Trainor thought about the comment and guessed he would feel the same way if he were in that profession. He sure didn't feel professional about his own investigative performance. He felt like an amature. Then again by not catching this perpetrator, it wasn't doing any harm. It wasn't the first time that Trainor had thought like that. There was a noticeable decrease in drug activity over the past few weeks and all the people being waxed were drug dealers. Most did have records. This guy was doing more cleaning of the streets than the justice system was. Maybe they should leave him alone.

Trainor decided to get off that train of thought quickly. To help Kurt out, he volunteered more information that he thought would be useful. "Both bullets went straight through the head and came out the base of the neck."

"So he had a high angle."

"It seems that way. When we questioned the occupants of the apartment building that the sniper was on, they had no idea what we were talking about. Besides, there was no evidence that somebody was in the building who didn't belong there. We figured that the perpetrator fired from the roof."

"Sounds right," Schneider confirmed. He looked up at the top of the crumbling billboard. "The escape route would be much easier. It is most likely that there were two of them"

"Two snipers?"

Schneider shook his head. "No, no. One sniper and a spotter."

"Come on, lets go up top."

No one paid much attention to the two officers and Dumptruck, though a few times Dumptruck stopped at a door when he got a sniff of marijuana. As soon as they reached the roof, Schneider commanded the dog to search. The shimmering heat that rose from the tar roof flowed like an angry wave and added twenty degrees to the heat.

Sniffing among the hanging laundry and debris that littered the rooftop, Dumptruck came up empty again. It was the same as the first time the police had swept the roof for evidence.

They came up with the same results at Lark and Third.

Saturday, June 13, 2:10 p.m.

The sleek Gulfstream IV aircraft descended on its approach to Dulles International. The loan passenger unbuckled the seat belt and rose from the leather chair once the wheels screeched and the plane shuttered as it touched down on the runway. It was late.

The plane rolled off the taxi way, maneuvered away from the main concourse, and came to rest in front of an inconspicuous hanger. A sleek, black limousine with its darkened windows was parked near the hangar doors.

The door of the jet opened and then Keith Bernard, descended the stairs to the waiting car. The driver got out and prepared to open the rear door. "Good afternoon sir," the driver said.

"I hope I didn't keep you waiting?"

"I didn't mind, but the Boss in the back is a little pissed."

Shock registered on Bernard's face. "He's in there?"

"Yep. Good thing the air conditioner is working." The driver

191

opened the door with a cheery smile.

"Hello, sir. Sorry about the flight." He said once he got into the limousine.

"It's nothing you could have controlled."

Paul McKnight, Deputy Director (Operations), Central Intelligence Agency, dressed in a tailored gray suit with a white button-down collar and a black and red paisley tie was seated in the back of the limousine. His brown hair was cut short above the ear, parted on the left side and starting to gray around the temples. At 49-years-old, he was as athletically fit and trim as a soldier half his age.

The last half-inch of an extinguished Arturo Fuente cigar was crushed in the ashtray, and a half-empty can of Coke was in his hand. He extended his free hand.

Bernard sat down and shook the outstretched hand of his boss. The driver started the car and drove off, heading nowhere.

"So, Keith, did you find where Koretsky is?" McKnight handed Bernard a Manila folder with red- and white- striped tape around the border.

"I know he's in Albany, and I have his location narrowed down to two locations." He glanced down at the top secret folder he was holding in his hand and read the name-Kaderri, Marcus A.

"Are you sure?"

"Yeah, I'm sure," Bernard said. "We found a guy down at the docks with traces of cocaine on him and two bullets in his forehead. The bullets came from a Makarov. And more importantly, he spent time with a hooker after the hit. She identified him by a photo."

McKnight drained his soda and popped the top of another. He handed one to Bernard. "I'm sending in additional people, can you find a place for them?" He offered a cigar.

"Yeah, thats no problem." Bernard popped the top on his soda, took a healthy swallow and held it up. "Thanks." He declined the cigar.

Bernard read the file on Kaderri and was impressed. The

man was one hell of a soldier. He read through the preliminaries of his date of birth, when he entered the service and the like. Then, he got to what he figured was the important information. Airborne and Ranger training, first in each class, Special Forces training, second in his class. U.S. Marine Corps sniper training, first in his class. All the training schools he attended he finished in the top three. Those also included jungle, air assault, and northern warfare. He was being groomed for Command and Staff School.

The more Bernard read, the more fascinated he became. Kaderri had received the Bronze Star and Silver Star for actions in Beirut, Lebanon. In Operation Urgent Fury, the assault on Grenada, Captain Marc Kaderri led a Special Forces A-Team and received the Distinguished Service Cross, the nation's second highest award for valor. In Afghanistan, where his involvement was unofficial and meant that he was unable to receive any official decorations, he received two more Silver Stars. He even had a couple of Purple Hearts.

Keith Bernard read on with even more fascination. As a sniper in Beirut, he had six confirmed kills, two confirmed kills in Grenada, and in Afghanistan he had eighteen. Twelve of those were Soviets, including one general.

After he left his assignment in Afghanistan, he had an artificial knee cap inserted to replace the original bone that had been shot away. He then completed his selection process to join Delta Force, the Army's top counter-terrorist unit. It was in that unit when Kaderri had a physical exam. A doctor who had a personality conflict with Kaderri found him unfit for duty and gave him a medical discharge. It didn't matter to the doctor that Kaderri passed his prescreening physical and had endured the long treacherous, training selection process. Despite the Unit Commander and the Commander of Joint Special Operations Command, going to bat for him, the doctor won and Kaderri was out. The doctor had friends in higher places.

"Impressive," Bernard said and closed the folder before he read everything. "Very impressive."

"Yes he is," McKnight said.

"How do you know him?" Bernard asked.

"He was my executive in one of my A-Teams." McKnight reflected on the young man he knew.

Bernard still held onto the file. "You said on the phone that I met him, where?"

"Beirut. Remember the day when you came to headquarters instead of meeting in town?"

Bernard searched his memory, "I remember. It was the day that the sergeant had said that the first lieutenant was going to have his ass."

McKnight smiled. "That first lieutenant was Kaderri."

"Now I remember him! He had the wound above the left elbow. I told him to get it checked out."

"Now," McKnight continued with the purpose of the meeting. "Why did you want his file?"

Bernard figured he'd cover all the bases, even though McKnight was the one who came up with the current operation he was working on to get Koretsky. "As you know, I'm posing as a detective in the Albany Police Department and there has been an unheard of rash on drug related murders in the city."

"Is that causing a problem?" McKnight asked.

"Yes and no. I'm trying to do my best by helping my partner out, but it's taking away time from finding Koretsky." Bernard stopped his train of thought. He knew he was getting away from the question. "Anyway, the people who were killed, with the exception of the guy who Koretsky killed, were shot by a sniper."

"Where does Marc fit into the picture?" There was an edge in his voice. "He is a good friend of mine and I don't like where this conversation is going."

"I've ran into him a few times. He beat the living shit out of a guy twice. Would have killed the man if the police hadn't shot him first. I was the investigating detective on the first beating."

McKnight cocked and eyebrow. "Why did he do that?" Marc

has one of the coolest heads I know. In order for him to do that, something must have gotten under his skin. And it must have gone real deep."

"His wife owns a fitness center—"

McKnight interrupted. "I know."

"He was in the locker room when a guy snorted some coke."

"Well that explains it. I never knew anybody more against drugs than him. Why the second time?"

"The same guy raped his wife."

"Sara? My God! How is she?"

"Recovering. He walked in on the guy and the rest is a long story but the perpetrator is dead. What can you tell me about Kaderri?"

Without thinking, McKnight rattled out. "Marc is a calm, competent man. He's very smart, determined and thorough. Rarely will he make a mistake. But don't get in his way. When he's on a mission, he doesn't stop. But he never takes any unnecessary risks. He's a warrior."

Bernard let what McKnight said sink in. He now knew who the murderer was. "Shit. It all fits."

"What fits?" McKnight asked. He shook his head. "What are you talking about?"

"Sir, I think Marc Kaderri has been murdering those drug dealers."

McKnight's eyes shot daggers. "What are you talking about?"

Bernard took a deep breath. He could see by the look on McKnight's face that he cared deeply about this man. He'd have to tread water in his explanation. "When the dealers were shot, all the money, drugs, and weapons were left behind."

"So?"

"So that means that the shootings weren't a turf war or a robbery. They were assassinations."

McKnight sat silent for a moment. He didn't know what to say. He knew Keith Bernard had one of the best analytical and problem solving minds in the Agency. He was rarely wrong. "I see your point. Do you have any supporting evidence?"

"No, I just figured it out. What do you want me to do?" Paul McKnight sat there for a moment, then lit up another cigar. "Nothing for the moment, especially since you don't have any evidence."

"What about my partner?"

"Let him figure it out. You drag your feet."

Bernard's face was impassive, he knew when and when not to question McKnight. This was a time when he shouldn't question him.

"Now, how close are you to catching Koretsky?"

Bernard was glad the subject was changed. "Close enough, I can taste it."

The two men drove in silence for another ten minutes, both thinking their own thoughts about their conversations and what it would mean to the Agency to catch Koretsky. It would be only a smaller feather in the Agency's cap but it would send a loud message to the Mossad, if not Israel, that they didn't have impunity to operate around the world. Especially in the United States without paying a high price. For the Agency nailing Koretsky was also personal. Like the sergeant in the Lebanese Armed Forces that Koretsky murdered, he did the same thing to a fellow CIA officer who happened to be a close personal friend of both Bernard's and McKnight's.

Bernard knew that Paul McKnight wanted Koretsky dead and he wanted Koretsky to know who killed him. It didn't have to be McKnight himself but Koretsky knew it was going to be the CIA.

"What about the FBI? We're stomping on their territory," Bernard said. The Federal Bureau of Investigation was charged with law and order inside the borders of the United States.

"They won't be bothering us. They were told by the President to back off."

Bernard smiled. He hated butting heads with the Bureau over territory. "I guess an order from the Man can't be ignored."

"No, it can't." McKnight smiled back.

CHAPTER THIRTEEN

Saturday, June 13, 6:00 p.m.

Michele Thorsen sat at the vanity in her bedroom and applied the makeup to her face. A little blush on the cheekbones and rose lipstick brought out her smooth tanned skin and flowing blonde hair. The light touch of purple eye shadow made her sparkling blue eyes deep and more seductive. She looked business-like and professional, yet sociable and appetizing to the opposite sex.

She rose from the chair and walked across the deep blue carpeted floor. She wore a purple cotton coatdress that had a deep "V" cut to highlight the roundness of her cleavage. The short length came to mid-thigh. On her left hip was the gold button that clasped the dress and accentuated her figure. Because of the heat wave that had moved into the area, she decided to forego pantyhose. The matching purple pumps gave her freshly shaved legs an admiring shape. There was no way that Gary Trainor would be able to resist her. Especially since he had already seen what was underneath those clothes.

She made a conscious decision to do whatever it took to get

the information from Trainor so she could run the story and get in the limelight. The last time she had tried to use sex to get information failed. Well, almost. Gary Trainor didn't immediately pull away from her advance and he actually kissed her back. She knew he would be interested in what she had to offer. This time he wouldn't be able to resist her.

The one thing that still bugged her was why he was treating her the way he was. Though she was grateful, she wanted more. She wanted all of it. Michele resented the fact that Trainor would only give her partial information on the investigation. She blamed him for not running her story on the air.

It was now planted firmly in her mind that she was going to air her story on the Monday evening newscast. Her decision was also helped when her boss put the screws to her run something. Besides, she thought, that airing her story would actually help the police by scaring the criminal into surrendering.

That night, she was going to try and get the rest of the information from Trainor. She was going to use her body to its fullest extent and she had the tape that geek ham radio operator had. She had her plan and was going to spring it on Trainor. So, when she went on the air Monday evening, she would have the whole story and she would be in the limelight. Maybe she could even help catch the killer.

Michele could see her name in lights. Headlines across the nation would read: *"Albany reporter helps nab Serial Killer!"* Job offers from the major networks would soon follow. Even though the police didn't have a suspect, Thorsen's skeptical, reporter's brain thought that the police were lying to her and the rest of the press.

Satisfied with her looks and ready for the evening, Michele Thorsen picked up her purse and left her house to pick up her victim, Gary Trainor.

The Troll sat where he was supposed to at Linda's News, the third stool from the right, sipping a soda. Moshe Koretsky had watched him for the past ten minutes from a safe distance across the street.

Koretsky had been in his position thirty minutes before the Troll showed up promptly at six o'clock. He checked to make sure he was clean and of course he watched to make sure his contact wasn't followed. With a nonchalant stride, Koretsky made his way into the café and took the empty seat next to Troll. He took a quick glance at him and determined that he really was an ugly man. Now he knew why he was called Troll.

The waitress behind the counter came over to the new customer. "What would you like?" She had flipped a page on her order pad and pulled a pencil out from her apron pocket.

"Coffee." Koretsky answered.

After the waitress left, Troll took a sideways glance at the stranger sitting on his left. "Hey, man," Troll said, "I'm waiting for somebody. You gonna have to move."

Koretsky took a sip from his hot coffee. "I believe I am that somebody, Troll."

"Okay, man, come with me." Troll stood, threw a few dollars on the counter to cover his soda and Koretsky's coffee and left.

Koretsky waited until Troll was at the door before he followed. He knew where to go since he had watched Troll get of out his car. The only thing he didn't know was where the transaction was going to take place. Then again, it didn't matter, he was ready for just about any contingency.

"How'd you know where to find me?" Troll asked once Koretsky arrived at the Chevrolet Camaro parked forty-feet down the street.

Koretsky ignored the question. "Where's my package?"

"In the car," Troll said and opened the door to get in. When Koretsky got in the passenger side, Troll started the car.

"What are you doing?" Koretsky's voice was calm and firm.

"I thought I'd take you to your car, man. That way you can put the merchandise in and leave."

"No. We do it here."

"Man, what if a cop comes by?" Troll was getting nervous.

"Do you have it in a gym bag like you were told?"

"Yeah."

Koretsky reached into his back pocket and pulled out an envelope and handed it to Troll.

Troll grasped it. Then, in an accusatory voice he said, "Hey, man, you got it all in here?"

Koretsky's eyes flared but kept his face impassive. "I don't think I heard you correctly."

Troll caught the meaning. "I said 'I got it all in here.'"

Koretsky smiled a malicious smile. "That's what I thought you said. Now where is my package?"

If Troll thought about doing anything, Koretsky gave him the smile that erased any doubts. Koretsky knew that his smile with just the edge of his lips curing up was evil looking. Troll reached behind the passenger side seat very slowly and retrieved the nylon gym bag.

Keeping the bag low so nobody could see into the car, Koretsky unzipped the bag and checked the contents. He counted three bags. He quickly closed the bag and reached for the door handle.

"Wait, man, I got something else for you from the Boss." Troll handed over an envelope. "He said it's something you would enjoy."

"Right." Koretsky took the envelope and left the car. He swung the bag over his shoulder and blended in with the evening crowd.

On his way back to his car, he checked and double-checked his route to make sure he was clean. Once inside the car, he held the envelope up to the light to make sure it wasn't booby-trapped. Since he didn't think Miller was capable of poisoning the envelope or its contents, he opened it. Inside was a photograph that Koretsky had taken of Joshua Miller with the woman's head buried deep in his lap. On the back was written: "Ariel, enclosed is the address of the woman in the picture, give her a try." This was clearly Miller's way of apologizing and Koretsky was going to accept it.

Shadows and Deceptions

Saturday, June 13, 7:10 p.m.

It was a typical Saturday night at The Steer House. The wait staff was working in high gear, earning their handsome tips. Seated in the dinning room at a private, cloth-covered table adorned with a single white candle and rose, sat Michele Thorsen and Gary Trainor.

Thorsen received many looks from men and women because of her beauty and profession. On the other hand, Trainor didn't receive any looks except for the few questioning glances of not a bad looking guy but she could do better. He was dressed in gray slacks with a white shirt and blue sport coat. His red and blue paisley tie was nondescriptive.

The ride over in Thorsen's car was awkward. Trainor hadn't said much and Thorsen wasn't sure how to proceed with her plan. She was starting to have second thoughts about tricking him. Inside her, she was starting to like him. So, they made a little small talk until they reached the restaurant.

Once they sat down at their table, Thorsen ordered a White Russian and Trainor a draft beer. Both had their menus opened and Trainor had a tough decision on his selection. The waitress appeared and asked for their order. "Have you made a decision?"

Michele spoke first. "I'll have the vegetable platter for an appetizer and the Norwegian salmon for the entrée."

The waitress turned to Trainor.

"That sounds good," he said, "but I'll have the onion soup and the New York strip—medium."

"And a choice of wine?" the waitress offered.

"None for me thanks," Trainor said. He didn't know much about wines and wouldn't know what to order. "I'll take another beer, though."

Thorsen thought about ordering a bottle for herself, but declined. She didn't want to look like a lush, so she ordered another drink.

"Well," she said, once the waitress left with her order and the menus, "What do you think of this place?"

"I like it. I've been here before."

That surprised Thorsen. "Oh, by the look on your face it all seemed foreign".

"I just have a hard time making a decision. . .with food I mean."

She smiled with a bright twinkle in her eyes. "I hope that's the only problem you have making a decision with."

"What is that suppose to mean?" Trainor became apprehensive.

Under the table, Michele kicked off one of her shoes and rubbed her toes up Trainor's leg. Her smile became mischievous. "You'll see."

"Now, Michele," he turned serious, "if you try any stunts."

"Shut up, Detective," Michele commanded. She removed her foot from his leg. "Hasn't anybody every told you not to pass up a good opportunity?"

"I know a good opportunity when I see one," he smiled, "or feel one, but you seem to have forgotten about your last stunt."

She looked right into his eyes. "I apologized for that, remember? That's why we're here."

The waitress arrived with their drinks just in time to get them off the subject.

Meanwhile, in the bar section of the restaurant, Marcus Kaderri sat at the bar waiting for Rufus "Ghost" Brown to finish a drink order.

Ghost was at the end of the bar placing the last of the six drink order on the waitress' tray when he glanced down the bar to see if there were any new customers. He saw Kaderri and immediately went over to him. "Hey Marc," Ghost said and extended his hand to his friend. There was concern in his voice and face. "How are you?"

"Getting better," Kaderri admitted as he took the outstretched hand.

"How's the head?" Ghost pointed to the sutured cut.

"I've had a lot worse."

"I swung by the hospital to see Sara after Bob called and told me what happened."

"Yeah, Sara told me. I just came from there."

"As far as I know," Ghost said, "she looks to be in good spirits. How is she?"

"Recovering. She's almost back to normal." Kaderri said with a heavy sigh, indicating that she would never be the same again.

Ghost was smart enough to know not to continue the conversation unless Kaderri wanted to, so he asked him the question that every bartender was supposed to ask. He put a smile on his face and asked, "What are you drinking? Samuel Adams?" He reached for a beer glass to fill it with Kaderri's favorite beer.

Kaderri stopped him. "No, Ghost. I'll have scotch."

That was extremely unusual for Kaderri. The only time he turned down good beer was when he had a lot on his mind. Considering the circumstances, it was understandable why he would want scotch.

Ghost replaced the beer mug. "Scotch it is. What kind? Good stuff or the blended?" He was determining if Kaderri was going to need a ride home or not by what scotch he ordered. If he ordered the blended, that meant he'd be getting drunk and would need a ride home. The blended scotches were made with a mixture of malts and were the only scotches that should be combined with mixers because it wouldn't hurt the taste.

Single malts, on the other hand, were the better scotches and the proper way to drink them was straight up with a splash of water. After drinking a few alcoholic beverages, the taste buds deaden and the senses loose the distinct taste of the whisky. Hence, the taste was no longer pure and perfectly good scotch was wasted.

Kaderri studied the rows of liquor on the shelves behind the bar. He found the dozen or so bottles of scotch and ordered the one he wanted. "I'll take the Macallan and a Poterhouse—medium."

Kaderri picked a single malt. Ghost sighed a sigh of relief, thinking Kaderri wouldn't be getting drunk and reached for the Macallan. It was twenty-five-years old and one of the best tasting scotches money could buy.

Ghost immediately delivered the drink and put the order in for the steak. He walked around the bar and came over to Kaderri. "C'mon, I have to talk to you."

Kaderri rose and followed Ghost through the kitchen and then outside. "What's up that couldn't be said in there?" Kaderri gestured with his thumb.

Ghost looked around to make sure nobody was watching or eavesdropping before he spoke. "I was in the office today and checked the tape recorder."

Kaderri gave Ghost his full attention. "Go on."

"There is another deal happening."

Ice and fire coursed through Kaderri's veins. "When and where?"

"Tomorrow morning. There was a deal that was to go off this afternoon that Miller was extremely happy about. He wants another one if it goes well."

Kaderri smiled. "He should be happy that his people weren't blown away. Who did it?"

"The guy that did it was named Troll, he's one of Miller's assholes. I don't know who the buyer was, but Troll is apparently going to sell him more."

"Where is the deal supposed to take place?" Kaderri asked.

"At the same place as the first deal. But I don't know where that was."

"Was it on the tape?"

"No."

Kaderri cursed. "Shit. Well, that doesn't help us out. Chalk one up for the bad guys." Kaderri turned back towards the door. "I need my scotch."

The dinner plates were cleared and the couple were deciding what to order for dessert. Many times throughout the course of the dinner and conversation, Michele Thorsen caught herself staring into the eyes of Gary Trainor. She found his brown eyes warm and inviting, but with a hint of skepticism and distance. When she got out of her reporter role, she realized that he was a real person with feelings and a heart, and a big one at that. He wasn't a neanderthal as she had previously thought.

Their conversation stayed away from the murder investigations, he made that clear the moment she tried to bring up the subject. Instead of talking business, Michele found it easy to converse like a couple who enjoyed each other's company and was interested in what the other person had to say.

She learned that Gary Trainor grew up in Rochester, New York and was the middle child with an older brother and younger sister. His father was a retired cop from the Rochester Police Department. Gary had decided early in life that he, too, wanted to be a police officer. Slowly, she tore down the tough exterior of the police officer and found a warm, friendly man underneath. She liked what she found and soon began having second thoughts about her plans for the rest of the evening.

Do you have a girlfriend?" she asked. She still found it hard to believe that he turned down her sexual advances on professional reasons.

Trainor looked up from his menu with one eyebrow cocked. "Where did that question come from?"

"I'm curious." Her eyes twinkled. For an unknown reason, she felt like a teenager waiting for the cutest guy in school to ask her out.

"Well," he said, then looked back down at the menu.

Michele watched his eyes become distant and knew she hit a nerve. She waited for him to do or say something. Then she had her recurring frightening thought. He may not have a girlfriend, but a boyfriend. She tried to take the uneasy look off her face. "I'm sorry, Gary, I pried too far."

Trainor looked up from the menu once again. "No reason to be sorry. To answer your question, no I don't have a girlfriend."

Oh, God! It's true, she thought. *He's a faggot!* And she had tried to seduce him, she thought frantically. That explains

205

why he turned her down. She cursed silently. What about the rest of the night? How was she going to be able to get information out of him?

"I was in a serious relationship for four years," he confessed, "but she couldn't handle the fact that I was a police officer and that one day I may not come home."

His confession was like music to her ears. She would be able to continue with her plans. "What was her name, and how serious?"

"Amanda. Amanda Wayne. We were engaged." He admitted. "She broke it off, but wanted to stay in touch and remain friends. I was in love with her and couldn't handle that type of relationship."

Michele was intrigued and felt sorry for the man sitting across from her. "What did you do?" She felt elated that he was unattached and couldn't explain why.

"I moved to Albany and joined the police force here."

Michele smiled. "And now you are a detective, moving up the ladder."

"So it seems. Now, why aren't you married or have a significant other?"

Michele was startled by the question, but knew she shouldn't have been. "I haven't found the right man yet, but I do have my sights set on one." That statement slipped out.

Now it was Trainor who smiled. "And who might that be?" He looked right into Michele's eyes.

After she made her statement, Michele knew she had backed herself into a corner.

For the second time that evening, the waitress arrived at the right moment, saving Michele from answering at least for the moment.

"Are you ready for dessert?" the waitress asked,

"I'll just have a cup of coffee." Trainor said.

"Coffee also, and a piece of cheesecake." Thorsen added.

Once the waitress collected the menus and left, Trainor looked at Michele and commented. "You won't be able to keep your figure if you keep eating that fattening stuff. Just look at my growing tire." He patted his stomach which wasn't that big.

Thorsen smiled and ran her foot up Trainor's leg again. "I plan to work it off."

The glass was empty again. It was the fourth time he drained it and signaled for another.

Ghost was on the phone. A moment later, he hung it up and walked over to Kaderri. "Another one?"

Kaderri nodded. "Yep."

Ghost smiled, took the glass and checked Kaderri's sobriety. "Marc, before I give you anther you have to say: Peter Piper picked a peck of pickled peppers."

With his glazed, bloodshot eyes Kaderri looked at Ghost standing behind the bar with his glass already refilled with the superior scotch. He really wanted the scotch and he knew Ghost was testing him. "There is no need to test me, Ghost."

"Say it."

Kaderri leaned back in the stool, took a breath and with a straight face said, "Peter Piper pickled his pecker and fucked a pepper." Still maintaining a straight face, he took another deep breath. "How many peppers did Peter's pickled pecker fuck?"

Ghost and the people at the bar who overheard the conversation burst out laughing. One man sitting next to Kaderri happened to be taking a sip of his beer when Kaderri said his tongue twister. The man choked and then sprayed his beer across the bar. That caused even more laughter and soon the entire bar had joined in.

When Ghost finally stopped laughing, he handed Kaderri his scotch and there were offers from other patrons to buy him his next few rounds.

"I can't remember the last time I laughed that hard," one patron said. "If you say another one like that, I'll buy you the bottle."

"I'll be a hot pepper if you want to be Peter Piper," a smooth, sensual voice said.

Kaderri looked over at the lady who sat in the recently

vacated stool. Through his slightly blurred vision he noticed that the lady was a pretty redhead and dressed in well-made clothes. "You are a very pretty lady with a dynamite body," he said with an exaggerated sweep of his head, "but by the look of you, you are too much for me to handle."

The lady leaned over and kissed Kaderri on the cheek. The patrons who overheard the conversation couldn't believe what they just heard. The pretty redhead just offered herself to the drunk at the bar and he refused.

Ghost burst out laughing again. "What'll it be?"

"Screwdriver please, Ghost."

"Just can't get away from sex, can you?" Kaderri said to the lady. "I turned you down and you order a screw. . .driver."

"Gotta screw something, so why not a driver?"

Kaderri laughed, took a sip from his scotch and excused himself to go to the bathroom. Many heads in the bar followed him.

Ghost delivered the drink. "Here you are, Louise."

"Thank you." Louise Faith, Kaderri's indispensable secretary said. Her face turned serious. "Bob called me about Sara and I tried to call all day but I couldn't get through. Do you know how both are doing?"

"Marc is doing better and Sara is still in the hospital."

"When is she getting out?"

"I think Monday," Ghost answered. "But he's taking her up to the cabin for a while."

Marc appeared at that moment. "I was going to call you tomorrow," he said through slightly slurred words. "Can you take care of the office for a while?"

Once Marc sat back down in the stool, Louise gave him a big hug. She whispered in his ear as she rested her chin on his broad shoulder, "I'm so sorry to hear about Sara. Is there anything else you want me to do?" She lifted her head and wiped the tears from her cheeks. She cared deeply for Marc and Sara Kaderri. Not just because she was employed by him, she knew they were great people both in and out of work. Something this tragic shouldn't happen to people like the Kaderri's.

"No, Louise, Thanks. Just take care of the office."

"For how long?" she asked. It wasn't that she minded, but she would need to tell his clients some date for his return. She pointed to the cut on Kaderri's head. "Did you get that from the accident?"

"Yeah," Kaderri replied quickly, then he answered the question about the office. "I don't know yet. Probably two or three weeks. I'll call from the cabin and let you know. And only in an emergency are you to call me." He drained his glass and put it out in front of him for a refill.

"Okay, Marc, sounds fine," Louise said. Then she caught Ghost's eye and gave him a concerned look. She had never seen Kaderri this drunk before.

Ghost refilled the glass and placed it in front of Kaderri, along with a basket of rolls to help absorb the huge influx of alcohol he was ingesting into his body. He reached out and grabbed Louise's hand and said in a low voice, "Don't worry about Marc. Bob is on his way over to look after him."

The relief immediately shone on Louise's face. "You guys are really good friends, aren't you?"

"Yeah, we are. Especially him and Bob. They've know each other for a long time."

"Hey!" Marc said a little loud and started giggling. "Peter Piper pickled his pecker—"

Ghost smiled and frantically waved his hand in an effort to keep him quiet. "Keep it down, Marc," Ghost said. Then he stood up straight as if he were at attention and put his nose in the air. "A couple of snobs are here and don't appreciate any 'vulgarity at this fine establishment.'"

Whenever someone cursed in the restaurant, which was rare in the first place, and one of the few patrons of the upper echelons of society were present, they would immediately run to the bartender or manager and complain.

Marc Kaderri was releasing the anger and frustration that had built-up inside him. At that point in time, he didn't care what he said. If it offended somebody so be it.

Before he turned around to see who Ghost was talking

about, he asked him, "Is it the guy with the nose hair that looks like a moustache?"

Ghost smiled and nodded.

Kaderri disliked him. His name was Daniel Sloan. He owned a chain of computer stores and was worth quite a bit of money. Standing at six-feet-two and in decent shape, he was a somewhat good-looking man in his early forties. He has black hair and one eyebrow that covered both eyes. On no particular day, Kaderri stopped by one of the man's stores to talk to him about doing some estate planning for him. Sloan told him flat out in a store full of customers that he didn't need the services of a crook and swindler. It was an embarrassing scene that Kaderri would never forget.

Instead of waiting for the waiter or waitress to take his drink order once he sat down, Daniel Sloan walked up to the bar to order his martinis. The only open spot at the bar was next to Kaderri. "Can you move over so I can get in here?" It was more of an annoyed statement instead of a polite question.

"No," Kaderri said flatly. He was in the mood to have some fun. Very few people knew the kind of fun he could have. And nobody in his present company were one of the few.

Sloan turned in disgust, appalled that someone said no to him.

"How dare you—" Sloan said. He paused when Kaderri glanced at him. "Ah, if it isn't Mr. Crook, oh, pardon, Mr. Kaderri."

It was Ghost who answered first in an obvious attempt to head off something he had no idea of what was coming. "Martinis, right, Mr. Sloan?"

"Better add water to 'em, Ghost, Sloan can't handle the alcohol." Then he added, "His wife gets upset with him after he drinks one. He can't get it up."

Sloan's face turned beet red.

Kaderri saw Sloan's reaction. His lips turned upward in a wicked smile and Kaderri continued. "Wait, Ghost, maybe you'd better give him a double, it may actually make his wife happy," he said meaningfully.

Ghost and Louise looked mortified. They had never seen Marc Kaderri act this way. Louise reached out and touched his arm. "Marc, is this a joke?"

He ignored the question.

"Now listen, Kaderri, who the hell do you think you are, talking to me that way?"

Kaderri stuck his nose up in the air in a perfect imitation of Sloan and said, "Sloan, we don't appreciate any vulgarity at this fine establishment."

Ghost turned away to hide his smile and to make the drinks. A few of the regulars at the bar who knew Sloan's reaction to vulgar vocabulary laughed at Kaderri's mimic.

The one patron who laughed uproariously at Kaderri's twisted Peter Piper ditty laughed loudly again. "Ghost," the man said, "I'm buying him that bottle." He clearly didn't like Sloan either. The man apparently knew his liquor because he threw down a hundred-dollar bill and a fifty to cover the cost of the half-filled bottle of Macallan. Then he added, "There should be enough to get him a cab ride home."

Ghost nodded, acknowledging the sale. "I'll bring your drinks to you, Mr. Sloan," he said in an attempt to diffuse the situation.

Sloan ignored Ghost's offer and kept staring at Kaderri."I want an apology from you, Kaderri."

"Don't like to be embarrassed in front of people do you?"

"I am not embarrassed, Kaderri, but you owe me an apology."

"Honey," Diane Sloan, a tall, pretty brunette said as she came up behind her husband. "What's going on?" Her blue eyes showed concern.

"Nothing important, why don't you sit back down."

Ghost appeared at that moment with the martinis in his hand. "I'll bring your drinks over, Mr. Sloan."

"Go ahead," Sloan said to his wife.

Just as soon as Diane left, Sloan turned back to Kaderri and said boldly, "Now, Kaderri, I believe you were going to apologize."

Kaderri decided his fun was over, he accomplished what he wanted. "Fuck off, Sloan, I'm not apologizing to you. I'm tired of playing games. Go back and sit down with your wife." Kaderri turned away from him and sat straight at the bar. He kept his eye on Sloan in the mirror on the back wall of the bar.

Sloan's face contorted into an angry grimace. He reached out and grabbed Kaderri by the arm and in low menacing voice he said, "Don't you turn your back on me!"

Slowly Kaderri turned to face Sloan. Looking him right in the eye Kaderri ordered, "Take your hand off my arm."

Sloan was too stupid to see the threat in Kaderri's eye's and refused to remove his arm. "You will apologize now!" he said.

"Excuse me," Ghost said from behind the bar. "Marc has gone through a very traumatic experience. I think it would be best if you sat down."

"Oh, poor man," Sloan mocked. "You had too much to drink and couldn't get it up, so somebody else got it on with your wife." Kaderri's warning went unheeded. Sloan tightened his grip on Kaderri's arm.

"Oh, shit," Ghost whispered and left to go to the far end of the bar.

Kaderri leaned over and whispered in Sloan's ear. "You were warned." Without saying another word Kaderri grabbed three of Sloan's fingers, and gave them a quick, powerful, twist ending in a sickening crunch.

Sloan screamed and recoiled in pain. The bar immediately went quiet and searched for the source of the disruption. Gently holding his hand he yelled out, "He broke my fingers, somebody do something." His eyes bore into Kaderri. "I'll have you arrested for that!"

Michele Thorsen and Gary Trainor were walking out the door when a man screamed. "What the. . ..I better see what's going on," Trainor said quickly to Michele. He headed for the bar, she was right behind him.

Trainor spotted a man holding his hand and a pretty brunette standing at his side, which he assumed to be the man's wife. A short, plump, female dressed casually was there, too. "What's going on here? Are you okay?" Trainor asked to the injured man.

"Who are you?" the man asked indignantly.

"Detective Gary Trainor. Who are you?"

"Daniel Sloan," he said.

He turned beet red again and yelled as he pointed to Kaderri. "That man broke my fingers, arrest him!"

Trainor went over to Kaderri, who was sitting nonchalantly on the stool. His face and eyes displayed a different posture, however.

"What's your name? Is what he's saying true?" Trainor asked. He studied the eyes they were cool yet hostile.

"Marcus Kaderri, and no." he answered.

Trainor looked at Kaderri and a bewildered look spread on his face. He looked over at Sloan's disjointed fingers. They looked broken. "Why did you do that to him?"

"He got pissed at me and grabbed my arm," Kaderri said. "I asked him to remove it, but he didn't."

Trainor shook his head in disbelief. "So you broke his fingers?"

"Hi, Marc," Michele said. She waved to Ghost behind the bar.

"Hello again, Miss Thorsen," Kaderri said.

Trainor turned to Michele and asked, "You know him?"

"I met him this morning. He's Marc Kaderri," She answered, emphasizing him name.

The name rang a bell. Trainor searched his memory for the connection, then it clicked. "A Better Body, right? You own it."

"No, my wife does."

"How is your wife, Marc?" Thorsen asked.

Marc tried to ignore the question but knew he couldn't. The incident last night was still something he didn't want to discuss, especially with a reporter. "Getting better."

"That's good to hear," Thorsen admitted. "You're looking

213

much better than before. How's the cut?"

For a moment Trainor was wondering what the hell everybody was talking about. Then he remembered the report. No matter how curious he became about the shooting, that wasn't his case and he had to clear up this thing in front of him. Besides, he knew Michele would know what was going on and would ask her later. "Okay, people, I need to know what happened here."

"That asshole broke my fingers!" Sloan yelled.

"That I know," Trainor admitted. "But why?"

Leslie Jackson, the short, plump, woman and owner of the restaurant answered from behind the bar. "I didn't see anything, I was in the back."

Trainor knew that to be true, he saw her come flying out the kitchen door after Sloan screamed. He turned to the bartender. "What did you see?"

Ghost also answered truthfully. ""I saw Mr. Sloan grab Marc's arm, but after that I didn't see a thing either. I was down at the other end of the bar."

The man who bought Kaderri the bottle spoke. "Detective Trainor, I saw the whole thing."

"Well?" Trainor said impatiently.

"They were bantering with each other and Sloan here grabbed Marc's arm. Marc asked him to move it but he didn't."

"I heard that also," Ghost said.

"Why did he grab your arm." Trainor asked.

Kaderri answered. "He wanted an apology, and he didn't get one."

"That's what this is about? A stupid apology?"

"I guess that's about it." Kaderri said.

"Aren't you going to arrest him?" Sloan reentered the conversation with a vehement temperament.

Trainor turned and faced Sloan, "No, actually, I'm not."

"What? He broke my fingers!"

"I only dislocated them at the knuckles," Kaderri said calmly. "They're not broken. If you want, I'll put them back in."

"Mr. Kaderri, be quiet," Trainor ordered. "Mr. Sloan, if I

understand the situation correctly, you grabbed Mr. Kaderri's arm, yes?"

"Yes," Sloan admitted.

"Now, Mr. Sloan, that could have been interpreted by Mr. Kaderri as a threat to his well-being."

Sloan's wife apparently caught on before her husband.

"C'mon, Dan, let's go to the hospital and get your fingers set."

"Absoluetly not,! I want that fucker in jail."

Trainor looked right at Mrs. Sloan and shook his head in astonishment. Then he turned to Dan Sloan. "It may be a good idea to listen to your wife."

Sloan pointed at Kaderri. "I want something done to him."

"Honey, lets go." She tugged at his arm.

"Let me explain it to you this way," Trainor said. "You physically grabbed Mr. Kaderri first. If he felt threatened in any way, he defended himself against you, the aggressor. That means I would arrest you on assault charges."

"You've got to be kidding!" Sloan said in shock.

Kaderri hadn't changed his facial expression during the whole ordeal. His face was blank and impassive, but his eyes were full of white-hot intensity. "Sloan, you scared me."

"Why you—"

Diane Sloan grabbed her husband forcefully and pushed him toward the door. "Will there be anything else Detective?" she said.

"Not as far as I'm concerned. But, you'll have to check with Mr. Kaderri to see if he wants to file any charges."

Kaderri shook his head.

"You can go," Trainor said to the couple.

After the Sloans left, Kaderri asked Trainor, "Could I really press charges?"

"Yes, you could, but I don't know how well they would stick. On the other hand—"

Michele wrapped her arm around Trainor's waist and whispered in his ear, "I want to work off my cheesecake."

As Trainor and Thorsen left, Bob Wolff entered the restaurant to take care of Marcus Kaderri.

It was a dull Saturday night sitting a lone and waiting for the stupid phone to ring. The only thing that kept Moshe Koretsky from giving up and leaving was the consequences he would have to pay if he didn't answer the phone. He wanted to go out and find Michele Thorsen. He tried calling all day to see if he could set up a late date with her, but her phone went unanswered. He desperately wanted to sleep with her again. He also wanted to pick her brain about the drug murders. He was especially interested to know how close the police were to collaring suspects in Pedro's murder. He knew that nobody saw him pull the trigger, and with Stroehmann dead, there was no link to him. He had made sure of that.

Finally, the secure phone rang. By the time the first ring ended, Koretsky had the phone pressed against his ear. "Yes?" He didn't know who would be calling, but guessed it would be the director.

"Hello, Moshe. How are things going?"

It was the director and Koretsky knew exactly what he was talking about. "Very well, I've re-established contact and the package left on time."

"Very good. What else?"

"I have another deal tomorrow, but I'll pay full price for this one."

"Keep up the good work."

The line went dead. Koretsky hung up the phone and sat there for a moment wondering what he was going to do with the rest of the evening. Deciding that he wanted to be fully awake for the deal tomorrow with the ugly Troll, he poured himself a scotch and water and then turned in for the night.

Saturday, June 13, 1015: p.m.

Gary and Michele were sitting on the sofa in Michele's living room sipping B&B from crystal snifters. Both were relaxed and enjoying each other's company and conversing about many things. She had the candles lit and classical music was playing on the CD player.

This time, Michele kept her shoes on and her feet off the coffee table. But she did let her legs show through the slit in her dress and allowed a spectacular view of her cleavage. She happily noticed the bulge in front of Trainor's pants and teased him a bit more. She wanted Trainor all night and didn't want to scare him off with her sexual desires. She didn't know how he would react if she came out and said, fuck me hard, like she had with Steiner. She wanted to ease Gary into it and control the entire night.

It seemed like it came out of nowhere, but Michele brought up the subject of the murders. "How's the investigation going, Gary?" The final stages of her plan were put into motion.

"What do you mean?' Gary had an erection ever since she whispered in his ear at the restaurant that she wanted to work off the cheesecake.

"Are you any closer to finding the culprit?"

"Perpetrator, we like to say. Off the record?" he asked. When she nodded he continued. "Now, which investigation are you inquiring about?"

It was a legitimate question. He was working on different murder cases.

Michele slowly and seductively crossed her legs to reveal more of her tanned flesh. She didn't make any attempt to straighten out the dress and moved her torso a bit so that more of her cleavage was visible to Trainor's eyes. "Pedro's."

"We don't have any solid leads, but it appears that the murderer spent some time with a prostitute."

"Have you talked to the hooker?" she took a sip from her snifter, leaving a lipstick stain.

"Yes, but I won't give you her name. So don't ask."

"Do you have a name?" Michele asked with a smile.

"Of her customer? That I won't tell you either, but we have an artist's rendering of him."

"How do you know he spent time with a prostitute?" she recrossed her legs to intensify his desires.

"We interviewed members of the crew of the Whispering

217

Sea. It seemed that when they come into port, there is a hooker waiting to fulfill certain desires of the officers. One of the officers gave the name and address of the prostitute to Pedro. Only, he didn't make it there. When we searched his body, the address was missing."

Michele reached over to Trainor and gently squeezed his groin. "Those officers want to put this to use."

Trainor was caught unaware and had no idea how to respond.

The CD ended. Michele placed her snifter on the coaster and rose to put on another CD. She knew she had a remarkable shape, especially from behind. The dress she wore flattered her figure and was as tight as a glove. There weren't any telltale panty lines and the matching pumps made the muscles in her calves more pronounced. Her hips swayed seductively as she slowly and deliberately walked across the living room to where the stereo was located in the entertainment center. The candles in the room emanated just enough light to highlight her moves, making her more seductive, and showed off her beautiful long, blonde hair.

"Anybody in particular you want to hear?" she asked once she reached the stereo. She stood with most of her weight on her right leg, her left leg was bent at the knee, lifting her heel off the ground. Her right arm rested on top of the entertainment center turning her torso back in the direction of Trainor. Her pose gave Trainor a perfect view of her best parts. The blonde hair framing the pretty face danced in the flickering candlelight. She thrust her large, firm breasts and tight, round buttocks in opposite directions, each taking on their own importance. Her legs flowing out from under her dress were perfect.

Trainor was speechless. She knew he was awed by the sight in front of him and he didn't fully comprehend her question. "Uh?"

"I like Rimsky-Korsakoff, you know, *Flight of the Bumblebee.*" She turned, bent over at the waist, and stuck her buttocks right at him. She took a few moments longer than was necessary, knowing he would be staring. Finally she found the CD she wanted and put it in the machine. She walked as seductively back to Trainor as she had walked away.

Soon, the music filled the room.

Michele stopped in front of the glass coffee table, her legs spread shoulder width apart. Her blue eyes were filled with passion and stared right into Trainor's. She unclasped the button on her hip, slowly pulling the coatdress open. She no longer had second thoughts about her plan. She was going full steam ahead.

Michele smiled. She watched his mouth drop while she pulled open her dress. Her breasts were gently cradled in a purple satin and lace bra. His eyes moved downward as she let the dress fall off her shoulders. The small material of the purple thong was the only discerning object that separated the smooth juncture of her waist and hips. The flickering candlelight glowed around her body, making her appear like an angel from heaven.

Trainor licked his dry lips and swallowed hard. "By the look on your face you approve of what you see," she said. With one hand, she reached for the clasp in front of her bra and with two fingers she unsnapped it. Her breasts were capped with pink, erect nipples. Before he could answer, she shed her bra, stepped around the table, and straddled Trainor's waist. She danced one of her erect nipples in front of his face, and when he eagerly took one into his mouth she pulled his head closer to her.

She had to do this part very carefully. She didn't want to scare him off with her newly fueled sexual appetite before she got all the information out of him. Her desires were calling out to get rough, but it wasn't time for that. For this round, as much as she hated it, she would have to relinquish much of her control and play to his desires.

Trainor was expertly sucking gently on her nipple, alternating between hard and soft strokes with his tongue. She wanted him to bite it. She pushed a little. "Oh, Gary, that feels good. Suck a little harder." With her free hand, she reached underneath her groin and unzipped his pants.

Trainor in turn put his hands on her tight buttocks and began squeezing and feeling their smoothness. He slid his hand forward over her hip and placed his hand inside the small patch of material that covered her groin. Her pubic hair was almost as soft as her skin. He probed the folds of her skin and then inserted a finger in her.

Michele moaned at the feel of his finger, but she wanted it hard. She could tell he was an expert lover. He was slow, gentle, deliberate, and took his time. But, she didn't like it like that. Steiner had awoken a hunger in her that had to be satisfied, and a gentle deliberate lover wouldn't do. She freed his erection and was exhilarated at his size. He was much bigger than Steiner. "Another one, Gary. Put another finger in me." She started to move her hips, driving his fingers deeper into her flesh.

His desires, she had to remember. Round two she would take control. Control as in telling him what to do, not letting him explore for her hot spots. As he complied with her wishes to insert another finger, she whispered in his ear. "What would you like to do?"

Trainor disconnected his mouth from her nipples and removed his hand from inside her. "Lay back on the couch." She moved off him and did what he asked. Trainor stood and removed his pants, his huge erection pointing. "You are truly beautiful, Michele," he said. He bent over and gave her a deep passionate kiss.

Michele spread her legs, eager for him to enter her. She pulled the thong to one side and with her free hand guided him in. He put his cock in and stretched her like she'd never been filled before. He was big and she loved it. Slowly he began moving. He would pull all the way out and then insert himself back into her tightness and slowly push all the way in.

Michele wanted it deeper and harder, but said nothing. She had to control herself. Most women would love to have a man like Gary Trainor. He took pleasure in a beautiful woman and gave her pleasure back. But Michele was no longer interested in that type of sex. She no longer wanted to make love, she wanted it rough. Though she didn't tell him to go harder, she could make him go deeper, and hope that he would go faster and harder in the process. She pulled her knees back to her shoulders, opening herself more to him, and by doing so, gave him more room to maneuver and limited her movements. To her delight, he picked up the pace and drove himself into her.

"C'mon, Gary, that's it. Oh, God!" She reached down and grabbed his hips pulling him harder and faster into her. Her long manicured nails dug deep into his skin.

"You like it like this?" he asked between thrusts.

"Yes, more!" she cried. Her moans drowned out the music.

Michele could feel him tighten up. "C'mon, Gary," I'm ready."

Trainor could hold back no longer, grunted, and came with a fury. He kept thrusting and Michele kept yelling in delight.

She was now in total control of Gary Trainor, and for the rest of the night he willingly complied with her wishes. They had sex three more times, and Michele got everything she wanted-rough, hard sex and Gary Trainor to reveal more information to run her story.

CHAPTER FOURTEEN

Sunday, June 14, 5:30 a.m.

There were a few exceptions but no matter what happened the previous night, Marc Kaderri awoke at his usual time without the aid of an alarm clock. This morning, he had a slight headache but that didn't deter him from his morning run. Swinging his legs over the side of the bed, he shook the cobwebs from his head and quickly dressed into his shorts and running shoes. Once downstairs, he set the timer on the coffee machine to finish brewing when he finished his run and began his fifteen-minute stretch on the thick padded carpet in his living room.

As he stretched his leg muscles out, he considered how lucky he was that he hadn't wound up in jail for the stunt he had pulled the previous night. Granted, Sloan deserved something, but dislocating his fingers was a little extreme.

Not bothering to lock his front door, Kaderri stepped out into the bright sunshine that set his dew-capped lawn a blaze. The fresh-air rushed through his nostrils and into his lungs with each deep steady inhale. Like it did every morning, the sensation made him feel alive. It was the start of a new day, a new beginning in a timeless world. After a couple of deep knee bends, he began his run by jogging down his long driveway.

Kaderri's five-mile road run coursed through tree covered roads that filtered out most of the sunlight causing patches of sunlight and shade dotting the pavement. Though the route that he traveled was all paved roads, it was rarely used by motorists. The lack of vehicles to watch out for enabled him to concentrate on the two deeds he had to do. First and foremost on his mind, was Sara. After her release from the hospital tomorrow, Monday, he was taking her up to the cabin for an extended period of time. There, they would work through her ordeal and determine if she would need professional help. Secondly, not today though, he was going to find Moshe Koretsky and kill him.

His plans for the day were to go to the hospital and spend the day with Sara. He hoped that he would be able to have a late breakfast with her. Prior to the hospital, though, he had to meet with Ghost to pick up the sniper rifle he asked him to get.

Sunday, June 14, 7:25 a.m.

"Are you going to explain to me how you know Marc Kaderri?" Trainor asked from the queen-sized bed in Michele's bedroom. The sunlight glowed around the edges of the window shades, casting enough light into the room so that a lamp wasn't necessary. He felt a little woozy from all the alcohol he had drank, though it appeared that Michele was unaffected by the amount she had. He didn't know that while he was drinking the B&B she was drinking iced tea.

She looked over at him and sat up. She allowed the sheets to fall off and expose her breasts, purposely shaking them. "I covered the story of the accident and fight he had with Greg Sander. I interviewed him at the hospital the following morning."

"What was your impression of him?" he asked and then sat

223

up, too. He couldn't help but notice her breasts, and her long blonde hair that fell over her shoulders. Even without makeup she was a beautiful woman.

She brushed her hair behind her ear before she answered. "He's very impressive. Quiet, but gentle and menacing at the same time. He's an intriguing individual."

"Why did you ask about his wife?" Trainor asked. He wanted to know who and how well connected both Kaderri and Thorsen were. If they were at all to anybody.

"She was raped by Greg Sander. Apparently, Marc walked in on Sander raping his wife. He chased him up and down 787 until they got into an accident. After the accident, Kaderri beat Sander up and was going to kill him. Then, the cops arrived and stopped the whole spectacle. While two Emergency Medical Technicians were attending Sander, he came to and beat them up. Then he beat up a couple of cops until they shot him."

"Interesting," was all Trainor could say. He thought about his ex-fiance' and what he would do if the same thing had happened to her while they were still together. Being a police officer, he knew the judicial thing to do was arrest the perpetrator. But he wasn't so sure if he'd be able to arrest the man. He may have done exactly what Kaderri did, or worse. He would have shot him.

Under the sheet, Michele slid her hand across Trainor's thigh. Her soft fingers stroked him until be became fully erect. With a twinkle in her eye and a sly smile, she said, "I think this is interesting."

With her free hand she pulled the sheet off Trainor and bent her head over his erection, teasing the tip of the cock with her tongue. The saliva and warm breath sent shivers throughout his body and then suddenly she took his entire length into her mouth.

"Would you like a cup of coffee?" Michele asked. She lifted the sheets off and climbed out of bed. She stood at the edge of the bed, giving Trainor another view of her naked body.

When Trainor didn't answer, she smiled and added, "I'll bring it up. I set the timer last night so it's already brewed." Not bothering to put on a robe or cover-up, she left the bedroom.

She brought the coffee, cups, and condiments up on a serving tray that she placed on the nightstand. Trainor still hadn't said anything. He was staring open mouthed at her. After seeing the look on his face and the information he spilled last night, she knew she had him.

She poured the two cups and handed one to Trainor, who normally took it with cream and sugar, took it black this morning to help his hangover. She climbed back into bed and took a sip out of her cup.

"So, Gary, you never answered my question. Why did you decide to give me the true information on the murders? I think it's about time you told me. Wouldn't you agree?"

Trainor furrowed his brow and nodded. "The story you did some time ago when one of the police officers shot and killed someone, I can't remember the guy's name. It was in self-defense and everyone in the press but you had determined on their own that the officer was a liar and a racist. Everyone said he'd shot the man because he was Asian."

Michele remembered the story well. She was the only reporter who researched the facts and as it turned out, the shooting was determined to be self-defense. As for the racist remark, the officer himself was married to a successful Korean businesswoman. No reporter took the few moments to research the officer's family and his work record, except Michele Thorsen. "I remember, but what has that got to do with me?"

"From that moment, I knew that you were a reporter that was honestly objective and would give both sides of the story a fair shake. And more importantly, you would tell the truth, not push some bullshit political correctness issue."

She immediately felt a slight twinge of guilt for what she had done and was planning to do. In so many words, Detective Trainor admitted that he could trust her. She sat silently for a few moments and let what he said sink in. The more she thought about it, the more she felt she had to follow through with her plan. The story had to come first.

Michele opened the drawer of her nightstand and took out a cassette tape, holding it up like a prize.

"What's that?" he asked and took a sip of his coffee.

"I think you should hear it. It's about the murders at the Preserve."

Trainor shot out of bed, spilling the black coffee across the new carpeting. "What?"

Michele rose out of bed, placing her coffee cup back on the tray. She walked over to the dresser where a stereo shelf system was located. She loaded the cassette and turned it on. "You're going to like this. I think it will help your case." Her confidence in her plan was as high as it could be.

Trainor didn't say a word. He felt a set up in the works and tried to keep an open mind. But the door was closing quick.

A crackle and a hiss signaled the beginning of the tape.

". . .clear."

"Let's reach. . .touch. . .one."

Michele reached over and stopped the tape.

"What the hell did you do that for?" Trainor asked.

"The entire tape is like that. The words are fragmented and in whispers, but you can piece together what is going on."

"Fine. Can you play the tape?" The anger was building.

She pressed play again and the hushed voices came back on. "Driver's first."

"Roger."

There was silence for a moment than a light metallic click. "Good shot."

"Second shot." There was another metallic click.

"Good. . .." Another click.

"Shit."

". . .right shoulder. He's. . .up."

"I got him." This time there was a slightly different metallic click followed by some noises that couldn't be distinguished.

"He's. . .away." A string of metallic clicks followed. "Got. . .in. . .leg." There was a silence and one of the voices came back on. "Need a spotter?" The voice was a little louder this time.

"No." There was silence for a few moments and then another indistinguishable sound. "We're pulling out."

"Roger. . .clear."

The tape ended.

Trainor had worked himself into a rage. He pulled the tape out of the cassette player and glanced at the clock. The tape had run for about three minutes. "How long have you had this?" His face was inches away from Michelee's.

"I got it the other day, Wednesday afternoon I believe."

"How?" he demanded. He narrowed his eyes into slits and drew his lips tight across his teeth.

Michele stayed silent for a moment, her eyes shifting nervously. "Some guy came into the office and said he had information that he thought I would be interested in. As it turned out, I was."

"Shit," he said. He was both angry and excited at the same time. Excited that he finally had a solid lead in the case, but extremely pissed at Michele for pulling this stunt. "What's his name, Michele, and where can I find him?"

Michele hesitated, obviously not wanting to give the answer.

"I'm waiting," he growled.

"I can't reveal my sources, Gary, you know that. Can't you be happy with the information. It's credible."

Trainor felt his face flush and he balled his fists to keep them from trembling. "Don't you pull that bullshit with me!" He moved closer to her, putting his nose right against hers. "You give me his name and address now. Or I'll haul your ass in for withholding information on a murder case, interfering in a murder investigation, aiding and abetting, and whatever else I can think of!"

"Doesn't last night count for anything?" She was looking for some sort of slack or break.

"No!" Absolutely not!" Trainor now knew he'd been had. The whole night had been a farce.

Michele was clearly shaken by the ferocity of his demand.

"His name is Richard Armstrong," Michelee admitted. "But, I don't know his address off the top of my head. It's back at the office."

Trainor searched for his clothes and found them draped over the chair at the vanity. He walked over to them and quickly got dressed. "Leave the address on my voice mail. He then turned and walked out the door, leaving Michelee with her blue eyes wide with shock. "You can get your car later at the station," he informed her from the front door.

Sunday, June 14, 7:35 a.m.

"Hey man, it's been cool doing business. We gotta do it again sometime." Troll held up his clenched fists to the newly established relationship with a fellow drug dealer.

Koretsky looked at Troll and wondered if he really knew what an asshole he was. Another deal went off as planned and Moshe Koretsky had handed over ten thousand dollars for the cocaine that would shortly ship out to New York City. The people down there would turn one hell of a profit for the Mossad by way of a sayan courier. This time, Troll wasn't as uptight as he was the first time and he didn't try any stupid stunts that would get him killed. Feeling smug and secure, Koretsky decided to stop at a diner on South Pearl Street, just a few blocks from the intersection where he had just completed his deal. He parked his car in a spot that had opened up in front of the diner and casually walked into the restaurant, taking a booth against the wall and sat facing the door. A pretty waitress appeared with a pot of coffee, a menu, and a big smile. "Would you like some coffee?" she asked.

"Yes, please, but I don't need a menu."

The waitress's smile faded, clearly trying to keep her professional appearance on, she poured the coffee into the cup she had turned over. "Cream?" she asked and held up the steel decanter.

"Please, and could you leave the pot?" he asked.

She shook the pot. "It's half full, or half empty depending on your outlook Would you like me to bring a full one?"

"Yes, and I'd like an order of steak and eggs."

"How would you like your eggs and steak?" The smile came back, but most of it was kept hid behind her professional face.

"Over easy, the steak medium, and a plate of white toast."

"Hungry this morning?"

"As a matter of fact, yes. May I have your phone number for dessert?" She seemed to be the type of waitress he could joke with.

"You are supposed to ask for that when I hand you the bill, not before you eat. If I refuse to give you my number, you may decide that you don't want to eat here and I lose my chance of getting a tip."

"Well put."

After she delivered the breakfast, he started thinking about all the people that Miller had lost. It was apparent that someone was informing the killer on the location of the deals. Miller didn't have a right hand man and his operation wasn't that big to create a power struggle. There was a great possibility that an informant from one of the local pushers had penetrated his intelligence, if he had any. If that was the case, he wondered why no one had taken a shot at him. Throughout his breakfast, he ran through scenarios to try and come up with the answer.

Sunday, June 14, 8:05 a.m.

The run and long hot shower that followed did wonders for Marc Kaderri. He felt revitalized. He was ready for his next and most dangerous challenge. Find and kill Moshe Koretsky.

His thoughts were occupied during the drive to Ghost's house. When he pulled up the driveway and into the garage, he noticed Bob Wolff's Mercedes was parked on the street in front of the house. He searched his memory for any reason why Wolff should be there at that time.

Kaderri walked up the stone walkway and was about to knock on the door when it was pulled open. "Hey, Marc!" Ghost said with a smile. "It's nice to know you're still alive,

229

and ten minutes early for your appointment."

"Shut up." Kaderri smiled and poked Ghost in the stomach with his finger, pushing him back so he could walk through the door.

"Jesus, it's alive!," Wolff said stepping from the kitchen with a steaming mug of coffee in his hand. "After last night, I was beginning to wonder if you would ever wake up."

Kaderri turned to face Wolff with a sheepish grin. "You shut up, too. And thanks, guys."

"Hey, what are friends for?" Ghost said. "Just one more time, Marc, can you say your Peter Piper—"

"No!"

The three men laughed heartily.

"Okay, guys, let's get on with it. I have to go to the hospital," Kaderri said. "Ghost, were is my rifle?"

"I'll get it. It's locked away."

As Ghost left to retrieve the rifle, Kaderri turned to Wolff and cocked an eyebrow. "Bob, what brings you down here?"

"Besides the fact that you asked me to come down here last night, I have a new toy for you."

"I asked you to come down last night?" Kaderri couldn't remember that. He shrugged. "What kind of new toy do you have for me?"

Wolff left for the kitchen with Kaderri right behind. Kaderri took a seat at the table while Wolff went to the counter and retrieved a plain, brown box roughly the size of a shoe box. With his coffee mug still in one hand he sat down across from Kaderri, opened the box, removed the foam protection and pulled out a dull black box.

"What the hell is that?" Kaderri asked as Wolff held it up.

Wolff smiled. "This, my friend, is a telescopic sight that mounts on your weapon." It was the size of a hand-held video camera.

"Oh, yeah? It looks like a box. Where is the eyepiece? Or is this one of your new fangled inventions and—"

Wolff kept on grinning. "It's one of my new inventions, and yes, it does work." He held the box and slid down two little doors. One in the front and one in the back. "Here is your eyepiece and this is the front. Underneath is the clasp to attach it to the weapon. Up top," he pointed to the mesh screen, "is where the power source is."

Kaderri looked the scope over. "It's solar?"

"Yes, and it can store the energy for up to six hours. That would come in useful at dusk and early evening. It also gathers the starlight for night vision and has a battery backup for those real shitty days."

"Okay, in a nutshell, what does it do?"

"Basically, it's a miniaturized version of the fire control computers on a M1 tank."

Kaderri was speechless. How Wolff could make such a complicated piece of equipment down to a fraction of this size and to fit on a rifle was remarkable. "It can do all that?" Kaderri referred to the deadly accurate fire control system that the M1 Abrams main battle tank used to assure a first hit when its main gun was engaged. The system was able to determine the distance of its target, and the speed that is was travelling. And it did it in all types of weather conditions, in a blink of an eye. Also, it could be done while the tank was travelling over forty miles an hour.

"Within reason, Marc. There aren't any stabilizers for your rifle like the main gun on the tank. You still have to control that."

At that moment Ghost came into the kitchen holding a plastic rifle case. "Here's your request." He placed it on the table in front of Kaderri. Then he saw the scope in Wolff's hands. "Another gadget, Doc?"

"Thanks, Ghost." Kaderri said, popping the two clips and opening the case. He stared at the rifle lying on the gray foam rubber.

"Yes," Wolff rolled his eyes at Ghost and smiled. "Now shut up." He turned back to Kaderri. "Marc, the scope's computer can track wind velocity and notify you of where and how much you have to adjust the rifle to ensure a hit. It works like a heads up display on a fighter. There are two crosshairs.

One that paints and locks on the target, that one is white. The yellow tracks wind and adjusts for elevation."

"How do I get the scope to tell me where to move the rifle?" asked Kaderri.

"After you mount it on the rifle, I'll show you how it works. The scope also has thermal imagery." He pulled down a little arm on the left side of the scope. "This arm here has your controls on it. There are three vertical buttons. Obviously, they are for different purposes. The top button is for night vision, the middle button is for thermal, and the bottom one is for wind and elevation adjustment. When the scope is mounted, this piece comes down and fits near the grip of the rifle. You operate it with your thumb. Now, on the other side, there is another arm that extends." He extended that arm. "The three buttons, again they are vertical, sit in front of the trigger guard. The top button is your on/off button. The middle button is your laser range finder and the bottom button is to lock on the target."

"Let me see that." Kaderri stuck his hand out and reached for the scope. He looked it over and was unimpressed by its appearance but very impressed by its capabilities. "What if I don't want to use all the wizardry?"

"Then it works like a regular scope. Up on the top is the wheel to adjust your magnification. It's fifteen power. That, you have to do manually if the power is off. If the power is on, it works automatically like a video camera, only a hell of a lot faster."

Kaderri took the scope and mounted it on the sleek rifle and walked through the sliding glass doors that opened on to the deck. Ghost's house was by no means secluded but he did have a ring of trees that made it difficult for anyone to see who or what was on the deck. Being cautious anyway, Kaderri pulled over a chair and sat in the doorway, keeping the rifle below the top of the deck's wooden spindle fence. Turning on the power, he sighted the scope on a bird sitting on a tree branch forty feet away. He pressed the range finder and an invisible laser shot out and marked the target. The number thirty-eight appeared in the bottom left hand corner of the screen, indicating how many feet it was to the target. He then pressed the bottom button in front of the trigger guard and the white crosshairs locked on the unsuspecting bird.

A slight summer breeze blew, tickling Kaderri's face. He took the opportunity to test the wind button. He pressed the button and the yellow crosshairs appeared instantaneously, almost super imposing itself over the white crosshairs but it was just enough off-center to allow for the wind adjustment. With an imperceptible touch, he moved the rifle to the left until the yellow and white crosshairs were super imposed. If he pulled the trigger now, he would get a hit in the center of the bird. A yellow number five appeared in the lower left hand corner under the distance number indicating the speed of the wind in miles per hour.

Kaderri took a few more minutes to operate the scope and was satisfied with what he had in his hands. He rose out of the chair and turned to Wolff. "Nice gadget."

"Why thank you, Mr. Kaderri. I thought you would like it. Now all that has to be done is zero it. You do that just like any other scope. Obviously, you only need all the bells and whistles on a target that's hard to find or in real shitty weather conditions."

Kaderri looked at his watch. It was time to go. "Gentlemen, it's been a pleasure. I'm going to the hospital to be with Sara."

"Give her our best, would you," Wolff said. "I'll swing by later before you head north."

"I may not have time," Ghost added. "I have some things to do."

Kaderri walked through the kitchen door and into the garage where his Jeep was parked. He loaded the rifle and scope in the back and covered them with a blanket. He looked both men in the eye and thanked them for their help.

Sunday, June 14, 8:45 a.m.

"That was good, Koretsky admitted as the waitress cleared the table.

"I'm glad you enjoyed it," she said with a smile.

"Now, may I have your phone number?" Koretsky started the game again.

"That all depends on what you want it for?" She was having fun also.

Koretsky motioned for her to lean down so he could speak softly to her. "I want to take you to bed."

She smiled and whispered in his ear. "Only on the condition that we tape record the sounds of our lovemaking. Then I could use it to blackmail you at a later date." That statement switched on a light bulb in Koretsky's brain. "You have a deal."

The waitress wrote out the bill and placed it face down on the table and then walked away picking up a tray full of dishes. Koretsky didn't bother to look at the bill and fished a fifty-dollar bill out of his pocket and threw it on the table. He never looked to see if he got her phone number, but he never expected to.

He walked out of the restaurant to the car that he's parked in front. He wanted to get back to the safe house on Morris Street to get some equipment and then head back to Miller's officer on State Street. He headed north on Pearl Street being cautious and watched for a tail. He made turns throughout the city and retraced some of his route to see if he was being followed. He wasn't. During one of his turns, he was forced by a car in the wrong lane to make a wrong turn and found himself in front of Albany Medical Center on New Scotland Avenue. He needed to turn around and head west instead of east, so he drove into the parking lot to make his turn.

As he pulled in, his gaze followed a man emerging from the steps that ascended from a side street. The man walked across the path of the car. He pressed hard on the break to avoid hitting the idiot that didn't look where he was going. He pulled the car along side the man and pressed the power button to lower the window. "Hey, pal," Koretsky said sarcastically, "watch where you're going!"

The man spoke as he turned to face Koretsky. "Pedestrians have the right of way, pal." Then the man turned and leaned toward the open driver's window.

At that moment both men looked into each others eyes and time seemed to stand still.

The other man was the first to react. His face drew tight and this soft steel-blue eyes immediately turned coal black. "Motherfucker!" he hissed through clenched teeth and punched Koretsky in the left eye.

The encounter came as a complete surprise for Koretsky, and the extra half second he took to recognize the man standing next to the window cost him. Koretsky turned just in time so he didn't catch the full punch square in the nose and caught it in the left eye, which immediately began to swell. The punch knocked him over so he lay across the front seats. He knew he had to get out of there and quick. Short of pulling out his gun, he was in no position to take on the man outside his car.

The driver's side door was suddenly pulled open and the crazy man's strong hands grabbed his shirt collar. The man hissed, "I promised if I ever saw you again, Koretsky, I'd kill you!" The man tried to pull Koretsky up off the seat, but the seat belt he was wearing prevented him from being pulled from the car.

Koretsky had to think fast and react to get out of the deadly situation he was in. His foot was still on the break and the car was in gear, he never put it in park, so he instinctively shoved the man in the stomach and slammed on the gas.

The force of the car pulling away tore the grip the man had on Koretsky's collar, causing him to jump away to prevent from getting ran over. Koretsky watch in his rear view mirror as the man turned to give chase, but another car coming up the drive cut him off.

Moshe Koretsky raced down the street as fast as traffic would allow him to go. He made turns at just about every intersection, doubling back to see if he was being followed by that crazy man. Koretsky wasn't thinking, he was going on instinct and training. His heart was racing and he felt an anxiety that he hadn't felt in a long time. After driving ten minutes and deciding it was safe, he pulled the car off the road and into the parking lot. He parked the car between the yellow lines and left the engine running. He wiped the sweat off his forehead in surprise. His shirt was soaked through as if he walked through a shower and for a moment he thought he had pissed in his pants.

Taking a few deep breaths to calm his nerves, he searched his memory for the face that had introduced itself into his open window. Those eyes, black and dreadful, were full of anger and death. They were eyes that he knew he'd seen before, but he couldn't place them. And then, when the man called out his name, his real name, that unnerved him even more. Koretsky's world had just changed. He reached up and with his fingers gingerly felt the swelling of his left eye.

Marcus Kaderri watched in anger as Koretsky's Taurus pulled into traffic and disappeared among the other cars. He momentarily thought about jumping into his Jeep and giving chase, but decided against it. He wouldn't be able to catch up to Koretsky, who would now be on guard and be hard pressed to find. And more importantly, he wouldn't leave Sara again like he had when he chased down Greg Sander.

The game had changed. Kaderri knew that Koretsky would now seek him out. He would wait for Koretsky to come to him. Now Kaderri had to keep his guard up, for his life was not now the only one in danger. Everyone who he had contact with was also in danger. He knew Koretsky wouldn't think twice about shooting anyone who got in his way.

Marc walked into Sara's private hospital room as if nothing happened, but the intensity of his eyes revealed a face of anger and concern. Sara was watching one of the Sunday morning news programs when Marc walked over and gave her a kiss. "Hey, babe, how are you?" he asked happily.

She smiled. "I can't wait 'til I get out of here." Then her face changed when she looked at her husband. "Something's wrong, what is it?" She was one of the few people that could read Kaderri.

He knew that he couldn't lie to her by telling her nothing

was wrong. She had always been able to read his face, if he tried lying now, he knew she would catch him. "Business, that's all," he answered. It wasn't a lie, but it wasn't about the insurance business either. "It's nothing to worry about." He quickly changed the subject, "how did you sleep last night?" He was concerned because she had said she'd had a few nightmares reliving the rape. He pulled up the chair that was in the room and sat down next to the bed and gently held Sara's hand.

"Soundly," she answered. "It was great."

"No nightmares?"

"No, honey, none. I just wish I could leave the hospital today instead of tomorrow. I long to sleep in my own bed in the arms of my husband." She flashed him a smile.

"Did you talk to the doctor about leaving today?" he asked.

"Not yet. The doctor hasn't examined me this morning. I just finished my breakfast, which wasn't that appealing."

Kaderri studied the beautiful face of his wife. Then he asked, "How's the face? Does it still hurt? The bruise has almost disappeared."

"It feels fine. The dentist came in yesterday, no last night, and checked on my tooth. He said its healing nicely and in a couple of days it'll be back to normal."

"That's good to hear, but you have to eat soft foods for how much longer?"

"Two days! I'm tired of the yogurt and the scrambled eggs were terrible. I'm dying for something with substance."

Kaderri smiled. He knew his wife's appetite could be pretty hearty, even though she ate a lot of healthy food. So, the food she had been eating the past twenty-four hours didn't do much for her. "Sara, you've been here for about thirty-five hours and most of the time you have been asleep. How much food could you have missed?"

"I want something that tastes good!" she said emphatically.

It was apparent that she was close to normal again. Her sense of humor was back and that was encouraging. "Speaking of tasting good," he wanted to rub it in, "I had a Porterhouse last night."

"Shut up." She smacked his arm and cocked her head. "And how much scotch to wash it down?"

"Uh,"

"I thought so. Who brought you home?"

"Bob did. And Ghost drove the Porsche back."

Sara laughed. "Ghost was probably in his glory. He's been wanting to drive that car since we bought it."

Just then, there was a knock at the door and in walked the doctor. "Good morning, Sara." Then she looked at Marc sitting in the chair next to the bed holding Sara's hand. "And good morning to you, too, Marc."

"Hi, Doc."

"You're not going to berate me again, are you?" The doctor smiled, but she seemed serious.

Marc had given this doctor a tongue lashing like he had to the emergency room doctor who first examined Sara. But, this doctor didn't deserve it. She was thorough and caring. And had sympathy for rape victims. She didn't just look at them as patients, she looked at them as violated human beings. "Not unless it's warranted," he said with a smiled. But he, too, meant it.

The doctor smiled awkwardly and turned her attention to Sara. "Okay, Sara, let's take a look at you."

Marc stood, "I'll wait outside the door." He bent down and kissed Sara lightly on the lips.

"You don't have to go," Sara said. "You've seen everything she's going to check out."

Both the doctor and Marc blushed at her remark. "I'll go outside."

Sunday, June 14, 9:30 a.m.

Gary Trainor replayed the tape of the murders in the car's tape deck on the way home from Michele's house. He could feel the anger and excitement building as he drove. Once he got into his house, he ran for the bathroom to shower and cooled himself down. As the powerful course streams of water pelted his body, he contemplated what he should do with that no good self-serving woman.

Stepping out of the shower and toweling himself off, he quickly combed his hair and brushed his teeth. Deciding not to shave, he reached for the telephone on the nightstand and dialed a number from memory.

"Hello?" the voice on the other end was groggy.

"Keith, I've got some stuff you got to hear." He said excitedly into the phone.

"Whoa! Slow down. What are you talking about?"

"About the murders in the Preserve! Get your ass out of bed, I'm coming over." He hung up before Bernard had a chance to say no.

Feeling a surge of adrenaline, Trainor threw on a pair of jeans and a golf shirt, ran downstairs to the kitchen and scooped up all the files on the murders on his way out the door. Trainor had a huge break in the case and he felt like he was floating on air.

The distance to Bernard's house wasn't far, but Trainor made record time anyway. He braked his Mustang to a screeching halt next to the curb in front of Bernard's house. He ran up the overgrown front lawn to the porch and rang the doorbell.

Keith Bernard, dressed in boxer shorts, opened the door as soon as the bell went off. "Jesus Christ, Gary, did you fly down here?" He moved to one side to let Trainor pass. "Now, what's got you worked up?"

Trainor held up the cassette. "This! This has the conversation of the murderers in the act at the Preserve."

"Are you sure?"

"Fucking A!"

Bernard grabbed the tape out of Trainor hand and led him to the family room where the stereo shelf system was located. He inserted the tape and pressed play. Three minutes later the tape was over. "Holy shit," Bernard said, rubbing his face wearily. He rested his chin in his hand and frowned.

"All we have to do is identify the voices and we got 'em!" Trainor exclaimed.

"Slow down, Gary. First of all, where did you get the tape? And second, how are we going to identify the voices?"

"I got it from Thorsen and I don't know yet how we can identify the voices, except for sending them to the FBI to see if they have a match on file."

That gave Bernard some time to think. He now had to place a call to McKnight. "Stay here." He bounded up the stairs to his bedroom and quickly got dressed. "Come on, Gary," he said when he came back downstairs. "Let's go."

"Go? Where?" He figured he's go over the files with Bernard at his house.

"The station."

Marc was getting fidgety standing outside the door in the hospital corridor. He kept looking down at his watch to make sure the time was right. He expected a five-minute exam at the most, but five minutes had expired fifteen minutes ago. Finally, the door opened and the doctor came out wearing a smile. "That's a remarkable woman you married," she said. "You can go in now."

"Hold on, Doc," he said as the door closed behind her.

"Yes?"

"What took so long? Is everything okay?"

"Physically she's almost one-hundred percent. The swelling in her face has subsided and the bruise should be gone in a few days. Her tooth is healing nicely and the stitches can come out in another six days. Bring her back Saturday and we'll remove them".

"Is there any infection of any kind?" Kaderri said sternly, enough to get the meaning across.

The doctor apparently knew what he was asking because she said, "The cut in her mouth is free and clear, and we had the rapist tested for numerous diseases. He came up clean except for large amounts of cocaine in his blood. The autopsy revealed that he had no needle tracks on his body so all the drugs that he ingested were taken orally or through the nose. He wasn't infected with HIV or any other sexually transmitted disease—or any other ailment for that matter."

Kaderri silently thanked God at the good news, but knew there was more. He figured it wasn't physical. "What else?"

In a professional, though caring voice, the doctor said, "It's going to take her a while to recover mentally. How long is anybody's guess. That's where you come in. She is going to go through some trying times and all the support you can give her will be a tremendous help. She is going to need you." She took a breath and continued. "But after the lecture you gave me, I think, you could provide most of the support that Sara needs."

"Thank you," Kaderri said and warmly shook the doctor's hand. He pushed open the solid pine door and walked in. Sara was bending over the bed, packing the small overnight bag that he had brought her the day before. She was dressed in a gray and pink jogging outfit and running sneakers, with her hair tied in a ponytail. "Whoa!" he said, surprised at the sight before him.

Sara turned, ran to him, and threw her arms around his neck. "I can go home!"

A warm feeling wrapped itself like a blanket around his body. Marc wrapped his arms around her thin waist and looked down into her beautiful, almond-shaped, brown eyes. She looked up into his eyes and they gave each other a soft passionate kiss. He tightened his grip around her waist with his right hand and quickly and effortlessly placed his other hand behind her knees and scooped her off the floor.

Finally, their lips parted and a tear clung to Kaderri's eye. Sara reached up and gently wiped it away with her thumb.

"Marcus Kaderri, I love you more than anything in this world. But, you are not going to carry me out of here!"

When they left the hospital, the door shut on a dark and horror filled incident. They could leave that one behind, for Kaderri knew that his wife would be able to overcome the emotional struggle to deal with the rape. She has always had the ability to rebound from misfortune and this time would be no different—except for maybe the length of time needed.

But, that was why he was taking her to the cabin in the Adirondacks, to give her that time. He also realized that the recovery wasn't going to happen overnight and it may take years for the scars to heal. Under the current circumstances, the cabin was also the safest place for her to be now that Moshe Koretsky was on the hunt.

And Marcus Kaderri knew he'd show up, he just didn't know when.

Moshe Koretsky took extra precautions to get home. From the location of where he wound up after fleeing from his confrontation with the crazy man, his drive should have taken him no more than fifteen minutes. Instead it took him forty.

Once he got home and realized he wasn't tailed, he sat down on his couch and drank a double scotch in one gulp and quickly poured himself another. He also lit a cigarette and took a long pull, savoring the taste of the smoke. Finally, he got control of his emotions and replayed the incident. It didn't take him long to discover that he'd let his guard down, and if it was up where it should have been he could've taken care of the situation. He had become too complacent in his dealing with Miller and his amateurs when he shouldn't have.

The eyes of the man that punched him brought back a memory that was still fuzzy. He remembered the eyes and the threat but couldn't put a name to the face and place where the words had been spoken. Before he had moved his operation to Albany, Koretsky had done a complete canvass of the area to see if any intelligence agencies had any people working in the area. The search had come up empty. The only law enforcement agencies he had to seriously keep an eye on were the State, County, and Albany Police Departments. The Federal Bureau of Investigation had a building in the city itself. He never had thought that a run-in from the past would put his operation and life in danger.

It was something he didn't want to do, but procedure prescribed him to call in for instructions. He picked up the secure phone that was connected to Mossad headquarters in Tel Aviv.

The phone on the other end was picked up before the first ring was completed. Koretsky didn't give the man on the other end a chance to say anything before he spoke. "I need to speak to the Man, I have a Flash message." He was poised to light another cigarette.

"You have the wrong number," the voice on the other end said. It was standard procedure to say that if the correct code words weren't spoken. It was a safety precaution that prevented the wrong people getting through.

Shit, he thought. Koretsky didn't recognize the voice and it was obvious that he wasn't recognized either. Usually, he knew who answered the phone and was able to go right through—especially when he had a Flash message. That should've put him right through. But it didn't and the watch officer wanted him to use the code words to get access. Dropping the lighter, he picked up his Seven Star and fumbled through the pages to find the right phrase before the line was disconnected. Koretsky got lucky. The operator screwed up and waited for a reply instead of immediately hanging up. Obviously he was new. "Mountains loom in the distance." It was the verification phrase that signaled there was an emergency and he needed to talk to the director personally.

"Big or small" the voice asked for confirmation.

"Snow capped ones." Koretsky answered angrily. That phrase was for his own personal use and gave away his identity. No other Mossad officer had that phrase.

"Wait one, I'll put you through."

"What's the problem?" the director's voice asked.

"I ran into a situation," Koretsky said. He picked up the lighter and stroked the wheel, igniting the fluid in a bright orange flame and lit his cigarette.

The director's voice was angry and concerned. "Obviously, or you wouldn't be calling. What type of situation?"

"I was recognized."

"Who saw you?"

Koretsky explained what happened and waited impatiently for the director to give him some direction of what to do.

Koretsky, himself, knew what he wanted and should do. Find and kill the man who punched him in the face.

"So, it wasn't anybody in the game?"

"No, sir. But, like I said, he's tied to the military. I don't think he's involved, because if he was, I wouldn't be calling."

"I'll call you back." The line was disconnected.

Koretsky knew he couldn't go anywhere, and that his plans to check out a few thing were now put off. He lit another cigarette and drained his scotch. The prudent thing to do would be to close up shop and get the hell out of there. But sometimes, things didn't always turn out the right way.

Five minutes later, the secure phone rang.

"Yes?" Koretsky spoke calmly into the receiver.

"Find him fast and take him out," the Director ordered. "I want to keep your operation up and running. I'm sending over some photographs for you to look at. If you recognize him, let me know immediately."

"Yes, sir."

Just as he hung up the phone, the secure fax machine beeped and whined and started spitting out paper.

Sunday, June 14, 4:35 p.m.

If Koretsky had to look at one more picture and read one more description that came along with the photographs he was going to scream. Forty-six photographs and profiles were faxed to him and for the past five hours he's been studying them and trying to determine if one of those men in the photographs was the same man that almost punched his lights out.

Mossad has a vast library of people from all works of life in their files and computer banks. Many of those people didn't even know that they had been targeted by Mossad. The first group of photos that were called up and sent to Koretsky were the more readily accessible. A computer operator punched some keys on a keyboard and spit out the information on the people that were known to be in Lebanon the same time Koretsky was and still in the intelligence field. A more ex-

244

haustive search was in progress for people who were there, but were no longer on any active list. That list would take some time to compile.

Koretsky needed a break, more specifically, dinner and female company. He also wanted to know if Michele Thorsen had any information that could help him out. He found her number and called.

"Hello?" Michele asked in a hesitant voice.

"Hi, Michele, it's Ariel."

"Hi, Ariel!" Her voice immediately became brighter.

"Is something wrong?"

"I've had a real shitty day. Anyway what's up?"

"Dinner at six-thirty? I'm buying."

"Sounds good to me. Are we going any place in particular? I need to know what to wear."

"Here at the hotel. I'll come by and pick you up around six."

"The Hilton, right?"

"Right."

"I'll meet you there. I have to get to the office early tomorrow."

To Koretsky, those words were as good as her accepting his invitation to pick her up. She just said that she would spend the night, and didn't want to put him out by having to drive her back to her house to get her car. He felt himself stir at the prospects that the night would bring. "I'll meet you in the lobby."

By making the reservations two hours from now, it would allow Koretsky time to get down to the hotel, check for messages and make the hotel room looked lived in. He'd shower in the hotel room and give his deception authenticity.

After looking in the mirror to inspect his appearance, Koretsky closed the door to the hotel room and walked toward the elevator. There were two couples conversing in front of the elevator doors and the down button was already pressed. He just stood in the back and waited for the car to arrive. When the car did arrive, he let the couples on first. When he walked into the elevator, he turned to the closing doors and looked at his watch. The hands read six o'clock. In his excitement to be with Michele, he had hurried himself along and was finished with the room early.

Before the elevator reached the lobby, he decided he would sit at the bar and nurse a drink or two, and think about the prospects the night would bring. The car stopped and Koretsky was the first one off. He headed toward the restaurant to grab a seat at the bar when he heard a familiar voice call, "Ariel."

He turned toward the sound of the voice and quickly scanned the lobby. He spotted Michele, dressed in a blue jumpsuit, rising from one of the lobby chairs waving at him. He wondered if she owned any clothes that didn't flatter her figure. He stopped and waited for her to come over. "Hi, Michele," he said. "You're early. I was going over to the bar to have a drink. The reservations aren't until six-thirty."

"Hi, Ariel," she said in return. "I could use a stiff drink."

A half-hour later, they chatted quietly over diner, not saying much of anything. It wasn't until dessert when Koretsky asked how things were going with the reporting on the murders. "Any progress on your work?"

Michele's eyes lit up at the question. It was obvious that she wanted to talk. "Yes! I'm going on the air tomorrow with the whole thing." She took a sip of her coffee and peered over the rim waiting for a reaction.

"And do I get a sneak preview?"

She nodded and swallowed her coffee. In a whisper, she declared, "I have a copy of a recording that was made of the murderers in the Preserve."

Koretsky stared hard into her eyes and slowly put his own cup down. "Say that again, please."

She leaned closer and talked in a soft voice. "I have a tape of the murderers talking when they were killing the victims. "I'm going on the air with it tomorrow. Actually, I'm going to break the whole story. There are no gang turf wars going on out there on the streets as the police claim. There is an assassin running amok."

"How do you know this?" He was listening very intently now. He figured he may be able to discover who was popping Miller's people, eliminate them and keep his operation running without any more problems.

"I have a well-placed source who knows all the intimate details of the investigation. He relayed them all to me. Most of the recent murders are connected and were killed by a trained sniper."

In a scope of things, that was pretty good news. There was only one man doing the killing, and it made it easier to find him. The odds were that there weren't too many trained snipers in the city. With the information that Koretsky now had access to, he knew where his search would begin.

"Why haven't the police said any of this?"

"Because they aren't one-hundred percent sure that it isn't gang warfare. The police are keeping all their options open. The information I have is my source's own evaluation of the evidence. I have to agree with him, especially after seeing the evidence."

It was obvious to Koretsky that her source was the detective trying to solve the crime. "How about the murder on the docks? Weren't you working on that one also?"

"On that one, the police have a sketch of who they believe the murderer is."

Koretsky's heart skipped a beat and his palms began to sweat. He fought hard to keep his composure. "I thought they said there were no witnesses? How could they have a sketch? I think your source is pulling your leg."

She shook her head. "No, he's not. Apparently, there is a hooker supplied for the enjoyment of the officers of certain cargo ships who pull into the Port. The victim was on his way to visit the hooker, but he never made it."

Koretsky interrupted. "I thought the reports said he was a crew member, not an officer."

"That's true, but one of the officers gave Pedro her name and address on a piece of paper, and that paper was missing from Pedro's body when the police searched him. So, they believe the murderer took the address off the body after he killed him and then went to the prostitute. The hooker identified two of her three customers from the ship. The last one wasn't."

Koretsky's head began to spin. How could he have been so stupid. His stomach began to churn and he fought down the acid that shot up his throat.

Koretsky regained his composure, it was jumbled internally, and his analytical mind changed gears. "Did you get a look at the sketch?"

"No, I haven't. For some reason, the police are keeping it under wraps from the public."

Koretsky breathed a sign of relief, thought a small one. He was now torn between inviting Michele up to his room, or getting back to the safe house. He decided to invite her up. He was safe for the moment. "How about a nightcap?"

Michele's eyes twinkled. "You lead the way."

Koretsky charged the dinner to his room, threw the tip on the table and led Michele out of the restaurant. Walking past the front desk, Koretsky stopped and asked if there were any messages for him. He didn't expect to have any waiting for him, but to use his cover as a wine importer convincingly he checked anyway.

"May I help you?" the desk attendant asked.

Koretsky held out his key with the room number and asked, "Any messages?"

"I'll check for you, sir." The attendant turned to the wall of square boxes behind the desk and located the box that corresponded with Koretsky's room.

To Koretsky's surprise the attendant returned with a folded piece of paper. He quickly opened the paper and read the note. It read "Wine Order." Turning to Michele he said, "I'm sorry, but I'm going to have to call it an evening. I wish it didn't have to end, but something important has come up."

Michele stepped forward, wrapped her hands behind his neck and gave him a deep passionate kiss, thrusting her tongue deep into his mouth. "Are you sure?"

Koretsky stepped back. As much as he wanted to take her back to bed, this was business and it came first. He told her the truth, "Michele, this is very important, and it can't wait. "I'm sorry." He turned and walked toward the elevator.

He got on the first elevator that opened. It was going down, and he got off at the basement where the gym was and exited the building.

Koretsky made it out of the hotel and into his car without being following or seen by Thorsen. He didn't really worry about that, she thought he was up in his hotel room. Before he drove out of the parking lot, he read the note again. It read "Wine order". Those two simple words made him alter his plans and get back to the safe house where he could use his secure telephone. Those words ordered him to call Tel Aviv immediately, which meant something important was happening.

He made it back to the safe house and immediately called the director. With his Seven Star opened to the proper page, he placed the call.

"Yes?"

"Spade," Koretsky said into the phone. It was his code word signifying he was returning the director's call and was to be put through to him immediately. He didn't have to wait long.

"Moshe, we narrowed down the list. "I'm sending four photographs and descriptions over. All these people are known to have relations in the field. All are very good. Let me know if one of them is him. Do you have anything else to add?"

"I may need some help in the near future. I think this guy I'm looking for is the cream of the crop. I also have to tie up a few loose ends.

"Such as?" the director's voice was concerned.

"That reporter I made friends with gave me some heavy information on the investigation of Stroehmann's carrier that I eliminated."

"What is that?"

"They have a sketch of the murderer."

"How the fuck did they get that!" the voice exploded. "You

told me there were no witnesses. How the fuck could they get a sketch of you?"

Koretsky explained what happened with the hooker.

"Fix it, Koretsky, your ass is out on a limb." The director hung up without another word.

Monday, June 15, 2:10 a.m.

It took longer than expected, but Koretsky broke into the office building at 60 State Street. Over the past few nights, he had studied the security guard at the front desk inside the building as the guard checked the building and monitored the closed circuit television system.

The security guard, a fragile man in his late fifties with silver hair and a gait that was slowed by a limp, made his rounds like clockwork. Twenty minutes after the hour and ten minutes to the hour, he left his desk and made his rounds that took twelve minutes. It was apparent that they didn't go all the way to the top floor and check all the doors in the building. The rest of the time, he monitored the security system, ate, watched the portable TV, or dozed. Since the building didn't have anything that would need armed guards on constant alert, the security was lax and didn't have to worry about break-ins. And for somebody with the talents of a Mossad officer, breaking into the building was a walk in the park.

Except for this night, the silver-haired man with the limp wasn't on duty and a different security guard was on duty. Under other circumstances, Koretsky would have welcomed the challenge the new security guard offered, but he was in a foul mood and had other things planned. He watched the short-haired brunette for two hours before he made his move. She made rounds every half-hour on the hour and also returned in twelve minutes. It was obvious that the guards followed a set course when they checked out the building.

At precisely two o'clock, Koretsky, dressed completely in black, watch the guard leave her desk and head for the stairs. Quickly he got out of his car and crossed State Street. After a few tense moments, he picked the lock and headed for the other stair case. He pulled the door open and closed it gently, careful not to make a sound. He quietly walked up to the next floor. He stood motionless on the dark landing listening for any sounds. The only light available was from the exit sign above the door.

Suddenly, the sound of footsteps and the rattle of keys echoed from below to greet him. The guard switched stairways in the basement and was now climbing up to his location. He was trapped. He couldn't open the door that was at his finger tips. The extra light of the hallway would give him away. Going down was definitely out. His only chance was to creep up one more flight of stairs and wait and see what would happen. He pulled the Makarov from his waistband and stealthily climbed the stairs.

As the footsteps climbed in a thunderous roar, Koretsky's heart beat faster. He cursed the exit sign for giving off too much light. Closer and closer they came. Then, they stopped at the second floor, the landing below where he was. He tightened the grip on the pistol and held his breath. The keys jingled and the grate of a key being inserted into a lock was a welcomed sound. The door opened and the guard disappeared.

Not waiting for any more chances, Koretsky ran up the stairs until he reached the eighteenth floor and law offices of Miller, Katz & Kaufmann. He picked that lock also and headed for Miller's office. Once inside, he pulled the blinds and turned on the light. Out of his pocket he pulled out a little black box and turned it on. He began his sweep of the office for bugs.

When the waitress in the diner had said that she wanted to tape their lovemaking, the pieces of the puzzle began to fall into place. Every time he and Miller talked about a trade, they spoke in the conference-room, never in Miller's office. Never was Koretsky a target for the assassin who killed so many of Miller's people. The people who were killed were directed from Miller in his office. That meant that Miller's office has to be bugged, either in the telephone or elsewhere. Koretsky knew that Miller wasn't smart enough to sweep his office and think the way a professional spook would.

Koretsky pointed the detector first at the telephone and got a negative reading and the same reading came up when he swept the desk. He then turned to the wall that was shared with the office next to him and he got a beep. He stopped moving. Slowly, he passed the detector from floor to ceiling and got another beep. Then, it became steady when he pointed it at the electric outlet.

He took a screwdriver from a pouch of tools he carried and removed the plate to the outlet. Staring at him was a microphone attached to a wire that ran through the outlet on the other side of the wall.

Koretsky replaced the plate and quietly entered the other office, being careful not to disturb anything. He located the outlet hidden behind the desk that was pressed against the wall, and followed the wire that was taped up the side of the desk and into the top left drawer. When he opened the drawer, he looked in and found a typical retail tape recorder. It was obvious that the equipment was amateurish, but it had accomplished what the people had wanted. Koretsky found the killer. He smiled wickedly as he closed the drawer and took a business card from the brass and glass card holder on the desk. He read the name, Rufus Brown.

CHAPTER FIFTEEN

Monday, June 15, 8:00 a.m.

Marc and Sara Kaderri left their beautiful Loudonville home right on time and settled in for their three hour trip to the cabin in the Adirondack Mountains. They held hands during the entire trip.

Heading north on the Adirondack Northway at this time of morning they encountered very little traffic. There was a huge traffic flow going south with commuters, all-heading into Albany. Marc was thankful that they didn't have to deal with that headache.

Continuing north in the Jeep, they drove past the city of Saratoga Springs. They had to slow down somewhat due to traffic, but once they drove past the last exit for the city, the traffic thinned out and the resumed their speed.

The Adirondack Mountains loomed to the north and west. The variations in heights of individual mountain peaks created breathtaking views of green as mountains cast shadows upon one another. As they approached Glens Falls, traffic caused them to slow down again, but that didn't last long.

Just north of Glens Falls they crossed the southeastern, jagged border of the Adirondack Park. The Park itself was six million acres that occupied most of Northern New York. Travelling further north and looking east, they soon came parallel with the resort town of Bolton Landing on Lake George. Past the eastern shore of the land was the southern tip of Lake Champlain and beyond were the beautiful high peaks of the Green Mountains in Vermont. It was a drive Kaderri never got tired of.

Finally, they turned off the Northway and took smaller roads through the mountains to their destination on Mt. Colden. That was where the Kaderris had their cabin and one hundred forty-five acres, most of it located on the southern slope that faced Mt. Marcy, the tallest mountain in New York State. Kaderri slowed quickly so as not to miss his driveway. The dirt road, was tree lined and covered and dense with brush. A small No Trespassing sign located at a small opening revealed that there was a driveway, and most of that was overgrown.

Carefully, Kaderri turned onto the two tire paths and made his way up the mile long tree covered driveway. About half way up, the trees thinned and bright sunshine baked the area in a warm glow. Straight ahead lay the two-story cabin. It sat on a flat grassy area with the slope of the mountain beginning two hundred feet from the rear of the house. A wrap around deck split the cabin horizontally.

Just in front of the cabin's one car garage was a patch of loose gravel, big enough to park two cars. That was where Kaderri parked the Jeep. Once the engine was off, Marc and Sara exited the Jeep and stretched their cramped muscles.

"I'm up for a steak for lunch, how about you?" Marc asked from the other side of the vehicle. He feigned surprise that he forgot she couldn't eat solid foods. He threw up his hands and said, "I forgot you can't eat that stuff yet"

"Make it a tender Filet Mignon and I can," she shot back.
"Deal!"

They kept the house furnished, so there was no need to

bring up any luggage. Marc fished the front door key out of his pocket, unlocked the door and walked in.

It took them no more than fifteen minutes to go through the house to check out everything. Everything was in order. The only thing they had to do was grocery shopping to re-stock perishable foods.

Monday, June 15, 1:00 p.m.

Gary Trainor didn't know if Michele was home or not, but his pounding on the front door went unanswered. An officer went around the back of the house to see if she was in the yard or ignoring the pounding on the front door. He came back and told Trainor that everything was locked up and she wasn't seen.

"Okay, let's pick the lock," Trainor said. He was pissed that Michele didn't call back with the address of the guy who gave her a copy of the tape. He was also pissed at himself for letting her get the drop on him. He's had too much to drink that night and knew he had blabbed about how far the investigation had gone.

One of the eight officers that was with him pulled some tools out of his pocket and went to work on the front door. He could have used a battering ram, and was tempted to use one to open the door, but he decided against it. As long as he got in, he was happy. It took the officer ten seconds to unlock the door. Gary Trainor was now going to execute his search warrant to find more evidence that Michele Thorsen was with-holding information on a murder investigation and obstruct-ing justice.

The backdrop for the television report was the front entrance to the police station. Civilians and both plain clothes and uniformed officers walked in and out of the building while a curious passerby stopped to watch.

"Are you ready for the real thing, Michele?" Tony Patten asked as he hefted the camera over his shoulder and settled it on a more comfortable spot.

This was the moment Michele had been waiting for. Her years of hard work were going to pay off. She was going to blow the lid off of this story and police misinformation. The white hot spotlight was hers and it was going to cast her silhouette on center stage for all the world to see. The consequences be damned.

"Yeah, Tony, let's go." Michele pushed a string of hair away from her mouth and readjusted her blazer and skirt. Over the past twenty minutes, she went through a couple of dry-runs and made few adjustments to her report. Her story would take less than a minute to tell. She had it set up that she'd go live now and then tell most of her story from behind the anchor desk on the six o'clock news where she could go into more detail. This segment was going to be broadcast as a special report and be the lead-in to the rest of the newscast. She tapped her earpiece connecting her to the station and the anchor a few times because the sound had gone dead. It was too late now to do anything.

Tony gave her the thumbs up, the red light on the camera came on and she began to talk to the camera.

"There have been startling new developments in the rash of drug murders that have swept the once peaceful city of Albany. Sources have revealed to me that the police have an artist's sketch of Pedro's killer, the man found brutally murdered among the containers of Stroehmann's Self Storage at the Port of Albany. This startling piece of the puzzle came hours after the body was found and the questioning of a prostitute that the suspect visited after the slaying. Why the police haven't yet released any of this information is anybody's guess.

"In related investigations concerning the drug murders, sources revealed that the victims in the separate incidents were assassinated, not killed over turf. One of the victims of the assassin's bullet was in fact Allen Stroehamm and one bit of information concerning the heinous killing at the Corning Preserve is that the police have a tape recording of the killers' conversation while the assassination was being conducted.

So, it appears that there are killers running amok. That's it from here, I'll have more information on the six o'clock news. This is Michele Thorsen for channel eleven news."

Keith Bernard sat next to Hank Warren, Michele Thorsen's boss, in the control room where the live feed of Michele's broadcast came in. He was a tall man in his mid-forties and balding. He held the tape in his hand that she planned to play later on the news cast. There was another man in there with them who didn't say much and didn't smile. He had come with Bernard. He stood at five feet ten inches with sandy brown hair and brown eyes and a trim physique. He was nondescript and could get lost in a crowd of two people. When Michele signed off, Bernard reached over and shut off the monitor. "I want that tape and you don't know it ever existed."

"What the hell are you talking about?" Warren demanded. He was still pissed that he'd let Bernard talk him into pulling the plug on Michele's live special report. "You have a search warrant for her desk, nothing else. This is a news story and we have the right to air it. I will do that later on. You can't come in here and make these demands without the proper authority. You got what you came for, Detective, now go."

Bernard kept his cool and his companion finally sat down. At the police station before they obtained the warrant, Gary Trainor explained to Bernard what had happened at Michele's house, omitting the steamy details. Bernard reacted immediately, got the warrants issued for Michele's house and desk, and raced over to the television station before she could do serious damage to his mission. Bernard was finishing their search of Thorsen's desk when he overheard one of the technicians tell Warren that they were ready for Thorsen's report. Politely, Bernard reminded Warren that he and his companion were expecting full cooperation from him and would like to sit in and watch the report. Warren reluctantly agreed. Bernard was thankful that he had been able to avert the certain disaster that would've occurred if he hadn't been there to put a stop to the live airing.

Bernard was about to do something that he didn't want to do. But, under the circumstances, he couldn't let this information get out and alert the wrong people as to what was really going on. He reached into his back pocket and pulled out what appeared to be a billfold and handed it to Warren.

Warren glanced at it and then read it more carefully. "Oh my God! Is this real? Is Michele in trouble?"

The other man in a tailored, blue pinstripe suit, white shirt, and conservative tie answered. "It's real." He said as he handed his identification to Warren. "My name is Wilson."

Warren looked over at Bernard and handed his identification back to him. "Which am I suppose to believe, that you are a detective in the Albany Police Department or an employee of the—"

"The Federal Government," Bernard said firmly, without a trace of humor in his voice. "And you are to forget that you ever saw this identification."

"Fine, but you can't come in here and tell me that I can't air Michele's story!"

Bernard deferred the answer to Wilson who said, "Under a threat to national security we can, will, and do."

Warren's face registered shock. "Are you fucking serious? Who do you think I am? You can't lie and threaten me like this. I have the power of the First Amendment—"

"Shut up, Mr. Warren," Bernard said. "We have the authority to do it and we will. If you want to attempt to prevent us from doing what we have to, you'll be taken into custody and I'll get the FCC to revoke your license. So yes, we are fucking serious."

Warren thought about that. Getting the station's license revoked wouldn't do his career any good. He highly doubted that Keith Bernard could get the license taken away, but if he did actually work for the Central Intelligence Agency, he could make life hell for a short while and get the FCC involved somehow. Warren agreed. "What has Michele gotten herself involved in?"

"That, Mr. Warren, is classified," Wilson stated.

Twenty minutes later, Michele, her face glowing and a huge smile that was all teeth, proudly walked into the room. She held her chin high, expecting profound applause, congratulations, and questions about how she obtained this information.

Instead she got curious glances.

"Michele," Hank Warren called from his office, "come here please."

Michele was bewildered at what was happening. She wondered why no one had congratulated her. She put her purse on her desk and noticed that everything was out of place. She opened her drawers and quickly determined that someone had gone through them. Now her guard came up and she started to get angry. Immediately, she knew that something was wrong and her broadcast didn't go live. She briskly strode over to Warren's office. "Hank, what the hell is going on? Somebody has gone through my desk and—" Michele stopped when she walked passed Warren and noticed the two men seated in front of his desk. "Hi, Detective," she said to Bernard.

He rose from this chair and didn't offer her his hand. "Hello, Michele."

"What are you doing here?" She still had anger in her voice, though it was somewhat tempered. Then she threw all caution to the wind and launched into a tirade. She turned to Warren who was still standing next to the door which he closed. "I wasn't live, right? Why the hell not! I busted my ass to get this story and you screwed it up for me."

"That's enough!" Warren yelled back. "Shut up, Michele. These two gentlemen are here for you."

"Michele," Bernard said, "why don't you come with me down to the station and keep you mouth shut."

Shock and silence enveloped her. She couldn't believe what was happening. "Am I under arrest or something?" She said half-jokingly.

"As a matter of fact, you are." Bernard then read her the

Miranda rights and put the handcuffs around her wrists.

Monday, June 15, 3:30 p.m.

Marc and Sara Kaderri were in the kitchen putting the groceries away after a satisfying lunch. The tender Filet Mignon that Sara desperately wanted was still a little too tough for her bruised mouth, so she ordered a quiche and decided to take the filet back home, hoping she would be able to saver it in a day or two. Marc had the doggie bag in his hand, and was wondering how good it would taste. "Hey, Sara, I wonder how good this filet really tastes?"

Sara, poised to put a bag of french-fries in the freezer, stopped her forward motion, and smashed the bag against Marc's chest. "Don't you even think of sniffing my dinner, let alone eating it. Hands off!" She grabbed the bag from his hands, put it in the refrigerator herself and then disappeared upstairs, leaving Marc to put the remainder of the groceries away.

Within five minutes, Sara came running back down the stairs wearing a pair of hiking boots and carrying Marc's special forces combat boots. "Where are we going?" he asked when she dropped the boots on the counter.

Her gaze became shifty and she lowered her chin to her chest. She slumped her shoulders and rubbed her eye. "Marc," she said. "I've been wanting to talk to you since....well, for a couple of days."

Marc gently raised her chin with his strong finger. "Sara, what's wrong?"

"Let's go for a walk, okay?"

Marc quickly shed his sneakers, shoved his feet into his combat boots and met Sara out on the deck. They instinctively grabbed each other's hand and walked silently across the grass and into the woods. Marc knew something was afoot, and knew it was damn important to Sara. Only when it was very important and personal did she want to walk and talk. Otherwise, she would just say what was on her mind where she was at that moment.

Marc was anxious to hear what was on her mind, but he didn't want to pressure her by asking. She'd start the conversation when she thought the time was right. In silence they hiked up one of the many trails that criss-crossed their property. This particular trail brought them on the western slope of Mt. Colden. Their footfalls crushed crumpled leaves from seasons past and brush that had over grown the trail. Small animals scurried out of their way, fearful of the strange intruders. Inside the woods, Kaderri was in his element. Here, he felt at home. This was a place that sharpened his senses, and heightened his awareness of his surroundings. It brought out the warrior in him. Forty minutes into the woods and up the slope of the mountain, Sara stepped off the trail and by memory made her way through a dense pocket of dark green pines. She pushed the low hanging branches out of her way and spotted the massive rocks on the edge of the mountain. Still holding Marc's hand, she guided him to the rock where they both climbed to the top. From their vantage point, the view was breathtaking. At twenty-five hundred feet, he felt like they could touch the azure sky and see a small puddle of clear blue water off in the distance. They were just a few of the twenty-five hundred lakes that dotted the impressive landscape of the Adirondack Park.

They made themselves comfortable on top of the hard stone. Looking at the mass and height of Algonquin and Iroquois Peaks, Sara finally spoke. She grabbed Marc's hand and averted his eyes. He was looking right at her waiting patiently. "Marc," she whispered as if people were around her that she didn't want to hear what she was going to say, "I'm not yet ready to make love to you." She let go of his hand to cover her face in an attempt to hide her tears.

Her statement didn't come as a surprise to him, but she should have known that he would already know that. The healing process had just begun and he was there to help her through it. He moved himself closer to her and wrapped his arm around her shoulders, pulling her in close. He kissed her on the head. "I brought you up here to heal, honey." He was trying to think of something that wouldn't come out the wrong way and sound stupid. He didn't want to say that it wasn't important that they make love, because both he and Sara knew that it was. And if he did say that, she knew he would be lying. "That's not important right now," he squeezed her tighter. "You take all the time you need, and when you're ready, let me know. I'm here for you, to help you both physically and emotionally. I love you, Sara."

She took her face out of her hands and looked up at him. Her cheeks were streaked with tears and Marc gently wiped them away. "I love you too, Marc. I just don't know how strong I am to get through this."

"You'll do fine, honey. Actually you're doing great. I spoke to your doctor. She was very impressed with the way you are recovering."

"She was talking about physically, not mentally."

"Sara, I have all the confidence in the world in you. You should, too." He took a deep breath and then asked, "Do you want to go for professional help?"

"No, I don't," she said not as confidently as she would have liked. Then she added, "At least not yet."

Once the nausea and shock of being taken into custody subsided, Michele Thorsen became more angry by the second. She had been locked in the interrogation room for over three hours. Three long hours. At a total loss of what was happening, she hadn't spoke to anyone that could give her any information. The only person who spoke to her was one of the officers who asked if she needed to go to the ladies' room. Other than that, she had the silent treatment. She couldn't figure out what she had done to deserve this. She wondered if Gary Trainor was behind this. Was this his way of getting revenge for what she done to him? Besides all the unanswered questions, she was also getting frightened.

The day had started out promising. Even though her night was less than joyful with Ariel Steiner, her excitement had been at the highest plateau. She had gotten out of bed early, eager to get this story on the air. This was her day. A day that would bring her fame and national recognition by catapulting her into the national limelight. It would be the start of a brilliant career. Instead, it brought bewilderment, anger and the realization that it wouldn't happen.

Unexpectedly, the door opened and in walked Detectives Keith Bernard and Gary Trainor. The light of her life just got dimmer.

Michele sprang to her feet. "What the hell is going on!" she said to Bernard. She wouldn't look at Trainor. "I've been here for over three fucking hours. I—"

"Sit down and shut up," Bernard commanded.

"You fucking whore!" Trainor spat. He took Bernard's advice and removed his sidearm before he entered the room. He seriously considered shooting her.

Bernard put his hand on Trainor's shoulder and gently pushed him into a seat. "You've had your say, Gary."

Michele shot out of her chair again. Trainor wasn't going to get away with that. She pointed at him and opened her mouth, ready to spew some vulgarity at him.

Bernard reached over the table and pushed her back down. "I told you to shut up and sit down." He then took the seat next to Trainor. "Now, Michele, there seems to be a problem that you have gotten yourself into."

"A problem? Yeah, you can say that." She pointed at the two detectives. "You two are my problem."

"Now, Miss Thorsen, we searched your house and desk at work for any other evidence that may have been withheld from our investigation."

"You did what?"

"We even had a warrant," Trainor added sarcastically. "We had a deal, Thorsen. I would give you all the information when it was the right time, but your ego got in the way. Now, you're in trouble. I told you not to fuck with me."

"So, it was you who had me brought down here."

"No," Bernard admitted, "that was my doing."

"Who was that other guy with you in Warren's office?"

she asked.

"You don't need to worry about that. Now, who have you told your story to? I need to know because it could be a matter of life or death, and I'm not being over dramatic." Bernard knew it wasn't necessary to let Thorsen in on what was really going on, especially since she was going on the air with her report when she pledged her word not to. She simply couldn't be trusted.

She thought it over and answered. "Nobody. I was keeping it to myself. I wanted to break the story myself and didn't want any leaks. I told nobody."

Bernard leaned closer and bared his teeth. "Are you sure?"

"Yes, I'm sure, and thanks for fucking up my career."

Bernard stared at her intently. Trainor turned his back on her.

Since they had no legal reason to hold her, and they had orders from a judge to let her go, they did. "You can go," Bernard said. "But, we may need to speak again."

She rose from her chair and walked out the door, never turning around to see the two detectives smile.

When she was gone, Bernard said, "Gary, meet me at my place at six." Then he added, "Bring half a dozen pizzas, too."

Monday, June 15, 5:10 p.m.

One of the final pieces of the puzzle was about to be put in its place, Koretsky thought. The plan was simple, grab the guy named Rufus Brown and interrogate him. Once again, Koretsky sat in his car on State Street and watched for Brown to exit building sixty. The rush of people exiting the buildings onto the sidewalks at the end of the business day resembled a Chinese fire drill. People seemed to pour out of every building. In a matter of minutes, the streets became clogged with traffic and pedestrians heading home or out to a bar for happy hour. The amount of people caused Koretsky to loose his line of sight and surveillance. He exited the car and put himself half a block away from the target building's door, giving him a good field of vision. As he positioned himself, he

thought about his current situation. This was not to his lik-
ing. Under normal operating circumstances, he would put the
target, Brown, under surveillance and determine his habits.
Once that was established, he would be able to grab him without anybody knowing or suspecting foul play until it was too
late. He was running out of time to do everything by the
book.

Within ten minutes, he recognized Brown from the framed
photo he had taken from the desk with the tape recorder. He
remembered crashing into Brown when he was getting out of
the elevator, and then remembered speaking to him when he
had met Thorsen at The Steer House. He guessed he had two
options with Brown. Either follow him home, or to The Steer
House where he bartended. Brown, with a garment bag slung
over his shoulder, stopped to say something to a woman he
walked out of the building with and then turned heading east
down State Street, right at Koretsky. Slowly, Koretsky turned
his back to Brown and waited until he crossed the street before he began to follow him. Brown was going to The Steer
House.

Since Koretsky knew that Brown was going to be in one
location until eleven o'clock, it gave him time to work on the
other piece of his plan. He walked back to his car and then
headed home to the safe house.

Gary Trainor was falling asleep at his desk listening to all
the tapes he had confiscated from Michelee's house. The boredom of some of the conversations she had recorded was making his eyelids feel like they were coated with lead. After two
hours of listening to the tapes, he made it through only six
cassettes, most were dated from mid-May and after the killings started. He was ready to give up for the night. His stomach seemed to be getting worse, so he chewed two more Tums
and made a mental note to go see a doctor. He thought the
possibility of an ulcer or two was great.

He picked up another six-minute cassette dated June 1,
looked at it and then thought better of it. The cassettes he

was listening to were mostly nothing but highlights of previous conversations. She seemed to have transferred them from one tape onto the cassettes, making a collection like a resume on tape. He tossed the cassette aside and picked up one of the half dozen micro-cassettes she had. He figured that these would have more interesting information on them. He rummaged through his desk and found his micro-cassette recorder, hoping the batteries still worked. Searching for a date that she wrote on the cassettes that was close to one of the murders, he found one that was dated June 13, the same date that he'd had his dinner and was given the shaft by Thorsen. It also had the name Kaderri scribbled on the label.

He put the tape in and pressed play, hoping there was enough juice in the batteries to play the tape. There was. Michele's voice immediately came on. "Oh, can you comment on anything?"

"Now, Michele," Bernard's voice answered, "you know we can't comment on a shooting that is under investigation, especially when a police officer is involved."

"Okay, but what about Kaderri?"

Trainor stopped the tape at that point. There was that name again and he knew that his guy Kaderri was the interviewee of the tape. That would explain why his name was on the tape label. He seemed to be popping up in the most unexpected places. What was his connection to Thorsen?" He put the tape back on. He listened for a few more moments and got disgusted when he heard Bernard's voice say to have fun at dinner. The anger swelled in him and he threw the tape recorder down on the desk. He started to mutter to himself and picked up the recorder to shut it off when he heard another voice play on the tape. This one gave him a chill that shivered along his spine.

The voice was menacing, yet calm. "What I was involved with last night was over and done with. It was nobody else's business. I saw you at the scene last night, Miss Thorsen, you know what happened. Why don't you leave it at that?"

The rest of the tape was blank.

That voice, Trainor thought, it belonged to Marc Kaderri. It was the same voice that was on the tape of the murders at the Corning Preserve. Trainor sprang from his seat and raced to the evidence room to retrieve the tap of the murders. He wanted to make sure that the voices matched. When he made it back to his desk, he reached for Bernard's boom box to play the tape. When the tape came on, one of the voices engaged in conversation that entered his untrained ear matched. He grabbed a stack of forms and filled them out. He prepared the tapes to send them on the FBI crime lab for a positive voice match.

He glanced at his watch and the hands read six fifteen. He cursed under his breath. He was supposed to meet Bernard at his house at six with some pizzas. He wanted to get to Kaderri's house and bring the bastard in for questioning, though. Pulling the telephone book out from under the phone, he looked up Kaderri's name and found it was the only one listed in the area. Right below the name was Kaderri Financial Services. He knew he had the right guy.

Grabbing his car keys, he raced out of the police station and into an unmarked car. Once he made it out of downtown, he tried to call Bernard on the cellular phone to tell him of his incredible find, and to ask Bernard if he wanted to meet him up at Kaderri's house and question him. The line was busy so Trainor turned the car around and headed back into the city to swing by Bernard's house to pick him up and go to Kaderri's.

Trainor slammed on the brakes and screeched to halt in front of Bernard's house. The grass still hadn't been cut and he had to high step it to Bernard's porch. Beside Bernard's, there were three cars in the driveway and he noticed they were all rentals. He paused and glanced around the neighborhood and noticed that there were two cars with federal government license plates. He filed that away in the memory banks.

He knocked on the door and it was immediately opened by Bernard who was wearing a broad smile. That quickly faded when he saw Trainor's empty arms. "Where are the pizzas

Gary?" he asked. "And besides, you're late."

"Keith, I found the killer!"

Bernard was immediately put at a loss of what Trainor was talking about. "I was expecting a comment about why the hot pizza's aren't in your outstretched arms." By the twisted look on Bernard's face, the comment that Trainor blurted out wasn't a comment that he was expecting. It took a moment for what Trainor said to slowly sink in. He furrowed his brow and stepped aside to let Trainor in.

Bernard led Trainor through the foyer and into the spacious living room where seven people, five men and two women were seated among the sectional couch, love seat and recliner. Trainor didn't recognize any of them. He also noticed that there was a lack of alcohol. Usually, when adults ordered that many pizzas, there was a generous amount of beer to compliment the large glob of oozing cheese and tomato sauce. There was something very strange about this gathering.

"Find a seat, Gary," Bernard said quietly.

One of the men sitting on the couch got up. "Here, Gary, take my seat."

Trainor stared at the man, wondering how he knew his name when he didn't know any of them. He gook the seat that was offered. "Thank you?" he said with a quizzical look, hoping the man would catch his drift.

The man did. "Wilson, Art Wilson."

"What happened to the pizza?" one of the females asked from the opposite end of the couch.

Bernard, leaning against the door molding with his arms folded across his check, interrupted the interrogation that was about to erupt over the missing pizza. "Gary, what do you mean you found the killer?"

The other female picked up the phone in the living room and ordered the pizza.

Trainor was dumbfounded that Bernard asked him that question, in front of all these people, and by the look on Bernard's face he expected an answer. "Um, Keith," he hinted that he felt he shouldn't answer in front of all these people.

"It's all right, Gary," he said shortly. "These people are okay"

Gary looked around the room and noticed all eyes were on him. He swallowed hard and began his answer. "I found the killer to the murders at the Corning Preserve, and I bet we could link him to the rest of the murders."

"Shit", whispered Art Wilson, who was now sitting in the recliner.

Trainor looked around and saw a lot of expressionless faces. Except for Wilson's, he looked concerned.

"Do you have the name of this killer?" Wilson asked as he rose from the recliner.

"Why should I tell you? I don't know you from a hole in the wall."

Once again Bernard interceded. "Go ahead, Gary, you can tell him. I want to know also."

"What's gong on here, Keith? I have no idea who these people are and you want me to tell them the name of a murderer?"

"That's exactly what I want you to do, Gary. There is a lot more going on here that you can imagine."

Trainor happened to catch the man named Wilson give Bernard a stern glance. "Like what, Keith?" The people in the room were dead silent.

Wilson spoke first. "There is something going on here that we can't tell you. You are going to have to trust us. If not, that's your decision. But, what about your partner? Do you trust him?"

Trainor thought for a moment. The past few months with Keith Bernard flashed through his mind and the bizarre acts he had performed. There was a shady side to him that he wanted to know about. "At times I do, and other times I don't. What the hell is going on?" He cast his stare at Wilson. "Who the hell is *we?*"

Bernard motioned for Trainor to follow him into the kitchen, "Gary, come over here please."

Trainor rose from the couch and followed him into the

kitchen. "What the fuck is going on, Keith?" he asked once he arrived in the kitchen. He stood behind one of the wooden spindled chairs and gripped its back.

"First, Gary, I want you to tell me who you think the killer is."

Trainor thought for a moment and answered. For Christ's sake, Bernard was his partner. "It's Marcus Kaderri, the guy who's wife owns A Better Body, and he's the owner of Kaderri Financial Services."

"How do you know this?" Bernard asked.

"I was listening to the tapes I confiscated from Thorsen's house. She had a tape of a partial interview she had with him. I wanted you to come along with me and pick him up for questioning."

"The interview was at Albany Med, right?"

"I don't know if it was in a hospital. How do you know anyway?"

"I interviewed him first, and she was following up on a story from the previous night."

"That's when he was involved in that serious fight with the guy who raped his wife, right?"

Bernard nodded. "But, how do you know it was him that pulled of the hits."

"I recognized his voice from the other tape that Thorsen received from that ham radio operator on the hit in progress. I'm sending the package down to FBI lab for a voice match."

"Did you send it yet?"

Trainor sighed angrily. He was getting the runaround and didn't like it one bit. "Why do you want to know if I sent it or not? I, we, have a bunch of murders to solve. Once again, Keith, what the fuck is going on here?"

"Gary, I have to make a few phone calls, then I'll explain everything."

Just then, the doorbell rang. Bernard handed Trainor a wad of bills to pay the pizza delivery man.

Once Trainor left to get the pizzas, Bernard opened a drawer and retrieved another telephone and dialed a number from memory.

"Yes?" McKnight answered in a monotone voice.

"Sir, it's Bernard. My partner discovered its Kaderri pulling off the assassinations."

"Does he have proof?"

"Yes, sir."

"Listen, is my aide with you?"

"Yes, Wilson is here."

"Ask him to explain everything to you. Tell him I said 'unveil.'"

"Yes, sir, "unveil.' After that, then what?" This information was all new to Bernard.

"Do you have assignments for everybody?" McKnight asked,

"Yes," Bernard said hesitantly.

"Send them on them. I'll be in touch."

Bernard wanted to get one last suggestion in before McKnight hung up. "Sir, I have a suggestion."

"What's that, Keith?"

"Gary Trainor is a determined cop. He won't stop until he gets his perpetrator. He's very good at what he does, and when he has his man in his sights, there is nothing that is going to stop him."

"What's the point? What are you suggesting?"

"We bring Gary in. Let him know what's going on."

"You're the man running the operation," McKnight said, "do you feel comfortable doing that?"

"Yeah, I do. I think he has a right to know why."

"Okay. You make the call. Anything else?"

"Actually, yes, sir," Bernard hesitated. "There is."

"What is it?"

"Why is Wilson here? Like you said, it's my operation."

"After he talks to you, you'll understand."

The line went dead and Bernard was at a loss of what else was going on. He had his suspicion thought. There had to be more to why McKnight was taking an interest in Marcus Kaderri than friendship.

Trainor walked back into the kitchen with the pizzas just as Bernard put the phone back in the drawer. "You want these in here?" Trainor asked.

"Yeah, just put them down on the table." Bernard opened the refrigerator and took out a few bottles of Coke. "When we finish eating, we have to talk."

"Damn right we do."

Monday, June 15, 7:15 p.m.

The phone ringing in the kitchen sounded like a klaxon blaring in a submarine when it had to dive below the surface. Marcus Kaderri was momentarily startled, by its ringing, because nobody was supposed to be calling unless it was an emergency. He shot from the recliner in the living room and ran into the kitchen before the second ring. Sara was asleep upstairs and he didn't want her to wake. "Hello?" he said into the receiver. His voice was full of concern and anger.

"Marcus, how are you?" it was a husky voice.

Kaderri thought for a moment and said, "Why are you calling?"

"I heard what happened to Sara, how is she?"

Kaderri's suspicion was confirmed. The man on the other end shouldn't have know what happened to Sara. There was only one person who would reveal the information. "She's doing well, thanks."

"You're welcome."

Kaderri started to get angry at the situation, but he kept everything in perspective. "Listen, there's only one person who knows what happened to Sara that could have told you. I think we need to talk."

"I agree, but it can't be over the phone."

Kaderri started getting an uneasy feeling, one that he felt only in dangerous situations. It was time to really put the guard up. "When? There's a lot going on here."

"It's complicated, Marc. I'll be out at your cabin tomorrow at eight."

"I think complicated is an understatement, unless there is a hell of a lot more going on than I know about."

"Yes, there is."

"One question," Kaderri said. It was more of a statement than a question.

"What?"

"He's up here. Do you know about it?"

There was silence for a moment and then the answer finally came. "Yes, but I'll talk to you tomorrow."

Before Kaderri could say anymore, the line was disconnected. He stood in silence after he hung up the phone and gathered his thoughts. That little piece of news that there was more going on was disturbing. Slowly, he put a few pieces together and came up with a scenario that made him even angrier. He hoped he was wrong with what was going on, but his gut instinct told him he was right. Engrossed in his deep thoughts, he didn't notice that Sara had come downstairs.

He ran his strong hands through his short hair and wiped his face. Trying to clear his mind and think, his thoughts were interrupted.

"Honey, what's going on?" Sara asked. She was leaning against the door frame in a short t-shirt, staring at her husband.

Kaderri spun around and stared at his wife. He didn't expect to see her there. She had a concerned look on her face. "Sara, what are you doing here, you're supposed to be in bed."

"I heard the phone ring, and came downstairs to see what was going on. What's the emergency?" She also knew that they were only to get interrupted in case of an emergency. When he didn't answer, she pressed him." "Marc was it Louise or Stephanie?" Stephanie was the club manager who had instructions to also call her in case of an emergency. Her eyes became hard but distant as she stepped over to Marc. "Marc, there's something going on and I want to know about it."

Marc looked hard at his beautiful wife and by the look on her face, he knew she wasn't going to take no for an answer. But, he was going to try. "Sara, I can't—"

"Bullshit, Marcus!" She pointed her finger at him and almost touched his nose. She only called him Marcus when she was mad. "Don't you dare pull down your curtain and withdraw into that damn shell. You and I are going to sit down and talk. I know you," she started to cry, "at least I thought I did."

Kaderri thought for just a moment, and made a decision. He could no longer keep his wife in the dark. "You're right, Sara, we have to talk." He grabbed her trembling hand and led her into the living room.

Monday, June 15, 7:50 p.m.

There was one pizza left and except for Bernard and Wilson, Trainor was the only other person in the house. After most of the food was eaten, Bernard simply told everybody that it was time to get the show on the road. In concert, everyone rose and left.

Trainor was standing in the kitchen and took a quick look around to make sure everybody had left. Satisfied that the three were alone he turned to Bernard. "All right, Keith, I've been waiting patiently all night. Tell me what the fuck is going on! I want to pick up this guy Kaderri for questioning."

Bernard sat down at the wooden kitchen table, and Wilson followed. Trainor remained standing. Pushing an empty box and one of the bottles of soda out of the way, he said, "Gary, sit down, it's going to be easier for you."

"What are you doing?" Wilson asked sternly.

Bernard turned his attention to Wilson and answered, "I spoke to the DDO, he said 'unveil'."

Wilson nodded, motioning for Bernard to follow him. Then turning to Trainor, "Gary, we'll be back in a few moments."

After ten minutes of letting his thoughts run the gauntlet, Bernard and Wilson returned to the kitchen and sat down at the table.

Bernard took a deep breath before he started. "Gary, first of all, what's said here, stay's here. Agreed?"

Trainor nodded.

"Good," Bernard said then continued on. "Art, and I work

for the Government. We are working on something that is very sensitive."

"What part of the Government? FBI?"

"Don't insult us. We work for the Central Intelligence Agency."

Trainor burst out in a scornful laugh. "Who the fuck are you kidding?" He looked at both Bernard's and Wilson's faces and noticed they weren't smiling. Their eyes didn't even betray them. "You're not kidding, are you?"

"No, we're not." Bernard answered.

"You're a spy? He asked Bernard. "You aren't really a cop?"

"We don't use the term spy, but, yes we are," Wilson said.

Trainor turned to look at Wilson, "You too, huh?"

Bernard continued, "No, Gary, I'm not a cop, and never was. Now, the reason why I am here is because I'm tracking a man named Moshe Koretsky. He sometimes goes by the name Ariel Steiner. Did you ever hear of him?.."

"No, who is he?"

"He's Mossad, Israeli Intelligence," Bernard said.

"He's a spy, too?"

"Yes, he is and he's very good—and dangerous." Bernard said matter-of-factly. "Actually, we believe he works in a unit called Al. It's a super secret unit within the Mossad that operates in the United States."

"What does that mean?" Trainor asked. "And more importantly, what does that have to do with me and Albany, and why are you telling me all this? Don't I have to be checked out first before you tell me any of this?"

Bernard thought a moment before he answered. He didn't want to reveal too much. "The answer to the first part of your question is that its too complicated to explain except to say that he's well covered. For the rest of it, well, he's running drugs out of here, and is responsible for the murder of Pedro."

"How do you know all this?" Trainor shook his head.

"Remember the ballistics report on the murder and the ammunition data that the type of weapon was a Makarov?"

"Yeah."

"Well, two shots to the head with a Makarov is his signature. And I also showed a picture of him to Betty Freeman, and she confirmed it. He was the last guy she slept with."

Trainor shot out of his chair, startling the other two to the point where Wilson went to draw his weapon. "You have a confirmed picture of this perpetrator and you haven't released it? Why the hell would you do that?" Trainor held his tongue for a moment, letting his mind work as he waited for an answer. He began pacing and tossed another Tums into his mouth.

"There is a reason, Gary," Bernard said catching his breath after Trainor's outburst.

"You also held up the artist's composite drawing of this guy, Koretsky. And, I bet you're responsible for all the misinformation that the Department is releasing, right?"

There was no way for Bernard to deny it, Trainor was right. "Yes, Gary, you're right."

"Why?" Trainor threw his hands up. "That guy out there is a drug runner and a killer. And he's doing it in my city! And, you withhold information that can get him arrested."

"National Security, that's why," Bernard stated.

Trainor stopped in mid-pace and faced Bernard. "What's that got to do with it?"

"If we pick him up on regular charges, he claims diplomatic immunity and gets away with it. The Israelis aren't going to extradite him, he's to good of an asset for them. They would do everything in their power to protect him. So, there is no way to bring him in on murder and drug charges. Besides," he said uncomfortably, "I haven't been able to locate him yet."

"Is that what all these other people were here for? They're trying to find him?"

"Yes, and I have him narrowed down into three locations, and all are too big to watch by myself."

Trainor let that go for the moment. Something that Bernard did not say previously caught his attention. "So, Keith, if you are unable to arrest Koretsky on murder and drug charges, how do you propose to keep him behind bars once you find him?"

Bernard looked right into Trainor's eyes. Without any emotion he answered, "We don't."

It took a moment for the meaning to sink in. "You plan to assassinate him?" Trainor stared hard at Bernard, unable to comprehend what he was hearing. "I may be a little naïve, but when has the United States resumed carrying out assassinations?"

"When it's a National Security concern and when it's a Presidential Directive. Koretsky is responsible for at least nine murders in the United States, and three of those were employees of the Agency. It was decided that it wouldn't stand that he would get away with it. We took the matter up with the Israelis, but they shrugged it off saying they knew nothing about the man. Moshe Koretsky is a danger to the United States of America and must be stopped. Besides being a drug runner, we're tagging him as a terrorist. In case you don't know what a terrorist is, in plain language it's someone who uses violence for political gains. Moshe Koretsky is one of the best, and he will do anything for Israel."

Trainor pursed his lips and let out a big sigh, acknowledging and accepting what he was told at face value. "This stuff is way out of my league. If you want to kill this spy, and have the authority to do so, that's your business. But, I still have this assassin running around the city. I believe it's my duty to bring him to justice. I want to bring this guy, Kaderri, in for questioning."

Wilson, who was sitting at the table with a stone face and hadn't said a word finally spoke up, "I have to fill you in on a few things."

Trainor shifted his stare to Wilson and thought, Oh, shit.

Marc and Sara went into the living room, where it was more comfortable to talk, rather than sitting at the kitchen table. Marc sat in the recliner opposite Sara who was sitting on the couch. The fan turning in the window cooled the room down and the noise drowned out most of the wildlife noise outside the cabin. "Would you like something to drink, Sara?"

"No, thanks, can we get on with this?" Her voice shook, betraying her fear. Her first thought was that he was going to tell her that he was having an affair, and that he didn't love her anymore and that their marriage was coming to an end.

Marc just nodded. "I have deep reservations telling you this, especially under the circumstances. I don't know if you will be able to handle it."

Oh, God, she thought, here it comes. "Just tell me, Marc." Her bottom lip quivered.

"I love you, Sara, but what I'm going to tell you is highly secret and cannot, I repeat, Sara, cannot be told to anyone." His voice was firm and matter-of fact. "In fact, you are going to have to forget what I say. Do you understand?"

"Marc, can you stop the theatrics and just tell me?"

"No, Sara. There are no theatrics involved here. If you can't commit to not repeating and forgetting what is said here, then this conversation stops." He waited for a sign of confirmation before he would go on any further.

Sara stared hard at her husband. This was getting beyond scary. She had never heard her husband talk like that before. Sure, they had their fair share of arguments like any married couple did, but the tone in his voice and the words used were authoritative and distinct. It was almost as if he were addressing soldiers under his command. "Okay," she said quietly. The fear that had wrapped around her in her office when Greg Sander was raping her regained its icy grip.

"Good." He rose from the chair and sat next to Sara on the couch. He cradled her hand and began to talk. "Sara, I'm a contract employee of the Central Intelligence Agency, and for the past couple of months I've been working on an operation."

Fearfully Sara pulled her hand away and moved to the other side of the couch. Her hands were trembling and she stared at her husband. "Marc, what do you mean by a contract employee of the CIA—and what's this operation?"

For Marc, this was the hard part. "When the Agency gets a job that needs to be done, and special people are required to get that job done, they hire those people for the length of time needed. I'm one of those people." He stopped and let what he said sink in. "Do you want me to continue?"

"Yes," her voice was quivering. She was petrified to listen to anymore of what he was going to say, but she had to know what her husband was doing. "What's this operation you are on?"

"I'm contracted to help win the war on drugs. The police are overwhelmed and the liberal judges and prisoner rights groups have gotten out of control."

"What exactly are you doing?" It was the question she had to ask, but she didn't want to know the answer.

"Sara, I'm a sniper, hired to terminate drug dealers in the city of Albany."

Sara quickly covered her open mouth and stared in horror. She couldn't believe what her ears had heard. Her head began to spin and her stomach started to churn and she ran into the bathroom where she immediately vomited. Wave after wave spewed from deep within and as she stared into the murky water, her mind tried to erase what she had heard.

After flushing the toilet, she knelt by it for long moments until a glass of water appeared in front of her from Marc's steady outstretched hand. She looked up into her husband's eyes and didn't see him. To her, the handsome, loving man that would do anything for her was gone. All she saw were the eyes of a killer. "No! No! No!" she screamed and knocked the glass out of Marc's hand. It shattered when it hit the floor. She quickly crawled past Marc, then stood and ran out of the bathroom.

"Sara!" Marc called after and then followed her up into the bedroom. He arrived at the door just as she was about to slam it shut.

"Go away!" she yelled and collapsed on the bed.

Marc sat on the bed next to her and picked her up into his arm. He didn't say anything to her, but gently cradled her head against his chest and stroked her hair. Her heavy sobs lessened and he held her tight until she fell asleep. There was a lot more he had to tell her, but it would have to wait until morning.

"Gentlemen," Wilson said, "Marcus Kaderri is off limits."

"Why?" Trainor demanded. "Is he one of you people also?" He said it as a joke.

"Yes, he is," Wilson confirmed. "Actually, Gary, you're right, he is the one killing the drug dealers. He's working on an operation that is separate from the one Keith is working on."

Bernard huffed and shook his head. "I can't believe he's one of us."

"Yeah, he is. He's a contract employee—"

"What's the operation he's working on?" Bernard demanded, raising his voice. He never knew about Kaderri.

"If you would keep quiet and don't interrupt anymore, I will tell you what I can. First of all, his operation is above your clearance and is on a need-to-know basis. You don't need to know. All that concerns you is that he is one of us and is off limits to the police."

"Who's his spotter?" Trainor asked in a quiet voice.

Wilson eyed Trainor. "Robert Wolff, Ph.D. He's off limits too. Like Kaderri, he's a contract employee, but he's—never mind."

Trainor let it go for the moment. "And the third partner? What's his name?" He remembered the third voice on the tape.

Wilson cocked his head. "What third partner?"

Trainor briefly explained what happened with Thorsen and the tapes he confiscated from her.

"If he has another person involved, that's his business. I know nothing about it. He has free reign on how to run his operation anyway he sees fit."

Bernard slammed his fist down on the table and stood upright, knocking his chair down in the process. "That's just fuckin' great! We got another guy running an operation in the same goddamn town and has carte blanche—" The telephone in the drawer rang, cutting off his tirade.

He reached over from his seat, opened the drawer, and answered the phone. "Yes?"

"Keith, put Art on." McKnight said.

Bernard handed the phone over to Wilson, "It's the Boss." Wilson took the phone and turned his back on the two men sitting at the table. Bernard turned his attention to Trainor. "You weren't suppose to get involved in my operation, Gary, but it's the only way to get Koretsky. I wish things had turned out differently."

Trainor remained silent. Though he thought he knew what Bernard meant, he wondered what he meant by "turned out differently." "I can't believe you're out to kill him. There has to be something illegal about this."

"No, there is nothing illegal about it. This is a high stakes. Higher than you can imagine. There's more to it than what we told you, but we told you what we could. What you are going to have to do is forget that this ever happened."

"That is going to be real hard," Trainor said sarcastically.

Bernard's eyes became hard, and he leaned slightly forward across the table. "Forget it, Gary."

While Trainor and Bernard were staring at each other, they failed to hear Wilson's side of the conversation with Paul McKnight. Only when he called for their attention, did they turn toward him.

"Guys, what's going on?" Wilson asked.

Bernard peeled his eyes away from Trainor and answered the question. "Nothing. What did McKnight want?"

"I'm going back tonight. He's meeting Kaderri tomorrow morning. In the meantime, you are to carry on your mission."

"That's it?" Bernard thought there would be more, a lot more.

"That's it."

"What the hell am I suppose to do?" Trainor said, folding his arms across his chest. "Let all of these murders go un-solved? What's my boss going to say?" Trainor started to work himself into a rage. He threw his hands up. "What the fuck are we going to tell the public?" He looked both Bernard and Wilson in the eye, and he wasn't going to look away. "I'm waiting for your outstanding answers to—"

"Shut up, Gary!" Bernard said as he stood. "You're working with me now. You're in this until the end. I don't need to hear anymore of this bullshit."

Monday, June 15, 11:45 p.m.

Suprisingly few motorists and pedestrians were out and about in the star filled summer night sky. The Steer House closed at eleven, and the staff was finishing it's clean up duties.

Moshe Koretsky watched the outside kitchen doors, waiting for Rufus Brown to exit. He had his simple plan set. As Brown walked toward his car, Koretsky would grab him long before he got inside the parking garage.

Parking his car a few blocks away from the restaurant, Koretsky stood in the shadows of the building and watched the door that led into the kitchen in the rear of the building. When the time was right to abduct Brown, he would make it appear as if they were two friends bar hopping for the evening.

Standing quietly, the rumble of his stomach caused him to cringe fearing someone would hear the noise. He purposely didn't bring anything to eat for fear of leaving a trace of evidence that could be linked to him. Flexing his fingers in the surgical gloves, he drew in a breath as the kitchen door opened and Brown stepped out.

He slowly began to move then stopped, when Brown was followed out by another employee, the girl in the photograph with him that was on his desk. Her presence created a major problem that could be addressed only one way. Koretsky began to follow and pictured the layout of the streets and alleys of the vicinity he committed to memory. Brown headed west on James toward the more crowded North Pearl, and finally to the parking garage on State. Koretsky had to make his move before the two of them reached North Pearl.

Remembering that there were a few alleys off of James, Koretsky quickly closed the distance. Silently he approached the happy couple and the entrance to the alley. He withdrew his silenced Makarov. With Brown on the left, they were engaged in happy conversation and holding hands like lovers. They were also oblivious to danger that was ready to strike.

Brown, pinched his companions ass. She giggled and moved closer to him. "Horny tonight, huh?" she said.

"You betcha, gonna give it to me?" he answered.

"Only if you give it to me first," she countered.

At that moment, Koretsky placed the barrel of the gun at the base of the lady's head. "Don't say a word. Keep walking and turn here down the alley."

Koretsky knew they were experiencing fear like they had never thought possible. It has enveloped them, cutting off all rational thought possible. The lady was shaking, too terrified to scream. Ghost turned to see the man holding the gun. He got a glance of the man before a quick slap turned his head. The party of three took fifteen steps down the dark alley to a dumpster. The light from the street lamps on the connecting streets made everything look eerie. "Stop here and face me," Koretsky ordered. Their backs were against the dumpster.

Both Brown and his companion obeyed his command. As the lady turned to face Koretsky, he kept the muzzle of the silenced weapon pointed at her. When she completed her agonizing, slow, trembling turn, Koretsky looked in her eyes and smiled a wicked smile where only the edges of his lips curled up.

He placed the weapon on her forehead and in rapid succession pulled the trigger twice. The only sound was the bullets exiting the back of her skull and along with the pieces of her head splattering against the dumpster. Her head snapped back and body fell straight down and landed in a seated position against the dumpster.

Koretsky turned to Brown and observed his reaction. Brown was obviously unable to comprehend what had just happened. Powerless to do anything about it. He stood there frozen in terror. The woman's eyes were still open and in the faint light, her face began to go pale as the flood drained from the massive hole in the back of her head where the skull used to be.

Koretsky turned the gun on Brown and spoke to him as he opened the dumpster lid, "Put her in here."

Slowly and gently Brown lifted her as if he were carrying her to bed. Blinking away the tears the flowed down his cheeks, his trembling hands lifted her above the edge, he kissed her cheek and dropped her in.

Koretsky closed the lid and motioned for Brown to walk down the alley. He walked beside him with the weapon, now concealed under hit light windbreaker, pointed at Brown's waist. He whispered in Brown's ear, "I guess you won't be getting any pussy tonight."

Like a lamb being led to the slaughterhouse, Rufus Brown was led to Moshe Koretsky's car.

CHAPTER SIXTEEN

Tuesday, June 16, 5:45 a.m.

Ghost had never felt pain like the pain he had been sub-
jected to just after one in the morning. Excruciating was a
fitting term, but it didn't do any justice to the real pain he felt.
He was surprised he managed to survive it. Ghost was hanging from a wooden beam in some basement. And from what
he could see, it wasn't an ordinary basement. It was a twelve
by twelve room with a concrete floor with a drain in the middle,
right below his swaying toes. The walls and ceiling were gray
and sound proofed without any windows. There was a single
recessed light directly in the center of the ceiling which gave
off enough light to see, but not to provide any details of the
room. It was as if it was a room within a room. He remembered being pushed and shoved down a flight of stairs and
stumbled through a couple of doorways. He couldn't see anything because he was blindfolded. Koretsky placed that on
him once he got in the car. For all he knew, he could be anywhere.

Once inside the room, Koretsky made him strip and then

sit down on a sturdy wooden chair. Ghost's hands were tied at the wrist and behind the back of the chair. His legs were tied directly to the legs of the chair, preventing him from escaping or striking back. When Ghost was tied firmly, Koretsky took off the blindfold.

"Hey, nigger," Koretsky started, "you remind me of those no good filthy Arabs. They're sand niggers. The only difference between them and you is they live in the sand."

"Fuck you, Jew asshole!" Ghost spat back. "You live in the sand, too, so you're also a fucking sand nigger." He was full of rage and fear.

Ghost watched with some satisfaction, as Koretsky was momentarily taken back by the fact that he knew he was a Jew.

Koretsky leaned closer. Ghost could get a good look at Koretsky's dark menacing eyes and smell his stale breath. "You're a tough little bastard, huh?" Koretsky said. "That should make this more enjoyable." He then took his fist and placed a punch directly on Ghost's solar plexus, causing a brief moment of intense pain that left him gasping for air.

As Ghost tired to catch his breath, Koretsky walked over to a little table that was in the corner and pulled a couple of two inch spindles about the size of a pencil out of the drawer. Koretsky shoved the spindles in Ghost's eyes, propping open the lids so he couldn't close them. Brown screamed in pain and vigorously shook his head to shake the spindles out, but they were wedged in between the bone of the sockets and wouldn't budge.

"Motherfucker!" Ghost yelled. "I'm gonna kill you, Koretsky!" He wanted revenge for the murder of Tanya Richardson, the woman he was going to marry.

Koretsky, who was standing behind Ghost and tying another piece of rope around his writs, immediately stopped what he was doing. "What did you call me?"

"You heard what I said," Ghost said triumphantly. "Or should I call you Ariel Steiner."

A deafening quiet settled in the room. Ghost knew he struck a sensitive cord. Suddenly, Koretsky cupped his hand and slapped Ghost on his ear, rupturing his eardrum and knocking the chair over. Ghost screamed at the pain. When he recovered, Koretsky spoke nonchalantly, "No you're not going to kill me, I'm going to kill you." He then righted the chair and Ghost.

Tightening the new rope around Ghost's wrist, Koretsky ordered him to stand. Koretsky then threw the rope over the beam running down the center of the room and pulled the end that dangled over the edge. The beam itself has a roller inserted in the middle of it, making it simple to pull a heavy weight off the ground that was attached to the other end of the rope.

As Koretsky pulled toe rope, it lifted Ghost's arms from his wrists that were tied at the small of his back. Inch by inch the rope raised his arms until they were perpendicular with his body. The pain he began to feel was extreme, burning as if his shoulders were on fire. Inch by the inch the rope was pulled, and Ghost's arm's moved higher and higher until his wrist's were as high as his neck. The white hot pain tore through his shoulders and across his chest as the muscles and ligaments fought against the direction in which they were being pulled. And because of the spindles propping open his eyes, he couldn't close them against the pain. At that point Ghost started to wail.

Koretsky stopped, wrapped the rope around a cleat cemented into the floor and then cut Ghost loose from the chair, He shoved a sock in his mouth to shut out the horrible noise that was emanating from deep within. Koretsky kicked the chair away and then pulled the rope in one swift long pull, lifting Ghost off the floor. In the process, Ghost's screaming muscles and ligaments tore, ripping both of his shoulders from their sockets.

He never felt pain that intense and didn't think he could stand much more. His screams became louder despite the gag in his mouth and his head began to spin as the agony intensified. Finally his eyes rolled into his head and he passed out. Moments later, he was awakened by a bucket of cold water thrown into the face. The water and sweat that trickled into his mouth that wasn't absorbed by the sock felt refreshing. But, it wasn't anywhere near enough to quench the dryness of his parched mouth.

"It's nice to have you back with us," Koretsky said. It was obvious that he was enjoying what he was doing. He walked up to Ghost's hanging body and gave him a push.

The shove on his body caused another wave of pain, that made his head spin and caused him to vomit, forcing the sock out of his mouth. Once he spit out most of the vomit that was stuck in his mouth, he gasped, "What do you want with me?"

"Ah," Koretsky said calmly, "you finally want to know what I want of you. That's good. I won't tell you now, I'm tired and am going to sleep."

Koretsky put the gag back in Ghost's mouth and then placed a floodlight in front of him and turned it on. Ghost looked directly into the brightest white light he had ever seen. The intensity of the light blinded him and made his eyes ache. And because Koretsky had propped his eyelids open, it made it impossible for him to close his lids to shield his eyes from the white-hot light. It also prevented him from getting any sleep. If he tried to move his body so it wasn't facing the light, the pain from his separated shoulders prevented that. Throughout the night, he moved his head up, down, and side ways so he wasn't looking directly into the light. At one point, he shook his body to cause the excruciating pain in his shoulders in the hopes that it would knock him out. It didn't.

Ghost spent the night looking directly into the spotlight, dangling from a rope.

When Koretsky re-entered the room through a concealed door, Ghost was still in a shallow form of shock from the physical pain and the murder of his girlfriend, Tanya. The only consolation was that his shoulders and arms were staring to go numb so that pain no longer mattered.

"Did you have a nice night? Get a good sleep?" Koretsky asked in a polite voice and removed the gag.

The voice startled Ghost since he hadn't heard a door open

or close. He was exhausted from the constant pain and light shining in his eyes. Koretsky asked if he had a good night, so that must mean it was morning.

"I did," Koretsky admitted. "I had a nice restful sleep in my bed, though it wasn't long enough." He walked in front of Ghost. "I have a deal for you, " he said menancingly. "And, you are going to truthfully answer all of my questions." Koretsky sat down on the chair that Ghost had been originally tied to and took a bit of his onion bagel smothered with cream cheese.

Ghost got a whiff of the bagel and the coffee and silently wished for some nourishment, especially water. He would do anything for a glass of water. But, he didn't say anything because he thought it would fruitless. He was trying to conserve his strength, for what he didn't know.

Koretsky shut the white-hot spotlight off, but Ghost didn't realize that. His eyesight was too far destroyed to take any notice. "Now," Koretsky said, "before we start this morning's session, would you like a drink of water?"

Ghost nodded. Koretsky removed the gag from his mouth and poured the water into his parched mouth. It was cool and refreshing. When the water was done, Ghost knew the torture would begin. So far, Mossad had taught Koretsky well in the fine art of interrogation.

As he swayed slightly, wondering what was going to happen, Koretsky moved behind Ghost and punched him in the bladder. A piercing paint shot through his body and caused him to lose control. He screamed as the pain raced through his internal organs and urine ran down his leg.

"Now, we begin." Koretsky still hadn't moved from behind Brown when he asked his first question. "Why did you have a tape recorder in your desk that led to a microphone in Miller's office?"

Ghost didn't answer. For his silence, he received another blow to the kidney that sent even more pain throughout his body

"I guess we're doing it the hard way," Koretsky said in an exhilarated voice.

Tuesday, June 16, 6:15 a.m.

Marcus Kaderri stood on his deck and gazed out. Morning in the Adirondack mountains was a beautiful exhibition of nature at its optimum moment. As the warm bright glow of the sun glistens across the eastern slopes of the mountains, its tentacles reach farther into the shadowy depth as it makes its timeless and predictable tract across the azure sky.

Kaderri's mind was ready to crash into the mountain's side with a fury because of the weight it was carrying. In light of the circumstances, would he be able to survive another day? What would Sara think about him when she woke up? How would she react when he filled her in on the rest of his mission and previous missions? Should he even tell her about those? No, he couldn't. They were still classified top secret. And what was the information that Paul McKnight had on Moshe Koretsky? And when would Koretsky make his presence known? It could be anytime.

Marc leaned his elbows on the railing, sipping his steaming coffee and surveyed the magnificent landscape. Suddenly, he felt a sense of foreboding and a black spot covered his heart. It appeared as if dark thunder clouds enveloped him, sending out a warning that there was one hell of a storm brewing. He knew that good people were going to die, and he may actually lose.

He would take the warning seriously.

A rattle in the kitchen signaled that Sara was awake and she was pouring herself a mug of coffee. Marc didn't move from his spot or say a word. He turned slightly and through his peripheral vision watched her through the screened window.

Moments later, Sara walked through the opened sliding glass doors and stopped next to Marc, brushing his arms. She stood there looking out at the scenery, not saying a word and holding her mug with both hands, took a deep swallow of her hot coffee.

"Pretty, isn't it?" Marc said. When Sara just nodded, he

decided that this was the time to tell her what was in store. He would go easy first. "How are you?" he asked, very concerned about her state of mind.

Sara took another sip from her coffee before she turned and answered. She looked up at him and moved closer. "Hold me," she said, leaning into his chest, almost as if she was trying to get inside him. "I'm okay, but I have a lot of questions and I would like to know the answers."

"I'll answer what I can, but some of them I won't be able to because they are classified." He pulled away slightly to look at her.

She looked at him briefly and then looked away. "How long have you been working for the CIA.? And what exactly do you do for them?"

"I've been working with them as a contract employee since I was discharged from the Army. And what I do for them is very selective."

"Like kill people?" The anguish and anger Sara clearly felt in speaking those words hung in the air like a cloud of dense fog.

"For lack of better terms, yes."

"So, you are a murderer for hire?"

Marc wanted to lash out at her remark, but he controlled himself. He could understand where she was coming from. "No, Sara, I'm not a murderer for hire. I don't go out and just kill people for the fun of it, or for money. I work for the United Stated of America. I took an oath when I received my commission in the United States Army to defend this country and the Constitution against all enemies foreign and domestic. This may sound like preaching, naïve, old fashioned, or whatever you want to call it, but I believe in this country and what it stands for. I believe in the Constitution and the souls of all the men who fought and died to make that piece of parchment a reality—and especially for the ones who made the supreme sacrifice to protect it.

"Right now the enemy happenes to be drugs, drug dealers, and users in this country and in the city of Albany. My job is

291

to help stop the flow of drugs on our streets, and to make people think twice about getting into the business. This isn't the only city that this is taking place in. What we're trying to do is prevent drug dealing from taking up roots in America's smaller cities like they have done in the larger ones. Those will be dealt with later. And forget about the court system. There are too many liberal judges and juries who feel for the goddamn defendant and what bullshit excuses they come up with to justify or excuse their crime. Until those judges are voted out and people's attitudes change, other ways are going to be used to crush this menace."

Sara stood silent, letting what her husband said sink in. "Is this legal, or is it something that is going on behind the backs of the Government?"

"It's legal, Sara. It was authorized by the President of the United States, and I believe the Senate Intelligence Committee knows about it. If they don't, so be it. The President has the authority to do so."

She leaned closer into him. She took a deep swallow of the coffee and then asked, "Marc, how may people have you killed?"

Marc knew the question was coming. He put his coffee down on the railing, moved away from her, and held her at arm's length. Holding her trembling body and looking right into her eyes he answered, "You don't want to know the answer to that question." He didn't know exactly the number of people he killed, but it was not a number he would boast about. He remembered as clear as his hand in front of his face the first three people he killed. He still has nightmares seeing their faces, especially their eyes, through his scope just before their heads exploded. He also clearly remembered the first ambush he'd been involved in where he had been able to hear the labored breathing of the soldier in front of him before he pulled the trigger and ended his life. The other faces blended together. But, if he thought hard, he could remember all thirty-eight killed as a sniper. He had no idea how may soldiers he killed in firefights. It was jut too hectic to try and count, not to mention it would send him to a padded room.

Sara looked again into his eyes. "One more question," she ventured.

"What is it?"

"Are you the one responsible for the recent string of murder-crime in Albany?"

"Most of them," he answered truthfully.

She let a big sigh and rubbed her face. "Okay, honey, no more questions." She leaned forward and wrapped her arms around his waist and laid her head upon his muscular chest. "How about another cup of coffee?"

"Sure, but I have to tell you, Paul McKnight is coming over at eight."

"Paul? Why is he coming over?"

Marc hesitated. "He isn't the real estate developer we led you to believe. He's the Deputy Director of Operations for the Central Intelligence Agency. Paul's my boss."

Tuesday, June 16, 7:05 a.m.

The broken body of Ghost Brown swayed over the drain in the interrogation room of 615 Morris. Urine, feces, teeth, and blood dotted the floor around the drain. Koretsky used a rubber mallet to methodically break the bones encased in the bruised and broken-skin. Koretsky started at the two bones in each leg that make up the shins and shattered them with one blow. He slowly worked his way up the legs, paying careful attention to the intricate structure of the knee and the knee-cap. He shattered them also with one blow. After the legs were broken, Koretsky worked the mallet over Ghost's lower back, concentrating on the kidney area and then the abdomen. It was when he worked over this part of the body that Ghost lost control of his bodily functions.

Having a prisoner piss and crap all over himself was nothing new to Koretsky. He's had enough experience in smashing people that he knew the moment when the person would lose control. He just stepped out of the way so he wouldn't get sprayed by any of the waster. When Ghost was done, Koretsky continued where he left off.

293

As for Ghost, besides being in agony from the broken legs, he also felt humiliated by the loss of control over his bodily functions. Exhausted and near unconsciousness, Brown silently begged for the one blow to put him into eternal sleep so he wouldn't have to endure anymore torture.

As the bones in his legs were being hammered, he screamed and screamed, but the pleas for mercy fell on deaf ears. From head to toe, Ghost was a carcass of broken bones, torn ligaments and tendons. He could faintly remember the question Koretsky asked and had a harder time remembering his answers. Despite the fact that he had been in good physical condition, he was totally unprepared for the rigors of torture at the hands of an expert.

Koretsky gave him a shove on his leg, releasing the scream he knew Koretsky wanted and expected and then said, "Let's take it from the top, Rufus," he dragged out his name, sounding like a mooing cow.

Ghost, despite all his pain, managed to shake his head and say through a weak voice, "I've told you everything."

"Bullshit!" Koretsky yelled and punched Brown in the jaw, knocking out another tooth. "So far, you've told me that you work with two other men. That you three are acting as vigilantes, because you are fed up with the court system and lack of resources to stop the drug trade. You want me to believe that?"

Ghost nodded. As far as he knew, that was the truth. They kept him in the dark for his own protection. They only used his office and closeness to Joshua Miller to get the information on the drug deals that were to take place.

"You lying piece of shit!" Koretsky hit him again. "Why did you bug Miller's office?"

"I overheard him talk on the phone about a deal, and..." his voice trailed off into an inaudible whisper. A slap from Koretsky brought his voice back.

"And what? You called your two friends to make the hit?"

"Yes."

Koretsky thought about that. "How many hits?"

"I don't know, maybe three," Ghost answered truthfully. Because of the beating, he honestly couldn't remember.

Koretsky change his tone of voice and asked quietly, "How do you know my name?"

Ghost didn't answer. The one thing he did not want to do was give Marc away.

When he didn't answer, Koretsky yelled. "Where the fuck did you learn my name?" He repeatedly hit Ghost in the upper torso and head.

Once again, Ghost didn't answer.

"That's it," Koretsky said. "I'm running out of time. I need those answers so I can continue with my mission."

Koretsky reached into his back pocket and pulled out a stun gun. When he pressed the button on the handle of the small device, a blue arching light danced across the opened front.

"Tell me how you learned my name."

Ghost managed to see the bright blue arching line through swollen eyes that were still propped up with the spindles and cringed. But, he wouldn't tell him the answer. He wouldn't knowingly betray his friend.

When he didn't answer, Koretsky put the stun gun in his groin and pressed the button, sending the electrical circuit through his testicles.

An animal-like scream erupted from Ghost. The pain felt as if someone was holding a blow torch to his groin. Koretsky kept the gun there for another three seconds as his body twitched from the influx of voltage.

"Name," Koretsky demanded.

Ghost refused to answer and another wave of electricity was sent through his groin. This time, the agony brought him on the verge of passing out and tears streamed down his cheeks. He was broken.

"Name," Koretsky asked once again.

Ghost, exhausted from the torture and on the verge of death, answered the question in a hoarse whisper, "Marcus Kaderri."

Koretsky stepped back and sat down on the chair that was against the wall. "You mean the guy who owns the financial services company in the same building as Miller?"

Ghost nodded, barely lifting his chin off his chest.

"What's he got to do with this?"

"Sniper."

"Why?"

"I told you," his voice was getting shallow.

Koretsky now accepted the fact that Ghost told him the truth about being vigilantes. "Was he in the Army with you?"

"No, he was SF."

Special Forces?'

Ghost could only nod.

"Where is he?"

Ghost's eyes started to roll and his head bobbed up and down. His speech and thought process severely weakened, he answered, "Adirondacks."

The light in front of his eyes began to fade and a warmth enveloped his body like a long sought security blanket, dissipating the enormous amount of pain that he thought would never end. Ghost took a deep breath and mustered all the energy that he had left. He lifted his chin, smiled and spoke in a hoarse whisper, "Yeah, sand nigger, Special Forces. And he said he's gonna get your sorry fucking Jew ass for killing that sergeant in—" Then Rufus "Ghost" Brown no longer felt any pain and his eyes saw no more.

Tuesday, June 16, 7:58 a.m.

After a quick shower, Sara joined Marc on the deck for a light breakfast that Marc had fixed of toast and scrambled eggs. Her mouth still ached and the stitches were a little tender, but it was noticeably healing on a daily basis. She was about to say something, but the sound of a car parking in front of the cabin and a door opening and closing cut her off.

Minutes later, light footsteps on the stairs introduced Paul McKnight. He was wearing a pair of brown Dockers and a white golf shirt that stretched across his broad chest. "Hi," he said with a smile. He removed his sunglasses and walked over to Sara and gave her a kiss on the cheek. He heartily shook hands with Marc. "Sorry to hear what happened, Sara. How are you?" he asked, sincerely concerned. He then put his eyeglasses on.

"Recovering, Paul, thanks."

"Coffee, Boss?" Marc asked and headed toward the kitchen before McKnight could answer. Kaderri and McKnight has a friendship besides a working relationship and he had the option of calling McKnight sir, boss, Paul or nothing at all. But, the last option could be deemed as insubordination, not to mention disrespectful. In most cases, except when he was really pissed, Kaderri used his first name, or the more affectionate and respectful, Boss. Not everyone could call McKnight Boss. That was also true with Kaderri when he had been running his A-Teams in Special Forces. He had the respect and admiration from his men that they called him Boss. Rarely did they call him sir.

"Thanks, Marc," McKnight said when handed the mug of steaming coffee.

"Want some breakfast?" asked Kaderri and pointed to the plate of food.

"No, thanks, I grabbed a bite on the way up." He then took a seat on one of the wooden Adirondack chairs that was against the house and looked upon the serene view. He took a sip from the mug of coffee and stayed quiet while the Kaderri's finished their breakfast on the deck.

Once their breakfast was finished and the dishes were cleared, McKnight sat down at the table and got down to business. "Sara," McKnight said, "Would you mind excusing us while we talk?"

As Sara rose to leave, Marc grabbed her arm and gently pushed her back down into the chair. The intensity in his eyes grew and his face hardened, "She stays and hears what's going on unless it's classified Top Secret or above."

McKnight's eyes hardened at the challenge. "No," he answered flatly.

"Paul, I told her the truth. She knows what's going on and who you really are."

McKnight's face registered shock and then quickly turned to anger. "You had no right to do that! This is classified information, and a lot more is at stake than you can guess."

"I didn't tell her everything, and I won't. But goddamnit, Paul, she's my wife and has a right to know certain things. And one of those things is that I'm a contract employee and she knows the mission that I'm on."

"Maybe I better leave," Sara offered.

The tension was building between Kaderri and McKnight. Both men stared hard at each other until finally, Kaderri conceded. He knew McKnight was right, Kaderri said to Sara, "I'll fill you in later, honey."

After Sara left, McKnight stood and blasted Kaderri. "What the fuck do you think you are doing? And who the fuck do you think you are? You can't tell anybody anything without my approval. Jesus Christ, Marc, you could jeopardize the whole goddamn project by running at the mouth!"

"Enough, Paul, enough." Kaderri lowered his gaze and his voice, but both were filled with coldness. "I didn't run at the mouth. She has a right to know that I'm working for the Government, killing people in the line of duty and that on one of these missions, I may not come back. I think she has a fucking right to know what's going on. My marriage isn't going to end up like yours."

McKnight had been married to a wonderful lady for more than twenty years, but his involvement in the Central Intelligence Agency took too much time away from her and they grew apart until they both realized that they didn't know each other anymore. That was aside from the fact the he couldn't talk to her about his day at the office.

"Okay, Marc, enough is enough. Let's get down to business."

Kaderri accepted the olive branch without any further comment.

"Now, Marc, what exactly have you told Sara?"

Kaderri gave him the run down and studied the face of his boss. It was evident that he was angry that he had told his wife that he was working for the CIA, but McKnight seemed relieved that he hadn't gone into any operational details.

"Now, why is Keith Bernard working up here? And more importantly, why is Koretsky here?" Kaderri's face became hard and the lines in his face deepened. He wasn't going to take a bullshit answer.

McKnight looked Marc in the eye. "First," he took his glasses off and wiped them with a handkerchief, "how did you know he's working for me?"

"He screwed up by not asking questions police detectives would. Besides Bob Wolff, he's one of a few people who knew what happened to Sara. So, when you called and asked how she was, it confirmed my suspicions."

"I'll have to talk to him about that. Okay, he's working on a different part of the same mission that you are. Where your job is to eliminate drug dealers at the local level, his job is to find and track the bigger wholesale operations, focusing on the ones sanctioned by foreign governments. While working on a mission in Colombia, he came across Koretsky. Curious to why he was there, he began a surveillance on him. In no time at all, Bernard discovered that Koretsky was involved in drug running. Why, we can only guess but its probably safe to bet that he's funneling the untraceable money back to Mossad where they can run their own operations without interference or approval by their government. I wouldn't be surprised if he's pocketing some of the money for himself."

"Why is he here?"

"Bernard tracked him to New York and called in the DEA and NYPD to take down the warehouse and Koretsky with all the other people inside. But, it went bust. Less than two hours before the raid, the warehouse was emptied and when the place was raided, there wasn't a scrap of evidence. Bernard didn't give up, I won't go into details, but he traced him up to Albany and it's now an Agency job. The DEA and FBI are no longer involved. They later found the bodies of the two cops who were supposed to be watching the warehouse."

Kaderri smiled upon hearing that. The amateurs were out of the picture and the professionals had taken over.

McKnight smiled back. "Now Bernard's mission is to hunt Koretsky down and eliminate him."

"Why didn't you eliminate him then and save all this trouble?"

"First of all, we wanted to see who he was connected with. And second," he ticked off his fingers, "we didn't have the authority to assassinate him. If he was killed in a shootout, fine. That was actually what we were hoping for."

"Why didn't you tell me this?" Kaderri demanded. "Why didn't you tell me that Koretsky was here?"

"First of all, it's need to know." Kaderri started to protest, but McKnight held up his hand and silenced him. "You know better. Second of all, we can't pinpoint him. We only find bodies that he leaves in his wake. Besides, I never thought that you two would cross paths. I wanted to take that chance." McKnight looked right into Kaderri's eyes, "More importantly, I wanted you to continue with your mission. If you knew Koretsky was operating in Albany, you would have disregarded your orders and went after him. Right?" McKnight knew Kaderri and of his promise to kill Koretsky if he ever saw him again.

Kaderri nodded. In fact he has already started to hunt down Koretsky. "I saw him twice," Kaderri added. "And so did Bob. Hell, Paul, I punched him in the face. If I were armed, I would've taken him out. I vowed to when he killed Hassad in Beirut."

McKnight bolted out of his seat when he heard that. Astonishment covered his face. "You did what? You punched him in the face? When?"

"Sunday in the parking lot of Albany Med."

"Did he recognize you?"

"I don't think so, but I called him by his name. By the look on his face, that hurt him more than the punch."

"Jesus H. Christ!" McKnight punched the table, knocking over his coffee mug. He'd had the opportunity to kill Koretsky and it slipped through his fingers.

"If he's the type of man I think he is," Kaderri said "I figure he's going to track me down and try to kill me before I get a change to take him out. Didn't you tell me that he's the type to take out the threat before the threat can take him out?"

McKnight remembered the conversation he's had with Kaderri in his field tent after the incident that Kaderri had with Koretsky in Beirut. "Yeah."

"Now, when I took this mission," Kaderri continued, "you told me I had free reign to work resources and recruit people at my discretion. Since Koretsky falls dead center into the objective of the mission, I'm going after him. Actually, I'll probably be lucky enough for him to come to me up here. It doesn't take a rocket scientist to find someone."

McKnight eyed him suspiciously, "Marc, who did you recruit and for what purpose?" "

Kaderri didn't hesitate to tell McKnight. It was a legitimate question. "His name is Rufus Brown, but his nickname is 'Ghost.' He was a friend of Steven Caron and was with us when he was gunned down."

McKnight knew Caron and knew that he had been killed, but didn't know all the circumstances and the people involved. "What is he doing for you?"

"After you contacted me about the job, he overheard a one-sided telephone conversation with his employer about setting up a drug deal."

"Who's his employer?"

"Joshua Miller. He's the founding partner of Miller, Katz and Kaufmann. A bunch of ambulance chasers." That was Kaderri's favorite phrase for all lawyers. "What we did was put a microphone in Miller's office, Ghost shares the same wall. We simply listened in on his conversations. Whenever he gave information on a deal, we set up at the sight and took out the targets."

"Is he in on the hits, Marc? What exactly does he do?"

"He's primarily the source of information for the hits, and sometimes he serves as a lookout. He has no idea that Bob and I work for you. He was also in the quartermaster corps in the Army and has access to weaponry. Before you fly off the handle, I can get it quicker from him than going through channels. In fact, I just picked up an M forty A one from him."

"Don't you thing that's dangerous? Not letting him know what's going on? Why are you using him?"

Kaderri's nostrils flared. He immediately stood, knocked the chair over, and pointed his finger at McKnight. "No, Paul, it's not dangerous and I'm not using him. How the hell can you say that? Since he's not on the payroll, he can be denied if he runs into trouble. And you know that would happen. Imagine if he gets caught without any safety net. The police call Langley and they say they never heard of him. He's up shit's creek without a fucking paddle in the water. If something happened to him, he knows to call Bob or myself. He has your number in case the two of us are killed. That way, we could get him out."

"If he called me, how would I know he's legit?"

"Because he would say 'Marcus told me to call because you could help me—Delta Sierra." Delta Sierra was the phrase that Wolff and McKnight invented in case they needed help.

McKnight had to smile. "Alright, Marc, sit back down. You made your point."

Slowly Kaderri sat back down, not taking his eyes off his boss. "When I tell you the rest of the story, you're going to eat that shit-ass grin you're wearing."

"What's the rest of the story?"

"Ghost spotted Koretsky in Miller's office."

Kaderri was right. The grin immediately faded from McKnight's face. That opened up a new can of worms and a lot of questions. "How secure is the microphone you placed in Miller's office? And when did Brown last see Koretsky?"

"The microphone is placed in the electrical outlet with a tape recorder placed in Brown's desk. It is immune from detection? No. But, it can't be seen with the naked eye. And I believe the last and only time Brown saw him was Friday, but I'm not sure."

"If Koretsky gets any suspicions, he's going to sweep the office, you do know that, don't you?"

Kaderri let out a sigh. "Yeah, I know that. We had the microphone placed before we knew Koretsky was involved. I've been playing with the idea of pulling it."

"That's a smart idea. If Koretsky finds it, you can write your friend off. He won't go quickly either. It'll be pure hell"

Kaderri knew exactly what McKnight was talking about. He, too, was trained in the field of interrogation, but not on the level as someone like Moshe Koretsky. He knew it would be brutal. Kaderri just didn't know precisely how brutal. "If I pull the microphone, what do you want me to do? It's going to take some time to get the kind of information we get now."

"Don't worry about that. We have plenty of options that we can get you involved in."

For a few long moments, the two men sat there in silence lost in their own thoughts. Finally McKnight spoke. "Listen, Marc, I want to pull you out until Sara is healed. It's just a matter of time until we get Koretsky. I have a bunch of people working on it."

"You know that he's going to search for me, and it's most likely that he and I are going to meet."

"That's if we don't get him first. I want him dead, Marc. He killed some of my people—some were friends of mine. And Koretsky knew exactly who they were. The best thing about the situation is that we have Presidential approval to take him out, and he is being treated as a terrorist." McKnight read the hands on his watch and stood. "I have to go. If you need anything, let me know. In the meantime, I'm going to sit down with Bernard and fill him in with what you told me. As a matter of fact, I think I'll have him come up here and talk to you. I'll keep you posted on what's going on. Do you have any questions?"

Kaderri's eyes turned black and his face hardened into a

stone mask, "One. Can I get Koretsky?"

"Sit tight for the moment on that. Let's see if we can get him with the people I have now. I want you to take care of Sara and not end up like me. If he comes after you up here, he's all yours." He paused to let his instructions sink in. He then asked, "Where do you have the tapes?"

"Locked away."

McKnight sighed and smiled. "Where, Marc, in case you can't get them."

"In the Loudonville post office. But don't worry, I'll be able to get them to put Miller behind bars."

Tuesday, June 16, 10:00 a.m.

Staring off into space with his fingers steepled under his chin, Gary Trainor wondered how he got himself into these situations. A cup of coffee and a half empty role of Tums were on his desk along with a pile of now useless paperwork. He had the murder investigations solved and couldn't do anything about it. He felt cheated for not being able to bag the murderer. The sweet taste of success and accomplishing his first murder investigation where he was the lead detective had turned sour.

On top of the sense of being cheated, he was now working for the Central Intelligence Agency. That, he couldn't believe. At this point, he was waiting for Bernard to call with some important information. That was what he had said when he called over an hour ago. Until that call came in with instruction for him, he would sit there with nothing to do. He couldn't go to the lieutenant and ask for something to do. The lieutenant was involved in the whole thing.

For the next hour, Trainor sat there feeling sorry for himself.

Moshe Koretsky had disposed of Brown's body. That was the easy part. He dismembered the body, put the pieces into garbage bags and threw them into a dumpster. He also needed to find the time to eliminate the hooker, Blossom. He couldn't believe how stupid, and on the flip side how lucky, he had been so far. If the police had a sketch of him, why hadn't they pictured it across the television or post it in stores and on telephone poles? He'd have to ponder the answer at a later date. He now realized the mistake he had made by taking the address of the prostitute.

Now, he was waiting for a call back from Mossad with an answer of who Marcus Kaderri was—if they had any information on him. Mossad's network of information gathering and storage process was excellent, but it didn't have all the answers. He was also pissed at Brown for dying to soon. He had a lot more questions that would go unanswered. Questions like where Kaderri lived, and who the third partner was.

Racking his brain to determine if he had met Marcus Kaderri and why Kaderri was going to kill him. He tried to remember who the sergeant was that Brown referenced to that he'd killed. He killed many people, but for some reason he couldn't remember the sergeant or Kaderri. The next best option was to meet Kaderri and try to remember who he was. Pulling the telephone book out from a kitchen drawer, he flipped through the yellow pages until he found Kaderri's number and dialed it.

"Kaderri Financial Services," the smooth voice flowed through the telephone.

"With whom am I speaking with?" Koretsky asked.

"Louise Faith," she answered. Her voice didn't betray any skepticism. "Who is this?" she asked in return.

"Louise," Koretsky began, "May I please speak with Marcus?" He didn't give her his name. If Kaderri was for real, he'd recognize his name and his plan would be shot from the start.

"He's not in, may I take a message?"

"When will he be back? I'm interested in sitting down with him to discuss some money I want to invest."

"He's on an extended vacation, I'll leave him your name and number and he'll get back to you."

"That's nice. Hopefully it's some place not as humid as it is here. Listen, Louise, I'm talking about a sizeable sum of money. He comes highly recommended and I'd like to talk to him." Koretsky didn't believe that Kaderri was on vacation, especially if he was the target in Kaderri's scope. He figured that Louise screened all his phone calls.

"Give me your name and number and I'll pass it on to him," she repeated.

He tried a different approach, this one more direct. "Give me his number and I'll call him to set up an appointment where he's vacationing. Once he hears the amount of money I want to invest, I'm sure he won't mind the phone call."

"I can't do that. Sorry. Like I said—"

Koretsky hung up in disgust and flipped open the telephone book again. This time, the search was in the white pages under the residential section. If he couldn't get a commitment from that woman to set an appointment with Kaderri, and couldn't wait to get an answer from Mossad, he wouldn't wait for anybody else's help. Koretsky would meet Kaderri on his doorstep and take him out so his mission could continue.

Tuesday, June 16, 11:00 a.m.

This time, instead of staring into space, Trainor stared at the composite sketch of Moshe Koretsky. He still hadn't moved from his desk, waiting for Bernard to contact him. The role of Tums was used up as was the coffee in the pot. He desperately wanted to hit the streets and pump people for information to find this guy, Koretsky. He had a face to go along with a name and someone, somewhere, would know where to find him. But, as of this point, that option was out. Preoccupied with his thoughts, he didn't notice the shapely smooth legs in front of his desk.

Slightly shaking from fear of once again feeling the wrath of Trainor, Michele whispered his name hoping he wouldn't hear it and she wouldn't have to go through with her self made commitment. "Gary."

"What?" Trainor barked without looking up from the sketch. When there was no response, he looked up from the paper.

His eyes first noticed the legs. By the shape of them, he knew who they belonged to. Michele, wearing black shorts and a white t-shirt and a pair of cross trainers, once again stood in front of Trainor's desk. Dabbing at the sweat that accumulated on her forehead with a handkerchief, she was breathing deeply. He dropped the sketch as the rage immediately began to boil, threatening to erupt like a volcano. "What the fuck are you doing here?" he said through clenched teeth. As he spat out the words dripping with contempt, he rose slowly from his chair to his full height.

Michele closed her eyes and instinctively took a step backwards away from his desk. His hatred hit her like the force of a hurricane. She put up her hands in surrender hoping it would stop the onslaught. She spoke first in an attempt to answer his question. "Gary, I came here to apologize—"

"Apologize?" he balled his fists. "You are way beyond the point of attempting to apologize you bitch. You took my trust and threw it our the window. I once respected you, and thought that maybe there could be something more between us. Believe it or not, but I started to like you. You used me, and that's all you had ever planned to do. The whole relationship between the two of us was just a farce. I should've seen it coming. You were good, real good at hiding it."

His voice became louder as he spoke and people began to gather outside his office. "Do you realize what you could have done? Thank God Bernard was there to pull your plug. You could have been the cause of a criminal to escape, and worse, gotten some innocent people killed. Why the fuck do you think there are rules. And you wonder why many people distrust the press. It's because pieces of shit like you who betray the trust to get better goddamn ratings. Thorsen, you're nothing but a whore." When he caught his breath, he stared at the crowd that had gathered to witness a royal ass chewing. Some of the cops even applauded. "It's over, people," Trainor snarled, "you can go back to work."

Michele stood there and took it all. The words he used were harsh and appropriate and she cried her eyes out. Wiping her cheeks between sobs, she managed to pull a tissue from her pocket and wipe her nose. Finally she said, "Gary you're right. I came here to apologize and I mean it."

Trainor was still standing and leaned over his desk to get closer to Michele, "Any smart ass remarks and I swear I'll punch you in the mouth."

At this point in time, there was no doubt that he would. She cast her glance down to his desk to avoid looking at his eyes.

"Gary," she said.

"Leave. I'm done with you."

"No, Gary, wait. That picture—"

"I said leave." Then he realized that she was trying to tell him something about the picture. "That's none of your business." He walked from behind his desk and grabbed her arm to escort her out of the station.

"Would you stop for a moment?" She pulled herself free and stopped walking. "I know who that is."

Trainor stopped in his tracks. "What did you say?"

"I know who he is."

He leaned closer and bent down until their noses touched and his eyes were boring holes into hers. "Are you shittin' me?"

"No, Gary, honest. His name is Ariel Steiner."

A million thoughts raced through his mind. First and foremost was how did she know. And he asked her. "Michele, how do you know him?"

Michele looked around and didn't like all the attention she was getting, which was a first. "Gary, can we talk private?"

Trainor eyed her suspiciously, but took her to one of the interrogation rooms after he grabbed a copy of the sketch and a notepad.

"So, Kaderri's got a hard on for Koretsky?" Bernard said to McKnight over a turkey club. Though it was a little early to eat lunch, he promised himself he'd work it off later at A Betty Body—that's if he got a chance to get there. As it appeared, he wouldn't get there for a while. This mission was getting more and more complicated and more dangerous. It was apparent that people were going to die. Bernard just hoped it wouldn't be more good guys than bad.

"He has this penchant for giving people what they have done to others. Especially when they are murdered and an American." McKnight didn't expect a comment.

"Do you want me to go up to his cabin and help him out?"

"Not yet," McKnight said. "I'm hoping that you'd be able to get Koretsky down here. If he's not caught down here, I can only imagine what's going to transpire. One thing that I do know," his face turned deadly serious, "if the two of them meet, there is going to be a bloodbath."

There was no movement around the beautiful three-story house. Patiently and thoroughly, Koretsky stalked the house and watched for any signs of life. He knew he had to be extra careful with this man, he could be a force to be reckoned with, especially if he had been a Green Beret. When he was sure that nobody was there, he took the bold approach and walked to the front door and rang the doorbell. He had hoped that Kaderri would answer so he could place his two shot signature in Kaderri's forehead.

After he determined there wasn't an alarm system, Koretsky placed the Makarov back in his waistband and easily picked the lock on the front door. That dumfounded him. It was in-disputable that this man had money and he couldn't understand why there wasn't some sort of alarm system to deter thieves. Not that a system would have posed any problems, it would just delay him until he overrode it.

Once inside, he took in his surroundings, careful not to move anything. This would be the perfect opportunity to determine who is adversary was. He walked through the foyer and under the crystal chandelier and emerged in the spacious kitchen. Taking a quick tour of the downstairs, passing through the richly decorated sunken living room with a ten-foot fireplace, and an elegant formal dining room. Bypassing the sunroom that opened out onto a huge deck, Koretsky made his way back to the kitchen and walked into the den that was converted into a home office. He could have used the door that connected the den to the sunroom, but he didn't want to touch too many objects, yet. By the looks of the den, it would be the logical place to start looking.

He figured that he had time to thoroughly search the house. So he left the den for the main staircase and took it to the second floor to see what was there. Stepping off the carpeted stair and into the hallway, he looked right then left surveying which way to go.

Taking two steps to the right, he arrived at one of the two full baths on the floor. He gave it a perfunctory glance and continued the search. The second floor consisted of three bedrooms and a library. The bedrooms were all the same size, big. There was one bedroom directly at the end of the hall with the other two occupying each side of the hall. The library was shaped like a horseshoe with the entrance from the hall in the center of the shoe with the two uprights coming back toward the center of the house. With a trained eye, Koretsky determined that the library appeared to be a second den. The walls, except for where the windows were, were covered with books neatly placed in elegantly carved mahogany bookcases. Looking around the corner, he noticed the two far walls at the end of the library were void of books. One was covered with military insignia, decorations, and pictures of someone receiving decorations. The other wall was covered with medals suspended from ribbons and pictures of one of the most beautiful women he had ever seen. He made a note to scrutinize the military wall after he searched the rest of the house.

The remainder of the library had a leather couch that faced the window overlooking the rear of the house. The window showed a commanding view of the small lake, and two wingback chairs placed at an angle sharing a small mahogany table in front of another fireplace. A mahogany desk that matched the ornamented table was placed in a corner at an angle, as if it kept watch over the rest of the library. A computer was perched on the right side. A forest green, leather wingback sat at its place behind the desk.

Koretsky had to admit, the place was beautifully decorated. Too bad, he thought, the man wouldn't live to enjoy it. The bedrooms on the floor were just as beautifully decorated, each with its own theme and queen sized bed.

Finished with the second floor, he bounded his way to the smaller third floor. Here was the master suite along with a dressing room/walk-in closet, and a hot tub.

Just as the rest of the house, this room was well decorated.

The decorations on the wall of the library drew his attention away from the bedroom. He quickly descended the stairs and briskly strode into the library. His eyes searched the "I love me" wall picking out the important awards. In the center of the wall, standing alone in a sea of awards and military accomplishments, there was a framed picture of a handsome man. He wore a Class A Army uniform and a Green Beret. The man's chest was filled with medals and ribbons, but the eyes were what drew Koretsky's attention. The were warm and gentle that matched his smile, but there was a hint that they could turn deadly.

This was the man who had punched him in the face and threatened to kill him. He reached up and rubbed the side of his face.

Next, Koretsky studied the medals and awards that were mounted on the wall surrounding the picture. Some he glanced over and others he read with interest. An award for the Combat Infantryman's Badge. This was an award one could only receive in participating in combat. Top in his class in three schools, one of those being the U.S. Marine Corps Sniper School. The description that explained how he won the Distinguished Service Cross read as if it were fiction. There was no doubt that the man was heroic.

It suddenly dawned on him. Everything came into focus as clear as the room he was in. Beirut. He remembered the confrontation he'd had with the American Green Beret over that stupid LAF Sergeant. He remembered the sergeant that he had accused of spying, and that the American had steadfastly denied. As it turned out, Koretsky was wrong and the American was right. He also remembered the threat and look in the eyes of that American. The man had vowed to kill him. For once in his life, that had been the only time Koretsky was ever frightened.

Koretsky found himself, being awed by Kaderri's achievements and credentials. They were definitely worthy of respect. Though he had had a run in with Kaderri, he didn't know him. But, he knew the type, and looked upon him now with due respect. Kaderri was a formidable adversary that would give him a challenge.

He tore himself away from the wall and opened the small closet next to it. He found a strong box, easily picked the lock and ruffled through the papers, most of which were deeds to the properties Kaderri owned. Quickly thumbing through them, he scanned the names of the town where the properties were located. He recognized most of them as being in the Capital District. One caught his eye, one with a name he didn't recognize. The deed was to the property in the town of Keene.

Locating a map of New York State, Koretsky unfolded it and searched the grid for the town. He found it in the Adirondack Mountains.

The desk has a telephone with preset numbers, and one of the buttons said cabin. Koretsky picked up the receiver and punched the button. After the fourth ring it was answered.

"Hello?" a female voice asked cautiously.

"I'm sorry," Koretsky said trying to sound truly apologetic, "wrong number." His wicked smile returned as he hung up the phone. He now knew where his target was.

At that moment, the battle had begun.

CHAPTER SEVENTEEN

Tuesday, June 16, 11:45 a.m.

Tom Washington threw the three garbage bags out the back door of The Steer House and into the alley. He was having a bad day that had started with a fight with his wife at six in the morning. One of six cooks, it was supposed to be his day off. He got called in to work at ten to cover for a cook who called in sick. He rushed over to get the restaurant opened by eleven thirty, but upon arrival he was told that one of prep cooks wasn't coming in that day either. That meant he had to pick up the other duties as well as his own.

His hand grasped something slimy on the outside of the garbage bag. He cursed loudly and wiped his hands on his already stained white overalls. Hefting the bags once more, he carried them the distance to the dumpster, cursing the owner of the restaurant for not spending the money to get a dumpster right outside the restaurant. Cursing once again at the idiot who closed the lid of the dumpster, he put the bags down and spotted a big pool of dried red brown liquid on the pavement and the dumpster itself. Not thinking much of it, the dumpster was used by the restaurant and a real estate office, he threw open the lid with a grunt and peered inside.

His eyes grew wide at the sight of the lady staring up at him with lifeless eyes and two holes in her forehead. His stomach churned and he felt the blood drain from his face. Leaving the garbage on the ground, he covered his mouth to cover the vomit that was racing its way out from his stomach. Despite being lightheaded, he pushed his legs and ran back to the kitchen to report the body of the bartender's girlfriend.

Her head and stomach were still churning. It had started from the moment that she sat down with Trainor in the room. He told her why the man in the picture, was being sought by the police. "Gary," Michele said in a somewhat tired tone that betrayed a hint of impatience. "We've gone over this for the past half hour." She really wanted to go home and sleep.

Trainor leveled his gaze. "If we have to, we'll go over it for the next six hours. I want to make sure you are telling the truth."

"I am, Gary, I swear."

"Why should I believe you?"

Michele didn't have an answer.

"You're sure his name is Ariel Steiner?" He didn't want to tell her his real name was Moshe Koretsky, but he wanted to know if she knew it.

"Yes, I'm sure."

"Positive?"

"Yes." Now that the roles were reversed, her being grilled as she had done to so many people, she didn't like it one bit. She wanted desperately to start asking some of the questions that had popped into her head. She had actually tried once, but Trainor cut that off with a curt reply. Now all she wanted to do was get out of there.

"Where does he live, again?"

"He told me he's staying at the Hilton downtown."

"Sure of it?"

"Yes, I am. I met him there for dinner and he picked up his

messages at the front desk."

Just as he was about to ask another repeated question, there was a quick knock at the door before it opened.

"Gary," another detective poked his head in. His head was shaved bald and he wore a blonde moustache.

"John, the door was closed. It better be important."

"It is. Can I talk in front of her?"

Trainor hesitated. He looked over at Michele and walked to the door.

Michelee watched and tried to read lips, they were talking too softly for her to overhear the conversation.

Trainor shook his head. "Shit!" he said loudly, ending the hushed conversation.

"Since it's the same pattern," John said, "I thought you'd want to know."

"Yeah, thanks."

"Don't you want to come to the scene?" John asked.

Trainor shook his head. "No, but can you give me a list of the witnesses when you're done?"

"Yeah, no problem." The detective turned and closed the door on his way out.

Trainor turned his attention back to Michele. "So, were you fucking Steiner, too?"

"What the hell kind of question is that? That's none of your business."

"Yes it is," Trainor sneered. "Because if you treated him the same way that you treated me, who knows what he said to you—or vice versa." He also wanted to tell her who this guy really is for her own protection, but dealing in matter of national security was above his pay grade.

She thought about what he said and knew he was right. He just could have asked her in nicer terms. Suddenly, Michele covered her mouth and her eyes went wide.

Alarmed, Trainor asked quickly, "What is it, Michele? What did you say to him?"

It took her a moment to collect her thoughts and she explained to Trainor her series of encounters and conversations.

As she explained what went on, he got more and more angry. "You've blown the whole fucking investigation! No wonder why we can't catch him." He threw his note pad across the table.

"That's not the worst of it."

Trainor's mouth dropped. "You mean there's more to this clusterfuck?"

She nodded. Unable to talk properly, she told him in a whisper, "I told him about the composite drawing and the hooker who gave the description."

Trainor bolted out of his chair, knocking it over in the process. "**You did what**?" Spittle flew from his foaming mouth as he leaped across the table.

Michele cowered in her chair fully expecting to be struck. She brought her knees up to her chest, buried her face in her lap, and used her hands to cover her head.

"You stupid ass!" There was no lull to the fury he was lashing at her. "Do you know what you have done? You just got that hooker killed! You, Michele Thorsen. You are responsible for the murder of an innocent human being because of your goddamn arrogance. Hope you're proud of yourself. Now get the fuck out of my sight!" He pointed to the door, but she didn't see. During his tirade, Michele hadn't moved. He walked over to the chair, gave it a swift kick knocking her off balance. "Get out of here before I shoot you!" She got up and ran out the door.

Trainor was so mad that he might have done it if she didn't run out of the room. Pacing bath and forth, he couldn't figure out who he was more upset with. He decided that he was more upset with himself for trusting and confiding in a reporter. He should have known better.

Pushing the door open in a fury he smashed into Keith Bernard, stopping him dead in his tracks. "Shit," Trainor grunted rubbing his nose and forehead until the stars faded from view.

Both being the same height, Bernard rubbed the same parts.

"Where are you going in such a hurry?" Bernard asked wearily.

Trainor grabbed Bernard by the arm, "C'mon, we got to see if we can find Betty Freeman." He glanced at the man standing behind Bernard.

"Wait," Bernard said as he was being dragged out of the police station. "What are you talking about?"

"First," he lowered his voice, "Koretsky got another."

Bernard stopped like he hit a brick wall. The man walking behind him just as fast smashed into his back.. "Whoa. When?"

Trainor didn't break stride and motioned for Bernard to follow. "I'll fill you in in the car. Who's that guy?" He pointed to the man following on Bernard's heels, rubbing his nose.

"Paul McKnight," McKnight answered for himself.

The name rang a bell. Then, he remembered Bernard and Wilson talking about him. He was somebody important. "Nice to meet you, sir. You can come, too."

It took less than ten minutes to get to the murder scene. During the entire frantic dash, Trainor filled both men in on what Thorsen had told him. Under the circumstances, it would be better to question the witnesses of the recent murder than to try to find a prostitute. They could sent uniformed officers to look for her while they tried to catch up with Koretsky.

The police had the area cordoned off with yellow tape. The three men walked up to one of the uniformed officers charged with keeping people out and showed their badges. "He's with me," Bernard said pointing to McKnight.

They lifted the tape and headed for the dumpster. The body was already removed, placed on the ground, and covered with a white sheet. The mobile crime unit technicians were busy collecting evidence as were the coroner and detectives assigned to the case.

McKnight and Bernard went over to the body while Trainor sought out the detective that had asked him if he wanted to go to the crime scene. He was directed into the restaurant where he found John questioning the cook who found the body.

"Hey, John," Trainor said quietly. The cook was visibly upset, shaken to the bone with his grisly discovery.

John excused himself and walked out of earshot. "What's up? I thought you weren't coming over?" John was wearing a blue short sleeve shirt and had loosened his brown tie.

"Change in plans," Trainor said. "What have you got?"

"Not much. Nobody saw a thing. The victim, her name is Tanya Richardson, left with her boyfriend after work as she does almost every night he works. He's the bartender."

"Where is he?" Trainor asked. The perception of the question would mean that he'd be a suspect. But in this case it wasn't true, and Trainor didn't lead John to believe otherwise.

"We haven't had a chance to look for him yet, but here is his name, address, and other place of employment." He handed Trainor the paper with the information from the personnel files in the restaurant.

"Thanks, John," Trainor said and turned to walk away.

"Gary," John called after him. "Do you think the boyfriend is the one responsible for all the murders?"

He shook his head. "No, he's not."

"What have you got?" Bernard asked as Trainor approached. They stood in the dining room near the kitchen doors.

"Name and address of the boyfriend."

"What's his name?" McKnight asked.

Trainor read the name, "Rufus Brown, but his nickname is Ghost."

McKnight hung his head.

Trainor immediately picked up of the distress in McKnight's demeanor. "What is it?"

"Brown's probably dead, too," McKnight said. "He was the target, and the girl was probably in the way."

Trainor became confused. "What are you talking about?"

Bernard answered the question. "Brown was the third partner with Kaderri and Wolff."

Trainor immediately knew what that meant. "Maybe he doesn't know. I'll try him at his office." He pulled the cellular phone out of his pocket and dialed the number that was written on the paper.

"Law offices," the professional female voice said.

"Rufus Brown, please."

"I'm sorry, but he hasn't reported to work yet. May I take a message?"

"No message. Is he usually tardy?" The voice sounded familiar.

"No, sir. He's usually early."

"Thank you for your time." He ended the conversation, re-read the piece of paper, and pressed a new set of numbers on the phone. There was no answer at Brown's house.

Following Trainor's lead, McKnight produced his own cellular phone and dialed a number from memory. The phone was picked up on the fifth ring.

"Hello?" Kaderri answered the phone in a reserved annoyance.

"Marc, its Paul. I'm sorry to have to tell you, but it appears Koretsky found the bug."

As soon as he heard McKnight's voice, Kaderri's gut told him the news was bad. "Ghost?" He braced himself for the bad news that was to follow.

"We haven't found him. But it doesn't look good. His girlfriend was found in a dumpster with Koretsky's two shot signature."

"Oh, shit. When?" He was immediately filled with anger and sorrow. He clenched his jaw and drew a breath.

"The coroner put time of death between eleven and midnight."

"Have you told Bob?"

"Not, yet. I'm going to call him as soon as I hang up with you."

"Don't. I'll call."

"Okay, Marc," a sense of urgency seeped into McKnight's voice, "he's coming."

"I'll take care of him.' Kaderri hung the phone up in silence, shaking his head because of another friend lost to the drug trade, and Moshe Koretsky. He knew McKnight would get some extra people to come up and help. But to be sure, especially knowing how bureaucracies worked, Kaderri decided to call for his own help.

Picking the receiver off the hook, he dialed the number for Crawford Enterprises and asked for Wolff's extension.

"Optics," a cheerful female voice said, stating department she was answering for.

"Doctor Wolff, please."

"He's in the firing range at the moment. Can I leave him a message?"

"No, it's important. Tell him Marc is on the line."

"He doesn't want to be bothered," the lady retorted.

"If you tell him my name, he'll drop his work no matter how important it is. Believe me." He heard a huff from the lady before he was put on hold.

Less than a minute later, Wolff picked up the extension in the firing range. "What's so urgent, Marc."

"Paul called," he said quietly. "Koretsky found the bug and Ghost is missing."

"Damn!" There was silence. "Koretsky probably got him." There was sorrow in his voice, too.

Kaderri took his mind off the death of his friend and focused on what was at stake. "If he got Ghost, he's no doubt on his way up here. How soon can you come up?"

"I'll leave here in two hours." Wolff's voice revealed the same thinking.

"Good, In my basement, there's a trunk with some equipment in it. Also, swing by Tommy's Shipping. He'll have something for you."

"What's at Tommy's Shipping?"

"He's an acquaintance of Ghost's, and was a good friend of Steven." He was the man who had provided the M40A1 sniper rifle, and had access to military equipment.

Wolff clearly understood the meaning, but also seemed uncomfortable. "Wouldn't it be safer going through McKnight?"

"Don't have the time. Tommy has the material in stock. I'll tell him you're stopping by in two hours to pick it up."

"See you in a bit." Wolff hung up the phone.

Kaderri pressed the flash button on the phone and dialed Tommy's number from memory. Once committing something to memory, he rarely forget it. It came in handy at a time like this. The conversation took less than ten minutes. Kaderri briefly explained the situation and told him what had happed to Ghost. Tommy assured him the items he wanted would be ready for pickup when Wolff arrived.

One phone call to go.

Four, five, six rings, ten rings, finally it was answered. "Hello?" an unexpected female voice answered.

"Hi, I'm looking for Jesse Hughes."

"Hold on, he's on his way back to work"

Kaderri could hear the phone being covered and Jesse's name being shouted. A moment later an angry male voice came on the phone. "What?"

"Jesse?" Kaderri asked hesitantly.

After a moment's hesitation, the man said, "Boss?"

"Yeah, it's me."

"Well I'll be dipped in shit! How are you? What's up?"

"I got a problem." As a commander of an A-Team, Kaderri never used the word "problem" unless he needed help. And help was something he rarely ever called for. When Kaderri said there was a problem, it was serious.

"What do you need?" Hughes asked without hesitation.

"You," Kaderri simply stated.

"When, where, and what for?"

"Now, at my place in the Adirondacks. I don't want to say over the phone." When Kaderri was commanding troops, he knew that his men would follow him anywhere. His men knew the mission came first, and that he may take casualties. But, they also knew that Kaderri would do his best to try and keep them to a minimum. He realized that he wasn't commanding troops in this situation and didn't know how Jesse would re-act. "Jesse, it's serious." Serious meant real danger.

He knew that the word serious wouldn't escape Hughes' ears. "Okay, Boss, meet me at Adirondack Airport at eight. I'll be flying a Jet Ranger."

"Thanks, Jesse. And, bring your medical kit," Kaderri said and hung up.

"What's going on, Marc?"

He whirled around to see Sara standing in the doorway to the living room with her arms folded across her chest and a beautiful face masked with fear.

"What did you hear?" he asked. He wasn't upset that she heard, he just wanted to know.

"Everything," she hesitated, "I think."

"It's more than likely that Ghost is dead."

"Oh my God!" she quickly covered her gaping mouth.

"Sit down, Sara, we have to talk." He grabbed her by the arm and led her to the living room.

"Not again, Marc. Are you going to tell me something else I won't be able to handle?"

He stopped and looked Sara right in her eyes. "This is serious."

Tuesday, June 16, 5:00 p.m.

Satisfied that the day had gone better than expected, Moshe Koretsky swung by a fast-food place to pick up a few burgers and fries to fill his growling stomach. He still had a lot of work to do and hoped that Mossad had information for him regarding Marcus Kaderri.

He immediately checked the fax machine upon walking into the safe house to see if something was there demanding his attention. There was. He picked up the one page in the tray, noted the time it arrived, and took it to the kitchen where he read the paper and ate his burgers.

He scanned the paper. To his dismay, Mossad said they couldn't find any information on Marcus Kaderri. Why they didn't he thought was odd. Not that it mattered anyway, he knew enough about the man from reading his wall that he was a force to be reckoned with. Because of his military training,

322

he knew why he didn't have an alarm system. Finishing his second burger, he washed it down with a beer and gave Mossad a call.

Opening his Seven Star to the proper page, he made the call and went through the identification and authenticity process before he was connected to the director.

"Moshe, what do you have for me?"

"I know who Marcus Kaderri is and where he's located."

"You know your orders, why are you calling me? Did you fuck something up?" the director said angrily.

"No, sir. The man has an impressive military record," Koretsky said. "He's a force to be reckoned with."

"What are you saying?" The director's voice changed to one of concern. "You can't take care of him?"

"I can, but I think that some backup would be helpful to make sure he doesn't get away. He's a serious threat."

"You want a Kidon team?" Kidon was responsible for carrying out assassinations and kidnappings.

"No, they wouldn't do. I need commandos, a dozen preferably." Koretsky wasn't pulling any punches.

"Are you fucking kidding? You want a team of commandos sent into the United States?"

Koretsky didn't even argue. He simply answered in a level voice. "Yes."

"That's an act of war, do you know that?" The director's voice was back to being angry.

"If this man isn't eliminated now, the whole operation will fold. He knows I'm here and is coming after me."

"What kind of man is this?"

"Special Forces, Delta Force, black belt in martial arts. He's one of the best."

"Okay, Moshe, you have your team. When do you want them?"

"I need them by Thursday at the latest. I have all the information that the commandos will need."

"Send it. I'll be in touch. Good luck."

Before the line was disconnected, Koretsky had a stack of

paper full of information ready to fax over to Israel. He had the entire plan worked out, except for the tactical aspects that he would leave to the commandos. He had the objective of the mission, a profile of the target, along with topographic maps of the target sight, airline routes' and anything else he could find in the local gift shop, library and one of the Park Service Ranger station in the Adirondacks. Everything he had obtained was accessible to the general public, except for the photograph of Marcus Kaderri that he took off the wall. The commandos would need a picture of their target. He didn't care how the commandos arrived, just that they showed up at the right place at the right time.

Tuesday, June 16, 6:30 p.m.

"What are your questions?" Bernard asked standing in the center of his living room. Usually after the type of briefing he just gave, people always had questions about their new assignments. Someone raised their hand.

"Maria?" Bernard asked the pretty brunette.

"Hal and I," she glanced over at the handsome officer, "are going to be watching the hotel where he will show up sooner or later to pick up his messages. Most likely, there are going to be a lot of people about, and instead of shooting to kill—"

Bernard knew where she was going with the question, and cursed McKnight for sending her. The best quality about her was that she played the role of a woman in love perfectly. Her acting would win her an Academy Award. But sometimes, she thought too much and had too liberal a view on some things. She was also an expert marksman. "Maria, you just act like a horny woman waiting to get into Hal's pants without drawing too much attention. When Koretsky appears, he'll look at you. Like most men, he admires a pretty woman. When either you or Hal has a clean shot, take it. Use your discretion. He won't be taken alive, and he won't think twice about shooting, no matter who is near him."

"Don't get too carried away, Maria," another officer said with a laugh, "we need you to keep you mind focused on work, not wondering what kind of pleasure you are going to get from Hal."

The group of CIA officers and Gary Trainor laughed at the joke, but the crowd in Bernard's living room quickly fell deftly silent. They were about to engage in a life or death operation that would most likely end within the next twenty-four hours.

"Okay, are there any other questions?" When nobody answered, Bernard dismissed the officers. "Let's get to work." Bernard put most of the officers in and around the Hilton. In all, not including Trainor and Bernard, there were four officers there. The rest of the officers were assigned to other location around the city keeping watch in case Koretsky made his appearance elsewhere.

When the last of the people cleared out, Trainor turned to Bernard. "Keith, why don't we let a SWAT team take him out?"

"First of all, this isn't a police function. It's national security. Second of all, how many SWAT member are reliable?" When he saw Gary's face twist in anger he put his hand up defensively. "I don't mean in doing their duty, I mean pulling the trigger to kill. I can't take the chance on having one of them freeze at the moment it's time to pull the trigger. Do you know how many of them have actually aimed their weapon at someone and fired?"

Trainor frowned. "No."

"Listen, the police function is to protect the public. This operation is simply about killing a human being. Let me ask you, have you ever shot someone, let along killed someone?"

"No, and I hope I never have to either."

"It's not a pleasant feeling. My people are trained differently from yours. I'd like to think that they would follow through with what they have to. More importantly though, SWAT is two visible. Koretsky would spot them immediately." Bernard paused and asked, "How's the search going for Betty Freeman?"

"I got three officers searching for her, and so far she hasn't turned up. Do you think he got her?"

Bernard shook his head and shrugged, "It's possible, Gary."

"I told Thorsen to leave town for a while. It would be in her best interest. Besides, her job is on shaky ground because of the stunt she pulled, so she has no reason to stick around."

Bernard chuckled. "To save herself from who? Koretsky or you?"

Trainor smacked Bernard's shoulder. "Shut up. Let's get to the hotel."

Tuesday, June 16, 8:15 p.m.

The Bell Jet Ranger helicopter touched down with ease on the tarmac. The pilot went through the motions of shutting the machine down. When the rotor blades finally stopped, the pilot exited the aircraft. Jesse Hughes stood at five ten with a slender figure and didn't weight more than a hundred sixty pounds.

Opening the side door, he pulled out some rope and tie downs, secured the rotor blades and secured the helicopter to the tarmac. He reached back into the cockpit and pulled out a duffle bag. Slinging it over his shoulder, he marched over to where Kaderri was standing. "Jesus Christ, Boss, you could have helped me secure the bird."

Kaderri looked him in the eye and said, "The last time I tried to help you do that, you chewed my ass off. Lucky for you, I liked you, because I'd never let a fucking sergeant first class talk to me like that." He held out his hand.

Hughes took the outstretched hand and shook it firmly. "It's good to see you, Boss."

"It's good to see you, too, Jesse. Thanks for coming." Kaderri led Hughes back to the Jeep that was parked next to a hangar.

Once they cleared the airport, Kaderri said, "Who was the lady that answered your phone?"

"Jill. Jill Watson, she's my fiancé and a hot little number." He beamed with pride and happiness.

"When did you get engaged?"

"Three months ago. She's a lawyer."

Kaderri slapped his forehead and dropped his mouth. "An ambulance chaser! I thought I taught you better than that."

"She's a corporate ambulance chaser if you must know," Hughes offered with a smile, taking the jab in stride. "Besides, she pretty and rich."

"Good. I'm happy for you. When's the wedding?'

Hughes shrugged. "That, we haven't decided yet." Now that the formalities were aside, the conversation turned serious. "Marc, what's going on? What do you need me for? I hope the situation is happier than the last time we met." He had been one of the pallbearers for Steven Caron. That was the last time they saw each other.

"Essentially, Jesse, I need you to protect Sara."

"Protect Sara? You want a bodyguard? Marc, you're more than qualified to protect her." Once the look of bafflement left his face, it quickly turned to anger. "You know I'd do just about anything for you or with you, but being a fucking bodyguard. For what? I hope there is a good reason for dragging me up here from North Carolina."

"You finished?" Kaderri asked sternly.

Hughes took a deep breath and let it out slowly. "Yeah."

"Bob and I, he's with Sara now, are involved in some work."

"You're contracted," Hughes said it like a statement instead of a question. When Kaderri nodded, Hughes nodded. "They asked me, but I turned them down."

"Anyway," Kaderri continued, "without going into specifics at this point, I'm being sought by a Mossad officer by the name of Moshe Koretsky."

"Mossad? What did you get yourself involved in?"

Kaderri ignored the question, but would answer part of it later in the conversation. During the rest of the ride back to the cabin, he explained to Hughes what had happened and was happening and how he planned to take out Koretsky. While he and Wolff were out in the field using their expertise, Hughes would remain in the house keeping Sara safe against any unforeseen development. And if needed, he could utilize his talents as a combat medic.

Tuesday, June 16, 9:45 p.m.

The three men sat around the kitchen table dressed in woodland pattern camouflaged battle dress uniforms. Kaderri's and Wolff's faces and hands were smeared with camouflage paint. The load bearing equipment that each man wore held a sidearm and extra magazines for their weapons, two hand grenades, and an assortment of other accessories necessary for survival in the field of combat.

Sara, being overwhelmed by the rape and the events of the past few days, was snoring loudly in the upstairs bedroom. Kaderri, Wolff, and Hughes drank coffee as they studied the topographical maps of Kaderri's property. They has an assortment of weapons scattered about, but all within arm's reach in case they were needed at a moment's notice.

"Bob and I set claymores and trip flares in these locations," Kaderri said pointing to spots on the map where the anti-personnel mines were set up. "We set them prior to your arrival, Jesse. With just the three of us, there is just too much territory for us to keep an eye on properly. If Koretsky comes from one of these routes, he'll run into the mines and hopefully they'll get him. If not, it'll give us a warning and time to get over there."

"Where the hell did you get claymores?" Hughes asked.

"From the same guy that we got the rest of equipment from," Kaderri answered.

Hughes knew that was all he was going to get as an answer. "Marc, don't you think you are going overboard with this? Are claymores really necessary? I mean, he's just one man."

Kaderri stared hard at Hughes and took a sip of his coffee. "I thought so at first, but if he's connected in the drug trade, he may bring in some extra people to make sure Bob and I cease to exist. And, he has to know about Bob if he got to Ghost. There's no way Ghost would be able to stand up to the interrogation that Koretsky would conduct. If he's that high up in the Mossad hierarchy, who knows what steps they'll take to protect him and this operation. Besides, if you were going after someone with our abilities, how would you go about it?"

"I'd bring a whole goddamn battalion," Hughes answered with a smile.

Kaderri smiled back and read the time on his military issue watch. "It's time to go patrolling." He pointed a steady finger on the map at the area on the mountainside above the house where he would be. The spot he chose would enable him to watch the house and all the approaches. "I'll be here." He pointed to another spot that covered the front of the house and the road. "Bob's over here." When Wolff nodded Kaderri turned to Hughes, "Jesse, take care of Sara."

"Not a problem"

Kaderri and Wolff slipped on their ghillie suits, and Kaderri slung his scope mounted sniper rifle over his shoulder. Next to be fitted in place were the AN/PVS-7A night vision goggles secured to their heads and the communication headset that allowed all three to communicate with each other. After chambering a round in their pistols, Kaderri chambered one in his Heckler and Koch MP5 submachine gun and Wolff did the same with his M16A2. Placing the weapons on safe they walked out into the night.

Tuesday, June 16, 10:40 p.m.

The heat and high humidity was still oppressive at this time of night and as a result, it created a massive thunderstorm over the Capital District. Fiery ribbons of lighting zigzagged across the sky immediately followed by ear ringing booms of thunder. Rain fell as if it was forced out of a fire hose, making driving extremely difficult and hazardous.

Despite the windshield wipers being on fast as they could go, Koretsky could barely see the front of his car. For a day that had gone so well, it hadn't ended on a positive note. He was in the process of remedying that.

He has spent two hours searching for the prostitute, Betty "Blossom" Freeman, but he came up empty-handed. He first went to the address where he'd had his encounter with her, but she wasn't there. His search on the streets ended up the same way. She had to be eliminated at all costs. According to Michele Thorsen, she could identify him. In all probability, she was right and he only had to blame his own stupidity for this intangible mess that he had to rectify.

The rain came down even harder and he decided the smart thing to do was to pull over until the rain subsided. Putting the car in park, he flipped on the dome light and pulled out his map and picture of the lady with her head buried deep in Joshua Miller's lap. He checked the address attached to the photograph and searched for it once again on the map. As far as he could tell from his present position, he was two streets and almost three miles from her house.

Within five minutes, the rain let up enough so that he could safely drive. He continued on the same road for another mile and a half and found the left turn where it was supposed to be. This brought him into a nice residential area that was easily tagged as upper middle class. Another half mile brought him to a road off to the right, which he gently turned onto. There were three houses completed and two more under construction. He slowed the car, searching for the right house number. Finally, he found it on the mailbox. It was the last house on the street.

The outside lights on the raised ranch weren't on. But there were two on inside the house. As he pulled into the driveway, he felt himself get hard at the anticipation of getting laid. Quietly, he closed the car door and sprinted to the house trying to keep as dry as possible. After two succinct knocks, the outside light was illuminated and the door was opened.

"Yes?" a pleasant voice said.

Koretsky still had the hood on his raincoat up when he laid eyes on the pretty redhead. The glare of the light made his eyes squint causing him not to be able to get a good look at the woman. He held out the picture and said, "Miller sent me over."

"Sure, come on in and go upstairs into the living room" The unexpected familiar voice said. She opened the door to allow Koretsky in and took the picture from Koretsky's out-stretched hand.

Closing the door, she quickly following him up the stairs where he already had his raincoat off, and was making himself comfortable on the overstuffed couch.

When Koretsky looked up to get a look at the lady he would be spending the night with, he recognized her. A smile spread across his face. "Well Miz Waters, we meet again. I must say, it's more of a pleasure meeting you this way than in Miller's office as his receptionist." He pointed to the picture she was still holding in her hand. "You come highly recommended. Will you do the same performance on me as you do with Miller?"

"How'd you get this picture?" she asked,

"That's not important, but I have a whole lot more." He unbuttoned his pants, ready for a night of pleasure.

As he got undressed, he carefully removed the gun from the small of his back. Koretsky noticed her hands started to tremble and she tried to keep her cool. He thought maybe she saw the gun, and it made her nervous. With trembling hands, she lifted her t-shirt over her head, exposing her bare breasts.

Koretsky's erection grew as he watched in delight as Miss Waters undressed herself in front of him. But, he noticed the fear in her eyes. Something wasn't right.

After she pulled her shorts off, she kneeled between Koretsky's legs and took him into her mouth. She twirled her tongue over the tip and sighed, "Mmmm, this is nice. It this what you like?"

Those words struck a cord. He heard those same words before while receiving a blow job. He let her continued for a while longer, savoring her expert mouth.

He pushed her off of him and guided her to the couch. "I want to fuck."

"There's more room in the bedroom why don't we go in there?" she suggested.

"No, I want to do it here," he snorted his answer.

"If that's what you want." She lay on her back and spread her legs. Koretsky moved between her legs and placed his mouth on her erect nipples, sucking them hard and biting them.

Moving away from her chest, Koretsky put himself in her and began to push in and out of unevenly. It didn't take long before he felt himself begin to come. Suddenly, he stopped and withdrew.

She looked up with terror filled eyes. "Why did you stop?"

He pushed away from her, grabbed his Makarov and stood above her. "You!" he yelled.

Her face twisted in fear as she still lay on the couch, trapped underneath, watching the muzzle of the gun point directly at her forehead. "What's going on?"

"You're Blossom aren't you?"

"No! " I'm Debbie Waters," she screamed. "I work for Miller."

"Don't forget prostitute." He lowered his voice and spoke in a measured tone. "I see it now. You were wearing a long, red wig and different makeup the last time we fucked. Pretty convincing, I must admit." He smiled evilly.

"No!" she covered her face with her hands hoping to shield herself. "Please, don't!" she pleaded.

"Damn, I really want to come, but I don't want to leave any evidence that could link me to your murder."

She attempted to scream, but the two bullets that slammed into her forehead prevented any sound from escaping.

Koretsky got dressed and smiled, knowing there was no longer anyone that would identify him as the murderer of Pedro. Miller may be pissed that his concubine and one of his paralegals were dead, but he'd get over it once he learned about the bug. He could always tell him that Debbie Waters was part of it.

Once in the car, he thought about giving Michele a call, but decided that he better just go home and prepare for the upcoming fight with Marcus Kaderri. Once Kaderri was dead, he would indulge in the pleasures of the flesh with her.

CHAPTER EIGHTEEN

Wednesday, June 17, 4:20 a.m.

The patrolling brought back many memories, for Kaderri, some good and some not so good. This was the third time he had swept his area and all was in order. He was tired, but for him, it felt good. He was back in his element, his world. The twenty-minute catnap he took while sitting against a tree was refreshing, but he still needed a decent sleep. He just wasn't used to this line of work anymore.

He sat down on a rock and gazed over the mountain tops on the eastern horizon. A pink line shimmered in the distance, signaling the rise of the sun and the dawn of a new day. Taking a long pull from his canteen, he surveyed the last remaining stars before they were swallowed by the morning light. Though he knew the constellation Orion wasn't visible at this time of year he still gazed upward seeing it with his mind's eye.

Orion the Hunter. He thought back to one of his instructors at the sniper school who gave a lecture about snipers and sniping. One speech in particular stood out where the instructor compared a sniper to Orion the Hunter. Kaderri remembered the man telling the class that the sole purpose of their training is to kill another human being, particularly with one shot and without being detected. As a sniper, they are the deadliest men on the battlefield. Like Orion, the greatest hunter of all, who lives forever in the night sky, they too, are hunters. The instructor went on, explaining that unlike Orion, who hunted animals, he focused on the point that they will hunt the deadliest creature on Earth. They will hunt human beings.

The instructor closed by telling them that Orion is immortal, and they are not. The translation meant that if they made a mistake, they'll end up in God's heaven. Unless they became immortal and had a constellation named after them, they will hunt under the shadow of Orion.

Kaderri remembered the speech as if he just heard it. He was the hunter, hunting a man named Moshe Koretsky.

"How's it going, Marc?" Wolff's voice whispered over the radio in Kaderri's ear, breaking him from his thoughts.

"All's well," he talked back into his microphone. "How's your area?"

"Clear. No sign of anything. It's getting light out here, and I don't think anything is going to happen. It would have happened by now. I'm heading in."

"Me too."

"I'll have the coffee ready," Hughes said suprisingly. He too could listen in on the conversation and talk to both men. "But, you cook your own breakfast."

Wednesday, June 17, 9:20 a.m.

The weather conditions hadn't changed from during the night. The rain came down just as hard and the thunder and lighting boomed and cracked. Moshe Koretsky walked into the lobby of the Hilton and swept the room with his eyes. As usual, the hotel lobby was busy. People dressed in casual clothes wandered aimlessly, searching the hotel as if to see what was there, while others dressed smartly walked with a purpose to a meeting or a breakfast in the restaurant.

Sitting on one of the love seats were two people who appeared to be in love. Their raincoats draped over the table in front of them. The lady, a pretty brunette with shapely legs, wore a pair of shorts and a golf shirt. The handsome man next to her with black hair wore jogging pants and a t-shirt. He ran his hand up and down her leg and every few minutes they would kiss. Sometimes passionately, sometimes not. The couple got stares and smiles from the people who noticed. They were obviously a couple in love.

Koretsky spotted them the moment he walked into the lobby. He had a keen eye for attractive women, and not completing his business with the prostitute last night, he couldn't help but notice the couple in love and envied the man that he soon would be in bed with her.

Tearing his mind away from them, Koretsky strode over to the desk to retrieve any messages that may be waiting for him. "Any messages for me?" He held out his room key. As the desk attendant left, he turned to watch the couple.

"No messages, sir," the attendant said when he came back.

"Thank you." Koretsky didn't turn to face the attendant. He was too busy watching the couple and noticed something was missing. He became suspicious and pretended to not look at them. Every time they kissed, the woman didn't close her eyes. Instead, she glanced over at his direction.

He moved over to the gift shop and picked up a copy of the Times Union and pretended to read the headlines. The woman's gaze followed him. He was being watched, but by whom? Was it one of Miller's people or a cop? He bought the newspaper and headed over to the elevators. All the cars were on the higher floors and Koretsky didn't want to wait for them. He turned and headed for the stairs.

"Kiss me quick!" Maria ordered Hal.

Hal closed his eyes as she put her lips to his. "What?" he muttered during the kiss.

She started to nibble on his ear. "He's at the desk," she

whispered in his ear between nibbles. "Wearing olive trousers and tan raincoat." She turned her head to get a better look, and then started kissing Hal again. "He's heading for the stairs."

Maria shifted in her seat, reached down onto the floor, and slung her purse over her shoulder. "What are you doing?" Hal asked.

Maria stood and waited until the door closed behind Koretsky. She zipped open her purse and took hold of her silenced .22 caliber pistol. Though it wasn't by any means a powerful pistol, with soft point bullets, it's ideal for close range assassinations. She spoke into the microphone that was attached to her bra strap, "He's going upstairs, I'm following." The other officers heard her, as did Bernard and Trainor in the van outside. Only her and Hal didn't have an earpiece to listen in on conversations and instructions. Bernard thought it would be too risky. Someone with Koretsky's talents would spot them immediately.

"Wait," Hal said, "he's going up to his room. Jerry and Lou are in there waiting for him." It hadn't been difficult to get Koretsky's room number. When they did, they had picked the lock and placed two officers in the room. When Koretsky opened the door, he would walk into a few well-placed shots.

"No, I'm following," Maria said and walked into the staircase.

"Maria, stop."

It worked, Koretsky took his time walking up the stairs, knowing at least one of the couple would follow. He was half way up the second flight of stairs pretending to read the paper. When he heard the door below him open, he withdrew his Makarov and hid it under the newspaper.

A moment after the door opened, there was silence. Obviously the person was listening to determine if they should go up or down. To help the person out, Koretsky shuffled his feet. He was ready. He wouldn't lose.

Koretsky saw it was the woman and thought it was a shame

for a pretty woman to die so young. Silently, she walked up the stairs. Soon, she was not more than ten feet away. Because he was higher than her and on a different flight of stairs, she couldn't get a good shot. She had to close the distance.

Out of the corner of his eye, Koretsky saw the pistol come up. He spun around, leveled his silenced pistol and paused a moment before he fired. The look of surprise in the lady's face was amusing to him. Her eyes and mouth opened wide, clearly knowing she was caught and would lose. The two bullets that he fired at less than six feet tore through her chest, one piercing her heart. Blood burst from the entrance and exit holes and her body fell backwards, down the stairs.

Koretsky followed the body down, already knowing she was dead. He needed to know who she was and if possible who she worked for. Noticing the pistol was a silenced .22, he knew she didn't work for Miller. The idiots that worked for him didn't know the first thing about assassinations. This lady did.

He had to think quickly. She had been with a man who no doubt worked with her. He would soon be following, and it was a safe bet that there'd be someone waiting in his room. He started downstairs to exit the building from the rear when the door opened. He stopped.

Koretsky couldn't see who it was, but he assumed it was the man with the lady in the lobby. The man burst through the door and practically stepped on the dead body. "Shit!" he said at seeing her. Regaining his balance, he searched the stairs. "This is Hal," he said into his microphone. "I'm—"

Koretsky, who was now on the stairs below the landing, was hidden from view because of the way the door swung open. He took two more steps, turned around and recognized the man as the one who had been in the lobby with the lady. When the door closed, he got a clear shot and fired. Koretsky ran down the stairs and out of the building.

Hal turned just as the bullets hit. One shattered his collarbone and the other grazed his forehead. The force of the bullets slammed his body against the wall and he crumpled to the floor. Before he passed out from the pain and loss of blood, Hal spoke into his microphone, "I'm...in....the...stair...well. Maria's dead, I'm hit. Koretsky...getting....away."

Trainor and Bernard sat on the vinyl seats in the van parked on Lodge Street outside the hotel listening intently to the disaster unfolding in the stairwell. There was one other man in the van besides Bernard and Trainor, and all three were wearing headphones. Communications gear of all types were bolted to the walls of the air-conditioned van. Reel to reel tapes recorded every sound the agents made.

"What the hell was that?" Trainor asked, at the strange hollow sound he heard after the stairwell door opened. He pushed the headphones closer to his ears to hear better.

"Shit!" Bernard yelled. "That was a silenced pistol being fired!"

"Maria's?" Trainor asked. He had never heard a silenced weapon being discharged.

The other man shook his head and adjusted some dials.

"Get into the stairwell people, Maria needs help," Bernard ordered the other officers. They were all wearing headsets that were linked together and with the van.

"Why hasn't she fired back?" Trainor asked aloud, but he already knew the answer.

The next sounds came from Hal in labored breathing saying the he was hit and Maria was dead and that Koretsky was getting away.

"Stay here, Doug," Bernard ordered. "Follow me, Gary." They exchanged headphones for the portable sets that the other officers had. They exited the van through the rear door and headed down the street in the pouring rain. They came to the corner of Pine Street and stopped. Bernard tipped his head and peered around the corner to see if Koretsky was working his way up the street or waiting in ambush. The rain was coming down too hard to tell, so they took a chance and ran down the street toward the back of the hotel.

Nervously sweating, Trainor felt the excitement and terror at the same time. He had never been in this situation before. He studied Bernard as they ran and noted how calm and cool he was acting.

Suddenly, Bernard stopped and dropped to one knee bringing up his pistol. A figure rounding the corner of the building slowed from a fast run and seemed to try to look inconspicuous. What gave the man away was his roving, predatory eyes and the tip of the silenced pistol protruding from the sleeve of the raincoat. Bernard regulated his breathing and fired. The driving rain forced itself into his eyes and distorted his vision. The bullets missed. One ripped through Koretsky's sleeve and the other ricocheted off the building.

Instinctively, Koretsky ducked, fired once and ran.

Once the bullets came in Trainor's direction, he involved himself in the firefight. He managed to squeeze off three rounds at the fleeing target before it disappeared around the corner. Trainor, with Bernard in tow, gave chase.

Koretsky fled back down the way he came, running at a dead run toward the rear door of the hotel. A burly figure smashed through the door with a pistol drawn and took aim at Koretsky. Koretsky was a half-second faster. He aimed and squeezed the trigger, hitting the man in the chest. Without missing a step, he turned and fired at Bernard and Trainor.

Trainor cursed the rain and watched in horror as Koretsky shot the other officer. Trainor, who wasn't accustomed to firing on the run, stopped and took aim. By the time he drew a bead on Koretsky, he felt as if he got hit by a baseball bat. He stopped dead in his tracks and was lifted off his feet as the first bullet ripped through his left shoulder. A searing pain stretched from the corner of his eye and across the top of his ear as the second bullet glanced off the side of his head. With a crash, his body and head slammed onto the wet pavement.

In a dream-like state, Trainor felt pressure on his neck and heard Bernard. "Gary, come on man, wake up," he pleaded. "Please, don't be dead." The pressure increased and then "Thank God, you're alive." Bernard tore open the shirt and placed his hand over the hole in his shoulder to stem the flow of blood.

"Get me some ambulances!" Bernard yelled into the microphone touching his lips. "I've got people down!"

"On the way," Doug, the driver of the van said over the radio.

Just then, the van pulled up onto the curb behind Bernard, and Doug got out and ran to the man shot in the doorway of the hotel. The sirens of the approaching ambulances and police cars grew louder.

Moans escaped from Trainor's mouth and his eyes fluttered open. His first sight was Bernard's round face smiling at him. "Oh, shit," Trainor said, "I fucking hurt." His fingers felt the warm liquid flowing down his neck and when he pulled his hand away they were red.

"You took two," Bernard said.

Trainor's head was swimming from smashing onto the ground, not to mention the pain in his shoulder and head. "Two what?"

"Bullets, Gary."

Fear gripped him. "Am I dead?"

"No, you're not," Bernard answered him assuredly. "Do I look like Saint Peter?

Trainor sat up with the help of Bernard and shut his eyes tight at the pain. "Damn, my head hurts." He rubbed the back of his head where it had struck the concrete. He moved his shoulder, but the wave of pain that struck made him grimace. It also put an end to any more movement. He opened his eyes once again an stared at Bernard, "Did we get him?"

Bernard shook his head, "No, Gary, he got away and killed some good people."

Sara listened, but the downstairs of the cabin was quiet, an eerie quiet that was unsettling. The only noise she heard was the slight creaking of trees bending in the wind and the warning cries from birds of the approaching storm. But for now, the sun was still shining, giving off a false pretense of paradise in the Adirondacks.

When she finally made it to the floor from her slow decent

on the stairs, she was startled to see a sleeping form of what appeared to be a man in camouflage clothing with a rifle laid across his chest on the couch. Because of the camouflage face paint, she couldn't tell who it was.

"Good morning, Sara," said a voice from the corner of the living room.

Sara jumped at the sound and covered her rapidly beating heart with her hands. She stared at another camouflaged figure sitting in one of the chairs. "Who are you?" she asked.

The figure rose and smiled, revealing clean white teeth. Besides the whites of his eyes, they were the only discernable features of the man's face. He still held onto his weapon. "Jesse Hughes, remember me?"

Sara nodded, remembering the name and face of the man at Steven Caron's funeral. But, she had no idea where he came from. "Where did you come from?" she asked.

He extended his hand when he reached her. "Marc picked me up last night. There's coffee in the pot."

Sara shook the outstretched camouflaged hand and looked into the eyes of the man. There were intense beside friendly and they unnerved her. They were the same eyes she had seen in Marc when he bet up Greg Sander. "Nice to see you again, Jesse. I think. Where's Marc?"

"He's on the deck out back keeping watch. I'm watching the front while Bob sleeps." He pointed to the form on the couch. His eyes never left her face. He was clearly studying the stitches and discoloration of her skin.

"Thanks." She turned to walked out when Jesse called.

"Sara, you better change your clothes."

She stopped and took in her attire. She couldn't figure out what was wrong with her white spandex shorts and crop top. "Why?"

"Too easy of a target," Marc said walking through the kitchen, He, too, was dressed in a camouflaged uniform with his face colored the same as the other two. He, too, was carrying a weapon. "Good morning, honey." He gave her a kiss. "Had a good night's sleep, huh?"

She nodded.

It was then that she took in her surroundings. There was military gear scattered about and an ominous looking weapon lying on the kitchen table. These men were serious, and the situation they were in was simply a matter of live or death. It appeared that they were prepared to go to all ends to make sure that they'd come out on the winning end.

She studied the eyes of Marc against his smile. The smile itself was genuine, as always when he saw her. But, his eyes scared her. The steel blue eyes were there, but they took on a dark shade. They looked like the eyes on a predator. This was a man that Sara didn't know. She felt frightened and secure at the same time in his presence.

"Are you hungry?" Marc asked, sounding as if nothing else was going on.

"A little," she admitted.

"So am I," Wolff said, rising off the couch. "If you can wait fifteen minutes while I take a shower, I'll cook something for the both of us.

"Sure," Sara said and walked over to the coffeepot and poured herself a steaming mug and one for Wolff. Dumping in some cream and sugar, she handed Wolff his. Again, she noticed the eyes. His were the same as the others. Intense, determined, and frightening. She has never seen men, especially men she knew and loved, look like this.

The wind from the south picked up in the afternoon carrying the gray storm clouds that gathered for their assault. Wolff and Hughes were out in the woods patrolling, making sure nobody could slip through unexpectedly. Kaderri kept track of their report on the map that was on the kitchen table. They would be finished in time for dinner.

Sara came in from the deck holding an empty glass of iced tea. "It's getting breezy out there. I think we're in for one hell of a storm."

Marc nodded, switching the microphone on his headset off, but making sure he could still hear if he was called. "I was watching the Weather Channel, we're going to get hit pretty hard."

"How long is it going to last?" she asked.

"It's suppose to start early this evening and last until some-time tomorrow."

Sara fidgeted, shifting her weight from one foot to the other. "Is this going to help us?"

"What do you mean?"

"Will Koretsky stay away in this kind of weather?"

"No. It he's smart, he'll use it to his advantage."

"Marc, he's one man," Sara stated. "Is he really this dangerous?"

He grabbed her hand and walked her over to the couch and sat down next to her. "Sara, listen to me. I've spent quite a few years of my life doing this and dealing with people of this nature. I'm very good at doing this and know what I'm doing. Moshe Koretsky is this dangerous."

"How do you know Jesse?" she asked. "I mean, beside being in the Army together."

Kaderri sighed and decided this was good time to finish the rest of his story. "He's the one who patched up my knee. He and Steven were on the same assignment with me. It was those two who saved my ass. Jesse was one of our medics."

"Where were you sent?" Shivers rocked through her body recalling the day he called saying he was in the hospital in Germany. Obviously, there was more to what really happened than what he had previously told her.

"I can't say," he said. "When Jesse gets back, I'll ask him to take out your stitches."

Suddenly, the phone rang.

Before the first ring ended, he had the receiver in his hand and spoke into it. "Yes?" a pause, then, "Who's calling?" Kaderri then put the conversation on the speaker.

"Keith Bernard. Listen carefully, Koretsky got away from me and killed two of my people. One more is in surgery at this moment."

"How long ago?"

"About nine-thirty this morning."

"Shit, eight hours ago?" Kaderri said appallingly.

"This is the first chance I had to call."

"I understand. Is your person going to make it?"

"It's iffy. Koretsky also shot my partner—"

"The real cop?"

"Yeah, his name is Gary Trainor. He's okay, banged up real good but okay."

"Anybody with him?" Kaderri asked, meaning Koretsky.

"He was by himself at the time and armed with a pistol. I don't know if he has help waiting in the wings?"

"Thanks for the heads up."

"McKnight gave me the location of your place, I'll get up there as soon as I can with more help."

"That's not necessary, we'll be able to handle him."

"I want the son-of-a-bitch," Bernard stated.

Kaderri sighed and assented. "I understand. Listen, don't come all the way up the driveway. When you turn into the driveway, don't go more than one hundred yards. Call me or you're not going to make it."

"Right. Good luck."

Kaderri hung up the phone and switched on his microphone, "How are things, guys?" he was silent as they must have responded. "I got info when you get back."

Sara sat looking at Marc, wondering what the hell was going on. She moved closer to him and began trembling in his arms. "He really wants you dead, doesn't he?" she said.

"Yeah, he does. But don't worry, he won't win."

"You're just as determined to kill him, aren't you?" She looked up into his eyes to gauge his reaction. When she saw the flash of steely determination and the steel blue eyes turned coal black, it put the fear of God into her.

"Yes, I am."

Sara buried her head in his chest and began to sob. She felt as if she were on the edge of a nervous breakdown.

"Sara, nothing is gong to happen to you."

"I'm afraid for you! I'm afraid for me, Bob, and Jesse!" She began to shake.

"Being here with us is the safest place you could be. We can handle anything he does. The only thing you have to do is listen to us."

Sara sniffed and wiped a tear off her cheek. She pulled herself away from the security of Marc's embrace. "I'll start dinner.

Wednesday, June 17, 6:15 p.m.

"Can I go now?" Trainor asked the doctor hovering over him. She finished inspecting his shoulder wound and put the bandage back in place. The wound on his head required some antiseptic and a bandage.

"No, Detective, you can't leave yet. I want you here overnight to keep an eye on you."

"Why? You fixed me up. I feel better and I can move my arm." He paused and then added, "Sort of."

Bernard was sitting in the chair away from the hospital bed and listening to Trainor's losing argument with the tall red headed doctor. He had to smile. "Gary, will you just shut up and listen. You've been shot for Christ's sake."

Trainor sat up closed his eyes at the pain. He pointed at Bernard and asked the doctor, "Can you tell him to shut up and mind his own business? He doesn't listen to me."

The doctor smiled. "Are you two always like this?" Then her smile faded and she said, "Gary, your wounds are fine and there is no permanent damage. You'll have your full range of motion back."

"Then why can't I go now?" He was almost whining.

"I'm concerned about your stomach. You have an ulcer." Her green eyes bored a hole in Trainor.

"I have what?"

"You have your friend over here to thank for alerting us to the amount of Tums you were eating."

"Is it serious?"

"All ulcers are serious, but you'll be fine. That is as long as you keep taking the medication I prescribe. You should be able to leave in the morning."

He sighed, knowing he was beaten. "Okay, Doc, thanks." He put his head back down on the pillow.

Before the doctor walked out the door, she turned and said, "Your friends can stay for a few minutes, then they have to leave. You need your rest."

"What friends?"

Just then, the doctor moved out of the way and a troop of police officers entered the room.

Finally Koretsky had gathered his wits from the narrow escape with death. Coming that close to death was something new to him and it was an event he didn't want to go through again. He sat in the motel room in the small town of Blue Ridge, also in the Adirondacks, about fifteen miles south of Kaderri's cabin. It was here that he, along with the commandos, were suppose to stage for the assault on Kaderri's cabin.

There was a lot going through his mind. First and foremost, was the botched assassination attempt on his life. It was apparent that more capable forces were on to him, and he would have to close up his operation in this part of the United States. He just wondered if it was Joshua Miller who had turned him in. But, that didn't make sense. He was providing Miller's firm with serious money and it would be stupid to bite the hand that fed it. That was unless Miller was pissed about him killing Brown and Waters.

Drinking the rest of his soda, he stood, checked his Makarov to make sure he had a full magazine and walked out into the rain. He would be meeting the commando team at a small private airport located northwest of Saranac Lake. Why they wanted to be picked up there, he didn't know, but when they called back with the location and time, all Koretsky could do was comply. He has no idea how the team was getting into the States and didn't care just as long as they arrived on time.

Koretsky had to ditch his car after the shoot-out and rented a U-Haul truck big enough to carry a dozen men. He started the truck and drove toward the airport.

Koretsky would also wait until after the assault to tell the commander of the commando team that he would be leaving with them at the conclusion of the mission. Otherwise the mission would be scrubbed and Koretsky wouldn't be able to settle his personal score.

Wednesday, June 17, 8:30 p.m.

The interior of the cabin was dark, and any movement from the people inside was limited and couldn't be seen from the outside. Anything that has a light was turned off and forbidden to be used. That included the coffee maker, digital clock radio's and even the video cassette recorder. Anything that could betray any information, such as what room was located where, or if a person walked in front of the digital lights of a clock radio would make that person a target.

The only light to see by was from red filtered flashlights. Sara was safe and sound asleep in her bed. Jesse Hughes guarded the interior of the house and monitored the progress of Wolff and Kaderri out in the nasty weather.

This was now the standard operating procedure until Koretsky showed his face and had it wiped off the face of the earth.

The men had exited with precision the aircraft painted with the Canadian flag on the tail. The plane came in, stopped long enough for the men to disembark, and immediately got back into the air. The less time on the ground, the better. Once the pilots were back in the air, the would have to radio the control tower that all was okay and turbulence pushed them down below radar coverage or a mountain blocked their radar signature.

Koretsky had the truck parked one hundred yards off the single grass runway and watched from the dry cab as the men moved away from the plane and runway and dropped to the ground. A pulsating strobe light guided the pilots to their destination. Once the aircraft was gone and the men were on the ground, Koretsky got out of the protection of the truck's cab, took a green filtered flashlight and point it at the direction of the men. He turned it on and off four times, signaling that all was well. He waited as two shadows hurried over to him.

"Nice fucking weather," one of the shadows said to Koretsky. "I got guys puking all over the airplane from the rough ride. This mission must be important. I was ready to abort and called it in, but the fucking director got on the line and said no." The other shadow kneeled to the ground, and unfolded what looked like an umbrella frame. He pointed it to the sky, twisted a few dials on the satellite radio, and spoke into the handset. Koretsky knew the man was letting the people back in Israel know they had made it to the ground.

"I'm glad you made it safely." Koretsky said with an edge on his voice.

"Right. I'm Major Yousef Meir," the shadow identified himself then extended his hand.

Koretsky shook it. "Let's get your men in the truck. I have some sandwiches for them in the back in case they're hungry. You can ride up front with me."

Meir rounded up his heavily armed men and got them into the truck and out of the weather. It took no more than five minutes from the time the men hit the ground to the time they loaded into the truck and left the airport.

Koretsky handed a turkey sandwich and a coke to Meir. "Thanks."

"Where do you want to go first, Yousef? Back to the motel and have the men get some rest?"

"Actually, I'd like to recon the objective, This is perfect weather for us." Meir then looked hard at Koretsky. "Moshe, I read that you were a naval officer."

Koretsky knew that Meir was getting at and didn't blame him for his concern. All Israelis were required to serve in the IDF and Koretsky had happened to choose the Navy. The operation they were going to carry out was purely a commando operation that had nothing to do with naval training. If he had some type if infantry training, he'd have been better suited to the rigors of the field. But he did learn something about field work in the Mossad Academy.

"I understand your concern, Yousef, but I promise I won't get in your way."

"That is the only thing I ask of you. Just let me and my men do our job without any interference."

Koretsky detected a hint of animosity in the man's voice and decided to call him on it. "Is there a problem that I should know about?"

Meir sat silent for a moment. "I was on one of these operations before—"

"Working for Mossad?"

"Yes, We had to extract someone out of Iraq and it was a disaster."

"What happened?" Koretsky asked, He knew what happened on the operation, his friend was the one who was rescued.

"We lost two people and the information that the man had turned out to be false. Your person," meaning Mossad's, "panicked. He could have gotten out on his own. We lost two good men for nothing."

Koretsky decided to say nothing in response to that particular operation, but commented on this one instead. "Don't worry, Yousef, this isn't an extraction mission."

It would be worse.

By the time they reached their assembly point, the weather had worsened. They had taken back roads and goat path to the north face of Phelps Mountain. Their objective now lay some three miles to the south in a somewhat westerly angle. It would take them a few hours to circumvent the mountain and reach their rally point on the military crest of the north face of Mount Colden.

Leaving Koretsky behind with the other eight men, Meir took three men and conducted the recon of the target. They sat quietly on the south slope of Mount Colden and prepared to descend further down to get a better view of Kaderri's cabin.

It proved to be harder than he thought it would. The forest

was denser than he had anticipated, creating a problem of using his shoulder fired anti-tank weapons from a higher vantage point. The density of the forest also created vision problems. From where he was, he couldn't see the forest floor where the cabin was.

Not deterred, Meir rubbed his eyes and fitted his night vision goggles back in place. In a whisper, he orders his men to move out.

The spacing between each man was ten yards. Slowly and stealthily, the four men picked their way through the forest and down the steep decline of the mountain. Thankful for the wet forest floor that masked their footsteps, they could make better time and the roar of thunder overhead helped also.

But the wet floor and the steep decline also made the footing slippery. Ben, the commando on the far right of the line, was taking every precaution like all the others, not to make any noise. He was trying to keep up the somewhat fast pace and wasn't paying enough attention to his footing. He already got slapped in the face by some foliage. One cut was deep enough that it drew blood.

Ben felt a rock under foot and momentarily feeling secure in the footing he put most of his weight on it. What he felt was the tip of a large rock that had sides that dropped a foot straight down into a collection of smaller rocks. When he put his weight on the slippery rock, he slipped off the side, twisting his ankle and smashing it on a smaller rock.

The man fell sideways with a crash, hitting the ground hard. His rifle clanked off another rock and his head, protected by his helmet, crashed into a tree with a dull thud. Using all his force not to cry out, he grunted and moaned at the pain that shot up his leg. He knew his ankle was broken.

The crash sounded like a rock concert. The rest of the recon team froze upon hearing the noise their companion had made. Meir was closest and slowly made his way over, picking his path through the rocky and uneven landscape. He arrived just as his man brought himself to a seated position.

"What happened, Ben? Are you alright?" Meir asked in a

whisper. He suddenly felt naked and exposed.

"I got my foot caught. I broke my ankle."

"Anything else?"

"I hit my head pretty hard, and I'm a bit dizzy," the soldier admitted.

"You know, you're not going to be any help. Can you make it back or do you need help?

"I can make it."

Meir thought for a moment. He really needed the extra man on the recon, but without help his injured many might not make it back. "David will help you." Meir rose to leave.

"No, sir, you need him on the recon. I can manage."

"Never mind," Meir said patting the man's head. "You stay put. We'll pick you up on the way back." Meir left to gather the rest of his men and continued with the recon.

Bob Wolff sat on a collection of rocks wearing his ghillie suit. The suit kept him somewhat dry and protected from the fierce storm. His senses were still in tune when the distinctive sounds of something big hitting the ground brought them up another notch. At first, he dismissed it as a deer or a bear, but the immediate sound of something clanking off a rock and a quickly muffled groan negated his first thought.

Quickly snapping his night vision goggles in place, he scanned the area for movement. His eyes quickly adjusted to the lime green light of the goggles that now painted the forest. He sat quietly and listened and heard more rustling, but this time it was not as pronounced and he had to strain to hear it. He had company and instinctively knew it wasn't friendly.

"Contact." He whispered into his headset.

"Where?" Kaderri's voice flowed into his ear.

"Off to my right near the rocks,: he answered in a barely audible whisper. The nervous excitement grew.

"Quiet here," Hughes said.

"You sure it's not an animal?" Kaderri asked.

"Positive," Wolff said, continuing scanning the forest. He couldn't see anything. "I'm going to check it out."

"Careful, Bob," Kaderri warned.

Wolff walked slowly and silently to the vicinity where he had heard the noise. Constantly on the alert with his rifle ready, he made sure that he made no noise and stopped every few steps to see if he was being followed or could detect any movement. He came up empty.

After two hours of silently stalking the woods, Wolff neither saw nor heard any of signs anyone else in the forest. The rain hadn't let up and the thunder still roared overhead. The green light of the night vision goggles was starting to put a strain on his eyes when he saw something flicker. He froze and regulated his breathing. His heart started to pound, pushing the adrenaline through his veins.

He studied the area that had moved, hoping that whatever it was would move again. It did. Now he could see it. It was a man sitting against a tree and he was rubbing his head. Wolff knew that this was the cause of the noise. The man sitting here had fallen and smashed his head.

Slowly, Wolff sank to a crouch and studied the man while listening to the sounds of the forest. He could clearly see the outline of a rifle in the man's hand. The hand dropped into his lap, picked up a helmet and placed it back on his head. Wolff tensed. A rifle and helmet meant only one thing. He prepared himself to either, stay and observe the man, or to take him out. Instinct told him to wait, he didn't have enough information of what was out there with him.

Suddenly, the crack of a branch came from down the hill followed by some soft footfalls. A figure instantly appeared five feet away. He too was armed with a rifle and also wore a helmet. His head swiveled back and forth, methodically searching the area. Wolff shifted his gaze to the man against the tree and noticed that he still sat there, but his rifle was up and pointing in the direction of the new man. Wolff's heart beat faster and sounded like a bass drum in his ears. He just hoped that the man in front of him couldn't hear it.

Suddenly, two more figures appeared. One was next to the man against the tree and the other was right behind the one who seemed to materialize out of nowhere. Wolff could see that these two were wearing night vision goggles. Without moving a muscle, Wolff watched as one of the soldiers handed his rifle to another and knelt next to their injured comrade. Wolff watched who appeared to be a medic fix a splint around the injured soldiers right leg. When he was done, the medic pulled the injured man up and over his shoulder.

As the medic settled the weight of his comrade, the other two kept watch. That, along with their movements, told Wolff that these guys were professionals. In single fine, the three men began their walk up the hill, with the last man giving the area one last look. Wolff thought about following, but Kaderri or Hughes weren't close enough to give him any support. Besides, he knew they would be back and he and Kaderri would be waiting.

Kaderri and Wolff met at the prearranged sight on the mountain to discuss what Wolff had observed. Without missing a single detail, Wolff relayed all the information without a single interruption. The men knew the drill. They had experienced it enough in training and actual combat.

"Did you get all this, Jesse?" Kaderri asked through the headset. He knelt on the ground with his MP5 submachine gun resting on his thigh and his eyes scanned the forest above them.

"I got it, Marc," he answered back.

"There's no doubt that they're Israelis," Wolff said. "And I bet they're commandos."

"And Koretsky wasn't there?" Kaderri asked.

"No, it looked like a leaders recon. They're going to hit the cabin, Marc."

"No," Kaderri's voice took on that menacing tone he used when he was pissed and determined. He turned to look directly at the spot in the forest where Wolff sat. "They are going to try and hit the cabin, but won't make it."

The next course of action was logical. "Where are we going to ambush them?" Wolff asked.

"I don't think they had enough time to properly scout the area. Since they didn't come by my way I think it's safe to assume that they'll come back the same way they came the first time. We'll hit them in the rocks where there is less coverage."

The microphone in Kaderri's ear clicked. "I thing we're dealing with the first string here, guys," Hughes' voice sounded in their ears.

"You're right, Jesse," Kaderri acknowledge. "Listen, Jesse, I want you to bring Sara downstairs, it's safer."

"Roger, Boss."

Kaderri turned his attention to Wolff. "Let's get into position."

The route back to the assembly point went smoothly. The men alternated between carrying their injured comrade and had stopped once to let the medic take a cursory look at Ben's ankle. Once they made it back to the assembly point, Meir gathered the men and disseminated the information. "Gather round, men," he ordered. Once the team knelt down, he spread a map on a poncho that someone had placed over the wet ground. Someone else held one over their heads to keep them protected from the rain. He turned on his red filtered flashlight and shone it on the map.

"Mister Koretsky, are you with us?" Meir asked.

"I'm here, Major," Koretsky said and kneeled down next to Meir.

"Everybody's here?" Meir asked. When he heard the murmurs, he continued. He pointed to the topographical map with his finger and laid out his plan. "After the briefing, we'll get some rest, I know everybody can use it." Meir stared hard at every shadow that was gathered round. "We hit the target in the morning."

He shifted his weight and continued. "Here is the cabin, in this little clearing at the base of this mountain. Because of the density of the forest and the lack of clearing on the mountainside, we'll be unable to use our LAWs until we get to

354

the edge of the clearing. We are going to travel in single file until we get to this point." He pointed to the map. "This is the objective rally point and once here, we'll break off into teams—"

Thursday, June 18, 4:30 a.m.

The knock on the door startled Bernard. It wasn't something he was expecting, and before he answered the door he drew his pistol.

"Damn it, Keith, open the door!" Trainor shouted, knocking even harder.

Bernard shook his head in disbelief and dismissed the other officer to go back and finish what they were doing. He placed his pistol back in his waistband and opened the door. The sight before him was something short of a joke. Gary Trainor stood there with a bandage on his head and his arm in a sling. He was wearing a pair of blue jeans, a black t-shirt and tennis shoes. He was soaking wet form the downpour and wore a blank face.

"Gary, man, what the hell are you doing here? You're supposed to be in the hospital. Does the doctor know you left?"

"Are you going to ask me in?" He took a step forward before Bernard could answer.

Bernard moved out of his way and closed the door behind him. "Gary, what are you doing here?"

"I want the son-of-a-bitch. I'm coming with you." His expression hadn't changed, but his eyes had hardened.

"What are you talking about?"

"Don't play the fool, Keith. I know you're heading up to the mountains to chase him. I'm coming with you."

Bernard knew he couldn't lie to Trainor. There was evidence that hey were heading up there all over the floor. There were M16A2's propped up against the wall with spare magazines lying next to them on the floor. There were also maps, ropes, first aid kits, and camouflage uniforms. "Are you sure you're up to this?"

"Yes."

"Well, you came at the right time, we're getting ready to leave." Just as he finished his sentence, two of the surviving officers that he met came out of the kitchen wearing battle dress uniforms. With grim faces, they nodded to Trainor and threw him a set of BDUs to change into. The other officers were at the bedside of their comrade who was clinging to life in a hospital bed.

Bernard changed into his BDUs and asked Trainor if he needed help.

"No. I don't need any help getting dressed." Trainor immediately regretted the sharp tone of his voice, but didn't apologize for it. He thought it better to just be quiet.

"Gary."

"Yeah." He looked up to see Bernard holding an M16A2.

"Do you know how to fire one of these?"

"Yeah, well no. I learned how to fire it's predecessor." He meant the M16A1.

"Close enough, except this one has a three shot burst instead of going on full automatic. The barrel is also heavier and the hand guards are round, not triangular."

Trainor nodded and finished getting dressed. Ten minutes later, the car was packed and the four men were off.

Thursday, June 18, 4:45 a.m.

Meir gave the signal to his men that they'd be moving out in fifteen minutes. The black night had turned to gray, but the sky was still dark from the thick cloud cover and the relentless rain showed no mercy. Time seemed to tick away slowly as Meir and his four men lay concealed in the underbrush on the south slop of the mountain. Two of the commandos had worked their way past the house and were adjacent to the driveway, preventing anybody from entering or leaving the property. If somebody ventured on the driveway, they'd be blown away. The remaining four commandos moved farther west and prepared to hit the cabin from that direction. That way, they could hit the cabin from two directions and support each other's fire if necessary. Ben, the commando that broke his ankle, was left at the objective rally point.

The cabin was surrounded.

Meir mulled over in his mind the mission. He wondered if he'd covered everything. The only thing that he and his men weren't allowed to do, unless it was necessary, was to kill the man named Marcus Kaderri. That was left for Moshe Koretsky, the man responsible for bringing them here. Meir had to give the Mossad officer credit and due respect. Koretsky didn't shy away from any part of the operation and didn't try to pass the proverbial buck. He let the commandos perform their duties the way they were taught and saw fit. Also, Koretsky personally thanked each man before they turned in for the night. He only left out his role in what brought the commando team to America.

Despite the intelligence that Koretsky had provided Meir with on Kaderri, Meir had told his men that this would be a simple operation and they they'd be back in Canada before breakfast stopped being served.

"Five minutes," he said into his own headset that connected him with the rest of the team.

Kaderri was too pumped up to feel tired. This was the moment of truth. It was going to be there, on his property, high in the Adirondack Mountains where his life was going to be in jeopardy. Death was something he had resigned himself to when he had taken his oath. He knew that someday it may come down to this. Here, he was avenging the deaths of fellow Americans, protecting his country from the scum like Moshe Koretsky, and protecting his wife and honor.

Bob Wolff lay next to him. It was something that he was used to and welcomed his familiarity. The two men worked as a team, and were an inseparable combination that worked like a perfectly tuned machine.

At the moment, Kaderri peered through his night vision goggles, taking one last look through them before they became useless in the growing light. Wolff had already discarded them, placing them in a bag that was attached to his LBE that was under his ghillie suit. He held binoculars to his eyes as he methodically scanned the forest and sparsely covered section of the forest where the rocks were.

The position that the two men occupied was forty feet away from the likely route that the enemy would be using. The plan of action was to hit them hard and violently, and run to new positions before they had a chance to recover. Since they knew the terrain, they'd have the advantage in escape and evasion and could set up to hit them again.

Kaderri and Wolff were undetectable in their current positions. Their ghillie suits hid them perfectly and they were disciplined enough not to move. Kaderri had his MP5 locked and loaded and his sniper rifle resting at his side.

"Here they come," Wolff whispered. He traded his binoculars for his M16. He saw the men as they emerged through an opening in the trees above the rocks. The path they were on wound back into a dense part of the forest before leading to the rocks where Kaderri and Wolff would hit them.

A sudden gust of wind drove the rain harder, blocking out any vision more than ten feet away. "How many did you count?" Kaderri asked.

"Five, they broke through the trees then disappeared. We should be able to see them any moment going over the rocks."

"I'm going to the rifle," Kaderri said. By doing that, he was going to engage them at a greater distance than originally planned. He placed his submachine gun on the ground in easy reach and hefted the silenced sniper rifle. He turned on the scope that Wolff had given him and sighted it on the rocks fifty yards away. Because of the wind, driving rain and the distance the enemy was, they wouldn't be able to hit the ambush as hard as they would like.

Kaderri turned on the scope and heard a barely audible whine as it spooled up. Since he couldn't see anything through the eyepiece, he pressed the thermal button on the extended arm. Green figures jumped into his view as he watched the unsuspecting men move through the woods. He counted five figures and concentrated on the last man. He sighted the scope in the upper torso of the last man and pressed the laser rangefinder. He now had the target painted and the number fourteen appeared in white in the left hand corner of the view screen. He pressed a third button, locking the target in the white crosshairs. Before he squeezed the trigger, he depressed the wind button. A yellow set of crosshairs appeared as did a measurement of the wind speed. He moved the rifle to adjust for the twenty mile an hour wind.

To Kaderri, the man in the sights was no longer a man. It was a target. Regulating his breathing, he took a breath and let it half way out. Looking through the scope, the crosshairs were still in place and Kaderri squeezed the trigger.

A barely audible sound signaled the exiting of the bullet. "I can't spot," Wolff said.

Kaderri watched in the scope as who he thought was the last man in line toppled over in mid stride. The other figures took one more step before they turned around to see what happened. Kaderri took another three second to go through the motions of chambering a round on the bolt action rifle, sighting the scope, depressing the buttons for the rangefinder, locking the target and adjusting for the wind. This time, the target was the first man in line.

Meir was walking second in line when he heard a grunt and the following crash of one of his men. He turned to see what idiot wasn't paying attention and saw Koretsky, who was last in line, work his way over to him. Then the man in front of Meir turned to see also. Meir held his ground as one of the other men made a move to help the man that fell. Meir heard another grunt and felt, the side of his face get sprayed with something gooey. He turned to his front in time to see the man's head explode in pink mist.

"Cover!" Meir yelled diving to the ground. He was covered in blood and brains and hadn't heard a shot fired. All that he knew was that he was ambushed and two of his men were dead without his team firing a single shot. Meir brought his weapon up and started spraying the trees in short controlled bursts.

Kaderri had a third figure in his sights when the returned fire sprayed the trees high and off to his left. Not wanting to be left out of the excitement, Wolff entered the firefight with short bursts from his rifle. Aiming for the muzzle flashes that betrayed positions, he squeezed the trigger. After the burst there was a high pitched scream, confirming that he had hit his target.

Putting pressure on the trigger, Kaderri was about to confirm his third hit when a sharp explosion off to the west tore his attention away. Someone had tripped a claymore mine on another part of the mountain. This one was closer to the cabin.

"Shit!" Kaderri hissed. "They split up! They're moving in from two directions!" Kaderri turned to see smoke rising from the detonated anti-personnel mine. Fear gripped him. He and Wolff were out of position, the team moving in from the west had a head start and would be able to take the cabin.

"Jesse, are you listening?" Kaderri called.

"I'm here, Boss." His voice was calm.

"They're coming in from the west." Kaderri got into a crouch and tapped Wolff on the shoulder. "We're moving."

Wolff fired off a few more bursts and followed Kaderri down the hill

A trip flare shot through the trees in the vicinity where the mine had gone off, it streaked red through the trees and into the sky, marking the spot where the men were. Kaderri was banking that the two teams would slow down from confusion, enabling him and Wolff to get into better positions to take on both of them. He was sure that the last thing the Israelis had figured on was to be ambushed, running into claymore mines and trip flares.

Kaderri had more time than he previously thought. The flare and mine were on the upper part of the mountain, giving him and Wolff time to move. They picked their way through the trees on a westerly course down the mountain so they could intercept the other unit.

Meir was momentary knocked off balance by the suddenness of the attack, and the detonation of the mine. He admitted to himself that he was totally unprepared for what had just happened. He had seriously underestimated his foe and found Koretsky giving a smug look.

He called for his other team to report in and expected the worst. One man had been killed and two were injured. But, the two who were injured could continue the mission. Meir shook his head and thought about the devastation of the claymore mine and what was left of his man. Probably not much after taking the blast of thousands of steel balls that were expelled from the mine when it detonated. After their wits were gathered, Meir ordered his men to move out once again. Only this time, they took precautions and moved carefully down the mountain. He had lost four men before he'd even seen his enemy.

Slowly and stealthily Wolff and Kaderri worked their way down the mountain to intercept the new threat. They would have liked to stay and finish off the men they had been firing on, but they had no idea how many men comprised the other group. For all they knew, the force that hit the mine was the main thrust of the attack, and the group they fired on was a diversion. From the profession that they had spent many years of their lives in, they had an assumed number of men they were facing. Special operations units usually didn't work in large numbers, and Kaderri doubted that the Israelis worked otherwise. But he hadn't really expected a commando unit either.

The growth became dense and slowed their progress. Kaderri slung the rifle across his back and carried his MP5 at the ready position across his chest. Because the growth was so thick, he'd be unable to work the long rifle properly. The short, stubby submachine gun was better suited. It also made more sense tactically. The Israelis would no longer be travelling in single file, they would be spread out, expecting contact. They would be too close for him to use the sniper rifle properly.

The rain masked most of the footsteps, but the sound of a branch breaking under the weight of a man was not. Kaderri and Wolff froze, searching their front. Slowly they sank to the ground, careful not to move too fast, trying to avoid detection. Out of the corner of his eye, Kaderri saw Wolff bring his weapon up to his shoulder. Kaderri quickly scanned the area where Wolff pointed his weapon and saw a figure move behind a tree and stop.

Where there was one, there were more.

When the man moved from behind the tree, Wolff fired. The burst of gunfire shattered the eerie silence. The soldier was hit in the chest by two rounds. Bright red splotches of blood burst from his chest as the impact of the bullets knocked him off his feet.

The rest of the unseen team dropped to the ground and returned fire in the direction of Wolff and Kaderri. They had wide spacing between them and kept their intervals, not allowing the ambushers to get the upper hand.

Bullets slammed into the ground in front of Kaderri, sending chunks of mud into his face. The next set of rounds went high. The Israelis clearly didn't know where the fire had come from and they were using short controlled bursts to find the target.

Kaderri saw a muzzle flash and turned his attention to the new target. He brought the submachine gun up and squeezed the trigger. The weapon jumped in his hand and another volley of bullets tore up the ground next to him. He rolled out of the way and when he checked to see if he hit his target, it was gone. He held his breath, wondering where the man had gone. Movement to his left caught his attention. The man he had fired at moved to outflank him. Kaderri had enough time to roll behind a tree when bullets slammed into it, sending bark chips flying in every direction. A quick search for Wolff found him taking cover behind another tree putting out a steady stream of controlled fire.

The Israelis had recovered and the remaining two men had excellent fire discipline. Suddenly, the returned fire stopped.

The smell of cordite filtered through the trees and brush, mixing with the scents of the forest.

Kaderri looked over to the tree where he had last seen Wolff and found him missing. "You okay, Bob?" Kaderri whispered into the headset. When he didn't get a response, be became concerned. "Bob, where are you?" Because of the ghillie suit, it made it twice as hard to see him.

A sudden burst of gunfire twenty yards to his right spun Kaderri around. The rain was still falling and he couldn't see what had happened. Wolff's voice sounded in his headset. "Shit, the fucker got away. I lost him."

"We gotta move," Kaderri said. He then saw Wolff heading towards him. How many did you see?"

"I got one and one got away." Wolff said. "What about you?"

"I saw one but missed," Kaderri admitted. "So, there was a total of three?"

"That seems right, there wasn't much return fire, but it was disciplined."

Kaderri knew the spot where Wolff had shot the first Israeli and thought about checking to see if the man was still alive, but dismissed it. They had more men to hunt before they reached the cabin.

"Where to?" Wolff asked changing his empty magazine for a full one.

"Back down there," Kaderri pointed. "I want to be able to cover both their avenues of approach."

They headed down the hill, hoping to reach their predetermined point before the Israelis could reach the cabin.

Finally, the two settled into a position that Kaderri thought would be advantageous to them. Throughout the course of the morning, they had hit the Israelis with deadly results. At most, they thought the Israelis had half a dozen men left, maybe eight. They knew they had killed five and were sure that the Israelis came in with about a dozen, not including Koretsky. Kaderri was wondering when he was going to make his appearance.

Fifteen minutes went by. That expanded to twenty. There was no movement except for the rain splashing off the leaves. The scents of the pine trees and moldy forest floor filled his nostrils. Kaderri unslung the sniper rifle and turned on the scope. He switched to the thermal imagery to see if he could spot anybody. Slowly he scanned the mountainside. He swept the scope back and forth up and down and came up with nothing. He turned his attention to his right and repeated the same procedure. Again he came up empty. He switched to the left and repeated the scan. Once again he came up empty.

"Jesse, how are things in there?" Kaderri asked.

"Quiet. Sara's doing fine, scared but fine. I'll let her know you two are okay."

"Thanks."

Kaderri brought the scope back and searched his right again. This time, four red blotches appeared. "Got 'em," he hissed and pointed in the direction. The images faded in and out because they were walking behind trees or rocks. Kaderri couldn't get a clean shot at that distance.

"How far?" Wolff asked, checking his weapon to make sure he had a round chambered.

Kaderri pressed the laser rangefinder on the scope and get his readout. "Two hundred," he said quietly. He pulled the scope away and looked with the naked eye of the location the Israelis were at.

He saw a puff of smoke immediately followed by another. Two flashed and red lights with smoky trails came from between the trees and raced toward the cabin. Kaderri could only watch in horror as the rockets raced toward the cabin.

"Jesse, get out!" Kaderri yelled into his microphone.

The first rocket hit the roof, exploding on impact. The explosion rocked the ground and a ball of flame shot into the sky. The second rocket nosed down and hit the foundation, blowing a gaping hole in the wall and a crater in the soft dirt.

Two more rockets were immediately fired after the first one exploded on the roof. The red menacing rockets flashed across the mountain and smashed into the side of the house.

A thunderous explosion rocked Kaderri and Wolff and blew the whole back of the house away. A small fire started in the house and quickly spread. Then the small arms fired rippled, throwing dirt and debris on the two men, signaling the Israelis final assault.

Bernard made incredible time racing up to the cabin. He maintained an average speed of ninety-five and having a red flashing light on his dashboard kept the state police at bay.

He turned into the driveway that led up to Kaderri's cabin. He stepped on the gas to get up the hill as fast as he could then immediately slammed on the brakes. Trainor slid forward on the seat, smashing his head on the dashboard. Only the tightening of the seat belt kept him from going through the windshield. The two men in back suffered the same fate at Trainor. Instead of the dashboard, they smashed their heads on the front seats.

Trainor shook his head. "What the fuck did you do that for? Jesus Christ, Keith, we're on the same team!"

"Kaderri said to stop once I went one hundred yards up the driveway."

"Why?" Trainor was still pissed.

"He said to call him once we reached this point or we weren't going to make it."

Trainor was about to comment when they heard the explosions up ahead and saw the fireball rise into the air. "Holy shit! What was that?"

"Looks like LAWs," one of the officers in the back said.

"What's that?" Trainor asked, still looking forward.

"Light anti-tank weapons," the same officer answered.

Trainor turned with a look of disbelief when two more rockets exploded.

Suddenly, the other officer in the back shouted a warning and started pushing the other officer out the opposite door, "Get out! Get out! Get out!"

Everyone in the car turned to see what the officer was screaming about when they saw two soldiers standing on the edge of the clearing off to the right. One was holding a LAW and the other a Galil assault rifle. They scrambled to exit the car when the Israelis fired.

Trainor was mesmerized as he watched the smoke from the back blast as the rocked ignited and exited the tube and raced for him.

Bernard, who had already exited the car reached back in and pulled at Trainor. The rocket suddenly nosed down and exploded in the dirt in front of the car. A huge mound of dirt and rock heaved from the ground, rocking the car. The glass shattered, cutting Trainor's back as he scrambled across the seat to get out.

The other Israeli opened fire with his rifle and peppered the car full of holes. The one who fired the rocket picked up his Galil assault rifle and started a slow walk to the car firing as he advanced.

The officers who were in the rear of the car were faster to get out. By the time the second Israeli opened fire, they were away from the car, had their pistols drawn, and returned fire. Their shots went wide, causing the Israelis to go to ground and giving Bernard and Trainor time to get away.

The Israeli's were better trained and armed. They took cover, found where the fire came from, sighted their weapons and fired. A burst caught one officer in the stomach and chest, killing him instantly.

Once Bernard saw that Trainor was clear from the interior of the car, he stood and ran toward the brush. He took three steps when a bullet tore into his back knocking him face down into the dirt. Trainor watched in horror as his friend slammed into the soft ground and didn't move. He had his pistol in his hand and knelt next to the front tire. He heard cautious footsteps approach. Closer and closer they came. Keeping his head low he saw a rifle barrel come over the hood, pointing toward the woods. It was now or never, he thought. Trainor sprang from his crouched position, brought up his pistol, and leveled it at the startled Israeli's chest. Without further thought, Trainor pulled the trigger, putting four rounds in the soldier's chest.

"Get down!" someone yelled from a distance.

Not having to be told twice, Trainor ducked behind the car as bullets slammed into the hood of the car and over his head. One bullet was deflected after hitting the car and smashed into his already wounded shoulder. Gunfire immediately eruped from up the hill and Trainor turned to see a camouflaged figure holding an M16 to his shoulder. The figure started moving down the hill toward him.

"Check the other one," the camouflage figure ordered as he went over to where Bernard laid. The man walked as if he were in a park. "You okay?" he asked after seeing the red stains on Trainor's BDU.

Trainor nodded. Running over to the downed man, Trainor found him in the fetal position. His hands were soaked with blood and he was clutching his stomach.

"Who are you?" Trainor asked the figure. He couldn't make out the man's face behind the camouflage paint.

"Jesse Hughes. How's that man?"

"Hit in the stomach, but still alive. Where did you come from?" Trainor said.

"Get him," Hughes said as he pointed to the man at Trainor's feet. "Leave the other one, we'll recover the body later. This one may have a chance." Hughes hefted Bernard over his shoulder and started up the hill and into the woods.

Trainor lifted the wounded officer who screamed in pain and followed Hughes into the woods.

The sound of another explosion down the driveway startled Kaderri and Wolff. The sound of gunfire that immediately followed was even more puzzling.

"What's going on?" Wolff asked.

"I have no idea," Kaderri admitted. Then he remembered the phone call from Bernard. "Wait, it must Bernard. He said he'd be coming up this morning to help out."

"The Israelis must have been waiting for him."

"Somebody made it out, there's a firefight." He turned to

look at the cabin. It was in shambles and on fire. Kaderri's stomach churned. Oh shit, he thought. He silently prayed that Sara and Jesse had made it out. He tried not to think otherwise.

"Let's finish this, Marc. Koretsky's still out here."

Kaderri nodded and rose from his concealed position. Obviously, the Israelis had linked up somewhere in the forest and were not one unit. That sat well with Kaderri and Wolff. Kaderri knew where that unit was located and didn't have to worry about an assault from two directions.

The hunt was in its final phases. Kaderri was sure that the Israelis knew he was in the forest hunting them. They would now be looking for him since the cabin had been destroyed. Wolff and Kaderri crept through the forest.

Kaderri's ear piece clicked. "Boss, are you there?"

A felling of warmth spread through Kaderri's body. It took all his effort from yelling out in joy. "What's going on, Jesse?"

"Israelis were guarding the driveway. They're taken care of, but we got come friendlies down." Then he added, "Sara's fine."

Thank God, he thought. A tear came to his eye. "Fill me in later. Thanks for the report." There were so many questions he wanted to ask, but it wasn't the time.

Hughes didn't comment any further and Kaderri had the information he needed. His wife and friend were alive. It was time to finish the job.

It didn't take more than sixty seconds for Kaderri to hear movement. The rain had slowed to a drizzle making visibility much clearer. They dropped to the ground and found cover.

The Israelis approached methodically, searching for signs of danger. Kaderri counted four and held up four fingers for Wolff who held up four fingers in return, acknowledging the number. Kaderri still had his fingers lifted. He pointed to his ring finger, indicating which man he was going to target. After Wolff acknowledged, he lifted his MP5 and took aim on the approaching soldier.

Wolff pulled a grenade off his LBE and pulled the pin.

Kaderri fired, saw that he dropped the man and immediately shifted his aim to the left. Before the rest of the approaching unit could dive for cover the grenade Wolff threw exploded, sending hot fragments of steel into the two men on the right. One died instantly and the other took the shrapnel in the right leg and rolled for cover behind a huge pine tree.

Major Yousef Meir tried to shrink his body. The tree he hid behind wasn't big enough to protect him from the bullets that would be coming his way. Blood flowed from a dozen holes in his leg and he had lost its movement. He wanted to extract his team, but he knew that they'd be pursued the whole way back to the airport. It was here, they were going to fight and try to kill the men that hunted them. If they could succeed in that, they had a chance of getting back to Israel. He tried to contact the men down by the driveway, but when they didn't answer after the firefight, he knew it was just him and the three men with him. Of course, he had Koretsky.

Meir knew the outcome of this fight. This was the place where he was going to die. He cursed Koretsky for dragging him and his team into this. And he cursed himself more for underestimating the tenacity and brilliance of the American, Marcus Kaderri, and the men he had helping him. He had been warned from Koretsky that Kaderri was a force to be reckoned with. He should have heeded the advice.

Wolff fired at the tree, forcing the man behind it to keep his head down. The shards of bark that blew off the trunk was a reminder that Wolff had his mark. Instead of playing with the man behind the tree, Wolff took his last grenade and tossed it at the tree landing far enough behind it that when it exploded, the man laying behind it would have no chance of escaping.

Kaderri stood for better vision, knowing that he had dropped the second target. He approached cautiously, his weapon pointed at the man in case he had to fire. The still form of the soldier laid there, sprawled in a grotesque manner. His chest

369

was crimson and his lower jaw had been shot away.

Silence filled the forest.

"They're dead over here, Marc," Wolff confirmed after checking the other three bodies.

"Here, too." The smell of death hung in the air with the coiled whisps of smoke that slithered their way through the trees.

The sudden rustle of a branch nearby and the figure of Moshe Koretsky aiming a pistol from behind a tree brought instant movement from Wolff and Kaderri. As they dove for cover, Koretsky fired twice.

Kaderri hit the ground hard and felt a stinging pain in his shoulder, by the time he landed, rolled and brought his weapon up to return fire, Koretsky was gone.

A strange noise came from Wolff.

Kaderri rushed over and rolled him on his back. Frothy blood dripped out of Wolff's mouth. "Oh, God! No," he said over and over, trying to fight back the tears. He pullled out his combat knife and cut the ghillie suit open. Wolff's chest was covered with blood and there was a sucking sound when he breathed.

"I don't think I'm going to make it out of this one, buddy." Wolff's voice was still strong, but he winced at the pain.

Kaderri rolled him over and felt for an exit wound. When he couldn't find one, he held out hope. The bullet was some-where in his right lung. "Yes you will, goddamnit! I'm not going to let you die." He gently rolled Wolff back over and pulled his first aid pouch off his LBE.

Since his days in Beirut, Kaderri always carried a twelve inch by twelve inch sheet of plastic in his first aid pouch for wounds like this one, a sucking chest wound. He unfolded the plastic and unwrapped his compress. Helping Wolff to a sitting position, he placed the plastic over the wound to seal it, pre-venting the air from escaping. "Hold this in place while I wrap the compress."

Wolff reached up and held the plastic in place. "Did you get him?"

Kaderri placed the compress over the wound and tied the ends around Wolff's chest. "Not yet," he answered.

"Get him." It clearly had become more difficult for Wolff to breathe.

Kaderri finished the knot and made sure it was tight. "How are you feeling?"

"Go get him, Marc."

Kaderri stared hard at his friend and said, "I'll be back to get you." He patted him on the shoulder and ran off.

"I know you will," Wolff said to his back.

Kaderri dashed after Koretsky. His trail was easy to find by the foot prints and broken branches he has left in his hasty departure. Kaderri stopped when he came to a break in the trees and saw Koretsky run into the clearing at the base of the mountain. He was making for the Jeep Cherokee in the driveway.

Kaderri stopped, dropped to one knee and sighed Koretsky in the scope of the sniper rifle. He didn't bother to use the wizardry of the scope, instead he relied on his instincts and training. Koretsky ran in a straight line, not even bothering to zig zag to make himself a harder target to hit. Kaderri let him take four more steps. He let his breath half-way out and squeezed the trigger. Before he let the rest of his breath out, the bullet struck.

Koretsky was hit mid stride in the base of the neck. His body fell forward into the soft, wet grass and didn't move.

From his position in the woods with Hughes, Trainor sprinted to head off Koretsky, but watched in slow motion as the bullet exited Koretsky's throat with a spray of blood and tissue. He smiled when Koretsky fell. The smile quickly faded when he realized that he had been cheated from getting his own revenge from Koretsky shooting him.

But, Trainor didn't stop running until he came to the motionless body. When he got there, he heard labored breathing and rolled the body over with his foot. What he saw made him gag. Koretsky's neck was gone, a gaping hole that blood flowed from. But, he was still trying to breathe and his eyes moved as if he could see. When they focused on Trainor, Trainor's smile came back. He would be able to get his revenge.

"Look's like Kaderri won, asshole," Trainor sneered. " My friend back there," he pointed over his shoulder towards the burning cabin, "wanted you to know Kaderri's CIA." Trainor pointed his pistol at Koretsky's head and said, "I won too, but I'm a cop." He fired three times.

Kaderri had Wolff slung over his shoulder and made it to the clearing. He adjusted his weight and saw Hughes and Sara walk from behind the burning house.

"We got him, Bob," Marc said. "Koretsky's dead." The house was still burning and the sounds of fire trucks were approaching. "It's over, Bob. I'll get you to a hospital."

"I don't think I can make it, Marc, I'm drowning in my own blood." He coughed and spit up some blood that dribbled down Marc's ghillie suit.

"Don't say that. Jesse's here, he'll stabilize you until an ambulance arrives." He was getting closer to the house and Sara.

Sara waved and covered her mouth at the sight before her. She started to run when a burst of fire erupted from the tree line. Her smile faded as she watched her husband stumble and fall before Hughes pushed her to the ground.

Marc heard the fire and felt the white hot pain in his leg and side as the bullets tore into him. He collapsed to his knees and felt Wolff's body jerk with the impact of more bullets.

Jesse saw the man who fired, an Israelis solder with a splint on his right leg. Jesse brought up his M16 and fired successive volleys of three round bursts. The first volley found its mark, but Hughes kept firing until he was out of ammunition.

Kaderri rolled Wolff over and looked at his face. It was ashen, even under the face paint. "No, Bob, don't go!" He cried out for his pain and for the pain of his friend. He grabbed Bob's hand and squeezed, hoping there would be a squeeze back. There was, but it was weak.

Above, the clouds parted and a ray of sunshine broke through, bathing the grass in a warm glow. Kaderri stared into Wolff's face, looking for signs of life. Bob turned on the wet grass, opened his eyes, and looked back at Kaderri. He whispered something and Kaderri had to lean closer so he could hear. He still held onto Bob's hand.

Wolff's warm breath flowed into Kaderri's ear. "I love you, man." Then his eyes closed.

"I love you, too, but you're not going anywhere!" He slapped Wolff's face a few times and saw his eyes flutter.

A hand grabbed Kaderri's shoulder and pushed him away. "Let me take care of him, Marc." Hughes had sprinted over to where Kaderri had fallen after he shot the last Israeli. When Hughes pulled his hand away it was covered in blood. He gave Kaderri a concerned look, "How many did you take?" He had his medical bag already open and began working feverishly to save Wolff's life.

"Three. Jesse, you have to save him."

"I'll do my best."

Kaderri watched as Hughes pulled out equipment from his bag and heard the sounds of helicopters approaching. He looked up and saw them slow to a hover and prepare to land. Some of the helicopters were gunships. Kaderri was getting weaker and his vision started to blur. He pointed to the sky and asked, "Where'd they come from?"

"Bernard called them in. They're here to take you guys to the hospital. They're from the Tenth Mountain Division."

But Kaderri never heard his answer. The sky went black and he collapsed.

Friday June 19, 4:05 p.m.

Marcus Kaderri awoke in pain in a hospital bed at Albany Medical Center. The pain was tolerable because it meant that he was alive. It took him a moment to focus his eyes. When he did, he saw his beautiful wife. She stood next to him, holding his hand. She had tears in her eyes and dried streaks down her cheeks.

"Hey, babe," he said. "May I have a kiss?"

Sara started crying and bent over to give him a tear-soaked

373

kiss. "Marcus, I love you."